# SEEKER

Douglas E. Richards

Paragon Press

# PROLOGUE

The clear, reflective spacecraft was the size of a softball while at rest. But since it was now very near light speed, its mass had grown and its length had diminished in dramatic fashion, as relativity demanded. It had raced through both the intergalactic and interstellar voids for more than two million years, but its tremendous speed caused time dilation effects, and as far as it was concerned the journey hadn't even been a hundredth this long.

A photon of light, of course, could do this trick far better, as it moved at a speed that caused time to stop dead in its tracks. The photon could be born on a star and travel for a billion years, at least as measured by an outside observer, before slamming into a distant telescope—not having aged a *second*. To the photon, this journey would be instantaneous. It would leave its star and die on the telescope a billion light years distant, with no time passing for it at all.

Interstellar space was cold beyond imagining, but the tiny probe was able to tap into the froth of the void, the particles and energy that appeared and disappeared at random, the ultimate quantum magic trick. Perhaps this was the Universe's way of providing the perfect energy source for those who could learn how to tap it.

Or maybe, instead, this energy froth was a gift from an all-powerful deity, yet another subtle clue as to its existence.

If only the Universe, or this deity, hadn't set such a limiting, and unbreakable, speed limit.

The probe possessed sensors of unbelievable power, and had recently detected radio signals, which it had quickly traced back to their planet of origin. The nature of these signals made several things clear all at once: Not only was there life on this particular planet, but it was intelligent life. And not only intelligent life, but life that had reached a basic level of technological sophistication.

Outstanding.

The probe, as satisfied as a probe could be, instantly made a course correction, now having accomplished at least the first stage of its mission parameters.

The interstellar softball continued to digest the ever-growing content being broadcast from this chatty planet as it hurtled through space, and with each passing second it moved almost a hundred eighty thousand miles closer to its target.

The planet, which the inhabitants called Earth, Terra, and dozens of other names in different language systems, was now just under three light years away.

Only three years until the probe arrived.

But much sooner as far as it was concerned.

It could hardly wait.

# PART 1

"To appreciate the nature and significance of the coming 'singularity,' it is important to ponder the nature of exponential growth. Toward this end, I am fond of telling the tale of the inventor of chess and his patron, the emperor of China. In response to the emperor's offer of a reward for his new beloved game, the inventor asked for a single grain of rice on the first square, two on the second square, four on the third, and so on. The emperor quickly granted this seemingly benign and humble request.

"One version of the story has the emperor going bankrupt as the sixty-three doublings ultimately totaled eighteen million trillion grains of rice, which would require rice fields covering twice the surface area of the Earth, oceans included.

"Another version of the story has the inventor losing his head."

—Ray Kurzweil, *The Law of Accelerating Returns*

# 1

Anwar Sadiq whispered a silent prayer to Allah, clutched the American-made M4 assault rifle strapped around his neck, and glanced at his watch. He estimated that showtime was now only ten to fifteen minutes away. His eyes gleamed in the darkness, twin beacons framed by the folded black scarf that covered his head and face, their intensity and shine indicating intelligence and zealotry in equal measure—a lethal combination.

Sadiq was one of the few leaders of ISIS to have survived the organization's decimation, during which time his brave and glorious brethren had been expunged from the many territories they had acquired through their early, spectacular rise, when they had spread like a brushfire across the Middle East.

In ISIS's heyday the lure of their grand cause, *the caliphate*—the purification of the Muslim faith and the setting of the world once again on a righteous course—was irresistible to many young men in Iraq, Syria, the Levant, and Europe, who had rushed in to be a part of the excitement. And ISIS leaders had instinctively known the best way to attract them, tapping into the same primal recipe that had worked countless times before.

Religion was the centerpiece of their movement, of course, but this wasn't what had lured in so many followers willing to kill and die in ISIS's name. Not really. The central cause could have been anything. Workers' rights. Racial purity. Revenge.

Humanity was fiercely tribal. And young men, in particular, were wired to seek out adventure, glory, and esteem. ISIS was cool. ISIS was a brotherhood fighting together for a glorious cause. Killing together, raping unbelievers together. What could cement fraternal bonds more completely than this?

And in addition to offering adventure, glory, and camaraderie, ISIS offered something even more important: *purpose*.

But while all of this was true, ISIS and Anwar Sadiq knew that the disaffected young men they sought to attract also needed to believe they were joining a winning team. To believe that their self-sacrifice would eventually achieve their goals and save the world. The more recruits and territory ISIS gathered, the easier it was to gain additional recruits and territory.

Nothing succeeded like success.

Which is why Sadiq's current operation was the most critical the organization had ever undertaken. Because the tide had turned against them many years earlier, when the US had finally begun to take them seriously, and what they had been so sure was an unsinkable ship was pierced by an iceberg. The Great Satan began to crush them, to cast doubt on their inevitability, and with this, the hopes and dreams of scores of young men who would otherwise have flocked to replenish their ranks.

The once swelling, pounding, lion heart of ISIS was grinding to a halt, and this mission represented a last-gasp effort to shock it back to life. It was time to give the US a black eye they would never forget. One that would inspire young men around the world to take up the fight once again.

Sadiq surveyed ten of the fourteen soldiers he had with him on this night, the ten who were within sight. Each was covered head to toe in black, as was he, and each fondled an assault weapon of his own. The four not present were carrying out important duties. Two were ready to block the long, winding entrance to the property on his order, while two others were manning two parked and hidden cars towing industrial-grade woodchippers behind them.

The plan was visionary and bold. Daring and audacious. Sadiq had been given the honor to lead ISIS's smartest, most capable men on its most important mission.

He stood in the still darkness, the calm before the storm, going through the mission in his mind one last time. Send a viral AI into the electronic security system to take control of it. Establish a roadblock to eliminate all chances that a newcomer might surprise them once the Op had begun. And finally, kill cell phone coverage in the area.

They would have to commence the attack within minutes of this last, as blocking cell phone communications would draw immediate attention. By rights, their targets shouldn't be using their phones on this night, but Sadiq knew that many would anyway.

In the West, the phone had become a drug even more addictive than opioids. In a culture becoming ever more secular, the phone had become a god.

But in the midst of the coming massacre, Sadiq had the feeling his targets were about to rediscover their true religion, just moments before he and his men ushered them all into oblivion.

# 2

Ben Kagan waited for his gray Hydro sedan to enter a vast limestone surface on the grounds of a mansion in Poway, California, and park itself. He took a deep breath and braced himself for the party to come. This was the last place he wanted to be.

He had never been the party type. He considered himself to be very much on the boring side. Even his car was boring. It was a Hydro, of course, since Norman Weiser had founded this particular company, among many others, and Kagan was one of Weiser's most valued scientists. But it was one of Hydro's most unexciting models, a mid-range four-door sedan.

Like Kagan, it was a brilliant performer. And fully autonomous, of course. But not too flashy. Dependable, but not racy.

Still, it was a luxury car by any measure, and the woman in the passenger seat beside him, looking breathtaking in her elegant blue dress, was stunning, an adjective that applied to her personality even more than it did to her firm, gym-toned body and incandescent smile.

It was hard for Kagan to complain. He was only twenty-nine, and his life was very full.

Maybe *too* full.

He hadn't watched a television show in years, or read any fiction. The closest he had come to a vacation was when he occasionally allowed himself to take an entire Saturday or Sunday off, instead of working for at least several hours. He had been the top player on Princeton's tennis team as an undergraduate, yet he was down to playing tennis once a month, and exercising twice a week on a treadmill in front of an expansive computer monitor so that he wouldn't lose even a moment of productivity.

Something had to give. Now that Cynthia Shearer, the remarkable woman beside him, had entered his life, the job he treasured and the woman he loved were competing for his attention. Even after jettisoning everything else in his life, there still weren't enough hours in the day to satisfy both.

It had been so much simpler before Cynthia had come on the scene. Simpler, but certainly not better.

He had been just a year away from completing his doctorate in physics and computer engineering from Carnegie Mellon University when he seized an opportunity to join one of Norman Weiser's first companies, Advanced Propulsion Technologies. Even though he had been forced to pull out of school just short of his doctoral finish line, it was an offer he couldn't refuse.

Weiser was a wunderkind, a man who had burst onto the scene from nowhere, and in just a few short years had managed to out-musk the great Elon Musk. His initial breakthrough had come when he had devised an ingenious method for creating stable metallic hydrogen, a material that had been pursued for decades for its theorized properties as both an ideal superconductor and a powerful rocket propellant.

The applications for stable metallic hydrogen and the room temperature superconductivity it made possible were as wide-ranging as they were breathtaking. A superconductor was able to conduct electric current with no resistance, making batteries more powerful and electromagnets so strong they could levitate heavy objects, basically defying gravity.

The first commercially operated high-speed magnetic levitating train, or *Maglev*, was built in Shanghai in 2004. This railway used superconducting magnets ten times more powerful than ordinary electromagnets to levitate and propel the train. But there was a catch—these magnets had to be cooled to hundreds of degrees below zero to achieve superconductivity, a difficult and pricey requirement.

Room temperature superconductivity had long been a Holy Grail, and Norman Weiser, brilliant, daring, and iconoclastic, had finally brought it home.

Production of high purity metallic hydrogen was still tricky, and the technology was still being perfected, but Weiser had sprouted more companies even than Musk, in a shorter time, with several of these in direct competition with the great innovator, including in rocketry, high-speed tunneling, and electric cars.

And soon Weiser's electric cars would become *Maglev* cars, which would be charged and propelled using low-cost superconducting electromagnets in his cars and in the streets. At this rate, Weiser was sure to obsolete Tesla and SpaceX, and all other car and rocket companies on the planet, for that matter, within the decade.

The world order, at least when it came to technology, had been relatively stable for thousands of years. But in modern times, industries were being birthed and obsoleted at a furious pace. Even technology that had seemed utterly woven into the very fabric of society was often relegated to the trash heap of history in the blink of an eye.

In 1996, Eastman Kodak was a hundred-year-old powerhouse with one hundred forty thousand employees and a valuation of twenty-eight billion dollars. Yet a mere sixteen years later, the company was filing for bankruptcy, a T. Rex dinosaur that had failed to fathom the disruptive power and game-changing impact of the digital photography revolution.

In contrast to this, while Kodak was on its last legs, a small handful of entrepreneurs founded Instagram, a photo-sharing service, which rapidly attracted as many as eight hundred million users. Eighteen months after its founding, the same year that Kodak filed for bankruptcy, these few Instagram founders sold their company for a billion dollars.

And Norman Weiser was about to unleash this sort of disruptive technological change on any number of industries, with him as Instagram and the rest of the world as Kodak.

Ben Kagan loved what he did with a passion, and would have paid Weiser for the privilege of working for him. Instead, he was paid handsomely to solve fun, challenging, and consequential problems. Since much of this compensation took the form of stock options, which were now worth well over a hundred million dollars and climbing rapidly, the word *rewarding* didn't go nearly far enough.

Then, fourteen months earlier, out of the blue, Kagan's life had become much more . . . complicated. Weiser had hired Cynthia Shearer as a consultant on one of the projects Kagan was heading, and he had become instantly and irresistibly enamored with her.

Since she had worked with him side by side, in the trenches, for six months, he had gotten to know her far better than if he had dated her for many years, and had used every last minute of his spare time to see her.

By the time her tour of duty was up, they had fallen in love. Kagan would have proposed marriage to her already if he thought there was any chance that she'd accept.

But he knew she wouldn't. Not until he could achieve a better balance between his first love and his second, and somehow find a way to spend more time with her now that they weren't working together. He was determined to do just that, no matter what it took. He would prove to her that she was his top priority, and get her to agree to spend the rest of her life with him.

Which is why he was with her now, despite not enjoying this kind of party, which he found empty, boring, and a complete waste of time.

But while parties weren't his thing, he understood why Cynthia wanted to be here. This residence, and party, belonged to Dan Vettori, the founder and CEO of a young company working on improving virtual reality technology. Cynthia had consulted for Vettori almost as long as she had for Weiser, and had always had good things to say about the man. Besides, this was a great networking opportunity for her.

As the car parked and shut itself off, Kagan leaned over and planted a brief kiss on Cynthia's soft lips. "Here we go," he said tentatively.

"It's a party, not a funeral."

He shrugged. "Either way, as long as I'm with you, it can't be all bad."

"You're going to have more fun than you think."

Kagan rolled his eyes. "That would almost *have* to be true."

She laughed. "You'll enjoy this. *Really*. Dan is very smart. He runs in different circles than you do, but his friends tend to be impressive. Trust me, conversation won't be limited to the weather and sports. Might even be what you'd call *scintillating*."

"Scintillating?" said Kagan, raising his eyebrows. He had never used this word in his life. He grinned. "Have you been reading my diary again?"

Cynthia laughed as they exited the car.

The party was already in full swing, and there were many dozens of cars lined up on the never-ending limestone pavers in addition to his own. Dan Vettori's residence was at the end of a long marble path that led from the parking area, and it loomed against landscape lighting in the distance, looking like a museum.

Cynthia checked the time on her phone. "We'd better get up there," she said. "I met Dan's wife, Kelly, when I was here for a meeting last year, but I really want to meet his kids. He couldn't stop raving about them when I was part of his team."

Kagan was confused. "Dan Vettori has adult children?" he said. "I thought he was still fairly young."

"He is. So are they. Amber is seven and Eric is nine. But they're both precocious. He told me he's letting them hang out at the party until ten, before he sends them off to bed. Most kids would probably want to avoid an adult party, but apparently they pleaded for more time."

Kagan groaned. He only wished he and Cynthia could be banished from the party at ten.

They neared the residence, which encompassed more than fifteen thousand square feet of living space. As they approached the immense front doors, Kagan noted a concert-sized grand piano framed in the picture window of the library, playing Billy Joel's "Piano Man" in automated mode, the keys bouncing up and down as though being played by an invisible maestro or talented ghost.

Kagan smiled, hoping that forcing his facial muscles into this posture would improve his attitude. He was doing this for Cynthia, after all, and while he would have greatly preferred a quiet evening with her at home, he vowed that he would have fun here—even if it killed him.

As he looked into Cynthia's beautiful green eyes, he made a final decision on a matter he had been contemplating for weeks. On the way home, he would promise to quit his job in just two years. He would promise to work from home, dedicating his efforts to developing technology that could improve the human condition. And he would promise to use some of his growing fortune to set up a charitable foundation with her, following a trail blazed by Bill and Melinda Gates, among others.

In short, he would paint a picture of a future life together that made *her* as much of a priority as his work. He would pave the way for a marriage proposal in the near future, one that she could actually accept.

He had already been counting the minutes until the party ended—before he had even arrived—but now that he had finally reached a decision on this, he *really* couldn't wait.

They entered the home and made their way to the grand room, which contained many throngs of partygoers, most holding wine-glasses or plates filled with bite-sized gourmet treats.

Cynthia surveyed the room, looking for miniature humans, but didn't find any. "We don't have much time," she said, a woman on a mission. She gestured toward the entrance to one of the other rooms. "We need to find Eric and Amber before they get sent off to bed."

Kagan eyed the open bar in the corner of the room. "Okay, but why don't you begin the search while I get us a drink," he suggested. "I'll catch up with you. White Russian? With a splash of Bailey's?"

Cynthia smiled. "You know me too well, Ben. Thanks. But don't take too long."

"*Never*," said Kagan, pretending to be dismayed at the very thought.

He watched her walk away before making his way to the bar. He placed his order with one of three bartenders, shoving a few extra cocktail napkins in his pants pocket as he did so, since minor spills were not beyond the realm of possibility, and watched while the drinks were being made.

He was still facing the bartender a few minutes later, his back to the room, when a series of high-pitched shrieks emanating from several rooms, including the one behind him, almost shattered his eardrums. A chorus of screams unlike anything he had ever heard.

His heart began to pump wildly as he wheeled around in alarm.

But before he had even completed his turn, his ears were further assaulted by staccato bursts of machine gun fire, coming from the library—bursts that must have been directed at the grand piano, as the music stopped abruptly. This was followed by several additional screams, which also ended abruptly, as the room he was in became eerily silent.

Kagan completed his turn and saw three men near the entrance to the room, dressed in black, including cotton scarves wrapped around their heads and lower faces, exposing only their eyes. Each was extending an assault rifle toward the partygoers, and each had dropped a green canvas duffel bag by his feet.

Judging from the location of the screams and the shots he had heard, Kagan realized that these three were just the tip of the iceberg. Others must have magically appeared in other rooms throughout the residence.

*Were they terrorists?* he thought.

*Impossible.*

But as much as his mind struggled to reject this interpretation, he knew in the pit of his roiling stomach that this must be the case. No other explanation made sense.

But if so, what were they waiting for? Why were Vettori and his guests still alive?

"Who are you?" demanded one of the male partygoers, breaking the silence. "What do you want?"

The terrorist in the middle of the three depressed the trigger twice, sending two quick bursts of gunfire toward the man who had asked the questions. The man's body erupted into mini-geysers of blood and gore, and he crashed to the ground, the wineglass he had been holding shattering on the hardwood floor.

Several more shrieks reverberated around the room but were cut off by the black-clad terrorist who had just fired his weapon. "*No one says another word!*" he shouted, his English accented but very good. "For once in your pampered lives you're going to *follow* orders, not give them! Listen, not talk! Understand?"

Some of the guests nodded, others seemed frozen in ice, while one woman in the opposite corner of the room vomited onto the floor.

"We are with ISIS," continued the terrorist calmly. "And we're here to show the world that our battle with you is far from over."

# 3

Ben Kagan was surprised that an unnatural calm had settled over him, and everything seemed to be happening at a slower rate than normal, which he immediately realized wasn't really the case.

The world hadn't slowed down. His mind had sped up.

He had no idea how he might react to something like this, but he had every reason to believe he would find himself more on the cowardly side of the ledger than the brave side. He was the opposite of an adrenaline junkie. Not only couldn't he ever imagine himself having the courage to strap a parachute to his back and jump out of a plane, he could barely bring himself to jump from the high-dive at the local pool.

He had always assumed that his instinct for self-preservation would overwhelm his higher brain functions. That when death was breathing down his neck, his emotions would rise up and leave him paralyzed, or quaking in fear. But it seemed as though his emotions had fled the scene, instead, leaving him with an almost superhuman focus.

Not that it mattered. ISIS wouldn't be taking prisoners. He should be dead already, but he had no doubt this would be corrected very soon.

He quickly considered his options, and realized he had none. Cynthia was in one of the other rooms, and he had no chance of getting to her.

As he thought of the woman he loved, his feelings of panic surged, threatening to breach the internal wall that held his fear and emotions at bay. But, somehow, he managed to force them back into their prison, and his resolve and focus actually intensified afterwards.

Two other black-clad men entered the room, both wielding video cameras instead of the machine guns that were strapped around their necks. The cameras swept around the room, taking clean shots of every guest and every square inch of the residence.

The man who had spoken earlier, clearly the leader, removed a phone from his pocket and held it under his mouth. "I'll be sending men around to collect your cellphones," he announced, and his booming voice was somehow transmitted through the mansion's speaker system and echoed loudly throughout the residence.

"Phones have become like gods to you," continued the terrorist. "But give them up anyway, or pay with your life."

One of the two newcomers continued filming, while the second held open a large empty duffle bag and made his way to various groups of guests, urging them on to rapidly deposit their phones in the bag, which began filling quickly. Kagan removed his own phone and deposited it in the duffel when it came by, his mind continuing to race.

"Your culture is corrupt," continued the terrorist leader. "Look at the decadence of this place. You could all choose simple lives of piety, but instead, you turn your back on God and worship excess and technology. But what has your technology brought you? Nothing but addiction and dependence. Only fidelity to Allah can save mankind."

He shook his head in disgust. "Since you represent the worst kind of infidel, we have chosen you to demonstrate our newfound commitment to bringing the war to your shores. We will destroy the Great Satan in your own lair. You were chosen at random from the endless examples of decadence in your country. And while you will be the first to fall, none will be spared. Ultimately, you and all other infidels will be exterminated, and the true followers of the word of Allah will finally heal the world."

With that the terrorist leader and three of his thugs began to spray the crowd with short, controlled bursts of machine gun fire, calmly marching forward like soulless machines from a Terminator movie, spraying anything that moved, while the fourth terrorist in the room continued filming.

It was absolute carnage. Horrific beyond imagination. Dozens of guests went down in seconds, torn to shreds, the floor becoming slick with blood. Shrieks of fear and agony punctuated the staccato bursts, and the room fell into instant pandemonium. Many of the guests were stunned, paralyzed, while others tried to rush the terrorists, or run, with both strategies being equally ineffective.

Kagan was at the far end of the room, and he crouched down low, heading for the nearby kitchen, which would be shielded by steel appliances and islands made of quartz and granite. All the exits from the room were blocked, and it was the only destination that offered any protection, scant though it was.

He scurried across the floor, while the men and women on either side of him literally exploded as he passed, spraying him with blood. There had been dozens of living souls in the room just moments before, and now Kagan was one of only a small handful still alive, the bullets hitting everyone around him but somehow leaving him unscathed. His luck was uncanny, one in a thousand, but he was under no illusion that it would hold.

And Cynthia was almost certainly dead, wherever she was.

One of the terrorists now rushed up a set of stairs, and Kagan had no doubt they would be very thorough, searching every room, closet, pantry, and desk—anywhere it was possible to hide.

Kagan dived behind a quartz kitchen island. Just as he did so, one of the partygoers in the room behind him, who had been carrying a concealed gun, managed to get off a shot, hitting the nearest terrorist in the thigh, but two other ISIS barbarians hit this shooter with such prolonged and concentrated bursts that his body was nearly vaporized.

Kagan ignited the stove, set a roll of paper towels on top, and then tore through several cabinets, looking for sprays that would make good fire accelerants. It was his only chance.

He'd have to grow the fire very big, very quickly, as the sprinkler system would make short work of it otherwise. Even if it were extinguished, rain from the ceiling would make the floor slippery. And if he could burn materials that gave off a thick smoke, he could impair the terrorists' line of sight and sow confusion.

From out of nowhere, a small girl appeared at the entrance to the kitchen, sobbing and shaking uncontrollably, her eyes seeming to be larger than her body. Upon seeing her, Kagan felt sick to his stomach for the first time, and the room seemed to spin around him.

The girl had to be Dan Vettori's daughter, the seven-year-old named Amber.

Seeing the extent of her suffering finally caused his emotional dam to burst. She was a tiny, helpless little girl forced to witness a gory massacre, experiencing enough pain and fear and suffering to break ten adults. The presence of this innocent child was beyond horrific, beyond heart-wrenching. Kagan had no idea where she had come from, but his plans changed in an instant.

He was fighting death the best he could, but he knew he'd never be able to save himself, or Cynthia. But maybe he could save this little girl. She was small enough to fit into places that the terrorists would consider too small to search.

He rushed over to sweep her off the floor and help her to hide, when a terrorist rounded the corner and spotted them both. He ignored Kagan, and immediately pointed his weapon at little Amber with clear intent to fire.

"Nooooo!" screamed Kagan in horror and disbelief, diving on her without hesitation and taking one of the three rounds that had burst forth from the terrorist's rifle toward this tiny, helpless target—one that would have hit her otherwise—with the two other rounds missing their mark by inches.

Kagan's head slammed into the hard kitchen floor while the rest of his body covered the girl, dousing her with blood and crushing her under his weight.

He felt his consciousness rapidly slipping away, but fought with his last shred of will to cling to life for just a moment longer. "*Close your eyes and play dead!*" he whispered into Amber's ear, hoping for a miracle, hoping the terrorist would assume he had hit them both and move on to other targets. "*When he leaves, hide in a tiny cabinet.*"

But Ben Kagan was not destined to learn if this plan would work, or even if Amber had heard him, as the relentless ocean of darkness he had held at bay could no longer be denied.

# 4

It was three in the morning, but Jesse Carter, Secretary of Homeland Security, was as wide awake as he had ever been.

"Did you review the footage I sent you?" asked Special Agent Karen Firth Morris. Carter's phone displayed her holographic image five feet away, and her expression was every bit as grim as her tone.

Carter looked ill. "I did," he replied. "And just when you thought they couldn't get any more barbaric. Please tell me we were able to get this expunged from the Web, Agent Morris."

"We were too late," she replied miserably, "It's already metastasized. It's destined to go viral in a big way."

"Goddammit!" snapped Carter. "Do you have any idea the shitstorm this is going to create? The panic?"

"I have *every* idea," said Morris. "Which is why ISIS filmed it in the first place."

Carter's hands balled into fists. He needed to calm himself or his rage would consume him. "So you're on site now?"

"Yes. For about thirty minutes."

"How many dead?"

"One hundred forty-eight as far as we can tell, based on those known to be going to the party, those seen in the ISIS footage, cars in the lot, and so on."

"Were there any survivors?"

"Just one. A little girl. The daughter of Dan and Kelly Vettori, the owners of the home. She was hiding in a tiny cabinet in the kitchen. She's still much too traumatized to tell us anything. We'll get her story as soon as possible, but I'm guessing it may take a while. She hasn't said a word. We've sent for a child trauma expert."

"Sounds like she hid when the carnage began and waited it out," said Carter.

"Not that simple. She had a lot of blood soaked into her clothing. So she was in the open at some point during the attack."

Carter nodded. He knew ISIS hadn't spared her out of mercy because she was a child. In fact, she'd have been a *favored* target for just this reason. Sick, twisted bastards! The video of the massacre they had posted made a special point of dwelling on the bullet-riddled body of her nine-year-old brother, wanting to emphasize their utter, unflinching savagery.

"Any dead terrorists?" he asked.

"None," replied the Special Agent. "It wasn't a typical suicide mission. The fact that they killed so many and escaped so easily suggests a change in tactics. Everything they did here was designed to send a clear message."

"No shit!" snapped Carter. "Message received."

He wanted to scream and keep on screaming. ISIS had outdone itself this time. As if gunning down more than a hundred people like fish in a barrel wasn't grisly enough, they had run them all through a *woodchipper*.

At first he had questioned this move. Wouldn't it evoke more terror, a more visceral reaction, for those on the scene to encounter a graveyard's worth of gory bodies, see the frozen looks of horror on so many faces?

But the footage had answered this question. By filming most of the downed bodies, some not even recognizably human, and posting the footage online, they could have their cake and eat it too. Without the footage, the first responders would be sickened, but no one else would ever see the aftermath of what ISIS had wrought.

*With* the footage, the world would not only see the looks of horror on dead faces, but also a bonus, something sickening beyond imagination, something no one should ever see. Apparently, beheading this many people was too much work, so ISIS had found a way to expedite the process. Everything else had become automated, so why not barbarism and savagery?

The woodchippers they had used were commercial-grade. Given that these machines could swallow thick tree trunks and turn them into sawdust in seconds, the effect they had on mostly soft human beings was *unspeakable.*

The footage showed body after body being fed on a short conveyor into the machines, turned from solid matter into a red, pulpy spray, accompanied by a ghastly grinding sound, guaranteed to be the stuff of nightmares for some time to come. Thankfully, the director of this soon-to-be-viral video had stopping filming after twenty victims, although the pulping had continued until every last victim had been liquefied.

This carnage was accompanied by a narration, in excellent English, describing the sins of the infidels and the Great Satan, and the great wrath that would soon befall them. It also contained the standard "rivers of blood" rhetoric, although this rhetoric had considerable impact when accompanying a video that showed the actual creation of such a river.

Carter knew that no news outlet would show the footage, even with most of it blurred out. This was video that couldn't be properly sanitized, even for cable viewing. But tens of millions of Americans would view it on the Web, and the entire nation and beyond would hear and read about the details.

They had found additional footage on site, which hadn't been posted online, showing every last guest at the party before the carnage had begun.

"Anything special about the victims?" asked Carter. "Why this night? Why this location?"

"Nothing stands out so far," said Morris. "The terrorists left a bag full of guests' cellphones in each room. We'll go through these carefully, but I doubt we'll find anything to suggest why they chose this particular party. Seems to be a target of opportunity. The party was at an isolated location, and was scheduled three weeks ago, giving them plenty of time to map out their assault. And some of the wealthiest, highest-powered people in the country were in attendance."

"Yeah," mused Carter, "talk about being in the wrong place, at the wrong time." He paused. "Any leads on the terrorists?"

"We're almost certain that the voice on the video is that of Anwar Sadiq."

Carter cursed. Sadiq was considered to be the best that ISIS had. Syrian born, but a graduate of Oxford University in England, he was a man as brilliant as he was ruthless. "How did we not know he was in The States?" demanded the Secretary of Homeland Security.

"They must have pulled out all the stops for this one. By far the most sophisticated attack they've ever done. Still not clear why they spent so much effort on a random target, rather than something bigger, more symbolic. Something that would better help them attract recruits."

Carter shook his head in disagreement. "Are you kidding? A video showing the massacre of rich, pampered elites—not to mention the woodchipper piece—will be a huge recruiting draw. No matter who the victims, or what the symbolism."

Morris shook her head in disgust. "I'm going to find these bastards!" she hissed through clenched teeth.

"I know you are," said Carter. "But do it quickly. We need to use these savages to locate and exterminate the rest of ISIS, once and for all. Let's make sure this attack blows up in their goddammed faces!" he finished.

"Roger that," said Special Agent Karen Firth Morris, and for the first time there was a hint of enthusiasm in her tone.

# 5

Ben Kagan awoke abruptly. But try as he might, his eyelids were too heavy to open.

He felt as if he was floating through space. Comfortable. Serene. Alive!

His memories came rushing back. He was still alive. How could that be?

And how was he entirely pain free? Better than pain free. He was feeling as relaxed as he had ever felt. Almost euphoric.

Perhaps he was still on the floor of Vettori's mansion. Perhaps the ISIS terrorists had miraculously left him for dead. He had now regained his faculties, but perhaps he was too injured to move, nestled in the nether region between sleep and full wakefulness as his body struggled to heal itself.

If he could have moved, he would have shaken his head. Too unlikely.

The luck this would require was too great. Blind luck did happen. Someone had to win the lottery. But he wasn't comfortable with theories that relied on something so utterly improbable, so he needed to explore other possibilities before he'd believe this as the answer.

Dan Vettori was the CEO of a VR company. So had the terrorist attack been nothing more than a virtual reality stunt?

Kagan dismissed this possibility before it was even fully formed in his mind. Impossible. VR wasn't nearly advanced enough to achieve this level of reality, and none of the guests had put on headsets or glasses.

Besides, this would be the dumbest, cruelest, most despicable publicity stunt in history. Vettori would be sued and worse. If you wanted to spring a surprise demonstration of VR, you whisked your guests off to a fantasy city in the clouds, or put them near a waterfall with lots of butterflies.

You didn't throw them into the center of a massacre.

Kagan was about to search for other explanations when he heard the sound of footsteps, the first sign that he was more than just a disembodied soul. Multiple footsteps.

"What is his status?" he heard spoken nearby.

The accent and voice were unmistakable. It was the terrorist who had led the attack.

Kagan couldn't move, but a chill flashed up his spine. If he *were* in the afterlife, then the presence of this voice certainly made it clear that he had missed heaven by a wide berth.

"I don't have a full lab," said a deep, unaccented male voice, clearly American, "but the results I get with the portable blood analyzer are very promising. The blood infusion went very well. Red and white blood cell counts are good. Platelet count is good. No sign of sepsis. Lactic acid levels are good. C-reactive protein levels indicate no inflammation beyond what would be expected. I'm confident that he's out of the woods and will make a quick recovery from here."

"When will he awaken?" asked the terror leader.

"The monitors show that he's awake now, and conscious. He can hear every word we're saying. But the anesthesia and paralytic agents I gave him haven't fully worn off, so he can't move. I can inject a reversal agent into his IV that will counteract these drugs if you'd like."

"Yes, please do."

There was a long pause. "He'll be able to move in a minute or two," said the American finally, no doubt having injected the reversal agent.

"Thank you, Doctor," said the terrorist. He went on to ask a man standing next to him to escort the doctor from the room, so he could have a private conversation with their captive.

"Before I go," said the doctor, "I think we can remove his IV, and the straps holding his legs to the bed. His ankles are still tethered to it, so he can't go anywhere, but at least he'll be able to sit or stand if he wants."

"Go ahead," said the terrorist. "Just be sure to take the IV needle and apparatus with you."

While the doctor completed these tasks, Kagan tried to move a finger. Nothing.

Less than a minute later, however, he tried again and was gratified to find that he now had control of his body once more. The reversal agent had worked as quickly as the doctor had indicated.

Ben Kagan took a deep mental breath. As much as he wanted to continue to play dead forever, eventually he had to face this new, harsh reality, and learn about the situation he was in. Part of him concluded that whatever he would face was better than being dead.

Part of him wasn't at all sure that this would be the case.

He opened his eyes slowly to find himself on a bed, as expected, in the master suite of a private home, which had been transformed into a temporary hospital room. His legs were attached to the bed with a zip-tie chain, as the doctor had indicated, and his wrists were cuffed, with a six-inch length of chain, sheathed in plastic, to give him play between his wrists.

He still wore the black cotton slacks he had worn to the party, but his attire above the waist had been replaced by a gray sweatshirt—one that didn't possess a bullet hole and wasn't drenched in his blood.

A lone man was with him, hovering overhead. The man looked to be of Middle Eastern ancestry, but was clean-shaven, no doubt to avoid looking like a terrorist so he could better blend in.

"Who are you?" said Kagan, his voice still soft and raspy.

"Anwar Sadiq."

"You're a *butcher*," whispered Kagan, hatred oozing from his every pore. "You killed them all."

"Well, not *all*, or you wouldn't be here."

This gave Kagan pause. "Did you spare any others?"

"Yes," replied the terrorist. "One other."

"So, what, you just chose two of us at random? Why? To torture?"

Sadiq shook his head. "What makes you think you were chosen at *random*?" he said. "On the contrary, *Mr. Kagan*." A slow, cruel smile spread over the terrorist's face. "The truth is, *you* were the entire point of the attack. Everyone else at the party died to cover *your* abduction."

Kagan's eyes widened in horror, but he also wore another expression. One of comprehension.

Sadiq nodded in satisfaction. "And I see from your reaction that you know *exactly* why this is," he finished.

# 6

Bile rose in Kagan's throat. Sadiq was right. He did now realize what this was all about.

But as horrified as he was, he allowed himself a glimmer of hope. Sadiq had said that one other had survived the attack. He had a feeling that this had to be Cynthia Shearer, to use as leverage against him.

Either way, whether the love of his life was a bullet-riddled corpse or was being kept as leverage, he forced himself to shunt her from his mind, to prevent his emotions from turning him into a quivering, exposed nerve-ending.

"Where am I?" said Kagan.

"Not too far from where you were," replied Sadiq, obviously pleased with himself. "In a rental, um . . . estate. Hidden in plain sight. The last place anyone would expect."

Kagan knew that the occasional Poway estate was available for rental, for the right money, sometimes ten to twenty thousand a month. One of these would offer great privacy and seclusion. And Sadiq was right—authorities would expect the terrorists to put as much distance between themselves and Poway as possible, not to brazenly stay in the neighborhood, so close to the scene of their crimes against humanity.

Kagan's eyes narrowed. "If I really *was* the goal," he said, "then why shoot me? Seems to me I'm lucky to be alive."

Sadiq snarled angrily. "The man who shot you was an *idiot!* We studied enough holographic images of you in preparation for this mission to recognize you in an instant. From any angle. My men were instructed not to shoot near you if there was *any* chance you could be hit. The man who shot you said you dived into his line of fire. Even so, this mistake was inexcusable. He paid for it with his life."

Sadiq's ire was still readily apparent. "We had to kidnap a doctor from a local hospital and steal some equipment to get you back to health. Complicated the mission. We've lost two days because of it."

Kagan stifled a gasp. He had been unconscious for *two days*? He wanted to ponder this further, but didn't have that luxury. "Does the doctor know you're with ISIS?" he asked.

"Of course not. I hid most of my men from him, and we grabbed him before the news of our attack on the mansion was made public. We made up quite a tale to explain things. In our version, we're the undercover agents, and you're the enemy of America. We apologized profusely for the need to press him into service, and we've treated him well. We'll release him shortly now that he's patched you up."

Kagan didn't believe this for an instant. He wouldn't have, even if he hadn't been witness to Sadiq's barbarism and utter lack of mercy. The fact that Sadiq had let the doctor see his face, and Kagan's—not to mention know the approximate location of their hideout—had sealed the doctor's fate. He would soon be exterminated, without remorse, since he was no longer needed.

Now that Kagan knew exactly what was happening, and why, everything made perfect sense. Chilling, horrifying, perfect sense. "I still don't understand," he said, feigning confusion. "Why am I so important to you?"

Sadiq simply smiled and shook his head. "*Of course* you know why, Mr. Kagan," he said. "But I understand why you might pretend you don't. Why offer up any information, just in case I'm, as you Americans say, barking up the wrong tree. So I'll spell it out for you, so you'll know there's no reason to continue to play dumb."

Kagan blinked stupidly.

"You're one of the top scientists at Weiser Technologies. That much is public record. Six months ago, you were working on a project involving Hydro's fleet of fully autonomous vehicles. I now know quite a lot about these AVs. Yours and everyone else's rely on a constant stream of inputs delivered wirelessly to the AI controlling the vehicle. These include inputs from sensors built into the car, sensors built into the roads, and communications *between* vehicles. And also inputs such as weather, road conditions, and traffic reports." Sadiq raised his eyebrows. "How am I doing so far?"

"So you know a little about AVs. Is that supposed to impress me?"

Sadiq continued as if Kagan hadn't spoken. "Six months ago, you were assigned to dramatically improve this system. Devise superior algorithms that would allow Hydro AIs to access this data more efficiently, and make more intelligent use of it. If everyone has access to the same data, the company who can do the most *with* this data emerges on top."

Kagan frowned and shook his head. "All of this is in the public domain. Norman Weiser discussed this initiative at the last annual shareholder meeting, including the fact that I'd be in charge."

"What he *didn't* mention was that a few months after the shareholder meeting, while working on this project, you became convinced there was a flaw in the system. Convinced that, in theory, a way could be found to burrow through the security wall that the auto industry and your government are so convinced is impenetrable. A way to bypass the safeguards mandated by your federal government.

"You sounded the alarm," continued Sadiq, "but no one took you seriously, since the accepted dogma is that AVs are absolutely hackproof. So you convinced Weiser to let you set up a task force to find the hack. To prove it existed. And then to fix it so it could never be used. You know," he added menacingly, "by people like me."

Thrilling hatred coursed through Kagan's bloodstream, and while not a man of violence, all he wanted to do was drive an ice pick through the terrorist's heart. Instead, he forced his face to stay relaxed and shook his head. "I have no idea where you got your information," he said calmly, "but it's only half right. I did try to find a hack. But I failed. I proved that all of the experts were right, and I was wrong. The system really is foolproof."

Sadiq stared at his prisoner for several long seconds, appraising him carefully. "You are not what I expected," he said. "I thought you'd be a sniveling coward. Book smart but not street smart. Instead, you are remarkably calm, and seem to think well on your feet."

Kagan nodded. No one was more surprised by this than he was.

"I'll have to be even more careful with you than I thought," continued the terrorist leader. "But it really is time to stop this act. I know that you're close to finding the hack." His eyes gleamed with a sudden fierce intensity. "So be happy," he growled, "because I'm here to help you achieve your goal."

Kagan cursed inwardly. He had been a *fool*. He had sounded the alarm about AVs, and had established a task force to prevent terrorists from carrying out an unimaginably devastating attack on America. But instead of *stopping* such an attack, he had sent the terrorists an engraved invitation to carry it out.

Fully Autonomous Vehicles had been on the road for almost four years now, vehicles that not only could drive themselves, but couldn't be driven otherwise, as they had no steering wheels, brake pedal, or gas pedal.

Ever since they had been perfected, a growing percentage of the seventeen million vehicles sold in America each year were driverless. And in ten or twenty years, when the last of the manual cars were sold for scrap, the ascendancy of AVs would be complete.

The best minds in the world had grappled with the many ways this would transform society. Most believed the rise of AVs would bring about a transportation paradise, a gift to civilization, allowing mobility for all, including the blind, handicapped, underage, and elderly—providing everyone with their own personal, 24/7 chauffeurs.

Travel would become less expensive, and far safer, with many thousands of lives saved each year. Traffic jams would become a footnote in the history books, and car travel would become a productive time for watching movies, reading, or catching up on work, rather than an exercise in concentration and keeping eyes forever glued to the road.

Fewer cars would be needed, and far fewer parking spaces, as all cars in America would communicate and interact cooperatively, in a grand and complex ballet, like an ant colony with hundreds of millions of members.

But others saw the rise of AVs as more alarming. Millions of Americans who made a living from driving would lose their jobs, including truck and bus drivers, delivery drivers, taxis, and Lyft and Uber drivers, among others.

As crashes became a thing of the past, the ranks of the half million people in the auto body repair business would become decimated. Auto insurance companies would go out of business. The real estate market would shift dramatically, as longer commutes became ever more tolerable.

At first Kagan was more alarmed than anyone about these developments, especially widespread unemployment, but further thought and study allayed these concerns. Automation had been predicted to have a devastating effect on human employment many times throughout history, yet this had never materialized.

In 1811, an organized group of weavers and textile workers, calling themselves Luddites, destroyed weaving machinery to protest what they believed to be job-killing automation. Because of this movement, the term *Luddite* had come to refer to anyone who was resistant to new technology and technological changes.

But the job losses the Luddites of England feared never came to pass. Because of greatly increased efficiencies and cheaper goods, by the end of the nineteenth century, there were four times as many factory weavers employed than there had been during this movement.

In 1830, America's farmers comprised *seventy-one percent* of the workforce. Yet, in modern times, this number had plummeted to less than *two* percent. Improved automation of farms had impacted a greater percentage of the workforce than autonomous vehicles ever could. Even so, society had readily absorbed the loss of these farming jobs, which had morphed into opportunities in other sectors.

Additional examples abounded.

But one risk that the rise of AVs brought about couldn't possibly be overstated—the risk that these self-driving cars and trucks could be hacked. Terrorists had long been using individual, human-controlled cars and trucks as the equivalent of ground-delivered missiles, ramming many thousands of pounds of steel into large crowds with devastating results, causing mass casualties and untold terror. And this was the result of using a single vehicle in this way.

But there were now more than twelve million driverless cars on American roads. Twelve million!

The potential for disaster was nearly unfathomable.

Yet experts insisted the cars, and system, were safe. They made assurances that the communication system AVs all used couldn't be hacked, that there was no way a hacker could take control of a single vehicle, let alone all of them.

Even if the unthinkable happened, and someone managed to take remote control of America's AV fleet, the hacker would still need to override the vehicles' safety features to purposely crash into buildings, or plow into crowds of pedestrians. Disabling these safety features was considered to be even *more* impossible than hacking into the system in the first place.

But Kagan knew otherwise. And now, so did Anwar Sadiq and ISIS.

If Sadiq got control, he could take over every AV now in use and insert an algorithm that instructed their AIs to seek out nearby populations centers and ram as many people as possible, focusing on crowded malls, outdoor gatherings, and other collections of helpless pedestrians. And unlike the previous use of cars as terror weapons, where the death of the driver would finally end the carnage, the vehicles would continue to seek out new targets until their very engines were incapacitated.

"Good thing Vettori had his party when he did," continued Sadiq. "It was the perfect cover for us, at the perfect time. If we had waited much longer, you'd have found what you were after, and plugged any holes." He shot Kagan a cruel smile. "But don't worry, I'll make sure you have all the tools you need to finish the job."

Kagan raged within, but continued to maintain an outward calm. "You've been misled," he said wearily, a teacher trying to be patient with an errant student. "I'm not close to anything. How many times do I need to tell you? I tried to do what you suggest, but failed. I was wrong. You may wish this wasn't true, but it is."

Kagan shook his head. "And even if, for the sake of argument, you *are* right," he continued, "which you *aren't*, by now the authorities have gone over the remains of the innocents you butchered. By now they know I was the only one at the party whose body is unaccounted for. If this mythical program of mine did exist, they would quickly guess why you want me and take precautions. Alert authorities. Add additional firewalls to the AV fleet that I don't know about. Even if a hack was possible yesterday, it isn't today. Not when they know you're coming."

Sadiq shook his head in disdain. "Do you think you're the only one clever enough to see that?" he said. "Do you think we're *stupid*? We knew that it wasn't enough to kidnap you. We had do it in such a way that no one would ever suspect you were the target, or even still alive. So, first, we made sure your authorities knew you were there, by taking footage of all guests, and leaving it behind. We also left all cell phones, including yours, for them to find."

He leaned in menacingly and raised his eyebrows. "Then we put all the bodies through industrial-grade woodchippers. To be certain there were no remains of *anyone* to identify."

Kagan looked as though he had been punched in the gut.

"That's right, Mr. Kagan," said the terrorist, relishing this reaction, "no one will have any idea that you're still alive, and not part of the bloody mess we left behind. America's AV fleet will not be on guard. No one will be looking for you. And without your skills, your project team back at Hydro has no chance of success."

Sadiq took a few moments to bask in the look of horror on his prisoner's face. "What's wrong, Mr. Kagan?" he taunted. "You don't look so good. You can claim you aren't working on this as much as you like, but your expression says otherwise. Not that it matters to me if you persist in denying the truth. I *will* get what I want." He smiled icily. "Do you want to know how?"

Kagan's lip curled up in utter contempt and hatred. "You can torture me to death," he hissed. "Do whatever you want. But you have to know I'll never help you."

"So predictable," said Sadiq dismissively. "Again, did you think we didn't know this is how you'd respond? Did you think we'd just rely on simple coercion?"

He leaned in closer to his captive. "There are two ways we can play this," he continued. "First, you can help us voluntarily. Why would you do this? Because much more than your life is on the line. Your girlfriend is in the next room. Refuse to help and we blind her in front of you. Then we see how many tiny cuts she can survive. You get to watch her suffering, hear her pleas, hear her shrieks, the entire time."

Kagan exploded, roaring out his hatred and pain and helplessness, the emotions he had suppressed bursting through the surface like an eruption of pressurized magma. Sadiq waited patiently for his prisoner's screaming and cursing to subside, looking pleased that he had finally hit such a sensitive nerve.

When Kagan had screamed and cursed himself out, the terrorist manipulated a phone, and a series of holographic images appeared in the room beside him, revolving rapidly. Images of Kagan's extended family. His two sisters, his brother, and their seven children. His parents. His aunts and uncles and cousins. His friends. They were all there. Their images captured while they were going about their daily lives, none the wiser—proof that Sadiq or someone he controlled was within striking distance of them at the time, and could be again.

"If you refuse to cooperate after your girlfriend has been sliced into hamburger, then you'll lose friends and family, one by one. Starting with little two-year-old Heather."

A tear came to Kagan's eye as he considered the picture that Sadiq had so vividly painted. Still, he had no choice. He gathered himself and shook his head. "Do what you have to do," he whispered wearily. "I won't help you."

He was ashamed to admit it, but if a thousand strangers had to be sacrificed to save Cynthia, save his family, he might have considered it. Maybe even five thousand. But Sadiq had made the math too lopsided. If Kagan did what this monster wanted, *millions* could die.

He wouldn't let that happen, no matter what tortures he had to endure, and even at the cost of the slaughter of everyone he had ever loved.

Sadiq simply smiled. "I predicted you wouldn't cooperate. Not yet. I still think you'd change your mind once the torture and killing began, but let's table that for a moment. Have you ever heard of a drug that English speakers are calling *EasyZom*?"

Kagan managed to shake his head no.

Sadiq placed a small tablet computer in one of Kagan's hands. "Go ahead and Google it," he said. "I'll wait."

Kagan did as requested, the cuffs providing just enough room between his hands for him to manipulate the device normally. Just when he thought nothing could horrify him more than what he was already facing, he soon learned otherwise.

The *Zom* in EasyZom stood for Zombie. The drug had been developed only the year before, in Iran, and was a variation of the drug Scopolamine. Injections would cause a subject to lose free will entirely, make him or her wide open to manipulation, to following orders without question. While drugged, a man would give up passwords, rob his own home, kill his own family, or do whatever else was commanded, a human turned into a puppet.

Thankfully, the drug was quite difficult to manufacture, and producing even the smallest amount was costly and time-consuming.

After a few minutes, Sadiq retrieved the small computer from his bound prisoner. "Let me give you additional inducement," he said. "Help me of your own free will, and I will treat you well. I swear to Allah to release you unharmed when you're done. Cynthia also. And no harm will come to any member of your family."

He shook his head grimly. "Refuse to help me, on the other hand, and I'll shoot you up with EasyZom each day until you've achieved success. You'll become absolutely pliable, putting your heart and soul into helping me. But before this happens, I'll torture and kill Cynthia in front of you. I won't kill your family until you've succeeded, in case the authorities connect the dots as to why everyone you care about is being killed. But I promise you, they will all die, horribly, when we're finished. Either way, I *will* get what I want."

"Then why not just use the drug in the first place?" said Kagan. "Why do you need my willing cooperation?"

Sadiq paused, as though considering if he should answer. Finally he shrugged, as if it didn't matter. "I didn't give you much time to research the drug," he said, "but I can tell you, it's hard to make and expensive. We've already made enough to get us through this operation, but I'd prefer to save it and use it elsewhere. Also, the drug dulls the intellect—just a tiny amount. It's almost imperceptible. And you have more than enough talent to find what I'm looking for, even at ninety-eight-percent capacity. But why not have you at your un-drugged best? Why not get to my answer as soon as possible?"

He shrugged. "So it's your choice. Cooperate and give me what I want. Or don't cooperate and do the same."

There was silence for several long moments. "Okay," whispered Kagan in surrender, his tone one of utter defeat. "You win. Since you'll get what you want either way, I'll help you. But neither Cynthia nor my family get as much as a single bruise."

"May Allah strike me down if I'm lying," said the terrorist. A knowing smile began to spread over his face. "And speaking of ly-ing," he added, "you agreed *too* readily. You do realize I don't in-tend to just take your word that you'll be cooperating. I plan to give you periodic doses of EasyZom along the way, just to be sure you're working in good faith. If it can turn you into a puppet, it can induce you to tell the truth—the perfect lie detector test. So if you were just agreeing to cooperate to stall for time, or to try to escape, it won't work. Or if you think you can sabotage the process, seal the AV breach as soon as you find it—think again."

Kagan's eyes blazed with hatred once again. Sadiq had seen through his ruse all too easily.

"And you can't get out of this by killing yourself, either. We'll be on constant suicide watch. Why do you think you're restrained the way you are? All sharp objects have been removed from this room. No string or chain or tape that you could use to hang yourself. Your handcuff chain is sheathed in smooth plastic and too short to strangle yourself with. Killing oneself is not as easy as you might think. Try to hold your breath or choke yourself and you pass out long before you die."

Kagan nodded wearily. "You're right," he said. "When I agreed to cooperate, I was bluffing. Stalling for time. Now that it's clear you've seen through me, let me consider your proposal for real. Give me an hour to think about it."

"You have fifteen minutes," said Sadiq firmly.

# 7

Ben Kagan pulled at his restraints the moment Sadiq left the room, but it was hopeless, as expected. He took careful inventory of his surroundings, but true to Sadiq's word, there was nothing within reach, or even in *sight*, that he could use as a weapon, or an instrument of his own demise.

If he could have killed himself, he would have done so. He was in the ultimate cage. No biblical description of hell could do his predicament justice. Death would be a blessing, his only escape.

Still, his mind continued to be unnaturally calm, especially under the circumstances.

He checked his pants pockets, his fingers just long enough to explore them thoroughly, despite the handcuffs. Along with his wallet, they had taken his keys. Probably concerned that one of them might be sharp enough to open a vein. They had left him only a stray twenty-dollar bill in his left pocket, and two small cocktail napkins in his right. The napkins were a painful reminder of the moment the attack had begun and his life had turned into a living nightmare.

His belt had been removed, as had his shoes and socks. He guessed his socks had been taken so he wouldn't try to shove them down his throat to suffocate himself.

His mind continued a calm but rapid assessment of his predicament. There *had* to be a way out, he told himself. He couldn't allow himself to believe otherwise, or all hope would be lost.

He considered what he had to work with once again, but it was perhaps the shortest list ever.

He gasped! A hint of an idea had entered his mind.

His eyes widened as he explored this idea further, and electricity rushed up his spine as he realized it just might work.

Perhaps he had everything he needed, after all.

He ran the plan through his mind again and again, making minor variations and refinements each time. It was an act of desperation, and the odds of success were impossible to know.

Still, if they were above zero, it was worth trying, no matter what the cost.

He brought himself to a seated position at the edge of the bed, and made preparations to carry out his plan. After one final check to be sure Sadiq wasn't returning, he drew in several deep breaths to psych himself up, and then shoved his index finger into his right nostril, pounding and clawing at it for all he was worth. He ignored the pain until he was rewarded with a nostril-full of blood, which immediately began dripping onto the bed like a leaky faucet.

When he was a boy, he had suffered from nosebleeds on more than one occasion, and had cursed the thin, fragile veins that caused him such embarrassment. But not today. Today, this array of thin, dense blood vessels were just what he needed.

Less than two minutes later he rose to his full height at the side of the bed, his restraints not allowing him to stand more than a foot from its base. He used his left hand to smear blood all over his face, making his situation look dire, rather than the result of a harmless nosebleed.

"*Sadiq!*" he screamed in alarm. "Bring the doctor! I need help!"

He ratcheted his volume up even further and repeated these words.

Moments later the terrorist leader burst through the door, the doctor in tow.

"Thank God!" said Kagan. "My eyes and nose are bleeding!" he added in a panic as the doctor neared to examine him.

When the man was practically on top of him, Kagan reached out with cuffed hands, seized him by the shirt, and yanked him down onto the bed, all in the blink of an eye. The moment the doctor was down, Kagan dived on top of him and began pummeling him the best he could in his bound state. His hands flew over the doctor's body, ending up near the man's waist, where he pounded at his sensitive groin area, screaming and cursing all the while.

Kagan had turned into a berserker, his hands a frenzy of motion. "You stupid bastard!" he thundered, all but frothing at the mouth. "You should have let me die! *Do you know what you've done?*"

Sadiq was initially stunned by Kagan's behavior, but this quickly grew into alarm. Kagan's face was covered in blood, and it appeared that he was trying to kill himself through blood-loss and overexertion, or was attempting to provoke the *doctor* into killing him.

The terrorist shouted for two of his men, who rushed into the room moments later. He issued quick orders, and the three of them began to pull their crazed prisoner off of the doctor. As they were doing so, Kagan jerked his body around to face them, and he reached for Sadiq's gun, still in its holster, all in one smooth motion.

Just as Kagan's fingers touched the gun, Sadiq batted his hand away, and quickly got a firm grip on the bound wrists of the prisoner, ending his pathetic attempt to turn the tables.

Seconds later, Kagan and the doctor were pried apart, and the doctor was removed from the room. The man was rattled and a bit bruised, but due to the limitations imposed by Kagan's restraints, was largely undamaged.

Tears of rage and sorrow began to pour down Kagan's face, diluting the blood that was still doing the same. A stream of tears that he had thought were bottled up. Tears that reflected the horrors he had witnessed at Vettori's party, the fear of losing Cynthia and his family, and the prospect of being turned into the instrument of the worst terror attack in human history.

Sadiq carefully restrained Kagan in a supine position once again, and ordered his men to clean up the prisoner's face. It soon became clear that Kagan was only suffering from a simple, harmless nosebleed, which a wad of tissue shoved into his right nostril quickly abated.

When Kagan's tears finally subsided, he screamed curses and threats until his throat was hoarse. But this, too, eventually stopped. Finally, he faced Sadiq, his eyes on fire and his face showing nothing but pure, distilled hatred. "Okay, you monster," he hissed. "I'll help you. Of my own free will. But you'll pay for your atrocities with an eternity in hell!"

"I guess we'll just have to see about that," said Sadiq smugly. "But in the meanwhile," he added with a self-satisfied smile, "welcome to our cause."

# PART 2
# Three Years Later

# 8

The AI, which the US military had codenamed *Watchdog*, was housed within a supercomputer in Colorado, but its range of vision was nearly infinite, and it could happily perform twenty-seven million trillion calculations each second.

And if a non-sentient AI could experience surprise, this one did now.

Watchdog was very good at calculating probabilities, but the probability that the phenomenon it had just detected was random was as close to zero as anything got.

It checked and rechecked its findings thousands of times, accessing enough additional data to choke millions of desktop computers, but came to the same conclusion each time.

Still, for a finding this special, this unusual, it needed to be even more certain, so it continued its monitoring for almost ten seconds—an eternity—and continued to crunch data and perform calculations before it decided it had checked enough.

Now it was time to contact the Secretary of Defense, as protocol dictated.

Watchdog's job was to take in inputs from telescopes around the world and in space, with or without the knowledge of those who were running them. Telescopes that measured visible light, gamma-rays, the ultraviolet spectrum, X-rays, microwaves, gravity waves, and radio waves.

The data generated each day by a single space telescope, taking in views of an incomprehensibly large swath of the cosmos, could keep an astrologist busy for centuries. So only a supercomputer-based AI like Watchdog could possibly make sense of the data coming from the many thousands of telescopes that it monitored.

Watchdog gave humanity its best hope of identifying threatening objects that might want to collide with Earth. The sort of object that had wiped out the dinosaur, a form of life that had reigned for roughly one hundred sixty-five million years. Or just over eight hundred times longer than haughty *Homo sapiens* had so far managed.

Officially, NASA's Planetary Defense Coordination Office was responsible for detecting Near-Earth Objects, or NEOs. The space agency's Jet Propulsion Laboratory maintained a Center for NEO Studies, which computed high-precision orbits for all objects detected in space to predict close approaches to Earth. Using its *Sentry* impact monitoring system, the Center performed long-term analyses of possible future orbits of hazardous asteroids, searching for impact possibilities a hundred years into the future.

Watchdog *began* its analyses by tapping into JPL's program and stealing its results, before combining it with its own. And unlike Sentry, Watchdog wasn't shy about illegally tapping into similar programs around the world. This military version of Sentry was also more sophisticated, making use of computer advances coming from well-funded military laboratories that were not shared with the public.

But before Watchdog communicated its findings to the Secretary of Defense, Admiral Chris Headrick, its programming demanded it perform one final task. It needed to delete certain data sets from Sentry's memory. That AI was slow, *plodding*, but given another 1.4 seconds, even this incompetent system could figure it out, and Sentry had been programmed to be a veritable blabbermouth, broadcasting a result like this to anyone who would listen.

Watchdog finished deleting the data, and then, finally—almost twelve full seconds since it had first detected the anomaly—it put in a call through a secure channel to the Secretary of Defense.

It was time to bring this finding to his attention at long last.

# 9

President David Moro was the last to arrive to the White House conference room, and looked harried. This was the first emergency meeting his Secretary of Defense, retired Admiral Chris Headrick, had ever called, and he was bracing himself for the worst.

He looked around the table and saw there were only five other attendees, a surprisingly small group for an emergency meeting called by the man who commanded all of America's armed forces around the world.

In addition to Headrick, Jesse Carter, his head of DHS, was in attendance, along with a woman he had only met briefly years earlier, Stephanie Annise, the head of NASA.

The head of NASA? He had expected the Chairman of the Joint Chiefs, perhaps, but not the head of NASA.

The president didn't even recognize the two remaining attendees, which was disconcerting given the nature of this meeting.

"Thank you for being here on such short notice, Mr. President," began Admiral Headrick when Moro was seated. He gestured to the two women in the room whom Moro had never met. "Allow me to introduce you to NASA's Planetary Protection Officer, Dr. Kim Buckner," he said, nodding toward a petite brunette, "and the head of the 527th Space Aggressor Squadron, Air Force Colonel Mary Bredlau," he finished, referring to a woman in her forties with steely gray eyes.

The blood drained from Moro's face. Was this a bad joke? Planetary Protection? Space Aggressor Squadron? Was he about to be told they were under attack by marauding aliens? He had no interest in being the star of a real-life recreation of the movie *Independence Day*.

The president's heart stopped pounding wildly as he realized that
if they were under attack, or soon to be, the military would be much
better represented at this meeting.

He nodded perfunctorily to the two women who had just been
introduced.

"I'll get right to the point, sir," continued the Secretary of Defense.
"A little over three hours ago, Watchdog, the classified military version of NASA's Sentry, detected a small object—I'm told a little smaller than a softball—just beyond the orbit of Mars. An object traveling
at *very* close to the speed of light. Detecting an object this small, this
far away, traveling at this speed, is an impressive feat, and I won't go
into the scientific details of how this was managed. Suffice it to say
that it would have been impossible without an ever-growing array
of telescopes examining the sky, and sophisticated AIs able to make
sense of it all. A human would have missed it entirely, because no
celestial object of this size can travel this fast."

"What does that mean?" said the president. "That it *isn't* a celestial object?"

"That's the conclusion we came to, yes," said Headrick.

This chilling statement hung in the air for several long seconds.

"So what are you saying?" said Moro. "That this thing is an alien
spaceship? The size of a softball?"

"I'm afraid that's exactly what I'm saying, Mr. President. There
can be little doubt."

Moro swallowed hard. "Isn't it possible there are astronomical
processes we don't know about that can propel a natural object to
this speed?"

"Great question," said Stephanie Annise, the head of NASA, genuinely impressed. "It is true that we learn things every year that alter
our perception of what is possible in the cosmos."

"Watchdog initially considered this possibility, as well," said
Admiral Headrick. "But five seconds after the object was detected, it
made a course correction, and then began to decelerate."

"Conclusive proof that it isn't a natural phenomenon," said Kim
Buckner, who apparently was something called a Planetary Protection
Officer, a position the president didn't even know existed.

"So it's an alien spacecraft," said Moro, almost to himself. "But surely it isn't manned. Not that *manned* would be the proper way to say this. But you get what I mean. *Occupied*."

Stephanie Annise shook her head. "You're correct," she said. "It's very likely to be an unmanned . . . unoccupied," she corrected, "probe. Although anything is possible. It could be a craft built by intelligent beings the size of fleas, who would find a ship of that size quite spacious. But we doubt it. So for the sake of this discussion, I think it's safe to call it an alien probe."

Moro cringed, almost imperceptibly. "When I hear the words, *alien probe*, why am I thinking more about the exploration of human anatomy than the exploration of space?"

The head of NASA smiled. "I said alien probe, I didn't say *probed by an alien*. I'm afraid that's what we call this type of object. Shorter than unmanned, robotic, exploratory spacecraft. We've launched any number of these ourselves, as you well know," she added. "Pioneer, Mariner, Cassini, and Voyager to name just a few."

Moro nodded. "Got it," he said. "So this alien . . . probe," he continued, "changed direction." He took a deep breath. "Let me guess," he added warily, "Watchdog reported that it's headed toward Earth."

Headrick nodded.

"When will it arrive?" asked Moro.

"Almost three hours ago, sir," replied Headrick grimly.

"Three hours ago!" repeated Moro. "Didn't you say that's when it was first *detected*? Beyond the orbit of Mars?"

"All true, Mr. President," confirmed the head of NASA. "It *was* detected three hours ago. But it also *arrived* here three hours ago. It made it to Earth minutes after it was spotted. The speed of light is plodding when it comes to interstellar distances, but it's plenty quick within a solar system. It only takes light a little over eight minutes to reach us from the sun. At the speed of light, Mars is only two or three minutes away."

"When it got to within four million miles of us," added Colonel Bredlau, "it underwent a spectacular deceleration, one that shouldn't have been physically possible."

"Where did it land?" said the president.

"That's a little tricky, sir," said Colonel Bredlau. "It was still traveling at ludicrous speed when it entered our atmosphere. Easier to track things going this fast when they're far away and in space. Harder to track their precise landing on Earth, especially when they're this small. We do know that, in general, it landed in the heart of the Amazon Jungle."

Moro shook his head in disbelief. "Did you say *Amazon Jungle?*"

"I'm afraid so, Mr. President," said Bredlau, as if she was having trouble believing the insanity of it herself. "We've narrowed its location, but that's the best we can do. We were only able to get the read we did because it has an energy signature unlike anything we've ever seen. But the moment it landed, the energy signature disappeared, so we couldn't pinpoint it more precisely. We've taken the coordinates of its most likely position and used this as the center of a circle with a nine mile radius. We're confident it will be found within this perimeter."

"Why nine miles?" said Moro.

Bredlau sighed. "I'm afraid it's very technical, Mr. President. But please trust me, there are good reasons for this belief."

"But it's most likely in the center?"

Colonel Bredlau winced. "Yes, but this actually doesn't mean much, because this is only slightly more probable than any other location within this circle. Roll two dice and you're more likely to roll a seven than any other number. Still, the majority of the time, you roll something else."

Moro considered. "I understand," he said. "But at least you've narrowed it down quite a bit. Finding it shouldn't be *too* bad."

Bredlau frowned. "I thought the same before I did the math. A circle with a nine-mile radius has a circumference of fifty seven miles. Which makes the area inside a whopping two hundred fifty-four square miles."

Moro's face fell. "Yeah, this math is more discouraging than I had imagined," he said. "What about our spy satellites? I assume you've pointed a number of these in the general area."

"We have, sir," affirmed Headrick. "Can't find a leaf or piece of moss that is out of the ordinary. And the canopy is so thick, it's basically impossible for a satellite, or anything flying overhead, for that matter, to see what's happening on the jungle floor. I've done some research. Apparently, in many areas of the Amazon, the trees are packed together so tightly that it can take ten minutes after a storm begins for the rain to finally reach the ground." He shook his head in awe. "This came as a surprise, to say the least."

"That does present a problem," said the president with a frown. As he rubbed his chin in thought, his gaze fell on the two women he had never met. "By the way," he said, gesturing to them both. "Who *are* you?"

He narrowed his focus to Kim Buckner. "What in the hell is a Planetary Protection Officer?" he asked her. "NASA really has a group whose job is to protect us from alien invasions?"

Buckner smiled. "Mostly I protect other planets from *us*," she said. "We've sent a large number of ships and probes into space. Especially lately, with all the private companies sending missions to the Moon and Mars. I make sure they're as sterile as possible. We wouldn't want to contaminate any planetary bodies out there."

"We're about to begin the settlement of Mars," said Moro. "Doesn't *that* count as contamination?"

"Well yeah," said Buckner with a grin. "I suppose it does. But we make allowances for human colonization. My job is to be sure we have a chance to scour a planet for alien life—*before* we contaminate it for good. If we find life on Mars, we want to know it really is Martian, and not just the descendants of microbes from Earth that managed to hitch a ride on one of our ships and survive there. And we don't want to send any plagues into space if we don't have to."

She paused. "But more relevant to the topic at hand, I *am* responsible for repelling alien invasions, although this is—usually—the lessor part of my job. But only invasions by *microscopic* aliens. Because of course it works both ways. As eager as I am not to have something from Earth wipe out a planet full of life, I'm even more eager not to bring back something from space that wipes out all life on this planet. We've begun to bring back a number of spacecraft and extraterrestrial samples, and I'm responsible for making sure they don't harbor anything um . . . *unhealthy* for us.

"I'm sure you remember how we survived the alien invasion in H.G. Wells's *War of the Worlds*," she continued. "Our bacteria got them. Given my job, the final passage of this novel is my all-time favorite. Wells wrote that the moment the invaders landed, and I quote, 'our microscopic allies began to work their overthrow. It was inevitable.'"

"That's good stuff," said Moro wryly. "If this Wells guy keeps at it, he might just make it as a writer."

Buckner laughed.

The president rubbed his chin in thought. "But isn't it unlikely that life would be similar enough for microbes from one planet to bother life from another?"

Buckner nodded, impressed. "Very true," she said. "But even if the possibility of interplanetary cross-contamination isn't likely, as you suggest, it isn't impossible. In the *War of the Worlds*, our bugs killed them. But their bugs could have wiped *us* out just the same. That's the scenario I'm in charge of preventing."

"I see," said Moro. "So you must really be itching to take a look at this alien ship."

"You have no idea, Mr. President," replied Buckner. "Before it fully decelerated, it was going so fast that any microbes on its surface would have burned up in our atmosphere. What I'm worried about are any that might be on the *inside*."

Moro nodded and then turned to face the colonel. "And you?" he said. "Tell me about the Space Aggressor Squadron?"

"We don't advertise much, sir," replied Mary Bredlau. "But we do have responsibility to plan for possible alien invasions. And this time not by microbes," she added pointedly. "By intelligent beings who might just want to use Earth as their vacation home."

Moro shook his head. He hadn't known the military had a division that prepared for a possible interstellar war, but he should have guessed. Better to be prepared and not need to be, than not be prepared and regret it.

But no matter how prepared Earth was, Moro decided, an alien species with the technology needed to cross interstellar space would likely find Earth's defenses laughably simple to defeat.

"However, like Dr. Buckner," continued the colonel, "this is the smaller part of the job. Our most pressing responsibility is protecting our satellite infrastructure from attack. For example, we have thirty-one GPS satellites up there," she explained. "Take some of these down and we're screwed. Goodbye electronic navigation. No more getting directions from your phone. And our military becomes crippled.

"And it's not just GPS satellites," she added. "We have many other vulnerabilities in space. Imagine losing the Internet, cell phone, television, and radio all at the same time. We're here to prevent that. Along with the alien invasion thing, of course."

"Of course," said the president.

The Secretary of Defense nodded solemnly. "So now you know why I wanted Dr. Buckner and Colonel Bredlau here for this," he said. "I thought it best that they be kept in the loop from the very beginning."

Moro nodded. It was a good call. And the presence of Stephanie Annise made sense as well, since NASA was NASA, and also ran the Sentry program, among many others. But while everyone else in the room had deep lines of stress etched on their faces, there were times when the head of NASA seemed almost giddy, although she was clearly trying not to show it.

"You seem a lot more relaxed about this situation than the rest of us, Stephanie," said the president. "Does that mean you're convinced this probe isn't a threat? Even if it harbors hostile microbes?"

"No, sir," she replied. "I'd never discount the possible threat. I'd like to think any aliens able to get here would be peaceful, but I know better. We don't even understand *human* behavior—and we *are* human. So I get that we can't judge their actions by human standards. But I can't help but be ecstatic, no matter what. This is absolute proof of intelligent life. I wondered if I'd ever see proof of even microbial life before I died. But this means that life must be common. It's a dream come true."

"I'm all for other forms of life," said the president. "As long as they don't do anything to interfere with *ours*. You know," he added wryly, "like driving us into extinction. That sort of thing." But even as he said this, he was well aware of how momentous a discovery this really was. He had been so busy trying to get up to speed and consider possible dangers that he had left his sense of wonder behind.

"So what do all of you think," asked Moro, addressing the entire group, "should public disclosure be on the table?"

"That is ultimately your decision, Mr. President," said Jesse Carter, who had been silently following the proceedings with great interest, but had yet to join in. "But Admiral Headrick and I did discuss this before you arrived. We agree that before we make any decisions regarding public disclosure—which would be the story of the ages—we need to find the damn thing. Actually, we need to find it before we do *anything* else. And quickly."

"To make sure it doesn't inadvertently cause a plague?" asked Moro.

"Much more than that, sir," said Headrick. "This thing has a propulsion system well beyond anything we've ever even dreamed of. We already know it can decelerate in a way that defies our understanding of physics. It's small, but what other secrets might it have? It could contain technology that could transform human civilization. Catapult us generations ahead of where we would otherwise be. Without hyperbole, this could be the biggest game changer in history."

The president's eyes grew steadily wider as the Secretary of Defense framed the situation in this way. "Understood," he said. "And I agree with you. Retrieving this thing has to be our top priority. We can debate public disclosure after we figure out what we're dealing with."

Carter swallowed hard. "I'm afraid it won't be that easy, sir. That's why the admiral insisted on an emergency meeting. We have no time to waste. Because we can't assume we're the only country to have spotted it. Just the opposite. We're nearly certain that others will have also."

"I thought this Watchdog of ours is the best in the business," said Moro.

"It is, sir," replied the head of DHS. "And while other countries are six months to a year behind us, we estimate they're just sophisticated enough to have picked up this probe. A year ago, no country on Earth would have detected it, and all of humanity would be completely oblivious."

"Maybe we *have been* until now?" mused the president. "Who knows? Maybe these things have been landing here for centuries, and this is the first time we've been able to detect one."

There was a long silence around the table as everyone considered this new perspective.

"While this is a fair point, Mr. President," said Admiral Headrick finally, "it doesn't change our current situation. Several countries are almost certainly aware of its presence. Others will learn of it soon. Every country is hacking every other country, and hacking offenses are beating anti-hacking defenses pretty regularly in this ongoing battle. It's gotten so bad that for several years now, we've been keeping our most important secrets in paper notebooks, never letting them touch anything electronic."

"Wow," mumbled Stephanie Annise, unable to help herself, "that's like the Dark Ages."

Headrick smiled. "Not at all," he replied in amusement. "Our people have learned how to use their quills at night, by torchlight, so we're okay."

The head of NASA winced, realizing how condescending her statement must have sounded. "Sorry. I was just surprised we've begun keeping secrets, um . . . the old-fashioned way."

"Me too," said the admiral. "But it's the only way to be sure right now. Information about this probe's arrival will have necessarily been detected by computers and communicated through computer systems in every country that detects it. So this knowledge is susceptible to interception. And even if only a few countries managed to detect the probe initially, intelligence this profound is like a sexually transmitted disease in a whorehouse. Others will catch it. And soon. If they haven't already."

"So which countries do you think are already aware?" asked the president.

"In Asia," replied Admiral Headrick, "China and Japan, almost certainly. Possibly Singapore, South Korea, and even North Korea, although this last would have to be through a computer hack of its neighbor.

"In the Middle East, Israel for sure, probably Iran, and possibly Saudi Arabia.

"In Europe, England, Germany, and Russia for sure. The other European countries either haven't upgraded their systems or don't have Watchdog programs of their own, relying on us and others to police space.

"Hell, there are probably five or ten more around the globe. Possibly even ISIS. ISIS has almost been snuffed out, but the hacking skills of those who remain are quite strong. They've been successfully getting secret intel they should have had no business getting. From our country and others."

The president shrank back in alarm. "So what you're telling me," he said, "is that this thing might have tech that could change the balance of world power overnight. And that a despotic regime might be as aware of it as we are."

"I'm afraid so, sir," said Headrick. "Which is why we need to get to it first. Right now we're at the top of the food chain. Tomorrow . . ." He let the thought hang and then shrugged. "Who knows."

# 10

There was a long silence in the White House conference room.

"Thank you for making the stakes so clear, Admiral," said Moro finally. "So I assume you're recommending that we send in an overwhelming military force."

Headrick and Carter exchanged quick glances, and then the Secretary of Defense stared steadily into the president's eyes. "Actually, sir," he replied. "Just the opposite. One man. Alone. At least for starters."

"One man?" repeated Moro incredulously.

"To begin with, sir, yes," replied the admiral. "We believe anyone trying to locate the probe will be in the same position as we are. Able to narrow its location to within a similar perimeter, but not being certain where it might be within this zone. So it's the ultimate game of *capture the flag*. Go into enemy territory, find the location of a hidden object, and bring it back home. But with many more than just two teams. An *unknown* number of teams. But still only one flag."

He paused. "Due to the thickness of the forest canopy, no team will have good intel from drones or space as to the activities of the other teams. Communications will have to be by satellite phone, since the center of the Amazon isn't exactly teeming with cell towers. We're talking about the largest tropical rainforest in the world," he added, "spanning nine South American countries and covering millions of square miles. *Millions*. An area nearly as large as the lower forty-eight states." Headrick shook his head in awe. "It's the most untamed place on Earth."

"Which is why we believe a small force is the order of the day," chimed in Jesse Carter. "An army platoon would be easy to spot, and would give off enough of an infrared signal to be trackable. And to underscore something the admiral just said, it isn't enough for our side to find and acquire the probe. They have to get it back to home turf without it being taken from them."

"A single soldier would be the stealthiest of all possibilities," said Headrick. "If the other teams are bigger, our man on the ground should be able to spot them before they spot him. He'll have an easier time tracking them, using sound as well as sight, since it's harder for twenty men to move quietly through the jungle than it is for one. No matter how cohesive a team, they'll move more slowly and be more unwieldy. I believe this strategy gives us the best chance of getting to the probe first. *And* getting it the hell out of there."

Moro considered. "You do realize we aren't at war with any of these countries," he said. "Yet you're acting as though violent en-counters are almost a certainty. Are you suggesting that if a group from the UK gets the probe first, our man should shoot them down?"

"Violence isn't inevitable, Mr. President," said Headrick, "and I sincerely hope it never comes to that. But with the stakes this high, the possible reward this great, we can't assume cooperation. From anyone. And no country will have to worry about retaliation from us, no matter what, which will make them more . . . aggressive." He raised his eyebrows. "You know what they say, what happens in the Amazon basin, stays in the Amazon basin. If our man were killed, we'd have no idea who was responsible."

"That doesn't entirely answer my question," said Moro.

"Right," said the admiral. "I'd say that if the UK or another of our close friends finds the probe first, and our man gets the drop on them, he'll try to forge an alliance. If it's Iran, or North Korea, or ISIS, he'll do what he has to do. China or Russia . . . perhaps a tougher call. He'll need to make quick decisions on the ground, so we want someone smart, compassionate, and ethical. But also someone who understands the real world, and can make the tough choices."

"And you have someone in mind?" asked Moro, aware of just how insane this mission really was. It was like something out of a high-concept video game.

"As a matter of fact, sir," said Headrick, "yes. But before I describe the man I'd recommend, I need to fill you in on a Black Ops program that Jesse and I put in place three years ago. Just the basics, since every second counts. A program you aren't aware of."

"And why is that?" demanded Moro sharply.

Headrick looked uncomfortable. "You obviously have the clearance and are entitled to know about it, Mr. President," he said. "But you've inherited a government that no one could possibly fathom. If you were to be briefed on every last ongoing military initiative and program, you'd have no time to do anything else. I don't even know all the offshoots these trees have sprouted. Apple has extensive operations in multiple countries, but as vast as the company is, it is tiny compared to the US government. But even Apple's CEO can't possibly know every skunkworks project in the company, and what every last employee is up to."

The president nodded, appearing to be somewhat mollified. "Okay. I'm listening."

"It's a program called EHO," began the admiral. "Stands for Enhanced Human Operations."

He paused to let the president consider this phrase.

"Although we try to avoid it," continued the admiral, "there's another term we could use to describe the program that's been popular in comics and science fiction for a very long time." He hesitated, as if he really didn't want to utter the term. "Super soldier," he said, looking as though he felt a bit silly.

Moro shook his head. "You've started a program to create super soldiers?" he repeated in disbelief. "What, like Captain America? Like Jason Bourne?"

The Secretary of Defense sighed. "Along those lines, yes," he said. "We decided such a program couldn't be put off any longer. It's coming, and we can either stay ahead of the wave, or get buried under it. Our goal here is to continue our doctrine of peace through strength. We want rival powers to continue to think twice before testing us. And this program will help."

"As long as it's effective," said Moro.

Headrick nodded. "So far it has been," he said. "If we can ultimately transfer some of these advances to the rank and file soldiers in the field, we'll lose far fewer men, and have a much more effective fighting force. Also, the men and women in our EHO program give us another option to counter threats that might be spiraling out of control. We can call on them during our gravest emergencies, and send them on missions critical to our security. Including missions involving the imminent use of WMDs against us."

The president stared intently at Headrick, but didn't respond.

"We have forty-three men and women in the program so far," continued the Secretary of Defense. "We're taking it slow and steady. Being careful. Don't want to create any Frankensteins. And while they are guinea pigs in many ways, they aren't expendable. Healthy and safe implementation of whatever enhancements we try is of paramount importance."

"So were these super soldiers all chosen from our special forces groups?" asked Moro.

This time it was Carter's turn to respond. "Some," he replied. "But not the majority. Since our ultimate goal is to make a soldier as close to invulnerable as possible, the participants were chosen with extreme care. If you create an unstoppable soldier, you'd better make damn sure he or she doesn't go off the reservation. So we took a page out of Captain America's playbook."

"What do you mean?" asked Moro.

"I've never read the comic," replied the Secretary of Homeland Security, "but in the first movie, Steve Rogers weighed about ninety pounds before he was . . . enhanced. He had no military training. He was chosen because he had a big heart, and was a good man. We decided that these should be the most important qualities in anyone we recruited.

"There are hundreds of thousands of members of the military we could have drawn from," continued Headrick, "and any number outside of the military. So to pass the bar, those we chose to recruit had to have it all: personality, intelligence, and morality. Compassion, and a devotion to helping his or her fellow man.

"Equally important," he added, "was that they needed a history of showing great *judgment*. They had to be quick on their feet and cool in a crisis. We can always teach fighting skills. And native ability is less important, anyway, with the proper enhancements. But the plan was to create the most formidable people on the planet, and get them used to the taste of killing. To send them on our most challenging missions. So we worked hard to include only those with flawless ethics, who we considered to be incorruptible."

Moro nodded. "Sound plan," he said.

Powerful members of the military were often depicted in movies as violent psychopaths and war mongers—arrogant, brainless, and immoral. And while these traits were exaggerated in fiction, they did exist. Moro was impressed with the care these men had taken to ensure this wouldn't be true with their EHO program. "So tell me about these enhancements," he said.

"We can describe them in as much detail as you'd like," said Headrick "But can you approve my choice first? I'd like to get him briefed and deployed as soon as possible."

"Of course," said the president. He had to admit he was eager to learn the identity of this man. A man the admiral trusted to be thrown into a massive shit-storm to retrieve the prize of the century. "So who do you have in mind?" he asked.

"Turns out," said Carter, arching an eyebrow, "he's a civilian. A top scientist and ex-executive. Have you ever heard of someone named Benjamin Kagan?"

# 11

The president searched his mind. Benjamin Kagan? The name did ring a bell. He vaguely sensed the man was in the tech sector. During Moro's non-stop campaigning, he had visited the headquarters of a number of tech giants, and had met with their CEOs and key members of their executive teams.

But he couldn't place the name further, and he could easily be mistaken. "Am I *supposed* to have heard of him?" he replied.

"No," said Carter. "I just thought you might have. The most important thing you need to know is that he was at Dan Vettori's party when ISIS struck three years ago."

Carter really only needed to say that Kagan had been at Vettori's party. The bit about it being three years earlier and carried out by ISIS would then be instantly understood around the globe. The phrase, *Vettori's Party*, had become a shorthand for the devastating events of that night, like *9/11* had become a shorthand for the attacks on the Twin Towers and the Pentagon.

The president blinked in confusion. "How is he alive, then?" he asked. "Only Amber Vettori survived that night."

The head of DHS looked decidedly uncomfortable. "I'm afraid that there's more to that story than is . . . generally known."

He went on to describe how the entire attack had been conducted so that ISIS could abduct Ben Kagan without anyone knowing, and the *true* purpose of this abduction—as though what was commonly known about it wasn't despicable enough.

The president was horrified by this revelation, but equally enraged. Once again, vital information had been kept from him. "Why am I only learning about this now?" he demanded.

"It was my call, Mr. President," admitted the Secretary of Defense. "I didn't want to risk widespread panic. Imagine if the public became convinced their driverless cars could be hijacked. Worse, imagine that they learned that ISIS had actively tried to do it. Millions of car owners, and every last pedestrian, would be . . . highly stressed. Commerce would grind to a halt."

Headrick noticed that the president's icy expression hadn't thawed even a little and hastened to continue. "And information like this leaks," he added. "Quickly. We all know that sharing secrets with the press has become our government's national pastime. I judged that the best way to keep this out of the public eye was to severely limit who was told. In fact, I limited it to only those who knew from the beginning. There were no exceptions. Not even for you, sir," he said solemnly.

"Next time I need to be in the loop!" hissed Moro. "*Is that clear?*"

"Yes, sir," replied the admiral.

"If you can't trust me with something like this," barked the president, "then maybe I shouldn't trust you with your *job*. You and I need to have a long conversation about this when we have more time," he added angrily. "And count on it being *unpleasant*!"

"Understood, sir," said Headrick, at least outwardly wearing a contrite expression. "I don't blame you for being angry. It was an error in judgment on my part."

"Damn right it was!" barked the president.

Moro took a deep breath to calm himself and gestured to the two other men in the room. "But go on," he said. "This alien probe matter is too important for me to allow us to be sidetracked. Even with respect to matters of gross insubordination."

After a long silence, Carter cleared his throat and took it upon himself to continue. "During the massacre," he said, "Kagan turned out to be cool under pressure. Under *immense* pressure. He later even described the attack as almost seeming to be happening in slow motion. There was zero panic in the man, which even he didn't expect."

Carter raised his eyebrows. "And he was the one who saved little Amber Vettori, by the way. She couldn't identify the man who had taken a bullet for her—probably because she had ended up under him. But once we learned that Kagan was that man, and why ISIS was after him, it became clear how events must have unfolded. Amber had said that the terrorist who shot at her had run from the room in a panic. Now we know why. He had accidentally hit Kagan, their Golden Goose. He was in a panic to get a medic and further help."

"And when he left the room," chimed in Headrick, daring to speak once again, "Amber had just enough time to free herself from Kagan and squirrel away in a tight space. Which she said Kagan had told her to do with what had appeared to be his dying breath. When the terrorists returned to give Kagan medical attention, she was the last thing they were worried about."

"What this man did to save her life," said Carter, "was an act of heroism that any soldier would be proud to call his own. Taking the bullet was heroic and brave in and of itself, but this didn't require a clear head and clear thinking. Giving Amber expert guidance as he was losing consciousness, on the other hand, did. Especially given the horrific circumstances that had come before, and how little time he had to think."

"But he was still captured, right?" said Moro. "He was wounded and in the hands of ISIS. So how did he survive?"

Carter quickly described how ISIS had kidnapped a doctor and medical equipment to ensure that their star prisoner recovered, and how Kagan was then revived and told of how he would be pressed into service, with no way out.

The DHS Secretary elaborated on the threats made to the woman Kagan loved, Cynthia Shearer, who was also taken, and his entire extended family, including children. He described the new designer drug the leader of ISIS was prepared to use on Kagan to ensure he cooperated, even if he chose to ignore the threats to his loved ones.

"At that point," continued Carter, "Kagan asked for a few minutes alone to consider his options. He realized almost immediately that escaping on his own was impossible. He had nothing to work with. And they had made suicide impossible too."

Carter nodded slowly. "That's when he reasoned that his only chance was to get a message to the outside world. He basically knew where he was. And he also knew that the doctor was a dead man walking, no matter what ISIS had told him. So he decided he had to use the doctor as an unwitting mule, as despicable as this was. It was a long shot, but the only chance he had."

"How did he manage that?" asked Moro, intrigued.

"Brilliantly," said Carter simply. "With great resourcefulness and efficiency. First, he gave himself a bloody nose. Then he painstakingly wrote a short message in blood on a cocktail napkin that he had in his pocket."

"I know what you're thinking," added Headrick. "Writing a message in blood is as cliché as it gets. But maybe it's cliché for a reason. When you don't have anything to write with, this is the only option. And the bloody nose thing was inspired also, since he didn't have anything to cut himself with to even get a small supply."

Carter nodded. "And I didn't use the word, *painstakingly*, to describe how he did this by accident, either," he said. "Kagan was bleeding steadily from his nose, so had to be sure none spilled on the napkin while he worked. And he had to form the most delicate letters, using the least blood possible, so he had enough room, and so the napkin's absorbency didn't make the letters unreadable. And he did all of this using a twenty-dollar bill as a stylus."

"I'm pretty sure that isn't possible," said Moro.

"He folded it up tightly into a triangle first," said Carter. "Kids still do this in grade school to play table football. He dipped one of the points of the triangle in his blood. Allowed him to form remarkably precise lettering."

"You really admire this guy, don't you?" said the president.

"Very much so," said Carter.

Moro nodded. "Go on."

"When Kagan's brief message was complete," continued the head of DHS, "he folded the napkin in half and hid it in his hand. Then he used his other hand to smear blood all over his face and he screamed for medical help."

Carter waited several seconds to let this image sink in. "When the doctor got close to examine him," he continued, "Kagan threw him to the bed and pretended to go after him in a wild, crazed frenzy, shouting curses at the doctor for keeping him alive. While Kagan was pummeling him with his cuffed hands like a rabid lunatic, he slipped the cocktail napkin deep into the doctor's pants pocket. Impressive beyond words. Not even the doctor knew it was there."

The president and the other attendees listened in rapt attention, spellbound.

"Just to minimize the chances that the terrorists would figure out what he had done," added Carter, "while they were trying to pull him off the doctor, he went for one of their guns, pretending this had been his plan all along. That the assault had only been a diversion to create this one opening."

"He seems to have really thought it through," said Moro.

"No doubt about it," said Carter. "And while his hidden message strategy may seem obvious in retrospect, believe me, only one out of a hundred might have come up with it. And only one out of a hundred of those who did would have had the guile and balls to pull it off so flawlessly."

"So what happened with the note?" asked Moro.

"Just as Kagan had predicted, the doctor had outlived his usefulness. A few of the terrorists drove him thirty miles away from where they were keeping Kagan, to the worst part of town, and shot him, gangland style. He was found without a wallet or car keys, and identified as Dr. Arnie Horowitz. No one had any idea what such an accomplished physician was doing in this part of town. It would have remained a mystery forever, but the detective on the scene found the note in the victim's pocket, just as Kagan had hoped."

"Can you paraphrase what he wrote?" asked the president.

"No need to paraphrase," replied Carter. "I can tell you exactly. I know every single letter." He then proceeded to spell out the message for them, since it contained abbreviations: *Kagan Pway rntl hm. Hydro AVP. Call N. Weiser!*

"Normally, the detective wouldn't have taken it seriously," continued the DHS head, "but this Arnie Horowitz was a physician, not a gangbanger." He raised his eyebrows. "And if a message written in blood doesn't pique your curiosity, nothing will."

"So he called Weiser?" said Moro.

"He did. The mention of *Hydro* left no doubt that the N. Weiser in the message referred to *The* Norm Weiser, the one who had founded this company and many more. The detective was reluctant to bother the tech mogul, but correctly decided he had no choice, since the rest of the message meant nothing to him. His police credentials allowed him to reach Weiser without too much trouble."

"And Weiser knew what the word *Kagan* meant immediately, of course," said the president.

"That's right," said Carter. "And he knew what *AVP* stood for: Hydro's *Autonomous Vehicle Protection* initiative, which Kagan had started in an effort to prevent a possible terrorist attack. Weiser had known Kagan was at Vettori's party, and had been sure that he was dead. But this cocktail napkin made it clear that this wasn't true. And given Kagan's knowledge of the gaps in AV security, the reason he was still alive was easy to figure out. In this context, the meaning of 'Poway rental home' also became obvious."

The president nodded. This Kagan was as impressive as advertised.

"Weiser called me immediately," continued Carter, "and I called Admiral Headrick. There were only a handful of homes that had been recently rented in Poway. It was a simple matter to check them out without the knowledge of the residents. The one ISIS was in was the largest of them all."

Moro turned to the admiral. "So how many soldiers did you end up sending in?" he asked.

"I'm pretty sure all of them," deadpanned Headrick. Then his mood quickly turned somber and he lowered his eyes. "We did succeed in extricating Kagan. But we didn't know ISIS had snatched his girlfriend to use as leverage. One of the terrorists, just before he died, decided to take her out—one last act of brutality."

"I was there," said Carter grimly. "She didn't die right away. She ended up dying in Kagan's arms." He shook his head, remembering. "He was devastated."

There was another long silence in the room as the attendees pondered Vettori's Party, and the needless, tragic loss of life that had occurred.

"Kagan's life had been shattered," continued Carter, "but he understood the importance of finishing what he had started. Now more than ever. He returned to Hydro—with greatly added resources and unseen security, I might add—and within a month managed to find the holes in the AV system and plug them. I promise, America's driverless fleet could not be safer. It's as un-hackable now as the experts *thought* it was then."

Moro frowned. "You kept the true purpose of their attack secret," he said, unable to keep from adding, "even from me. So how could Kagan possibly go back to Hydro? Everyone would know he had survived, and would guess why."

"Well, Weiser knew everything, of course," replied Carter. "But Kagan hadn't been on any of the footage ISIS posted online. He was on the footage they took of the guests before the shooting began, which we found on-site, but we kept that under wraps. So Kagan told everyone that he had never made it to Vettori's party. That he had stopped at an ATM beforehand and was robbed, and that his girlfriend, Cynthia Shearer, was killed during the assault. We made sure this story would hold up to scrutiny."

"I see," said the president, intrigued. "How did you convince Kagan to go along with this lie?"

"It didn't take any convincing," said Carter. "He didn't want to panic everyone any more than we did. And well over a hundred people were butchered, just to get to him. Hard to imagine surviving something like that, knowing it wouldn't have happened if not for you. Bearing this burden alone was backbreaking for him. The last thing he could handle was this becoming public knowledge."

"After these events," said Headrick, "it occurred to us he might be an ideal candidate for our Enhanced Human Operations program. And the more we dug into his past, the better we liked him. Everything we learned suggested he was well-liked, decent, compassionate, and charitable. That he had exhibited great judgment and decision-making throughout his life. Brilliant in general, but especially so with advanced technology. No one better suited to becoming tech-enhanced, or to wield this tech effectively."

"And now he had been tested under merciless pressure," continued Headrick. "The rest of his qualities were great on paper, but this was the most important. How would he act when he had a gun to his head, and the fate of millions in the balance? And he was a good athlete, as well. Tennis star in college. So while he had zero combat training, or military training of any kind, for that matter, we had no doubt he could pick this up quickly. It was clear that if we could get him to do it, he'd be the perfect candidate."

"It's obvious he joined you," said Moro. "But I'm surprised. He must have been worth a fortune. And you said he lived for science. He's the guy you'd expect to be *inventing* the technology, not taking it into battle. Nothing in his background would suggest he'd ever do something like this."

"It took us a while to convince him," said Carter, "but we were persistent. As we've said, his life had been shattered. He was witness to the Vettori Party massacre. The love of his life had died in his arms. He was almost forced into helping unleash a weapon of mass destruction. Talk about the course of a life being forever changed."

He shook his head in disgust. "Kagan had been exposed, first-hand, to the threats the US was dealing with," he continued, "rather than just at an intellectual level. Threats that a super soldier with the right creativity and bravery might be instrumental in stopping. And we were offering him the chance to experiment with the world's most advanced technology, up close and personal. He loved tech beyond all else, and was a disciple of Ray Kurzweil, as many who work at the tech giants are."

"Kurzweil," repeated the president, lost in thought. "The name is familiar, but remind me who he is."

"An inventor and futurist," offered Stephanie Annise, who, along with Kim Buckner and Mary Bredlau, had been silent during this part of the president's discussion with his two cabinet members. "One of the best-known proponents of what he calls the *technological singularity*. This can be roughly defined as the point at which man merges with machine and reaches the point of runaway advancement. A huge, exponential burst forward that quickly leads to superintelligence, as man becomes some sort of super-entity. Basically with the capabilities and immortality of a god. A super-species that is unfathomable to *Homo sapiens*."

"Thank you," said Moro. "It's coming back to me now."

"Most believe the electronic component of the merged entity will lead the way to human superintelligence," added the head of NASA. "But there is also the possibility of humanity optimizing its own gray matter—with the help of technology—to the point where we get an explosion of superintelligence just as vast on the biological side."

She paused to let this sink in.

"Kurzweil has studied the exponential growth of technology," she continued, "and predicts that this singularity will happen a lot sooner than almost everyone thinks. He tells this story about a chessboard, and that if you start with a single grain of rice on the first square, or a penny—I can't remember which—and double it every square, by square sixty-four you end up with some absurdly huge number. It's his way of demonstrating the power of exponential growth."

Moro nodded. "So those who follow this guy, like Kagan, see the marriage of biology and technology as the natural next step, rather than being appalled by it?"

"I couldn't have said it better myself, sir," replied Annise.

Moro tilted his head in thought. "So how long has this guy been part of EHO?" he asked.

"Almost two and a half years," said Headrick. "Given the trauma he had been through, we checked possible damage to his psyche *very* thoroughly before we accepted him. He was stable before, but there's no guarantee anyone stays stable after going through what he did. And we put all possible recruits thought a gauntlet of psychological testing as a matter of course. Kagan suffered severe emotional scarring, no doubt: depression, anger, hostility—the works. But after a time, most of his personality and innate optimism returned. Our testing showed him to be resilient by nature. We were satisfied that he hadn't become jaded or accepting of violence."

"So why *him* for this mission?" asked Moro. "Why not one of his forty-two fellow agents?"

"Each of the others are impressive by any measure," replied Headrick. "And each have compelling backgrounds and heroic stories of their own. They've all excelled since being chosen. But Kagan is one of our top performers. He's taken to this like a fish to water. He'd be one of my top five choices for this mission no matter what.

But he's currently in Brazil on a case, which makes him the closest geographically."

"What's he doing in Brazil?" asked Moro.

"We've gotten wind of an unusual and suspicious operation there," replied the admiral, "which is off the grid, under cover of a massive coffee plantation. We've traced sophisticated biotech equipment there, and lots of it. Kagan just took a job there as a helo pilot for the plantation so he could investigate from the inside for a few weeks."

"When did he become a pilot?" asked the president.

"These men and women weren't all soldiers when we recruited them," said Headrick, "but we didn't just enhance them with tech toys. We trained the shit out of them."

Moro nodded slowly. "Lucky we have one of your people this close," he said.

"Not really," said Headrick. "We have them on assignments all over the world. One of them was bound to be close. But like I said, Kagan would have been on my short list regardless, so it's a happy coincidence."

"I'm glad to hear you have so much confidence in this guy," said Moro.

"He's earned it," replied the admiral. "But I also recommend we send four others. We rush Kagan there, but we'll give these others more time to prepare. Since they're also farther away, he'll be on his own for the first six to fourteen hours. We can spread these reinforcements out within the target perimeter. They'll have comms to communicate with Kagan and each other, and Kagan will be in command. Having five of our people in all, each working alone, will multiply our chances of finding the probe. Even with five, this is a needle-in-a-haystack problem. They'll all have advanced sensors, but these aren't likely to help at the start. Our only real hope is that a sensor begins to pick up a signal when one of our team gets close."

The Secretary of Defense paused and stared intently at the president. "So do I have your approval to go forward with Kagan and these others? More to the point, do you approve of Kagan making command decisions on his own, based on the situation on the ground?"

Moro considered for several long seconds. "I do, Admiral," he said finally. "Let's unleash this guy, this team, and see what they can do."

"Thank you, sir," said Headrick.

The president nodded absently, deep in thought. "I'm going to operate under the assumption that Kagan will end up winning this surreal game of capture the flag," he said. "So while you're deploying your people, I'll work with the others in this room to assemble a team of scientists to study this probe. Quietly."

Moro blew out a long breath. "The moment this guy brings us back our prize," he finished, "let's be sure we're ready to find out what makes it tick."

# PART 3

## From *Popular Mechanics*, December, 2015

U.S. adversaries are already working on something America is reluctant to: Enhanced Human Operations (EHO).

EHOs entail modifying the body and the brain itself, creating what some have called 'super soldiers.' At a press conference laying the Defense Department's future research and development strategy on Monday, Deputy Defense Secretary Bob Work warned that America would soon lose its military competitive advantage if it does not pursue technologies such as employing artificial intelligence.

'Now our adversaries, quite frankly, are pursuing enhanced human operations, and it scares the crap out of us,' Work said.

Altering human beings from the inside to more effectively fight in combat presents ethical dilemmas for American scientists and military planners. Work says those ethical concerns typically don't apply to authoritarian governments, but their lack of hesitation in developing EHOs may force America's hand.

'We're going to have to have a big, big decision on whether we're comfortable going that way,' Work admits.

## From the "about" section of MIT's Institute for Soldier Nanotechnologies website (2018)

The Institute for Soldier Nanotechnologies is a team of MIT, Army, and industry partners working together to discover and field technologies that dramatically advance Soldier protection and survivability capabilities. Team members collaborate on basic research to create new materials, devices, processes, and systems, and on applied research to transition promising results toward practical products useful to the Soldier. Army members of Team ISN also give guidance on Soldier protection and survivability needs, and the relevancy of research proposed to address these needs.

# 12

It was three full hours until daybreak, and Benjamin Kagan was wide awake.

He had been lucky to infiltrate his target, but he had made agonizingly little progress since. But this might be about to change. Finally.

US Intel had been keeping careful track of the highest end biotech equipment for several years now, although soon, even this wouldn't be helpful as biotech progressed to a level that the bag boy at the local grocery store could practically create designer humans of his choice. CRISPR-Cas9 technology had revolutionized genetic engineering, making it so powerful and so simple that even the inventors of the technology had raised alarms.

Which meant that anyone with questionable motives who did purchase the best, most advanced biotech-related equipment money could buy needed to be watched. Carefully.

Recently, US intel had determined that a mother lode of such tech, purchased from various companies in the US and around the world, had eventually all ended up in Brazil—one of the six largest countries in the world in terms of both land area and population. The equipment had taken circuitous, tortured paths to get there, and whoever was using it had done a masterful job of covering their tracks.

Just not quite masterful enough.

US intelligence had finally cracked the sophisticated scheme and had ultimately tracked this equipment to its final destination: Cardoza Coffee Enterprises, a holding company whose primary assets consisted of a number of large coffee plantations spread throughout Brazil.

When a coffee plantation was using more sophisticated biotechnology equipment than multibillion-dollar pharmaceutical companies, one had to wonder if this was really about the beans. When further digging by intel agents had revealed a possible connection to the small group of survivors who still called themselves ISIS, this had sent a shock wave through the upper echelon of American Intelligence.

Like all EHO agents, Ben Kagan had been given considerable autonomy to choose his own missions, and given ISIS's possible involvement in this case, nothing could have kept him away. ISIS was on its last legs, to be sure, but the remaining members of this savage organization were sophisticated and highly intelligent, the only way these last few had outlasted all of the rest.

Kagan could only imagine what they might want with biotech equipment this advanced. But it couldn't be good. Bioweapons were much easier to produce than nuclear weapons, and could arguably present an even greater threat to the world.

Perhaps they were trying to design a plague that would be deadly to all non-believers, but not to them. Or a pestilence for which they held the antidote, putting them in position to blackmail powerful Western countries once the disease-ravaged bodies of their citizenry began to pile up in streets and homes like putrid garbage, like something out of an over-the-top zombie movie.

It was also possible that ISIS wasn't involved at all. Regardless, Ben Kagan needed to get to the bottom of what was going on here.

Five days earlier, he had gotten a lucky break and had wasted no time taking full advantage. He had been looking for a way inside Cardoza Coffee Enterprises, or CCE. When the company had advertised for a native English-speaking helo pilot, he had fallen all over himself to apply, with a fake resume designed to match the precise qualifications they were seeking. After a brief interview and a thirty-minute flight, during which he had shown off his piloting skills, he was hired.

CCE had six pilots in total, each speaking numerous languages. But CCE management believed that when an American came to visit and needed to be flown around, having a fellow American as pilot and escort—or perhaps *butler* would be the better word—would make their VIP visitor as comfortable as possible. Kagan wasn't sure he agreed with this assessment, but he wasn't about to argue.

But so far, he had yet to fly a single mile. Instead, as per his contract, when he wasn't engaged in piloting duties, he was expected to do whatever other jobs were assigned to him, however mundane, tedious, or secretarial.

For days now, while the luxurious private helicopter he was supposed to be flying accumulated dust at a private helipad, he had worked a desk job in a small CCE-owned office building fifteen miles away.

Which was doing him no good at all. He already knew that working a computer wasn't going to get him what he needed. The best hackers in The States had tried and failed to discover CCE's secrets, and the company-issued computer he was given had no better access. Field work was the only way forward. He needed to visit CCE's plantations, where the bioweapons facility was almost certainly hidden, safely out of sight and off the grid.

He was convinced that something dark was brewing at one of these plantations. And it sure wasn't coffee.

While Kagan waited for an opening, he was being trained and supervised by a woman named Ella—no last name offered—whom Kagan judged to be in her early thirties, like him. She was an American, but had spent considerable time in China as a child, where her father had taught English at a university in Beijing.

How she had gotten any job within CCE, let alone a job supervising Kagan and others, was beyond comprehension. It seemed impossible. She was quite attractive, but she was also dumb as a rock. Scary dumb.

Kagan prided himself on being open-minded and non-judgmental, but these traits were being severely tested when it came to Ella. He knew that a person's intelligence was largely out of his or her control—so this wasn't her fault—but try as he might, he couldn't help but find her maddening.

She also seemed to be troubled emotionally, although he couldn't put his finger on why he had become so convinced of this. Then, to top it off, the day before she had made sexual advances toward him. He pretended to be oblivious to them, and had the distinct impression that her interest wasn't genuine. He had a feeling that she wanted something from him, and believed that being sexually intimate with him would help her get it.

The loss of Cynthia had torn a gash in Kagan's soul that would never fully heal. But after a year of mourning, of nightmares, of missing her so fiercely that it hurt, he had forced himself to date again. In the three years since her death, he had slept with two other women, most recently with a fellow EHO agent during extended training sessions.

And this Ella-without-a-last-name had a body that was as appealing as her face, toned and athletic. Still, even if he forgot about the impropriety of her advances, and how much he stood to lose if he was fired for sleeping with his boss, he found her simplemindedness and incompetence unappealing. Even if the circumstances were ideal, which they decidedly were not, he needed to have at least some respect for a woman, no matter how beautiful, before he could sleep with her.

The biggest question in Kagan's mind was how Ella had possibly landed her current position. He knew he was being piggish to think it, but had sex played a role? How could it not have? Her *abilities* certainly hadn't.

The only other explanation he could think of was nepotism: perhaps her father or other close relative owned the company. Still, he believed that hiring someone so demonstrably incompetent, regardless of motive, was a big mistake.

Thankfully, blessedly, the night before, he had been given an assignment that actually involved piloting. Later that morning he would be flying to the main plantation to shuttle a VIP to several other sites. With luck, perhaps he could begin to get a feel for how to unravel this ball of yarn. He needed to do this soon, as he could almost hear the clock ticking away in his head.

ISIS or no ISIS, he couldn't afford to get mired down here for more than a few weeks. There were always other pressing missions where his special abilities were needed, and he was well aware that scores of other talented, unenhanced agents were waiting in the wings to spend as long as it took to get to the bottom of Cardoza Coffee Enterprises.

Even after two years in the field, what he now did for a living still seemed unreal. Impossible. And while he missed the rewards of blazing new trails in science and technology, he wasn't ready to go back. Knowing he had almost been responsible for the death of millions had had a tremendous impact on his psyche. Knowing also that he had found a way to save these same millions with bold, decisive thinking, had also had a profound impact on him.

When Carter and Headrick had first approached him with an offer to join EHO, he had thought it ridiculous and shot it down, but he soon realized that his old life came with too much baggage. Working on familiar problems, in familiar settings, around familiar people—but with Cynthia glaringly absent, and the massacre he had witnessed forever playing in his mind—brought too many unwanted emotions to the fore, highlighted his loss too severely.

It was time for a dramatic change. And what could be more dramatic than becoming a glorified soldier in a group calling itself Enhanced Human Operations? He would be putting himself in a series of life-and-death situations that would give him no time for mourning or reflection. He would have the chance to protect innocent lives. And what could be more intriguing than getting up close and personal with technology that could usher in the next stage of human evolution?

So he decided to give it a go for at least a few years, and then decide what to do with the rest of his life. He was still relatively young, and would be welcomed back to the tech community with open arms whenever he decided to return.

The real question was, would *EHO* let him *go* with open arms? And if they did discourage his return to civilian status, just what form would this discouragement take? Even if they let him go without a fuss, they would almost certainly strip him of his enhancements, which would now seem like having his limbs amputated.

He would miss his onboard supercomputer-based AI the most, which he called Ory.

This AI partner had become more addictive than phones and Google and all other electronic tools combined. Like a second brain. A constant companion and friend, even though he was well aware that Ory wasn't conscious—nothing more than a very advanced tool.

"*I sense that you're awake, Ben,*" said the very AI he was thinking about, almost on cue, the pleasant male voice coming through the tiny comm that had been surgically implanted in his inner ear. The comm was invisible, and by directly stimulating the cochlear nerve that carried auditory information to the brain, its communications with Kagan couldn't be heard by anyone else, no matter how close they were standing. "*And an urgent matter has arisen.*"

"*Go on,*" said Kagan subvocally, creating tiny movements in the muscles of his mouth and throat that were amplified by minuscule embedded sensors and sent on to Ory, who deciphered them with perfect accuracy. This hadn't been the case in the beginning, since Ory needed to master the individual peculiarities of Kagan's subvocalizations, and Kagan needed to get used to making them. But now he could communicate with his AI in this manner effortlessly, with the ease and accuracy he might have achieved had the communication been telepathic.

Not that actual telepathic computer/human communication was far off. EHO had been working feverishly to perfect an AI supercomputer that could be embedded in the skull and pick up thoughts directed at it, and this goal now seemed within reach.

"*You've received an urgent communication from Admiral Headrick,*" continued Ory. "*Would you like me to read it to you, or send it to your lenses?*"

"*I'll read it myself,*" replied Kagan silently.

Ory transmitted the urgent communication to both of Kagan's contact lenses, which each contained nearly microscopic onboard computers and antennas, and the document now seemed to hover in front of him in perfect 3D clarity.

Kagan read it quickly. It was basically a set of orders and a backgrounder. Once the situation and the mission had been described, Headrick provided GPS coordinates that outlined a large circle in the heart of the jungle, many hundreds of miles away, and ordered him to haul his ass there at best possible speed. The admiral assumed that he would borrow CCE's helo, since this would get him there the fastest.

Kagan frowned upon reading this instruction. CCE's helicopter was opulent to the point of being garish, with a custom interior that included six cushioned leather captain's chairs, a wet bar, and even a slender private room filled entirely by a custom bed, four feet wide by seven feet long. This opulence by itself wasn't a problem, but the large size of the aircraft would be a hindrance. Still, it was blazing fast for a helo, and had a seven-hundred-mile range. All in all, the pros outweighed the cons, and he would have to find a way to make it work.

His last instruction was to call the Secretary of Defense, himself, once he was en route, for further clarification and instruction. But not until he was en route. Apparently, Headrick didn't want anything to delay Kagan's preparations and journey.

Kagan couldn't blame him. *Holy shit!*

As pressing as the matter was, Kagan couldn't help but read the communication a second time.

An alien probe that had traveled at speeds just a hair below the speed of light, and that had made physics-defying maneuvers before landing on Earth.

Tech that could possibly revolutionize the world.

A likely scramble by major world powers to get to it first.

This was surreal and unbelievable, but Kagan also found it electrifying and awe-inspiring.

He had resigned himself to using his abilities as an EHO agent to fight the powers of darkness, to engage in warfare to defeat the forces of hatred and destruction.

But if he succeeded in the mission he had just been given, it would be about *discovery*. About *possibility*. He could be the first man to bring a space-faring object, one that was inarguably alien, into the light of day. It was impossible to overstate the importance of what he had been asked to do.

Not that success would be easy. If he was entering a mad and potentially deadly scramble among world powers to find this probe, he would need to bring his A-game.

But how amazing would it be if he did get his hands on it? What if it did have the ability to upend physics, to send civilization down uncharted scientific and technological pathways?

What if the tiny spacecraft could inspire humanity to think about the universe in entirely new ways?

How could it not? Just its presence here, alone, if it became known, would do that. It would represent absolute proof of the existence of intelligent aliens with vastly superior technology. It would answer age-old questions about mankind's place in the universe, shaking philosophy, cosmology, and religion to their cores, at minimum.

When Ben Kagan was only eight, he had wondered what he might do if he were alone and spotted a UFO hovering nearby. He quickly decided that he wouldn't run away or be afraid. Instead, he would walk toward the object. Calmly. Guided by nothing but wonder and curiosity.

Before Vettori's Party he had always fancied himself a coward at heart.

But even as a boy, he had known he would gladly risk death for the chance to discover new wonders, to dramatically expand his horizons with respect to science and the nature of the cosmos, and especially to confirm that humanity was not alone.

The admiral had chosen the right man for this job, Kagan knew. He would find and retrieve this probe no matter what it took.

He had never been more certain of anything in his life.

# 13

Benjamin Kagan threw two large duffel bags into the back seat of his leased SUV, each bag stuffed to the gills, and jumped in next to them. "Ory," he whispered, this time aloud rather than subvocally, "how far to the nearest jungle outfitters store?"

"*I assume that you mean a store selling supplies that are beneficial for survival in the Amazon rainforest,*" replied the AI through the comm in Kagan's ear. "*I also assume you're aware that no such store will open for business for at least six hours.*"

"How far?" said Kagan irritably.

"*A store called Pedro's Premium Jungle Gear is eight miles away.*"

"Have the car drive us there at best possible speed," said Kagan.

He had already brought several items with him to Brazil that would help him survive the coming mission, including a recent invention that could pull drinkable water from the air, but he would need much more.

"Also," he added, "scour the Internet for guides on how to survive for extended periods in the Amazon, and prepare a list of recommended supplies. Make sure you take the mission parameters as you know them into account as you decide. I also want to know your rationale for each choice."

"*Roger that,*" said Ory.

Kagan ordered the car to turn off all interior lights so he couldn't be observed by the sparse collection of drivers who were also out at this ungodly hour. His contact lenses could operate in full thermal imaging mode, giving him true night vision, but they could also greatly amplify ambient light, which they did now, allowing him to see inside the car without too much trouble.

The contacts could be controlled by blink patterns and could sense subtle contractions within the complex array of muscles that controlled the human eye. After wearing the lenses for a few months, Kagan could control them without thinking, switching to night vision when he needed to, zooming in on distant objects, or switching to full augmentation mode.

In this mode, anything he examined was annotated by his personal AI. If he looked at a flower, its name and relevant information would appear beside it. If he focused on one particular word or phrase of this augmented content, additional information relevant to this word or phrase would appear—the equivalent of clicking on a hyperlink.

As the car started itself and began driving, he unzipped the first duffel bag and began sorting through its contents, which consisted of weaponry and high-tech equipment. He considered each item carefully in turn, leaving those items he chose not to take with him on the SUV's floor.

This completed, he unzipped the second duffel and removed various articles of clothing, thankful that he had chosen to lease a driverless car, one that possessed the ironclad safeguards that he, himself, had perfected.

Kagan stripped down to his underwear and prepared to suit up with his EHO Sunday-best. He had no idea what he'd be facing, and needed to be ready for anything and everything.

He glanced down at his naked upper leg out of habit, studying what looked to be a skin-colored adhesive bandage, or patch, four inches long and two wide, wrapped partially around his inner thigh. He really didn't need to perform any kind of visual check—Ory would have told him if the adhesive seal had been compromised in any way—but when you had a twenty-million dollar prototype supercomputer taped to your leg, it was hard not to take a quick peek whenever it was exposed.

The computer that the bandage concealed was Ory's home, and incorporated a number of breakthrough developments. The computer itself was bendable, to a limited degree, enough so that it could contour to the curve of Kagan's thigh. It was constructed using carbon nanotubes, allowing its architecture to be built in three dimensions, with each layer only five nanometers wide, or twenty thousand times thinner than a human hair.

The 3D-nanotube design allowed both processing power and memory to be interwoven into the same tiny space, increasing its performance exponentially, and substantially decreasing its need for power.

In 1969, NASA had sent two astronauts to the moon, using multiple IBM mainframe computers, each costing millions of dollars. In 1997, a supercomputer called Deep Blue had defeated Gary Kasparov, the world chess champion, with a processor capable of evaluating two hundred million chess moves each second.

But by 2014, the tiny internal computers in cell phones were more than ten times faster than Deep Blue, and millions of times more powerful than all of the computers available to NASA during the first moon launch, combined.

And by late 2017, Apple had come up with a small watch that contained all the functionality of a stand-alone phone, including the ability to make calls, and send and receive texts.

Now, only a handful of years later, the computer that Kagan had bonded with—almost literally, since the bandage that concealed it was bonded to his skin—was tens of thousands of times more powerful even than the best available smartphone, and even smaller. In fact, the majority of the area under the bandage wasn't even computer, but batteries, antennas, and a wide array of sensors.

The bandages that EHO had developed to conceal these computers were engineering marvels in their own right. The material appeared to be a standard bandage but was impervious to the sharpest scissors or knives and could withstand unbelievable abuse, protecting the computer within.

The adhesive bond to the skin was unbreakable. No application of water, soap, or random chemicals could loosen its grip one iota. Only a highly specialized reagent manufactured solely by EHO for this purpose could do the trick. The material allowed air to flow through, but its pores would slam shut in the presence of any moisture, including sweat, and it was absolutely waterproof, even when fully submerged.

EHO scientists had designed a small contact plate that could be plugged into a wall outlet and attached to the outside of the bandage, magnetically, to recharge the computer's batteries. The recharge took just under ten minutes and would sustain Ory for two or three days due to the system's miserly power requirements.

EHO had considered a variety of options for ensuring its agents were teamed with advanced AIs at all times, but without the need for a remote connection. Tapping into a remote computer could introduce small delays in communication, along with the possibility of total disruption. Eventually, the computer would be carried by each agent internally, either subdermally or inside their skulls. But until such time, the bandage method worked spectacularly well.

Even if an agent stripped naked, the computer would still be with him or her. If the bandage was seen by another, perhaps during a sexual encounter, the agent could explain it was needed to cushion a minor wound. If it was about to be seen by an enemy, the AI could release a small amount of blood-red dye onto its surface, allaying any possible suspicions as to the bandage's true purpose.

"Ory," said Kagan as he began slipping into the clothing he had selected, "we won't have an Internet connection in the jungle. So I want you to scour the Web for anything and everything that might be even *remotely* useful to us on this mission, and store it in memory."

"*This will take at least an hour, even for me*," said Ory.

"Then you'd better get started," said Kagan, allowing himself the hint of a smile.

"*I just wanted you to be aware*," said Ory, and Kagan could have sworn that it was saying this sheepishly—but of course he was just reading his own human emotions into its words. "*I'll get on it right away*," the AI finished dutifully.

"Err on the side of being *too* thorough," said Kagan as he began to suit up.

The clothing he had chosen was as impressive as the bandage and computer it was about to conceal, consisting of a tight jumpsuit that would serve as an undergarment, with two separate layered components, and an outer shirt and pants, in this case printed with jungle camouflage. Each of the three layers were breathable, lightweight, and waterproof.

The first layer of the jumpsuit undergarment clung to his skin and provided greater protection from bullets than a Kevlar vest. Years earlier it had been discovered that when sudden mechanical pressure was applied to two flexible sheets of graphene—which were honeycombed arrays of carbon, one atom thick—they would instantly stiffen, becoming harder than *diamond*. A fabric constructed of a million layers of such graphene was only a millimeter thick. While the manufacturing of such body armor was still prohibitively difficult and expensive, EHO was able to supply it to all of its agents in the field.

The second layer of the undergarment was a soft endoskeleton of fabric and carbon fiber, with an electroactive coating. Human muscles exerted their force through controlled expansion and contraction, and this flexible woven material could do the same. In 2017, researchers in Sweden had demonstrated that such a fabric could be made to expand and contract in response to the application of a low voltage, giving it the ability to actuate the same way as muscle fibers.

The version Kagan had been issued was a greatly superior version of this technology, and Ory could precisely control where and when current was applied to the material, amplifying Kagan's muscle power whenever the AI sensed this was required. All in all, with Ory's help, Kagan could almost triple his strength for short periods of time. This didn't exactly turn him into The Hulk or Captain America, but he would gladly take it.

Finally, the outer shirt and pants of his outfit, while waterproof and peppered with pockets and hidden compartments, appeared completely unremarkable to an outside observer. But this too, was covered in hidden sensors of astonishing variety and sensitivity, some removable, to be used to aid in interrogations in the field, among other things.

"*We are now two minutes from our destination*," reported Ory, just as Kagan finished dressing.

"Good. When we arrive and park, I want you to scan the store and its security, and hack its records if you can find them online. I'll want a recommendation for the most efficient way to break in, without attracting attention."

"*Understood*," said Ory.

Kagan sighed. He hated to have to steal from this poor merchant, but since the alternative was to wait around until the store opened, he had no other choice. When this was all over, he'd be sure to anonymously send the owner enough money to cover his losses many times over.

# 14

Kagan finished a thirty-minute sat-phone conversation with Admiral Chris Headrick from the cockpit of the helo as the aircraft continued to scream through the air toward the GPS coordinates he'd been given, high above the jungle canopy.

Hours passed, and the scenery changed little, if at all. Before daybreak hit, he was immersed in a sea of darkness, with not a single light of civilization below. After daybreak, there was nothing but a green ocean of towering trees as far as he could see in any direction.

The Amazon was truly awe-inspiring in its vastness, in the mile after mile of uninterrupted trees reaching hungrily for daylight, packed together like commuters in a Tokyo subway car, forming what looked like an impenetrable canopy. It was possibly the most spectacular view Kagan had ever witnessed, and without a doubt the most intimidating terrain he had ever crossed. This was a jungle that could swallow Texas as if it were a light snack, and was so dense that if he suddenly needed to land he was as good as dead.

Occasionally the green ocean would be interrupted by a muddy brown river, slithering like a snake through the jungle, or by an exotic bird or two, winging above the trees and displaying an array of brilliant colors.

"Ory, how much longer until we arrive?" he asked out loud.

"*At our current speed, one hour and seven minutes.*"

"Analyze all visual data from my contact lenses during this flight," said Kagan, knowing that as long as his lenses were in, Ory saw what he saw. "Based on the terrain I've seen, calculate our chances of finding a clearing within our target perimeter large enough to land this thing."

Kagan already knew the answer he would get, but it didn't hurt to have it confirmed.

"*Less than three percent,*" came the reply.

Kagan shook his head in frustration, even though these odds were better than he had expected. "Our only chance is to locate a river and hope we can find enough space on one of its banks. If not, I'll have to set down in the water, as close to land as possible, and risk a swim. What do you think?"

"*I agree that a riverbank is our best option,*" said the AI. "*But this could be inherently unstable. Stability would depend upon the amount of sand present in the dirt, length of time since the river last receded, time since the last rain, the consistency of the dirt or mud, and so on. So even if you did find a bank to land on, the helicopter might sink in enough to make taking off again impossible.*"

Kagan nodded. After seeing for himself just how dense the jungle truly was, he had already concluded that if he did find a place to land, taking off again might not be an option. Especially since this helicopter didn't have landing skids—essentially two elongated steel rails extending along the entire length of the frame—but instead landed on three sets of paired rubber tires, which would tend to sink in more forcefully.

Not that it would really matter. Once he had his prize, he could count on the entire US Air Force to be available for exfiltration on his command.

But now it was time to ask Ory the million-dollar question. In order to land on a riverbank, you needed a river. If there wasn't one running through the target perimeter, this would be bad. He'd have to then try Plan B, which was both risky and reckless.

He had packed an air-ram parachute for the trip, and would be forced to try a treetop landing. This was a technique long used by special forces for jungle insertion, but it was highly dangerous, even for those with great skill and experience. An air-ram parachute didn't open into a dome shape, but into the shape of a canopy or wing, and could be steered using handles, called toggles. An air-ram enabled a jumper to glide to a destination and control his or her speed rather than landing according to the dictates of the chute.

Plan B would well and truly suck, Kagan decided.

He was the guy who was afraid to jump from a diving board, so it was a miracle he had found the guts to skydive at all. But while he had been trained on an air-ram chute, even under the best conditions he wasn't very skilled, and landing on the treetops of a dense jungle was a dicey proposition, with too great a chance that he would end up injured—or dead.

If he was able to land without killing himself—a big if—the rest would be simple. He had a hundred foot length of rope he could use to rappel down to the forest floor. Still, even if this worked, it bothered him that under this scenario the helo would most likely crash into the jungle. Not that he wouldn't attempt to guide the autopilot to a far distant river, perhaps hundreds of miles away, so it could sink in peace, but this was also a dicey proposition.

Kagan knew he couldn't put this question off any longer. He took a deep breath, asked Ory about the presence of rivers within the target zone, and braced himself for the reply.

"*I can confirm there is a river within the perimeter specified by Admiral Headrick,*" it said.

"Yes!" said Kagan ecstatically, blowing out the breath he had been holding. Outstanding! He had dodged a bullet there, or, more accurately, a tree. One with his name on it, which would have likely worn him as an ornament had he been forced into trying a crazy skydiving jungle insertion.

"*I'm sending you the GPS coordinates now,*" said Ory, and tiny numbers appeared at the bottom of Kagan's contact lenses, available if he chose to focus on them, but not obstructing his field of vision otherwise.

"*While this is the closest we can get,*" it added while Kagan banked slightly to the north to take them to these new coordinates, "*it's still at the outskirts of our target circle. The circle has a radius of nine miles, and unfortunately, the river is just over eight miles from the center at its closest point.*"

"Believe me," said Kagan, still feeling giddy with relief, "I'm not complaining. I think we're lucky there's a river within a *hundred miles* of where we need to be."

"*Actually, this isn't true*," said Ory, who had been programmed to make conversation and volunteer information, mimicking a human—albeit one with an immense store of knowledge and superhuman speed of calculation. "*The odds were in our favor. If you were to study the ground we've flown over more carefully, you would have noticed some narrower rivers that aren't as visible from our current altitude. We've also taken a route over an improbably small number of tributaries. Statistically, these types of anomalies are bound to happen occasionally,*" it added, and Kagan imagined it shrugging.

"So you're suggesting I've gotten a false impression of the scarcity of rivers in these parts."

"*Exactly.*"

Kagan shook his head, still not convinced. "The Amazon River may be enormously long," he said, "but it's still nothing compared to the area of the entire jungle."

"*This is true,*" confirmed the AI. "*But while the river is only four thousand miles long, there are about fifteen thousand tributaries flowing into it, and they're spread across the jungle as densely as capillaries throughout the human body.*"

Kagan smiled at this turn of phrase. As always, he was impressed with Ory's programming. He knew it wasn't sentient, but there was no doubt it could fake this well enough to pass a Turing test. Not that this had been considered adequate evidence of consciousness for some time now. Ironically, if an AI *were* truly sentient, as Ian MacDonald had once pointed out, it would be smart enough to know that it should *fail* such tests of sentience—on purpose.

"As dense as capillaries," repeated Kagan in amusement. "Nice analogy."

"*Thank you, Ben,*" said Ory, and Kagan could have sworn it was pleased by the compliment. "*Just to give you a sense of the magnitude of it all,*" it continued, "*the longest one percent of these fifteen thousand tributaries, alone, wind through more than sixty thousand miles of jungle. All in all, the Amazon River system contains more than twenty percent of the Earth's fresh water, and the jungle generates more than twenty percent of the world's oxygen. The Amazon River itself is many miles wide in some places, and over a hundred miles*" *wide where it meets the ocean, gushing fifty-five million gallons of water into the Atlantic each second."*

Kagan whistled. "You should have been a tour guide," he said in amusement. "So tell me about the river that we're heading toward."

*"It's a very minor tributary. Only about sixty feet wide. I'm only aware of it because I stored the latest satellite imagery of the target area, and a hundred-mile radius beyond it, before we left. The dry season began a few weeks ago, and there are places where it has receded enough for a landing, but dense and uneven vegetation has already grown in these areas. Also, it rained there yesterday, dry season or not, so the ground will be less firm than is optimal."*

Kagan thanked his AI companion for this information and flew on in silence, performing a visual inspection of his gear as he did so. The bottoms of his pants were tucked into rugged rubber boots, which themselves were zip tied tightly around his upper calves—and he had packed plenty of extra zip ties. He was covered head to toe in bug spray. And along with the rest of the weapons he was carrying, both evident and hidden, he had a fifteen-inch machete hanging from his belt inside a nylon sheath, although the machete could be folded and stored inside his backpack if need be.

He felt absolutely ridiculous. But the Amazon rainforest wasn't about fashion, it was about survival, and he fully intended to get out of it alive.

Forty minutes later the muddy-brown artery he had been seeking finally came into view, and he followed it for almost a mile at high altitude before Ory instructed him to descend.

He lowered the craft over the water, below the height of the trees on either side of the river, and hovered, before inching the helicopter forward. Less than three minutes later he spotted a section of bank large enough to land on.

Bingo!

Moments later he was down. The riverbank was uneven and the landing was jarring. As Ory had warned, the rain the day before had left it more on the muddy side than Kagan would have liked, and he knew that the helicopter's tires had sunk in to the point of almost disappearing entirely.

But no matter. Any landing you could walk away from . . .

Kagan felt lucky to have gotten this far. The scary thing was that his insertion into the rainforest, as challenging as this had proven to be, was only the *beginning* of his mission, not its end.

He blew out a long breath, threw back his head, and closed his eyes in elation. In the brief time he had been a pilot, this was the happiest he had ever been to land.

His happiness was very short-lived.

He heard a sound behind him in the passenger's compartment and launched himself to his feet. The door to the enclosed area that served as a narrow sleeping quarters was coming open.

Kagan felt his stomach clench. Someone had hidden away in this claustrophobic compartment the entire time, waiting for him to land to make their move.

He drew a gun, ready to cut down any hostile who might emerge.

Kagan's jaw dropped open as the woman he knew only as Ella appeared behind the opening door, rubbing her eyes, and looking as content as a cat that had just awakened from a nap. She didn't even notice his gun, which he quickly holstered.

"Kind of a shaky landing, Ben," she said, as if it was the most natural thing in the world for her to be there. "But it's good that you woke me up."

# 15

Kagan was so stunned it took a moment for him to find his voice. "*Noooo!*" he screamed, as if in pain. "It can't be! What are you *doing* here?"

"Yeah, sorry about that," she said. "I guess I probably surprised you, didn't I?"

"*Probably?*" screamed Kagan "You *probably* surprised me? Are you kidding? *What are you doing here?*" he demanded for a second time.

"If you're not going to calm down, I'm not going to tell you," she said petulantly. "You know I'm your boss, right? So stop yelling at me."

Kagan heard a primal scream, only to realize a moment later that the scream had originated from his own throat. He managed to choke it off while his hands clenched into fists, and then unclenched again, over and over again, as he tried to find the strength not to strangle her.

He took a deep breath. "Okay, Ella," he managed to get out, forcing calm words through clenched teeth. "I'm not yelling, okay? But I need to know what you're doing here."

She looked outside, as though for the first time. "We seem to be in the jungle, Ben. Aren't you supposed to be flying to a CCE plantation?"

Without saying anything further, she threw open the door and made her way down two small steps to the drying, but still muddy, riverbank, wearing nothing but a blue pants suit and a pair of flats. Kagan followed her out in frustration.

The air was warm and muggy, even in the early hours of the morning, and the humidity was like a living creature. At the same time, the air was so rich with oxygen it was invigorating, intoxicating. Smells came at him from all sides, a potpourri of trees and flowers and de-caying leaves and a dozen other scents he couldn't place.

A steady chorus of sound surrounded them, the river moving la-zily onward, birds chirping nearby, and in the distance, the buzz and click and hum of insects, along with movement in the nearby under-brush as a universe of hidden life left evidence of its presence.

"*Ory,*" said Kagan subvocally, "*extend auditory monitoring to maximum. I want to be notified of anything coming toward me—hu-man, animal, or mineral.*"

"*Done,*" replied the AI simply.

The comm embedded in Kagan's ear could pick up and amplify sound well beyond the ability of human hearing, allowing him to eavesdrop on whispered conversations a hundred feet away. But the larger the field of hearing, the harder it was to monitor and focus on the incoming sounds.

It was well known that the human subconscious could absorb many times more information than the conscious mind, and acted as a sentry, deciding what inputs were useful to elevate to the con-scious mind for further attention. An exhausted, sleeping mother could ignore jarring thunderclaps, but would awaken immediately at the whimper of her baby. Her subconscious had taken in both the whimper and the thunderclap, but had known that only the whimper needed to be elevated to headquarters for further conscious attention.

This was called the Cocktail Party Effect, after a phenomenon that was well known to those who attended crowded, noisy parties. A woman could be at such a party with a dozen unlistened-to conversa-tions swirling around her, but if her name was mentioned in one of these conversations, her subconscious would alert her, and she would magically hear it as it suddenly stood out from the din.

In this case, Ory would play the role of the subconscious, monitor-ing far-off sounds so Kagan wouldn't have to, allowing him to focus his normal hearing as he naturally would.

While he was issuing this command to Ory, Ella was frowning and crinkling her nose up in disapproval. "Is it always this hot and hu-mid?" she complained, removing her pantsuit jacket to reveal a blue blouse underneath. She tossed the jacket unceremoniously into the open helo and then spun slowly around to take in her surroundings in their entirety. "What are we doing here?" she said with a frown.

Kagan scowled. "You first," he said. "Tell me why *you're* here, and then I'll do the same."

She sighed and lowered her eyes, and a palpable sadness came over her. "I wanted your help," she said simply.

She went on to explain how she had been involved in a torrid affair with the married owner of CCE, Carlos Cardoza, and how he had started mistreating her horribly, beginning several months earlier, including both physical and verbal abuse. She was miserably unhappy and feared for her life, but she also felt trapped, with no way out.

Cardoza was so wealthy, powerful, and ruthless that no one dared cross him, which meant that no one would help her. He had eyes and ears everywhere, and was extremely possessive. And he definitely seemed to think of her as one of his most prized possessions. She couldn't possibly leave the country without him being alerted and stopping her.

"But then you came along," she said. "Not only an American, but a pilot. And you had no idea that you should be, you know, afraid of Carlos. At least not yet. So I thought, you know, maybe you'd be willing to help me get away from him."

"But instead of just asking for my help," said Kagan disapprovingly, "you decided to try to seduce me first."

She nodded, as though she couldn't imagine having taken any other approach. "Men seem to be more willing to help me after I've had sex with them," she admitted.

Kagan shook his head. Using sex in an attempt to gain personal advantage was what had gotten her into her current predicament with Carlos Cardoza in the first place. Unsurprisingly, this irony was lost on her. "So you hid in the helicopter to what, try to seduce me again?" he said.

Ella shook her head adamantly. "No, that would be stupid. When it didn't work the first time," she added with a shrug, "I knew you were gay." She sighed. "I like gay men okay. They just don't seem as willing to help me as straight guys."

Kagan rolled his eyes. He had been surrounded by so many refined, educated, brilliant people in his adult life that it was hard to imagine someone like this woman could really exist. "So why *were* you hiding, then?"

"Carlos has listening devices everywhere. But not in this helicopter. I knew you had a job this morning, so I thought I could ask for your help while we were in the air."

She turned her head away and a tear rolled down her cheek. As off-putting as Kagan found her to be, she was obviously suffering, and he couldn't help but feel sorry for her.

"I haven't been sleeping well," she said, and, thankfully, this single tear didn't turn into a flood. "I was wide awake at two in the morning. So I thought I'd, you know, hide out early and try to take a long nap while I waited. I had no idea I'd fall this soundly asleep. That room is like a coffin with a mattress inside. But it's super comfy, and really dark and soundproof. I don't know how they manage the whole soundproofing thing when the helicopter is flying. Anyway, I must have been even more tired than I thought."

"Why wait to ask for help until I was in the air? Why not ask me before I took off?"

"I didn't want to risk that you'd kick me off the plane—um, helicopter."

"Right," said Kagan. "Because I'm gay and all."

"Exactly. This way, you'd pretty much, you know, *have* to take me along."

Kagan shook his head. "And why would you *want* to come along?" he asked. "How would that help you? I'm not flying to America. As far as you knew, I was only going to a plantation that Carlos owns. Into the belly of the beast as far as you're concerned."

"I don't know," replied Ella, looking as if she would burst into tears. "I was desperate. I guess I didn't think it through."

Kagan sighed. No kidding. Par for the course. "And why did you think I might kick you off, anyway?" he said. "As you pointed out, you're my boss."

"I don't know," she repeated, still distraught. "I had to do *something*."

Kagan shook his head in disbelief. This answer had nothing to do with his question.

This woman was absolutely maddening, but Kagan continued to feel somewhat sorry for her. She had been out of her depth her entire life, and her timing to try to get help from him could not have been worse.

Or maybe not.

Maybe, by inadvertently making herself the fly in the highest-stakes ointment ever, it would work out for her, after all. The very definition of dumb luck. He had to get her out of his hair, even if it delayed his mission by many hours.

"Look," he said, motioning to the open helo door, "I am going to help you. I'll take off again and deposit you in the nearest safe location I can find. I have a sat phone, and I can call some connections I have in America. If you stay put where I drop you off, I'll have . . . " He paused, considering what he should say. "I'll have an Air Force buddy of mine come and get you. He can make sure you put Brazil and Carlos Cardoza in your rearview mirror."

"Rearview mirror?" she said, blinking in confusion.

"He'll get you safely to America," said Kagan in frustration, failing to keep the irritation from his tone.

"But why are you here in the first place? You said you'd tell me."

Kagan sighed. "Yeah, but I'm not going to, after all," he said. "Since I'm helping you get beyond the reach of Carlos Cardoza, you'll just have to live with that."

Ella opened her mouth to protest but closed it again. It must have finally sunk in that it was a mistake to bite the hand that was about to feed her. "I guess I should thank you then," she said. "If you can get me to the US, I'd really owe you."

She paused. "In fact," she added, "why don't you do whatever you came here to do. I'll wait. You're doing me a huge favor, and you don't even want to fu—well, to you know, have sex with me. So I shouldn't make you leave before you're finished here. Don't worry about me."

Kagan issued a derisive snort. "Don't worry about *you*?" he repeated incredulously. "You do know where we are, right? In the middle of the Amazon *rainforest*. If you stayed, worrying about you is *all* that I'd do." He shook his head in disgust. "See the shoes you're wearing? Now see what I have on? Do you even have any idea why I'm wearing rubber boots?"

"I'm not stupid," she protested stupidly. "I know some places in the jungle are wet and swampy. Your boots will keep your feet dry."

"That's true," said Kagan. "But notice I have my pants tucked into them and the tops of the boots zip tied around my calves. That's to protect me from spiders and scorpions and other nasty little creatures. Nothing can crawl up my pant leg, and nothing can crawl inside of my shoes. Including two-inch-long bullet ants, which have a very painful bite that can cause swelling and fever. And leeches. Not to mention that most of the snakes here are ground dwellers. Disturb one by accident and they'll strike at your ankles. But when they strike at *mine*," he added pointedly, motioning to his boots, "all they'll get is a mouthful of rubber."

He raised his eyebrows. "You see where I'm going with this?"

"Yes. I didn't bring the right footwear."

"No!" he barked emphatically. "It's that you're a huge liability. It will save me time to leave and come back, rather than have to hold your hand while I'm here." He motioned toward the open helo door. "So let's go. The sooner, the better."

She looked as if she might argue further, but didn't, dutifully climbing back inside instead, this time sitting beside him in the co-pilot's seat. Judging by how stimulating previous conversations with her had been, this was going to be the longest flight of his life. If he was on a commercial flight, at least he could pretend to be reading a book and ignore her.

"Buckle up," he told her. "This might be a rough takeoff."

Kagan gathered himself. "*I've never taken off with wheels sunk in mud before,*" he said to Ory subvocally. "*When you stored information from the Web that might prove useful, any chance that this included advice on a mud take-off?*"

"*It did,*" replied Ory simply. "*As we've discussed, you may not be able to get unstuck at all. In a place like this, where mud can have a more quicksand-like consistency, that isn't a given. But to answer your question, the biggest danger is becoming unstuck asymmetrically. This would lead to a dynamic rollover. So you have to gingerly apply power and try to wiggle all three sets of wheels loose at the same time, using a little yaw."*

"*Thanks,*" replied Kagan, starting the rotor spinning. The massive blades roared to life and cut through the thick, clammy air.

"*I should also tell you that the sat-phone stopped working as soon as we landed,*" added Ory. "*Something down here is actively blocking the signal. It could be foreign agents, or it could be the alien spacecraft. I'm not sure. I do expect it to begin working once we get out of range of whatever is suppressing it.*"

Kagan thanked him for this information and mentally walked through his strategy for working the craft free, thankful that the roar of the rotor was keeping Ella temporarily quiet. After three or four minutes, he knew he couldn't stall any longer, and bent to his task. It was time to get rid of the albatross that had planted herself around his neck.

Gently, patiently, he began to apply the tiniest amount of lift and yaw to slowly pry the craft from the riverbank mud.

Gently. Gently. Gently.

Then, just like that, they were free. All three wheels came loose at the same time.

But the instant the aircraft began to rise, just as he was about to celebrate success, the unmistakable sound of extended machine gun fire broke through the protective shield of noise caused by the beating rotor. Kagan had just enough time to look down and see that four men who had emerged from the jungle were firing extended bursts of automatic fire at the rotor and engine, clipping the helo's wings almost immediately.

Only seconds after the firing had begun the helicopter dropped from the air like a lead safe, falling almost twenty feet onto the riverbank. The craft fell at a slight angle, causing it to slam hard into the ground and then tip onto its side, the dying blade biting into the mud and then stopping, but not before vibrating the craft like a beaten drum for several seconds.

Finally, the aircraft came to a complete rest. After the roar of the rotor and barrage of explosive sounds, the resultant quiet was profound. Even the jungle had been cowed into a temporary silence.

Kagan was disoriented and couldn't quite gauge his own position within the cockpit and with respect to the ground, but he glanced over to Ella and noted that she, too, looked to have survived the fall intact. Thankfully, the craft had held together well and hadn't burst into flames.

A shouted voice swept through the bullet holes now punched in the craft's side windows, breaking the temporary silence. "Come out with your hands up!" bellowed the voice in accented English. "Or I'll send a grenade in! You have one minute!"

# 16

The two inhabitants of the fallen aircraft managed to release their seatbelts and climb outside, although Kagan pushed out the stuffed backpack he had brought with him before he did, making sure his machete still filled the sheath strapped to his side.

As they rose to a standing position on the riverbank, their hands over their heads, the four hostiles formed an armed wall, twenty feet away, each with their machine guns pointing forward.

Kagan fumed. As if Ella's appearance here wasn't unlucky enough, now he had to deal with *this*.

With his hearing extended, and an ever-vigilant AI set to sound an alarm, he was nearly immune from a surprise attack. But because Ella's presence had caused him to take off again, the roar of the chopper blade had simultaneously drowned out his comms' ability to pick up distant sounds, and had advertised his position to nearby hostiles. In the four or five minutes the blade had been going, these men had raced here undetected.

What hurt the most was that, in the final analysis, this was *his* fault, not hers. He should have taken the time to psych himself up for the attempted takeoff *before* he had turned on the rotor and created such a mighty din.

He had been careless and had let down his guard. He couldn't think of a worse start to this mission than the presence of Ella and a stupid, unforced error on his part.

Now, not only didn't he have a helicopter, his sat-phone was also apparently inoperable.

So much for calling in the Air Force for exfiltration.

*Just perfect*, he thought in frustration.

Kagan blinked in a way that put his lenses into full augmentation mode and zoomed in on the faces of the four men who had attacked him. Only one was identifiable within the scaled down database now residing within Ory, a tall, wiry Iranian named Kazem Abdi.

The annotation now floating near the man's face described Abdi as Counselor to the Iranian Ambassador to Peru, stationed within the embassy there, a man who had come up through the military, spoke nearly perfect English, and who was long thought to be an intelligence operative rather than a diplomat.

Interesting.

Kagan took the time to finish scanning them from head to toe, his contacts providing information about their clothing and weaponry, as well as the size and make of the rubber boots they were wearing. Like him, they had familiarized themselves with the basics of jungle survival before their arrival. He glanced back down to Ella's shoes, the first time in augmented mode, and shook his head once again.

As usual in emergency situations, Kagan's mind was a picture of calm, and events seemed to be unfolding in slow motion. This happened to him naturally, but Ory had also automatically triggered several of the nearly microscopic implants embedded in his brain, which had amped up his mental and physical acuity even further.

The military had been experimenting with transcranial electrical brain stimulation for some time, after experiments had demonstrated the cognitive enhancement potential of the technology, and had field tested the technique with multiple Navy SEAL units in 2016. Originally, the stimulation was broad, rather than specific, and had been applied by a headset rather than implanted electrodes.

Even so, the results had wowed military scientists. So EHO had taken it several steps further, including the painstaking positioning of microscopic electronics within the brain itself, and fine-tuning the voltage, duration, and location of the stimulus to achieve even greater effects. Not only did this increase focus, it dramatically increased reaction speed. When combined with the instant boosts to muscle power provided by EHO-issued undergarments, this made EHO agents the most formidable soldiers ever fielded.

As Kagan stood poised to strike like a coiled snake, Ella stood beside him, a quivering mess. "Don't hurt us," she pleaded to the men facing them. "*Please.* I have some Brazilian money," she added. "Worth about eighty dollars American. You can have it."

"Very humorous," said Kazem Abdi, shaking his head.

"I wasn't trying to be funny," replied Ella in confusion.

"Sure you weren't," said Abdi, rolling his eyes. "Okay," he added, "I'll play along. Yes, you're right. We're a team of bandits. We like to fly to the heart of the rainforest to rob people, because there are such big crowds here. And so many valuables."

Ella grimaced. Even she now realized just how stupid this had been.

"Keep your mouth shut!" hissed Kagan beside her, knowing she could only make things worse—or more annoying at the very least.

The most diminutive of Abdi's men began speaking to him in Persian, which Ory translated instantly and fed to Kagan's contacts, so it was as if he were watching a foreign-language movie with subtitles scrolling across the screen.

Basically, the man was all but drooling over Ella, and was asking permission to keep her alive after they had killed her male companion, so they could rape her when they had the chance. Kagan was sickened by this vile request, even more so than by their clear intent to leave him dead, but managed to keep a neutral expression.

Abdi, on the other hand, barked back at his underling, his furious tone evident without need of translation. His words were the Iranian equivalent of, *Stop thinking with your dick, or I'll have it cut off.*

This said, Abdi turned to Kagan and switched to English. "Who are you, and why are you here?" he asked.

"Tourists," said Kagan simply.

"*Two* comedians, I see," snapped the leader of the four-man team, the flash of anger on his face showing that his patience had run out. "I better get a straight answer to my next question," he whispered, "or I'm going to put a bullet through your knee. Understand?"

Kagan nodded. While he outwardly appeared calm, even bored, his mind was assessing the situation and various possibilities at great speed. The pieces were coming together. The Iranian government had no idea what was going on here. This was the only explanation for why Abdi hadn't killed them immediately. Instead, the Iranian operative had asked why Kagan was here, as though he truly didn't know.

Iranian intelligence, tapping both electronic surveillance and human sources to spy on the upper echelons of numerous foreign governments, must have learned that countries around the world were sending teams with great urgency to these coordinates within the jungle. But they had no idea why. There was a grand gala being held, and they hadn't been invited.

So Iran had decided to invite itself. To find out what had caused this frenzy of activity. To learn what within the jungle had kicked a global hornet's nest so hard. Based in Peru's Iranian embassy, Abdi and his team were the closest to the action, like Kagan, and had been rushed there to investigate.

They all had military training, no doubt, but these were not Iran's best people—not by a long shot. You didn't station your best operatives in Peru.

But these men had been nearby and expendable. If they were able to learn what all the fuss was about without the need of additional resources, so much the better. If not, their sacrifice would hardly be noticed.

Abdi had been clever in one respect, Kagan decided. He had known that some of the teams would need to land a helo. Either because the bulk of the equipment they had brought with them necessitated such an approach, or, like Kagan, because they didn't have the skill or spare pilot to facilitate a treetop insertion. And if a team did need to land, they would most likely try to do so in the river, or on its bank. Abdi's own helicopter was probably parked in a similar riverbank location fairly close by.

All Abdi and his men had to do was identify other probable landing sites along the river and wait, hoping to ambush new arrivals. Kagan had been a fool not to consider this, compounding his error.

The EHO agent pondered all of this and more in just a few seconds as Abdi angrily awaited a reply to his question.

"I'm a member of French Special Forces, stationed in Brazil," replied Kagan, doing his best to put on a French accent in case this detail was important. Abdi, not being a native English speaker, would be less likely to pick up on just how fake his attempted accent truly sounded. Fortunately, Kagan had only spoken a single word, *tourists*, before pretending to be French.

"As to why I'm here, mon ami," he continued, his arms still raised above his head, "I was hoping you could tell *me*. Our intelligence agencies indicated multiple countries had suddenly put this wild area of the jungle on their radar. For unknown reasons. But based on your question, I think we're in the same boat, oui? Neither of us know what all the excitement is about."

Kagan lifted one eyebrow. "So why don't we team up and find out together?"

America was Iran's fiercest rival on the world stage, and would be the country *most* likely to know what was really going on here. Kagan had made a snap decision that playing dumb was more likely to succeed if he carried out the deception under the false flag of France.

"If you're in the French military," said Abdi suspiciously, "then why are you teamed with an American woman?"

Kagan resisted a frown. Apparently, Abdi was familiar enough with American English to know that Ella had spoken it without an accent. "S'il vous plait!" replied Kagan, shaking his head adamantly. "We *are not* a team. Long story, oui? She hid on my helicopter, and I didn't know she was there until now. She's a civilian."

The Iranian looked insulted. "You really expect me to believe she could remain hidden on a helicopter?"

Kagan sighed. Why was it that the only true thing he had said seemed the most ridiculous?

"As you can see," he said, gesturing with his head toward the downed craft, "it's a civilian luxury model. It has a custom sleeping quarters, which I didn't check. Sleeping quarters that are like a slim, glorified luggage compartment with a mattress. She was in there."

Abdi stared at Kagan in contempt and then turned to his companions. "The time for games is over," he said to them in Persian. "I think he's an American and knows exactly what's going on.

"Omar," he said to the tallest of the four. "Remove his weapons and tie him up. We'll cover you. This guy is too clever for his own good. We'll see how clever he is when I'm burning my initials into his arm with a lighter," he added with a sneer. "He'll be begging me to kill him before too long."

Kagan sighed. It was time to end this. He had hoped to extricate himself and Ella from these men without the need for violence, but he refused to apologize for what was about to happen. The Iranians were planning to torture and kill them both without mercy, so they deserved whatever they got.

He considered his options. "*Ory, can I assume these men are wearing comms?*" he asked subvocally.

"*That is correct.*"

"*Unprotected comms?*" he added.

"*Affirmative,*" said the AI.

"*Outstanding. I want you to take control of them and hit these men with a debilitating frequency. On my mark.*"

"*Understood,*" said the AI.

The man named Omar lowered his weapon and prepared to make his way across the mud and vegetation to carry out his orders.

"*Mark!*" said Kagan subvocally.

All four Iranians screamed in agony at the same instant, like a carefully choreographed musical number from a horror-themed musical. They dropped their weapons and brought their hands to their ears to rip out the comms that had suddenly turned so fiercely against them, issuing a shrill, head-splitting screech that stabbed at their heads like ice picks.

Kagan lowered his arms and drew his gun as quickly as the fastest gunslinger from a Western movie. His focus and reflexes were amped to their maximum by the electrical stimulation of his brain, and he planted a bullet between the eyes of the most diminutive of the four, the man who had asked permission to rape Ella once Kagan had been killed. The man's dead body fell to the mud, less than two seconds after Kagan had subvocalized the word *Mark*.

Kagan snatched up his backpack from the mud just as rapidly. "Run!" he yelled, grabbing Ella's hand and sprinting off toward the all-enveloping jungle.

Just as he was about to cross the threshold and disappear completely, Abdi succeeded in tearing the comm from his ear, and even though he wasn't fully recovered, he sprayed automatic fire in Kagan's direction, with one stray round slamming into the American's back.

Even though Kagan's graphene chain mail undergarment became diamond hard and prevented the slug from piercing his body, the force of the impact was immensely painful, and Kagan issued a short scream just as he made it to the thick of the jungle.

He had miscalculated. Abdi was better than he had thought, and this miscalculation had almost cost him his life.

There was a lesson here. Compassion could get him killed. And with the stakes this high, this was a risk he couldn't afford.

Which meant he had made yet another mistake. He had chosen to take the life of the Iranian behind him, whose blood was still pouring onto the mud, to give Ella a chance to survive.

His heart had made this decision, but it was time he started making decisions with his *mind*. It was time he used the cold logic that this situation demanded.

If he cut Ella loose and let her fend for herself, *he* would be much better off, but it would mean almost certain death for her. So even though he knew what he *should* do, he couldn't bring himself to do it. At least not yet.

But for every minute he delayed, his chances of accomplishing his mission fell ever lower.

# 17

Ben Kagan charged through the jungle with Ella in tow, his senses hyper-focused, his lower back bruised and aching. He ignored the pain and caught his companion's eye, putting his index finger across his lips to make sure she wouldn't decide it was time to get chatty, and focused on putting as much distance between them and the men following as possible.

After only twenty yards of progress the jungle became so thick with prehistoric-looking tropical leaves, tree trunks, vines, and other foliage that Kagan was forced to remove his machete from its holster and hack his way forward. He allowed his fabric endoskeletal suit to augment his strength just enough so that he could continue this strenuous activity for extended periods without risk that his muscles would become fatigued.

He had always thought the rugged explorer hacking his way through dense jungle wilderness was just an old Hollywood meme, like cars that exploded at the slightest provocation, a way to make a movie more interesting visually. But Ory's research had suggested this was very real, and very necessary, and Kagan had already realized his machete was indispensable here.

Whenever they came to an area that wasn't quite as dense, and progress could be made without his new favorite tool, Kagan returned it to its sheath, making sure anyone following wouldn't have a cleared path to guide them. To Ella's credit, she hadn't attempted to speak since he had shushed her.

"*Abdi just tried to report back to Tehran on a sat-phone,*" announced Ory in Kagan's ear.

"*Can I assume that his sat-phone is as inoperable as ours?*" said Kagan.

*"Yes. But from his ensuing discussion with his men, I learned that they were told hours ago to expect a six-man team of reinforcements later today. I don't think the exact time was specified."*

Kagan nodded. This made sense. He had already guessed that Abdi and his men had been deployed because of their proximity to the rainforest. But apparently, Tehran wanted to send others along.

America was doing the same. Kagan had been closest, but Admiral Headrick had told him that four other EHO agents would be joining him later that afternoon or night.

With any luck, when the six Iranian reinforcements arrived, they would join their comrades. If all nine Iranian's congregated, Kagan's early warning systems—amplified hearing, advanced sensors, and micro-drones—would be that much more effective. Given this technology, the larger the team, the less chance for stealth, which would render the most potent armed force virtually harmless.

After he and Ella had traveled almost a mile due south, according to Ory's compass feature, Kagan held up his hand to call a halt, already drenched in sweat from his exertion and the steamy, boiling-hot conditions. He put a finger to his lips once again for Ella's benefit, a reminder that the edict of absolute silence had yet to be lifted, and ordered Ory to use his comm to conduct an extensive survey of the surrounding area.

The AI began immediately, using copious amounts of computing power to filter out the wide variety of jungle noises, and also to determine the directionality of the sounds being picked up. After Ory listened for several minutes, it indicated that the Iranians following had mistakenly veered due east about twenty yards behind them, and were now getting farther away every minute.

Based on Kagan's research, and now from personal experience, he wasn't worried about being followed. At least not for too long. Not only was it extremely difficult to follow someone through the densest parts of the jungle—especially when they had a head start and weren't laying down an obvious track every step of the way—it was extremely challenging to even stay on course.

Amazon survival guides warned about the dangers of traveling in broad circles. The jungle terrain had a way of all looking the same, turning the rainforest into the ultimate minotaur maze. A poorly illuminated maze at that, as the canopy was so tight that light itself had trouble making its way to the jungle floor.

Guidebooks stressed marking a trail behind you, to make backtracking possible, and so you could tell if you had accidentally circled back to your starting point after hours of arduous labor.

Had it been necessary, Kagan could have activated one of a dozen drones he had brought, each the size of a dragonfly. Each drone contained a complex computer and had numerous impressive capabilities, including the ability to mimic his and Ella's voices. He could have sent one of these drones flying, with instructions to locate Abdi and his gang and lead them on a wild goose chase.

Fortunately, as expected, they had lost the Iranians without need of a high-tech decoy.

Kagan proceeded for a few more minutes until they came to a large fallen tree, lying on the jungle floor, bald of bark and leaves. He inspected it carefully with his lenses still in augmented mode for dangerous insects and then motioned for his companion to sit, placing his heavy backpack on the jungle floor and taking his own advice.

While they rested, Kagan removed a canteen from his backpack, took a large mouthful, and handed it to Ella, who seemed grateful to do the same. He then examined her shoes, which were covered in mud and already scratched and cut by some of the sharper undergrowth. Another day or two in the Amazon and they'd be shredded.

"*How long before Ella and I can talk?*" he asked Ory subvocally.

"*I'd give it five minutes,*" replied Ory. "*By that time, even if the Iranians are using the most sophisticated sound amplification technology in existence, they won't hear you.*"

Kagan leaned forward and cupped his hands around his companion's ear. "We can converse normally in five minutes," he whispered faintly.

Ella nodded her understanding.

He then removed a soda-sized can of industrial-strength bug spray from an outer pocket of his backpack and handed it to her, pantomiming spraying it over any exposed skin.

While she was covering herself in bug spray, Kagan rested and took the time to marvel at his immediate surroundings, as well as the amazing displays of nature at its grandest that he had already seen during the hour or so since they had left the riverbank.

The Amazon was deadly, but also a paradise. The Garden of Eden writ large.

Just the day before he had known very little about the rainforest. He was aware that it had been shrinking for some time due to mankind's encroachment, although the speed of this encroachment had thankfully tapered off. And he had known that it housed an untold number of different species, making it a bastion of biodiversity, with ten percent of all Earth's creatures calling it home.

Mind-boggling didn't even begin to describe it.

And Kagan now realized that no amount of reading fascinating facts, or watching jungle movies, documentaries, or *YouTube* videos could possibly do it justice.

The Amazon was total immersion in wilderness. It was humidity, and rich oxygen, and smells and sounds that no video could truly capture.

It was an explosion of green everywhere, in multiple shades, from dull, to vivid, to neon, with many leaves and plants growing so large it seemed as if he had traveled back in time to the prehistoric age.

It was a constant array of brilliant colors, displayed on birds, bugs, frogs, flowers, butterflies, and fruit. It was moss and mold. It was giant fungi, looking like massive misshapen mushrooms. It was waterfalls cascading down rock faces, and swampy areas appearing next to dry areas, seemingly at random. It was magnificent foliage, including the giant taro plant, whose leaves could measure ten feet across, maximizing the surface area available to capture the limited light falling to the jungle floor.

Already Kagan had seen and heard monkeys in several banana trees overhead, the creatures unaware of how stereotypical they were being, and spiderwebs that looked expansive and sturdy enough to snare a flying dog. He had passed a tree packed with squawking green parrots, thick as bats in a cave, making an unholy racket that was truly indescribable. Until that moment, having only seen parrots one at a time in cages, he had no idea that they ever congregated, or that there could be as many parrots packed onto a single tree as he had previously thought existed on the entire planet.

Ten feet away from where he sat contemplating the Amazon, he spied a dozen leaf-cutter ants, dutifully marching along the ground, the leaves they were clutching towering above them like giant parasails.

The variety of insect life he had seen in the past *hour* already surpassed the variety he had seen during the past thirty-two years of his life. They came in a dazzling array of sizes, colors, and body shapes, from species that looked exactly like a leaf or a twig, to those whose appearance defied description.

This reminded him of the many strategies that creatures here used to avoid detection. He had been fortunate not to see any snakes—at least as far as he could tell. But he could have passed many of them hidden in the undergrowth. He and Ella could well have missed disturbing one, and being struck, by a matter of feet, or even inches.

"*Ory*," he subvocalized, "*I want you to focus on my field of vision as part of your standard duties. I want you to watch for dangers I might miss, for camouflaged creatures, and so on.*"

"*Understood*," came the immediate reply.

Kagan shook his head, annoyed at himself once more. This should have been the first command he issued.

As he continued to explore his surroundings, he was struck by just how infinitesimally tiny a fraction of reality the average man was exposed to, or could access. There were universes within universes, realms within realms, well beyond the range of human experience.

The microscopic universe was one such example. The inhabitants of this realm were engaged in a constant struggle for survival, waging warfare on a more epic scale than any man could ever imagine. And all of it happened within a universe that human beings were part of, but couldn't sense. A single human body harbored *five thousand* times more bacteria than there were humans on Earth, making the total worldwide population of these organisms truly unfathomable.

The oceans represented another largely unseen universe of life. More than ninety-nine percent of the world's biomass resided in the oceans, which not only covered the majority of the Earth, but did so to an average depth of *two miles*.

The insect world was yet another epic realm, a universe almost entirely invisible to the self-proclaimed dominant species.

And so was the Amazon. Here, billions upon billions of creatures battled for survival every day in an environment as removed from the experiences of the average city-dwelling American as was an alien planet.

And most of humanity was oblivious to all of these realms, the microbial, insect, ocean, and rainforest—not to mention many others.

Even beyond this, the species was only beginning to comprehend just how limited its senses, its experiences, truly were, relegated to a small fraction of the visual and auditory spectrums, to macroscopic sizes and pedestrian speeds.

The two revolutions that had rocked physics had proven this point, revealing realities at the level of the very small—the realm of quantum mechanics—or the very fast—the realm of relativity—that could not have been more bizarre or counterintuitive.

The reason for this was simple. *Homo sapiens* weren't built to fathom anything beyond the infinitesimal range of reality needed for survival. The species was grasping an elephant's trunk and only able to sense a snake, completely missing the massive pachyderm behind it.

"*You should be clear to converse now,*" announced Ory, breaking Kagan from his reverie.

Kagan thanked the AI and turned to his human companion, still seated and now fully covered in bug spray. "Okay," he said, "We're clear to talk now. No one can hear us. But let's try to keep our voices down."

"How do you *know* that no one can hear us?" she asked. "They could be, you know, right around the corner."

"All I can do is ask you to trust me," he said. "We're safe. For the moment. And at least from them. But this jungle is full of insects and animals that are more deadly than those men by the river."

Ella swallowed hard. "Who were they?" she asked. Before he could answer she added, "You killed that man, didn't you?"

"They were Iranians, and they were planning to kill *us*. And yes, I killed one of them, but I did it for a reason. After we have a brief conversation, I'll tell you all about it."

"What happened to them? Why were they grabbing their heads and screaming?"

"They had communications devices in their ears. I happened to have a device in my pocket capable of broadcasting a debilitating sound through these earpieces. All I had to do was press a button, and you saw what happened."

She crinkled her forehead in confusion. "But your hands were over your head. You never pressed anything."

"I'm a trained magician," he lied. "You know, the hand is quicker than the eye. I pressed it, all right. I did it too quickly for you to see, but the results speak for themselves."

She nodded appreciatively, clearly buying this ridiculous assertion. But the wheels continued to turn within her head—however slowly—and another questioning look appeared on her face. "It took us, I don't know, seven or eight seconds to get to the real jungle," she said. "Seven or eight seconds before they started shooting. You shot that guy so fast I didn't know it was happening until he was dead. So you could have easily killed them all. Why didn't you?"

"Do you think I should have?"

She thought about this for several seconds. "I don't know. If you say they would have killed us, and maybe are still trying to, it would have been safer, right? And you screamed just after the gunfire began again. You got hit, didn't you?"

He shook his head. "No. One of the bullets hit a branch that ricocheted into my lower back. Hurts like hell, but I'll be okay."

Ella motioned to his backpack. "Do you have a painkiller in there?"

Kagan smiled. "I do, but it's special. Experimental. It takes all pain away—totally and completely throughout the body—for about six hours. Which means it can only be used when pain becomes too great to endure, and survival depends upon erasing it entirely. Otherwise, it's too powerful to use."

"What?" said Ella, blinking rapidly. "Sounds like a miracle drug. How could pain medication work *too* well?"

Kagan sighed. This was his fault for describing the painkiller with this level of detail. "Well, most people don't think about it," he began, "but we feel pain for a reason. Evolution didn't just add it to the mix to torture us. When you put your hand on a hot stove, pain gives you an instant signal to move it. A signal that's impossible to ignore. If you felt no pain at all, you'd just leave it there until it went up in flames. If you broke your leg and it didn't hurt, you might never know it, so you'd keep walking, making it a lot worse." He paused. "Turns out that pain keeps us out of trouble."

Ella thought about this for a second. "Yeah, maybe," she said. "But it still sucks," she added with a grin.

Kagan couldn't help but return her smile. "I can't argue with that," he replied.

"So why *didn't* you kill them all?" she persisted, returning to her original question.

"I don't take life lightly, human or otherwise. Even if that life is set on killing *me*. I knew they wouldn't be able to follow us for too long once we made it into the jungle. They won't be a threat from here on out—or rivals. They're the least of our worries."

Even as he said this, he knew it wasn't entirely true. The reality was that he *should have* killed them. The ache in his back was a constant reminder for him not to underestimate his adversaries.

Ella looked confused once again, an expression that she wore all too often, but this time she had good reason for it. "So if you weren't worried about them as a threat, why did you kill the one guy you did? You said you had good reason. What was it?"

"I killed him for *you*," he said simply. "So you would have a chance to survive here."

She stared at him as if he had just escaped from an insane asylum. "For *me*?" she said in disbelief. "How does killing one guy out of four change my chances of survival?"

Kagan sighed. "Because, of the four of them, his shoe size was the closest to yours."

He rose from the log and gestured for her to follow. "Come on," he said. "It's time to go back and get you a proper pair of rubber boots."

# 18

Kagan still knew he had made the wrong call by going to such great lengths to help his unwanted companion, but Ella was growing on him. On the other hand, given what he had thought of her in the beginning, she had nowhere to go but up.

Even so, he was about to waste several hours making sure she had the proper footwear, critical if she was going to last more than a few days. Even if wildlife didn't get her, if her feet became torn-up and bloody, she wouldn't have a chance of keeping up with him, and he would be forced to leave her behind, marking the beginning of the end for her.

He regretted the need to kill the Iranian for his boots—which seemed like something a villain might do in an old Western—and he would be better off leaving Ella to her fate. But if he had to trade one life for another, she deserved to live a lot more than Kagan's victim had.

She wasn't the sharpest knife in the drawer, but she wasn't cruel or sadistic, either. The Iranian had been perfectly willing to torture and kill them both, but not before raping her. So maybe it was fate that his feet happened to be the smallest of the four men.

Ella's eyes were wide as she rose from the log to follow him. "You really did kill him for me, didn't you?"

"Yeah, pretty much. I thought it was less likely he would wait around for us to take his boots, otherwise."

She digested this for several seconds. "So you had this planned all along, didn't you? From the moment you saw they were wearing rubber boots."

He nodded.

"Thanks," she said slowly. But a moment later she frowned. "I know that guy was the smallest, but do you really think his boots will be a close enough fit for me to wear?"

"I'm positive," replied Kagan. "Turns out I'm an excellent judge of shoe size," he added with a smile. "For instance, I'm guessing you're a women's nine."

"Exactly!" she said in surprise.

He smiled. Shoe sizes had been one of the easier things for his AI companion to get right as he had studied all footwear on the riverbank with his augmented contact lenses.

"Well, just like I was right about *your* size," he continued, "I'm confident that the Iranian's boots are the equivalent of a women's ten. A wide ten. But if you put them over the shoes you have on now, they'll be a little loose, but will work just fine. I have extra zip ties so we can fix you up like me. So nothing . . . unwanted . . . can possibly get inside your boots."

"Thank you!" she said, this time more enthusiastically.

They hiked in silence for several minutes before she spoke again. "Ben, are you sure we're going the right way? You didn't machete this section, and I don't remember going through here at all. Not that I would. A lot of it looks the same."

"I'm sure."

"But how? You aren't even, you know, checking a compass."

Kagan shook his head. He wasn't about to tell her about Ory. "I can act like a *human* compass," he lied. "I have a perfect sense of direction. It's a thing. Like being a mathematical prodigy."

"What's a prodigy?"

"Not important. Just trust me. We're going the right way."

She frowned deeply as they came to a denser section and Kagan unholstered his machete.

"You keep telling me to trust you," she said. "But here we are in the middle of nowhere. And guys from Iran are, you know, trying to kill us. So come on," she whined, and this time he couldn't blame her, "it's time for you to tell me what's really going on. No more stalling. I have a right to know what I've gotten myself into. None of this is normal, you know."

Kagan couldn't help but laugh. No, he couldn't argue that any of this was normal. He considered what he should tell her, finally deciding that this might be an opportunity to get a lead on his first mission, if he survived to return to it.

"Okay," he said, hacking a thorny branch to the jungle floor, "I'll level with you. I'm a consultant, working with the CIA. We've become aware that sophisticated biotech equipment, and lots of it, has ended up somewhere within Cardoza Coffee Enterprises. I joined the company to do some undercover work."

"Like a spy?"

He shrugged. "Close enough."

Ella nodded slowly. "Why would a plantation, you know, need biotech equipment?"

"Exactly," said Kagan. "That's why I was sent. To try to find out."

"And have you?"

"Not yet," said Kagan. "But I'm hoping you can help me with that. Carlos Cardoza has made your life miserable, and trapped you in Brazil. So you and I are on the same side. The CIA isn't sure Cardoza is involved, but it's likely he is. Can you shed some light on any of this?"

As Kagan said these words, he removed a dime-sized sensor from inside his shirt pocket, one of many he had hidden on his clothing. The sensor could attach itself to any surface, like a post-it note. He stopped and turned back toward Ella, brushing against her and depositing the nearly weightless sensor on her blouse, near the small of her back.

The tiny device could detect heart-rate and respiration, along with other measures of health, such as blood oxygen saturation. But these other signals could only be measured if the device was stuck to her skin, rather than to fabric. EHO was in the process of perfecting a sensor that could detect all vital signs from several feet away, even without the need to attach to the subject's clothing, but this was still months away.

"I'd help you," she said, "but I have no idea what you're talking about."

Kagan sheathed his machete for a moment and stared intently into her eyes. "Did you ever notice any strange equipment at any of Cardoza's plantations when you were with him?"

She shook her head. "To be honest, I wouldn't know biotech equipment if it, you know, bit me in the ass."

He smiled at her blunt reply. "I'm not sure if I'd be talking about getting bitten in the ass around here," he said, "but I get your point."

"*Ory*," he said subvocally, "*is she telling the truth?*"

"*Given the limited sensor data I'm receiving, I'm less certain than I would usually be, but the odds are very good she is. Her heart rate was fifty-one beats per minute before the question, and held perfectly steady as she answered. Her respiration was also steady.*"

When most people told a lie, they subconsciously couldn't hide this fact. Their pulse and breathing rate changed, along with levels of perspiration and blood pressure, although the sensor wasn't well placed enough for Ory to measure these last two. State-of-the-art lie detector equipment could measure all of this, and more, with greater precision than Ory. But the AI also used a complex algorithm that could pick up on subtle facial tells, which is why Kagan took care to point his contact lenses in her direction.

"*The facial cues are mixed,*" continued Ory, "*and inconclusive. All in all, the odds that she is telling the truth are greater than eighty percent.*"

Kagan pressed her for several more minutes, trying to learn if she had seen *any* equipment she didn't recognize. Or if she had seen or heard anything else out of the ordinary, for that matter, that didn't seem to have to do with coffee. Unfortunately, this questioning got him nowhere.

She didn't know anything useful, and Ory hadn't flagged anything she said as having a good chance of being a lie.

So much for helping him with the Cardoza case.

Ella had begun this mission as nothing more than a liability. And now it was clear that she was destined to stay that way.

# 19

Ben Kagan and his companion hiked in silence for several minutes before Ella realized that he hadn't answered her original question. "Okay, so you're spying on Carlos and CCE," she began. "But why did you come *here*? To the Amazon? And why did those men want to kill you?"

"*Ben, freeze!*" shouted Ory into Kagan's ear before he could respond. He halted in mid-step. Ella, who had been following close behind, plowed into his back, pushing him one step forward.

Kagan glanced upward and saw the reason for Ory's high-decibel command. A slender green snake was hanging down from a branch, and it didn't look happy that they were a few steps away from invading its personal space. It had tiny black spots peppering its green skin, and yellow lips that had opened wide to reveal dagger-like fangs, which were an instant away from burying themselves into the neck of the man who had dared disturb its peace.

If only Kagan still had his machete in hand, but the terrain had been more forgiving of late, and he had folded it and put it away in his backpack.

"*Back away!*" shouted the AI. "*Slowly.*"

Kagan stared the snake in the eyes, and it stared back, both animals equally alert. He backed away, reaching behind him to contact Ella and push her back at the same time.

*See there,* he thought at the reptile, hoping it could sense telepathic intentions, *I'm leaving. No need for alarm. If you don't bite me, I won't bite you.*

Kagan continued easing back, one small, careful, non-threatening step at a time.

"*You're clear,*" announced Ory an instant later, although this announcement seemed to take forever. "*Beyond its striking range. But it wouldn't hurt to back up farther.*"

"*Yeah, no kidding!*" he replied subvocally.

Now that he was safe, he focused on the text, images, and graphics that appeared beside the snake he was still watching, annotations that were faint and unobtrusive, but vivid if he chose to attend to them.

Apparently, his green friend was a two-striped forest pit-viper—or more properly, *Bothriopsis bilineata*—a venomous snake that was considered one of the most dangerous in the Amazon. Most snakes in the rainforest were ground dwellers, but not this one. A nocturnal hunter—or ambusher would be a better description—it liked to hang out in trees, literally, and would strike if disturbed, day or night.

Something Kagan had been in the process of doing. And rubber boots wouldn't have saved him from this beauty.

"What's going on?" said Ella anxiously.

Kagan pointed to the snake, now eight feet away but continuing to face in their direction. It blended in with the tree, but when her eyes widened in horror, he knew that she had managed to see it.

"It's a two-striped forest pit-viper," he told her. "Very dangerous."

"So you know all about the wildlife here too?"

He nodded.

"So let me get this right," she said. "First, you're a magician. And also a CIA consultant. Who turns out to be a human compass. And now you're also an expert on the rainforest?"

Kagan couldn't help but grin. "Don't forget pilot," he added.

She shook her head and blew out a relieved breath. "I don't care what you are, it's a miracle you saw that thing before we hit it headfirst."

Kagan began moving forward once again, giving the pit-viper a wide berth. He had to admit, Ella was handling herself reasonably well here. In his college days, he had dated a woman who would panic over the most harmless spider or wasp, pretending to be terrified until he could defend her from these seemingly insurmountable menaces.

He had never been sure if her terror was real or faked. Perhaps she thought it would be endearing to him, playing frightened so he could play heroic. But he had always found this behavior anything but endearing. Instead, he found it annoying, irrational, and childish.

The way Cynthia had handled insect and rodent pests was one of the things that he loved about her. If a large spider emerged from a corner of a room, one large enough to worry even Kagan, she would either capture it and set it free outside, or kill it, depending on what tools she had available. She didn't cower, freak out, or insist that he rescue her. She handled the situation with calm and a complete absence of drama.

So while Ella had her share of issues, at least she seemed to have a backbone when it came to dealing with this sort of thing. Thank God. The Amazon represented the greatest density of large, scary-looking creepy crawly insects, scorpions, and the like on Earth, so a woman who would run screaming from a room because of a harmless spider would be a nightmare to travel with here.

Not only that, but the climate was blistering hot, and as humid as a sauna, and they were sweaty and muddy and grimy. Yet Ella had barely complained.

As difficult as she could be to take, he was better off with her than with a companion who was brilliant, but terrified of bugs and prone to constant complaining.

"So let me finally answer the question you asked before we were . . . interrupted," said Kagan. "Why am I here?" He paused for effect. "Turns out the CIA called in the wee hours of the morning."

Had it really been earlier that morning when this had all begun? It seemed like ages ago.

"They told me an important, top-secret American satellite had been struck by fast-moving space debris. It lost altitude, and eventually landed very near these coordinates. They asked me to drop everything and retrieve it. I was relatively close by, so I got the call. That's about the size of it."

"And the Iranians?"

"Other governments would like a peek at this satellite themselves," he said, satisfied that this was close enough to the truth that it would serve to explain their situation nicely, without him having to delve into the alien technology aspect. "It's pretty advanced. So the Iranians aren't the only bad actors likely to be in the jungle right now."

"Bad actors?" she said. "What do you mean? The Iranians weren't putting on any kind of act as far as I could tell."

"Not *actors*, like in a movie. You know, *bad actors*. Meaning, uh . . . troublemakers. People acting badly. You've never heard that expression?"

She shook her head no.

"Well, no matter," he said. "The point is that I'm here to get this satellite and leave."

"So this thing managed to land?" she said skeptically. "Wouldn't something that fell from space, you know . . . crash?"

Kagan sighed. "No. It landed."

"How do you plan to carry something so big?"

"It's very small," he said as a toucan squawked in the distance, the fabled loudest bird in the Amazon living up to its billing. "So I'll be able to carry it."

She appeared to be deep in thought as they continued working their way through the jungle. "But now your helicopter is, ah . . . broken," she pointed out. "So how are we going to get out of here?"

Kagan frowned, annoyed that she had suddenly started to ask good questions. "I'll cross that bridge once I find the satellite," he replied. "But I need to be honest with you," he added, knowing that this was a speech he needed to give, anyway, and taking advantage of the opening she had just given him.

He blew out a long breath and stopped his movement near an array of bright flowers that he suspected were larger, brighter cousins of the birds-of-paradise plants he had seen in The States. "It's doubtful we'll be leaving here anytime soon."

He paused to let this sink in. "I don't have the exact coordinates of this satellite, and it could be anywhere within an area of over two hundred miles."

"So how are you *ever* going to find it?" asked Ella. "You could be here a hundred years and not find it."

"I'll find it," he said forcefully, trying to convince *himself* of this as much as her. "Don't worry about that. But the point is that it might take a while. And this mission is critical to America's national security, so it takes precedence over everything else. I shouldn't be wasting time with you at all, let alone making sure you have boots. So let me lay out the ground rules for you."

His eyes locked on hers, and his expression turned grim. "First, you do what I tell you. *Immediately.* Without argument or complaint. Understood?"

She opened her mouth to protest, but decided against it, nodding meekly instead.

"Good. I'll share the rations I brought with you, but it won't be long before we'll have to live off the land. This being said, we should be able to manage just fine. I have a device that produces purified water. I also have plenty of water purification tablets, just in case. And there are more than three thousand edible fruits here. We only eat about two hundred in the West. But I know which are edible, and which are poisonous."

Ella rolled her eyes. "Of course you do," she mumbled under her breath.

"Second," continued Kagan, "I'm going to have to invoke the law of the jungle—literally. I can't let you slow me down, or interfere. Remember, I didn't invite you on this little outing. You stowed away. I'm sorry that it's come to this, but you shouldn't be here. So if you can't keep up, I'll have to leave you behind."

Her face fell. "You know I wouldn't last a day by myself," she said. "You're the expert. I don't know the first thing about surviving here."

He nodded. "I know that. And again, I'm sorry. But there is more at stake here than just you and me. Not to mention dangerous people from multiple countries who might want to kill me. And this doesn't include the hundreds of indigenous tribes that live here, including about fifty that are believed to have never had contact with the outside world. To this day."

"I don't believe that."

"Believe what you want. I'm telling you the facts. I'd have thought after living in Brazil for this long, you'd have heard about these tribes."

She shook her head. "Not so much," she replied.

"Back to my point," said Kagan. "I can't afford to be compassionate. So do what I tell you, don't complain, and keep up. Stay very close to me and you'll be okay. If not, if you fall behind, or we get separated . . ." He winced. "I won't be able to waste time retrieving you. Are we clear?"

She swallowed hard. "I thought you valued all life."

"I do. And I hope like hell you'll be able to keep up and we both get out of here alive. But I have to do what I have to do. Don't say I didn't warn you."

She glared at him, hurt as much as she was scared. "I'll keep up," she said, a determined look in her eye.

Kagan nodded and began moving forward, pulling out his machete, as the jungle had become too dense for easy movement once again.

Maybe she *would* be able to keep up. She seemed remarkably fit. And while he was exerting himself to clear the path ahead of them, and carrying a heavy backpack, she had the easier job of following. Despite his externally enhanced muscles, he was dripping with sweat, while she seemed fresh as a daisy—or whichever flower was the jungle equivalent. Given the muggy conditions here, her present condition would be remarkable, even if she were only lounging by a pool.

Her body appeared quite toned, and this wasn't by accident. She had probably done a lot of Pilates and jazzercising over the years.

For someone who had long used her looks to get ahead, this made sense.

"Ory," he said subvocally, "*What is Ella's heart rate now?*"

"*Still at about fifty-one beats a minute.*"

Kagan considered this. "*I meant to ask you before, but forgot. Isn't a heart rate this low dangerous?*"

"*Not at all,*" said Ory. "*It's an indication of exceptional fitness. She has the kind of pulse you'd find in endurance athletes. Steady as a metronome. I think the word you're looking for is* impressive."

Kagan nodded to himself. Good. Maybe she really would be able to keep up. He hoped so. But only time would tell.

And he had been deadly serious about the consequences for her if she fell behind.

# PART 4

# 20

The interstellar probe, which called itself *Seeker*, had abruptly slowed its massive speed to a crawl as it descended through Earth's atmosphere, finally breaking through the rainforest canopy at turtle-like speed to gently come to a rest on a bed of thick, aboveground tree roots.

All objects moved through space-time at the exact same rate. The probe had been moving through space at such a high velocity, it had barely moved through time at all. Now the reverse was true. Since it was no longer moving through space, its movement through time was occurring at the highest possible rate.

With respect to time, at least, it and the inhabitants of this planet were now in perfect synchronicity, and Seeker had kept itself quite busy in the hours since it had landed.

The softball-sized probe, constructed from an insanely resilient reflective material unknown to human science, contained an internal computer brain the size of a golf ball. But what a brain it was. Only a hundred-billion-fold less efficient than the theoretical maximum.

Even a single pound of inert granite was a wonder of complexity, containing roughly a trillion trillion atoms that were each a cauldron of activity, with numerous spins, electromagnetic fields, and electrons. All in all, the theoretical computational capability of this pound of granite, provided it could harness all of these atoms and all of these differing properties as computational nodes, was a million trillion trillion trillion calculations per second. Since this theoretical maximum was roughly a trillion times more powerful than the combined minds of every human who had ever lived, Seeker's ability to attain even a hundred billionth of this capability was truly extraordinary.

After coming to a rest, Seeker had released millions of microscopic nanites into the rainforest, which immediately went to work, burrowing into the soil and vegetation and scavenging for the molecular building blocks they would need to carry out the first part of their instructions, which Seeker had programmed into them upon landing.

Each nanite was a complex nanofabricator, capable of tapping into the quantum foam, just as Seeker's star drive had done, to unleash all the energy it would need for its task.

First, the nanites had been instructed to make additional copies of themselves. *Many* additional copies. Each nanite converted rocks, and dirt, and roots, and the complex array of elements within the biological organisms it invaded into the raw materials it needed to reproduce, chewing through matter at the molecular level with effortless ease.

And each copy that was completed immediately went to work making *more* copies.

In only a matter of hours, the millions of microscopic nanites Seeker had released had grown into a thick carpet of silver moss, clearly visible to the naked eye, many hundreds of trillions of members strong.

These nanofabricators, also called micro-assemblers, were nothing less than a long-held dream of scientists and science fiction enthusiasts come to life. A dream that had been in the human imagination since Richard Feynman's talk in 1959 entitled, "There's Plenty of Room at the Bottom."

During this groundbreaking lecture, Feynman had speculated about a technology capable of moving individual atoms about, manipulating them like so many Legos to build any item imaginable out of its constituent atoms—from the bottom up.

And since the turn of the millennia, Nanotechnologists had made great strides creating ever-tinier machines, and advances in 3D printing had demonstrated the power and versatility of this approach at the macro level.

But being able to perform this function at the elemental level was another thing entirely, requiring a microscopic machine that could carve up complex molecules to get to raw materials in their most basic state. And such a machine would not only need *this* capability, but also the wherewithal to reconfigure these materials precisely as needed.

The level of engineering sophistication this would require was almost *inconceivable*.

How could such a fabricator find the materials it needed so unerringly? How could it know how to build a copy of itself so precisely? Or how to build anything else, for that matter? How could it do this reproducibly, and with the extraordinary efficiency required?

Such a capability was absurd. Ludicrous. *Impossible*.

Except that this is exactly what biological machinery had managed to do on Earth for billions of years.

When a human sperm and egg came together to form a single cell, this cell possessed the programming and technical capabilities needed to self-assemble an entire human, the perfect example of nanofabrication in practice. This single cell used raw materials found in its environment to quickly produce an identical cell, which then became four, which then became eight—eventually multiplying into the *trillions*.

And each duplication event along the way required a cell to find the molecular constituents of its DNA and assemble a perfect copy, three-billion letters long, something it did with astonishing fidelity.

Then, as if having a single cell direct the manufacture of trillions of others wasn't impressive enough, these identical cells would begin to specialize along the way. Following the dictates of a complex set of instructions, some miraculously transformed into eye cells, some into brain cells, some into heart cells, some into muscle cells, and so on.

The automated self-construction of a human being from a single cell, including a working brain hundreds of billions of neurons strong, was a staggering, mind-boggling feat of engineering. But since nature made this look relatively easy, it was largely taken for granted.

Those who celebrated mankind's engineering genius as being incomparable, raving about the magic of a 3D printer capable of creating tiny plastic action figures, almost never considered the miracle of complexity and precision that allowed hundreds of thousands of 3D human babies to arrive in hospitals each day, factory fresh.

And this process didn't stop once a newborn baby was deposited into the world. As this infant grew from an eight-pound bundle of helplessness into a two-hundred-pound wrestler, it converted breast milk—and later, pizza, beer, and potato chips—into the raw material needed to produce such dramatic growth.

Seeker's nanites had taken several pages from this biological playbook. After replicating to sufficient numbers, which had taken about four hours, they began to follow a supplemental set of instructions, quickly finding raw materials they needed to build the sophisticated equipment Seeker had specified.

All Seeker had to do was release these nanofabricating dynamos into the environment, and then sit back and wait for them to do the rest. This was the equivalent of a human planting a single giant sequoia seed into the ground, no bigger than a flake of oatmeal, and then waiting for what would become the heaviest living organism on Earth to emerge from the seed and self-assemble.

Unlike the construction of a sequoia tree, however, the atom-by-atom assembly of the equipment Seeker needed took place in hours rather than years, as the hundreds of trillions of nanites worked in perfect concert to complete their task.

One of the first instruments completed allowed the small alien craft to tap into the Internet and download content at unimaginable speed. Seeker had tasted Internet content while still in space, but this had been a relatively slow process, and it had only scratched the surface.

But now it was able to take the deepest of dives, digesting every word and image from billions upon billions of online pages, including every last blog, vlog, website, and advertisement, in every language.

It devoured the content of millions of books, magazines, and scholarly journals accessible online, stealing from Amazon, Google, and many others, hacking their systems in seconds so that the theft was undiscovered.

It read every last social media post ever made, a daunting number that was growing by over a million posts, worldwide, every *minute*, and raced through endless hours of YouTube videos, which themselves were growing by almost a million hours *each day*.

Voraciously, tirelessly, Seeker plowed ahead, sucking down every email and text message it could access, which, combined, were now being produced around the world at a rate of more than two billion per day.

It examined all of the photos and images ever posted to Instagram and other such sites, now more than a million per hour, as well as all tweets, which themselves were growing by hundreds of millions per day.

Corporate computers and the entire cloud were also raided and picked clean. Massive storehouses of data on products and customer preferences, stock market trades, traffic and security cameras, government data from DMVs, the census, phone conversation surveillance, and mountains more.

The Library of Congress maintained a collection of almost two hundred million items. This included forty million cataloged books and other print materials, in almost five hundred languages, and more than seventy million manuscripts.

Yet for many years now, humanity had been collectively generating enough data—*each second*—to fill *four* of these libraries.

And the AI that had landed in the Amazon rainforest now methodically consumed it all.

Even given Seeker's vast computational capabilities, digesting all of this content, saving it, and organizing it for better analysis, was taking additional time.

But it wouldn't be long now. It was almost done with its preparations.

And the show would begin very soon.

# PART 5

# 21

Kagan and Ella continued hiking back to the river, accompanied by the symphony of the jungle, which was never silent. Birds chirping, monkeys screeching, insects clicking, lizards darting off through the underbrush, it was a steady barrage of mostly soothing sounds that pulsated with the heartbeat of life, accompanying the vivid colors and varied aromas of the rainforest.

There were sixteen thousand different tree species in the Amazon, totaling four hundred billion individual specimens, and Kagan was pretty sure he had already seen every last one. The term *never-ending* was no exaggeration here.

"What's that smell?" asked Ella, crinkling her nose as they entered an area infused with an odor more pungent than the norm.

"*Ory?*" asked Kagan subvocally, knowing that his AI companion had odor sensors that were nearly as impressive as a dog's. Not that anything it smelled could evoke a reaction, good or bad, in the AI. Ory experienced the smell of freshly baked cookies and rotting, maggot-infested flesh with the same clinical detachment.

"*It's H. brasiliensis,*" said the AI.

"*Stop showing off,*" replied Kagan. "*You really think Ella wanted the scientific name?*"

Kagan listened for another moment to his AI and then turned to Ella. "You're smelling a rubber tree," he told her.

"A *rubber* tree?" she repeated. "You mean condoms actually grow on *trees*? I always thought that, you know, you had to get them at the pharmacy."

Kagan laughed. "Very funny," he said. Then, suddenly uncertain, he added, "You *are* joking, right?"

She smiled. "Of course I'm joking," she said good-naturedly, somehow not taking offense at the question. "But back to what you just said, this doesn't smell like rubber."

"Well, these trees do produce natural latex sap, which itself smells really bad. But that's not what you're smelling. Turns out when the tree is in bloom, the flowers are pretty pungent too."

"How did you get to be such an Amazon expert?"

"I have a really good memory," he replied as he turned with his machete to continue moving forward.

A massive beetle passed by, the size of an adult human hand. Ella looked disgusted, but she didn't shrink back or scream.

"That's what's called a *Titan beetle*," said Kagan, parroting what Ory was now telling him. "It's mostly harmless, but its jaws are strong enough to break a pencil in half, so probably not a good idea to pet it."

"Yeah, you read my mind," she said, rolling her eyes. "I was just about to do that."

Kagan laughed.

"Why are some of the bugs here so huge?" asked Ella.

"Good question," replied Kagan. "Hold on a minute, let me catch my breath," he added, his way of stalling until Ory finished giving him the answer.

"Bugs don't breathe like we do," he began finally. "Air comes in through holes in their abdomens and shuttles along tubes."

"You mean they don't breathe in and out, right?"

"Right. It's passive. The air just kind of travels through them. Which isn't as efficient as our system. So the bigger the bug, the harder it is for it to get the oxygen it needs. In prehistoric times, the oxygen content of the atmosphere was fifty percent higher than it is now, so the bugs back then could grow a lot bigger. Hundreds of millions of years ago, there were dragonflies with two-foot wingspans."

Ella curled up her nose in disgust. "Glad I didn't live back then," she said.

Kagan smiled. If she *had* lived back then, giant dragonflies would be the least of her worries. "Prehistoric bugs could have evolved a better breathing system and gotten even bigger," he added, unable to keep from sharing this fascinating tidbit of information that Ory had just passed on, "but birds evolved first. They were faster and more agile than bugs, so they outcompeted them in this niche—and also preyed on them."

Ella blinked in confusion. "But we're not in prehistoric times. So why are they so big *here*?"

"Right," said Kagan with a sigh. He should have known she couldn't connect two dots just one inch from each other. "Sorry. The Amazon is the most oxygen-rich region of the planet. So bugs can get bigger here than elsewhere. Not nearly as big as in prehistoric times, but still pretty big."

Ella nodded, apparently satisfied, although Kagan wondered if she truly got it, or had just decided not to pursue it further.

Minutes later, as Kagan was cutting through the thick foliage, Ory announced that it could hear a helicopter in the distance, more toward the center of the perimeter they'd been given rather than the river. It was the third helicopter the AI had detected since they arrived. No doubt dropping off one more team to add to the mix, who would rappel into the jungle, rather than attempting the tamer riverbank landing that Kagan had made.

A short time later, the AI announced that they were approximately fifteen minutes from their destination, so Kagan called a halt. He rested against the trunk of yet another tall palm tree, a mainstay of the jungle, facing what his augmented lenses told him was aptly named a *Walking Palm*. This tree's trunk was supported by a bundle of long, stilt-like roots, reaching up like legs. Vines had attached to nearby branches, with growths that looked like enchanted toilet brushes, with beautiful, vividly bright, orange-red bristles sticking out on all sides—a vine that was nicknamed *Monkey Brush*—and several hummingbirds were hovering nearby, feeding.

Kagan removed a canteen from an outer pocket of his backpack, took several long swigs, and handed it to Ella. "Go ahead and finish it," he suggested.

"Do you plan to fill it up again at the river?" asked Ella. "And use one of those purification pills you talked about?"

He shook his head. He had already told her about the advanced device he had with him, but this had apparently failed to sink in. "The purification tablets are just for emergencies," he said patiently. "In case I have an equipment breakdown. But I have a, um . . . *CIA-issued* device that pulls uncontaminated water right from the air. It contains a block of porous micro-material with a massive surface area. The technology allows it to capture water molecules in this material, and then flush them into a container. It's revolutionary. It can pull water from the most parched desert air, so in a place this humid . . . " He let the thought hang, seeing no need to finish the sentence.

"In a place this humid, what?"

He groaned inside. Apparently he did need to finish it. "In a place this humid, we'll have all the drinking water we need. No need to conserve."

She nodded and handed him back an empty canteen. "That's lucky. Especially since you have no idea how to find this spy satellite you're looking for."

"Well, not at the moment, anyway. I'm hoping that when I get closer to it, I'll be able to detect it with sensors."

"What sensors?"

"In my pocket."

"Along with that device you used to make those Iranians start screaming, right?"

He nodded.

"That's quite a pocket," she said. "I don't suppose that phone you told me about is in there too. What'd you call it? You know, the one you were planning to use after we took off to contact your friend to come get me."

"It's a sat-phone. Short for satellite phone. Why do you ask?"

"Maybe you can call your buddy to come get us *here*."

Kagan frowned. "It isn't working. Something here is suppressing it. I'm hoping that we'll get beyond the range of whatever is responsible, so we'll be able to use it again."

"What do you mean, suppressing it? What can do that?"

"Maybe some other group that's trying to steal the satellite," replied Kagan. He shrugged. "Or, more likely, something emanating from the satellite itself."

"It's one of *your* satellites, right? So don't *you* know if it can do this or not?"

Kagan sighed. "I'm afraid not," he admitted.

"But you at least know if we're going in the right direction to be able to use your phone, right? You know, if you're getting more bars as we travel—or not."

"It isn't a cell phone, and there aren't any bars," he said dismissively.

A surge of adrenaline coursed through him and his eyes widened. Out of the mouths of simpletons, he thought, as a smile spread over his face. She had given him an idea, one so obvious that it occurred to him that *he* had been the simpleton.

If the suppression field was emanating from the alien probe, perhaps it *did* have a strength gradient. In which case, doing the opposite of what Ella had suggested might allow him to find it. Instead of trying to determine where his phone might work, he could try to determine where it was suppressed the *most*. This could well be the center of the field, which, in this case, could be the probe he was looking for. The only question was if Ory's sensors had the enormous sensitivity that would be required.

"Stay here," he said excitedly, and then immediately communicated instructions to Ory subvocally. He traveled ten feet in each compass direction and then returned to Ella.

"What was that all about?" she asked. "I don't—"

"Hold on," he said, interrupting her, his face a mask of concentration.

"*Ory,*" he continued subvocally, "*Were you able to detect a gradient in the strength of the suppressor?*"

"*Yes. Infinitesimally small, but I was just able to sense it. It was stronger due east and weaker due west. But we'd have to keep checking as we go.*"

"Yes!" said Kagan triumphantly, ignoring Ella's confused look.

This would work. It would be slow, like a game he had played as child, in which a friend would hide an object and tell him if he was getting *warmer* or *colder* as he moved to find it, telling him he was *burning up* as he came ever closer to his goal, or getting *ice cold* if he was going in the wrong direction. Direct coordinates would be preferred, but this was a huge leap forward, giving him his first and best chance to actually find this thing.

"Ella," he said happily, "you're absolutely brilliant!"

She blinked absently for several seconds. "Sure," she said finally, a wry smile creeping over her face. "I get that a lot. If I had a nickel every time someone told me I was brilliant, I'd have, you know . . . a nickel."

Kagan laughed out loud at this display of self-deprecating humor, which was actually funny.

She may not have been terribly bright, but at least she didn't pretend otherwise.

He sighed. The time for rest was over. The direction they were moving in to retrieve the Iranian's boots was taking them farther from the probe rather than nearer, colder rather than warmer.

It was time to get going again. Now that he had an actual strategy that went beyond just moving randomly through the jungle and hoping to get lucky, the urgency was greater than ever.

# 22

As they neared the river, the distinctive sound of yet another helicopter cut through the music of the jungle. It was still a ways off, but it was the first helo close enough to be detectable by unenhanced human hearing.

"*Is it dropping off rappelers, or landing?*" asked Kagan subvocally, already suspecting the answer. Rappelers would be inserting themselves in a more central location than the river.

"*It's landing,*" replied Ory. "*It's roughly the size of the one you brought, but I can't tell its country of origin from the sound alone. It's setting down about half a mile upriver from where you did.*"

"*Keep me posted,*" requested Kagan unnecessarily.

He turned to Ella. "How are you feeling?"

She shrugged. "Okay, I guess. I run eight miles a day, so I'm pretty fit. But that's mostly on a treadmill inside an air conditioned building. And, you know, wearing running shoes." She looked down at her own shoes, which were becoming increasingly worse for wear, and frowned. But her frown slowly grew into a smile, and then into actual laughter.

"What's so funny?" asked Kagan.

"I was just thinking about the exercise I do back at home versus what I'm doing here. In these darn flats. Instead of fantasizing about how great it would be to have my running shoes, I'm fantasizing about how great it would be to have big rubber boots. That are the wrong size. Taken from a dead guy."

Kagan grinned. "I see your point. When you get back home, you should try wearing the boots at your club. Who knows, maybe you can start a whole new exercise craze."

Ella laughed again as they cleared the last bit of dense jungle and returned to where their ruined helicopter had fallen onto its side. Ory's guidance had been perfect, as Kagan had come to expect.

Kagan blew out a long, relieved breath as he spotted the Iranian he had shot earlier, still lying dead in the hardening mud. He had been worried that the corpse might have been dragged off or devoured. There were any number of animals who could have managed this trick, like a caiman, a close cousin of the alligator. Or a jaguar, a lethal predator and the third largest cat in the world. Or perhaps even an anaconda, which could grow to five hundred pounds, liked to patrol rivers, and would have swallowed the man whole, rubber boots and all.

The dead man's comrades could also have spoiled Kagan's boot hunting expedition had they taken the time to return to bury him. Fortunately, their mission had come first.

Kagan removed the man's boots as quickly as he could, ignoring the dozens of flies and ants that were already going to work on his corpse, beginning the process of decomposition.

He put some distance between himself and his victim, and helped steady Ella as she pulled the rubber boots over her shoes. He then knelt beside her and began securing her pant legs inside her boots to make both her pants and boots pest-proof.

He noticed some movement eighty yards or so down the riverbank, and his contacts zoomed in on this precise position, without being consciously aware that he had squinted in such a way as to make this happen. Four black caimans, far larger than alligators, had just finished a bloody meal on the riverbank, and were entering the water to swim in his direction, each fifteen to twenty feet long.

He and Ella had arrived at just the right time, he realized, as the dead Iranian would barely make a light snack for these brutes. He took one last look at these magnificent dinosaur-like animals and then turned his attention back to Ella and her new footwear.

*"During the last several minutes,"* reported Ory through Kagan's comm, *"the helicopter landed. Four men, speaking Japanese, exited, and were immediately ambushed by the Iranians. But only those that you encountered. Apparently, the reinforcements they are waiting for*

*have not yet arrived. The Iranians must have realized that they had lost you and doubled back to the river to await more prey. They are now holding the Japanese at gunpoint."*

"Good thing this guy's feet were so small," said Ella. "You know—"

"Quiet!" hissed Kagan, holding out a forestalling hand. "I need to listen for something."

*"The Iranians have learned from their experience with you,"* continued Ory. *"They didn't replace their comms, and they've frisked the Japanese and confiscated their weapons. They're now beginning to tie their prisoners with zip ties."*

A single crack of a rifle shot rang out in the distance, scattering nearby wildlife, and Ella eyed Kagan in amazement. Was his hearing really good enough to have known something like this might be coming?

She opened her mouth to speak, but Kagan caught her eye and shook his head, warning her to remain silent.

*"They killed one of the Japanese contingent to prove their seriousness,"* reported Ory.

There was a long pause. *"The others are about to cave,"* continued the AI. *"They've discussed the situation in Japanese and have agreed that the Iranians must know as much as they do, already, so staying silent isn't worth dying for."*

Several minutes passed. *"The Japanese have now told their captors what little they know about the alien spacecraft, using English, which both sides seem to understand. And they've insisted that they don't know anything else."*

After another long pause, Ory continued. *"The Iranians are speaking in Persian now. They believe the Japanese are telling the truth. Even so, Kazem Abdi has just ordered them to—"*

Another burst of gunfire reverberated throughout the jungle, this time an extended one, and Kagan didn't need to ask Ory what the Iranian leader's order had been. It was all too clear. They had killed the remaining Japanese agents in cold blood, just as they had intended to do with the two Americans.

Kagan rose from the riverbank and faced Ella. "We need to go," he said grimly.

"What was that all about?" she asked, gesturing toward the sound of the gunfire.

"The Iranians who ambushed us did the same to a group of Japanese. They're all dead now."

"*Who's* all dead? The Japanese or the Iranians?"

"The Japanese!" he replied, failing to keep the irritation from his tone.

Her eyes narrowed. "And you know this *how?*"

"I have really good hearing."

"Crazy good hearing," seconded Ella.

"It's a gift," he replied. "But come on, we need to go." He didn't see the need to tell her about the four approaching caimans, another good reason to be on their way.

"You know, Ben, you probably should have killed these Iranians when you had the chance."

He sighed. "You're right. But I don't have the time to correct that mistake now. With hearing like mine, though, I'll be able to tell if they're trying to sneak up on us," he added, trying to be reassuring.

They hiked back into the jungle, soon veering off toward the east, guided by Ory and its *hot* or *cold* pronouncements.

After several hours, and draining and filling Kagan's canteen twice from the device that pulled an inexhaustible supply of drinkable water from the air, they came to the densest section of jungle they had yet to encounter. The going became slower than ever, and Kagan had to rely on increased assistance from his powered undergarment.

Kagan had been hacking away at the suffocating greenery for almost fifteen minutes when Ory's voice issued through his comm. "*Ella has fallen behind, Ben,*" it said, its tone urgent. "*I should have caught this sooner. She's trying to find you, but she's moving more quickly than I would have expected she could, and going in the wrong direction.*"

Kagan stopped and shook his head. He was killing himself playing machete man and she couldn't even do the easy part and keep up.

"*If I shout for her,*" he asked Ory, "*what are the chances a possible hostile will hear me?*"

"*Very low, using their own hearing. But sound amplification technology is common, and most of the agents here are likely to have brought this with them. I wouldn't recommend taking that risk.*"

Kagan frowned. "*Which way is she going?*" he asked.

"*Southeast. But she's a surprisingly quiet mover. Unless she starts speaking or calls out, I won't be able to hear her for long.*"

"*What about the sensor I put on her? Can't you track her by that?*"

"*It fell off an hour ago,*" said Ory. "*I didn't want to bother you about it, since I know it served its purpose. She's been plowing through countless branches, and the adhesion is weak, so it's surprising it stayed on her as long as it did.*"

"Goddammit!" fumed Kagan aloud.

He had warned her. He had told her the consequences of falling behind. How had she not called out when she realized she was lost? She knew that his hearing was exceptional.

He sighed, trying to give her the benefit of the doubt. Maybe she was afraid of attracting dangerous animals. Maybe she worried that the Iranians were too close for comfort, since they had seemed to be within shouting distance ever since Kagan had landed.

It didn't matter how this had happened, anyway. The question was, what should he do now? Would he really just leave her?

He shook his head almost immediately. He had to give her one more chance. He was beginning to warm to her, although he wasn't sure why. He had no patience for the small-minded or the slow-minded, and she had proven to be both of these things.

And yet there was some quality about her that partially made up for this, in addition to the sense of humor she had recently revealed, although he couldn't put his finger on it. And she *had* given him the clue he needed to find the probe, however inadvertently.

Not that this was why he would make sure he found her. He would do this because he couldn't help but feel it was the right thing to do, regardless of how much the stark math might suggest otherwise.

Besides, his mission wasn't about being the first to acquire the alien craft, it was about being the one who left the jungle with it. For all he knew, he would get to it first, even *with* the delay that Ella was causing. But even if he didn't, it could well be that *not* getting to it first was the better strategy, if he could take it from the group that did.

Ory soon announced that Ella was beyond the range of its comm-assisted hearing, at least given how quiet she was being. Upon learning this, Kagan removed all twelve of the dragonfly drones from his pack and had Ory deploy them in a coordinated search pattern. They were tiny enough to navigate the tight jungle far better than he could, and they could fly to superior vantage points. Better still, Ory could control and monitor all of them simultaneously.

Even so, it took almost six minutes before one of them finally spotted the target. As soon as this happened, Ory began to transmit the drone's video and audio feeds to Kagan's contacts and comm. Ella was approaching what looked like a small lake that had materialized in the middle of the jungle, still off in the distance.

While there were trees and jungle foliage not only surrounding it, but emerging from the shallow water, as well, the jungle was as sparse here as he had seen. The surroundings were still not open enough for a helicopter to land, but fairly long-range visibility through the trees was possible here.

"*Is that a swamp?*" asked Kagan.

"*No, it's part of the river. In the wet season rivers here flood the jungle for miles. When the dry season comes, they recede, but they leave pools behind. As pools like this one get shallower and shallower, scores of fish become highly concentrated. If you want to catch fish, this is your chance, Ben. Given their likely density, even someone inexperienced could stab as many as they wanted with a sharpened bamboo pole.*"

Kagan nodded. Good to know. Hunting here would be the Amazonian equivalent of shooting fish in a barrel. He watched as Ella approached the small lake, the drone showing several exotic birds gathered around it to feast, which his augmented contacts identified as herons, egrets, and storks. It was a beautiful sight, but he recognized the danger immediately.

Kagan ordered the drone to fly near Ella's eyes, and when she noticed it hovering in front of her, he had Ory transmit his voice through it. "Ella!" he said firmly, and the volume was set high enough for her to easily hear. "This is Ben. You're looking at a tiny drone I sent to find you. It's now broadcasting my voice."

This last was obvious, but Kagan had to remind himself that even the obvious sometimes escaped his one-time boss.

"If you speak, I'll be able to hear you, also," he added.

"Ben?" she said, and the relief in her voice, and on her face, was palpable. For a moment he thought she might tear up, but she managed to get control of her emotions. "Where are you?"

"First, you need to reverse course. Immediately! Follow this drone. The birds and water you're nearing might look tranquil, but they'll attract dangerous predators. Most of these prefer not to attack humans, but this isn't something you'll want to test."

Ella swallowed hard. "Good point," she whispered, and dutifully began to follow the drone away from the water.

"I'll head toward you as quickly as I can," he said, "and we can meet in the middle."

"I never thought I'd see you again," she said. "You said you'd leave me if we ever got separated."

He shook his head. It probably wasn't the wisest move on her part to remind him of this until *after* they were reunited.

"I did say that," he replied. "And I meant it. But I've decided to give you one last chance. But you'll need to pay better attention. I know you can keep up physically. Once we're reunited, just be sure to keep your eyes on me at all times, and don't let your attention wander."

Suddenly, abruptly, the connection to the drone ended, and Ella's image vanished from his vision.

"What happened?" he said to Ory out loud.

"*I've lost contact with all of the drones. I need some time to investigate the situation and conduct further experimentation.*"

Less than two seconds later, the AI was back. "*Apparently, whatever was blocking the sat-phone is now blocking everything. And I mean everything. As far as I can tell, all drones are now grounded, ours and those belonging to any other party. The sound amplification technology in your comm is no longer working, either.*"

"How is that possible?"

"*Unclear.*"

"If this field suppresses all signals of every kind," persisted Kagan, still speaking out loud, "then how are *we* still in communication? Even though you're positioned on my leg, you still speak to me using a wireless signal."

"*It appears that the suppression is a function of distance between the sender of the signal and the receiver. So we, and other groups in this sector, can communicate as usual, and control drones and other remote technology as usual. But only as long as the drone or team member is within fifty or so yards of the origination of the signal. No farther.*"

"But how can this be killing sound amplification technology?" asked Kagan.

"*As I said, that is unclear. But it appears to be blocking the amplification at the source, at the comm itself, but without impacting your normal, biological ability to hear. And without impacting my ability to use the comm to communicate with you.*"

"Do you know of any country that has tech that might be able to do this?"

"*Negative,*" replied the AI simply.

Kagan's eyes narrowed. Not only had the suppressor field become more debilitating, it was now clear beyond a shadow of doubt that the alien probe was responsible. So what did that mean? Was this an accident? Had something within the probe malfunctioned after its landing, with this strange suppressive activity being an unfortunate side effect?

Or had this been done on *purpose*? And if so, *whose* purpose?

Was this action a part of the probe's landing protocols, like certain rote activities that NASA probes automatically engaged in after setting down on Mars?

And regardless of whether it was passive or active, automatic or mindful, how far did this field extend? And to what end had it been generated?

Kagan sighed. There was no way to know the answer to any of these questions at the moment, and he had other, more pressing issues to attend to. All he knew was that he could no longer extend his vision or hearing, meaning that his early warning systems were gone. *Everyone's* early warning systems were gone, increasing the likelihood that various factions in the area would ultimately clash.

He wondered what Ella was doing now that the drone had fallen to the jungle floor. Did she know to stay where she was and wait for him? He was about to find out.

"Lead me to Ella's last known position," he ordered the AI. "How long should it take me to reach her?"

*"Approximately seven minutes, provided she hasn't moved."*

Kagan moved quickly to join her, surprised to feel a hint of panic in his gut. His senses continued to be artificially heightened by transcranial brain stimulation, so he should be at his sharpest and *least* emotional, but this wasn't the case. Anyone would be horrified by the thought of a woman getting lost in the jungle, basically being given a death sentence, but his feelings were more visceral even than this.

Somewhere in his subconscious, Ella, who was still an albatross around his neck, had taken on far more importance to him than his conscious mind could account for. While it was true that she'd been growing on him steadily, she was still a clear liability, not to mention highly annoying more often than not.

Even so, there was more to her than he had originally thought. More potential. More heart. Perhaps she brought out paternal feelings in him. He wasn't sure.

All he knew was that he was suddenly prepared to go to great lengths to save her, when by rights he should be following through on his promise to leave her behind.

He passed a dense thicket of tall green bamboo and arrived at where Ella had been when the drone signals had died. No one was in sight.

"Ella!" he called out, much more loudly than he would have liked.

"Ben?" came an excited reply, from just beyond where he could see. "Ben?" she repeated, her voice getting closer. Moments later she broke through some thick, waxy leaves and came into view, throwing her arms around him like a giddy schoolgirl. "Thank you so much for coming for me," she whispered.

"I'm just glad you're okay," he said into her ear as they continued a long embrace. "Let's both make sure that this doesn't happen again."

They separated at last, only to find themselves surrounded by four Caucasian men. Each of them were armed to the teeth, and each had a gun trained on them at point-blank range.

# 23

"What a beautiful show of affection, mate," said a distinctly Australian voice, spoken by a tall, muscular man who looked highly formidable. "You're going to make me tear up. Really."

He waved the gun in his hand. "But why don't you both raise your hands where we can see them first."

Both pairs of hands shot up into the air. Kagan's lenses, still in augmented mode, identified the speaker as Major Jack Wilson of the Australian army's 2nd Commando Regiment, a crack special forces unit. The man's record was truly exceptional.

Kagan queried Ory subvocally, asking if the Aussies' comms could be hacked like the AI had done with the Iranians, just in case this proved necessary. But, as Kagan had expected with a team this competent, their comms were protected against such an assault.

"We're Americans," said Kagan simply. "Australia and America are close allies, remember?"

The Aussie leader laughed. "How could I forget? You must be here to get a look at this tiny alien spaceship like the rest of us. I thought you Yanks already had one of these in Roswell. Or maybe Area 51. Don't you think it's time to let someone else have one?"

"Alien spaceship?" said Ella. "What are you talking about?"

"Well aren't you a looker," said the major appreciatively, as if noticing her for the first time. "We've been following your mate for the past five minutes. Should have been following *you*. Love the blouse."

"You're joking about a spaceship, right?" said Ella, ignoring his comment. "I mean, the thing that fell from orbit is, you know, not your property. You have to know it's an American spy satellite, right?"

Aussie Special Forces Major Jack Wilson laughed once again. "Sure it is," he said. "An object coming in from deep space, traveling near the speed of light. Fast enough to circle the globe seven times a second. And then, just a little while ago, knocking out all signals beyond a tight radius. You Americans have balls, but trying to claim this as one of your satellites is bold, even for you. And ridiculous."

Ella tilted her head in confusion. "So you're saying it's *not* an American spy satellite? Are you *certain?*"

"I'm certain," said the Aussie with a grin. "And kudos on your acting ability. If I didn't know any better, I'd think you were genuinely surprised."

Ella considered Wilson for several seconds and then turned her gaze on Kagan, who was making no move to dispute anything the Aussie had said. She glared at her companion with a blistering intensity. "You've been keeping secrets from me, haven't you, Ben?" she hissed angrily.

"It's time you told me what the hell is really going on!"

# 24

Jack Wilson chose to ignore the woman's strange outburst, probably designed to confuse him and throw him off his game. "Look," he said to the two Americans, "you're outgunned and outmanned. And we *are* allies. So if you promise not to try anything funny, you can at least put your hands down."

Kagan lowered his hands and Ella followed suit.

"Thank you," said Kagan, noticing that the four Australians made no move to lower their weapons.

Wilson holstered his gun and walked the short distance that separated them, extending a hand. "I'm Jack Wilson," he said, and then introduced his three comrades in turn. Kagan and Ella introduced themselves as well, but there were never fewer than two guns pointed in their direction.

"We might as well be civilized about this," said Wilson. "Let's take a load off and talk this out. See if I can find a way to trust you." He couldn't help but notice that the girl named Ella continued to eye her companion angrily, and her companion's expression suggested that he wasn't surprised.

What was the point of their charade? Was there really some truth to it?

The major turned to Kagan. "Does your mate seriously not know about the alien spacecraft?" he asked in disbelief. "How can that be?"

"I'll tell you all about it," replied Kagan. "In fact, I like your idea of sitting down and comparing notes. I'm as eager for you to be able to trust us as you are. With long-range communications and sensors down, don't you think we'd be better off teaming up to get to this probe—before anyone else does?"

Wilson considered. "Possibly," he replied. "It all depends on how our little discussion goes. And just so you know," he added, "while we're having our conference, my men will be covering you. Just in case you forget that we're allies."

Kagan lowered his backpack carefully to the jungle floor under the watchful eyes of the Aussies, while the major walked twenty feet to a clear patch of dirt and sat down, motioning for them to join him.

As Wilson repositioned himself, his boot hit one of several small, hollow branches on the ground nearby, disturbing a huge, hairy spider that darted out with blazing speed and alarming ferocity. It headed directly toward Wilson's upper thigh, its five-inch-long legs churning in a blur of motion, and its red fangs standing out even from a distance.

"Major, move!" shouted Kagan, drawing a silenced gun and using augmented focus and reflexes to perfect his aim, hitting the speeding spider dead center, just as its first two hairy legs touched Wilson's thigh. Wilson jerked himself away, but only after Kagan's shot had long since turned the fist-sized predator into spider paste.

The Aussie closest to Kagan reacted immediately as Kagan fired, shooting him in the chest with a silenced gun of his own. The American screamed in pain and fell to the jungle floor.

"Cease fire!" screamed Wilson, jumping up from the ground. "He was trying to help me!"

Kagan pulled himself to a sitting position, groaning. Wilson's eyes roved over his body, searching for blood. "You okay, mate?" he asked in surprise.

"I'll live," croaked Kagan, still clearly in pain.

Wilson extended a hand to help pull Kagan to a standing position, but the American waved him off and rose on his own power.

"Sorry, mate," said a man named Liam Collins, who had shot him. "Thought you were trying to kill Jack."

Kagan grimaced in pain once again. "No worries," he hissed through clenched teeth, purposely using an Aussie expression that had migrated to America. "Easy mistake to make."

"That thing was really hauling ass," said Wilson. "What *was* that monster?"

"A Brazilian Wandering Spider," replied the American. "One of the deadliest animals in the rainforest." It was so deadly, in fact, that

Kagan had made certain he could recognize it on sight before they landed, without need of his AI companion. "It's the most venomous spider on Earth, and one of the most aggressive. It doesn't spin webs. It just wanders the forest floor in search of prey. And it has a bite that's potentially deadly to humans if left untreated."

"From just the brief look I had," said Wilson, "I don't doubt it. Thanks for shooting the bloody thing."

Kagan nodded.

"What would have happened if it had bitten me?"

"It injects a neurotoxin that causes loss of muscle control, eventually resulting in paralysis and asphyxiation." Kagan raised his eyebrows. "In some men the bite also causes an unwanted erection lasting for hours. Apparently, the venom is being studied by pharma companies as a possible treatment for erectile dysfunction."

"I'm sure it is," said Wilson. "What better cure for erectile dysfunction than death by asphyxiation?" he deadpanned. "I have to admit, I've known women who thought death by asphyxiation would be the perfect way to cure me of my *proper* erectile functioning," he added with a grin.

Kagan laughed.

Wilson paused for a few seconds and then sighed, all traces of humor now gone. "On another note," he said, "I'm afraid this spider blew your cover, mate."

Kagan put on a confused expression, but in truth he wasn't at all surprised. Wilson was nobody's fool.

"While it was kind of you to save my life," continued the tall Aussie, "when you shouted for me to move, you called me *Major*. Not Jack. Major. Turns out I *am* a major. But I never told you that. None of my men used our military titles when we introduced ourselves. And you should have no way to know mine."

Kagan shrugged. "You're an Aussie named Jack Wilson, dressed in jungle fatigues and armed to the teeth. And you're out here searching for the alien probe. Who else would you *be*? Of course you're Major Jack Wilson of Australia's 2nd Commando Regiment."

Wilson shook his head, clearly not buying it. "Good try," he said. "But I don't flatter myself. I'm not someone you'd know of off-hand, just someone likely to be stuck in a computer database somewhere. No one has that kind of knowledge of the special forces personnel of every country. And your description of that spider sounded like it came out of an encyclopedia." He stared into Kagan's eyes for several long seconds. "You have a supercomputer in your brain, don't you, mate? One that you can talk to telepathically. That's how you knew who I was."

"Are you out of your mind?" said Kagan, shaking his head in disbelief. "That's the most delusional thing I've ever heard."

"Enhanced Human Operations," said Wilson, undeterred. "We've heard rumors about this unit. The agents have AIs in their heads, and are loaded up with other goodies, too. I've never seen anyone move as quickly and decisively as you just did, nor shoot so accurately at a small, fast-moving target while doing so. You were a bloody blur. And my colleague didn't miss you. You're wearing graphene chain mail body armor, am I right? We've heard rumors about that too. Harder than diamond when it's hit, but dissipates the force enough that you don't end up with multiple cracked ribs."

"You've been reading too much science fiction," said Kagan.

The Aussie laughed. "Yeah, only science has caught up with it." Without waiting for a response, Wilson turned to his men. "Holster your weapons," he said.

"Major?" said Liam Collins.

"You heard me, Captain," said Wilson. "He probably saved my life. And you saw how fast he moved. Once I let him put his hands down, do you have any doubt that he could have shot us all before we knew what hit us? Which tells me he won't try anything shady. Besides, I've heard other rumors about America's so-called Enhanced Human Operations program. They take care to weed out possible psychopaths. Apparently, only well-intentioned souls with big hearts are allowed to become super-heroes."

Ella was listening to every word of the exchange with rapt attention, and fascination, but remained silent, quietly soaking it all in.

All three Aussies considered what their commander had said and finally did as he had ordered, no longer training their guns on the Americans. Each reintroduced themselves, this time with their military titles.

"Does this mean you're willing to work together to find this probe?" asked Kagan.

"Why not?" said Wilson. "We'll have a better chance if we pool our resources."

"*Ory?*" said Kagan subvocally. "*Truth or fiction?*"

When he and Wilson had first shaken hands, Kagan had placed a tiny sensor on the major's shirt, which Ory had been dutifully monitoring.

"*Most likely truth,*" replied the AI hastily. "*His heart is steady at fifty-eight beats per minute, down from one hundred sixty during the spider incident. His facial cues also suggest he's being truthful.*"

"Excellent," said Kagan out loud, responding to the Aussie's willingness to team up. "So what happens when we acquire this thing?" he asked. "I have full authority to make decisions in the field, decisions that are binding on the American government. This authority was granted to me by President Moro himself. I say we bring this probe out of the jungle together, and our countries then study it together. Assuming we can't convince our governments to open the tent even wider."

Wilson considered. "Agreed," he said finally, offering his hand.

Kagan stared into his eyes as they shook hands. "So just to be clear, once we find it, you won't unilaterally decide to abandon our partnership and take it for yourself?"

"You have my word," said Wilson.

"*He's most likely lying,*" said Ory.

Kagan digested this troubling information. Did it still make sense to team up with the Aussies? He quickly decided that it did. He'd have a better chance of finding the probe by working with this group, and he was now warned that Wilson was planning to stab him in the back once they succeeded. He would just have to be sure that he made the first move.

"So are you going to admit that you're part of America's EHO program?" asked the Australian major.

"You know I can't do that," replied Kagan, not about to confirm it, and not about to correct the major's misconception that EHO had already perfected intracranial AIs and telepathic communication.

The tall Aussie nodded toward Ella. "So what's the deal with her?" he asked. "How does she fit in?"

"She stowed away on the helicopter I brought here. She knew nothing about any of this."

Wilson rolled his eyes. "Look, mate, if you don't want to tell me, that's fine. But don't take me for an idiot. No way she was able to stow away on your chopper without you knowing it."

Kagan sighed. "Thanks. As if I'm not embarrassed enough about it. The helo had a sleeping compartment. Custom. Like a coffin room. She was quiet, and it never occurred to me to check it. Really."

Wilson considered. "So is she your girl, then? Is that why she stowed away?"

"No!" said Kagan emphatically. "She's not my *girl*. But it's a long story."

"That's okay, mate. We could be in this jungle for weeks. So there's plenty of time for you to tell us all about it. No matter how long it takes."

# 25

The two men continued to face each other, ignoring the sweat that continued to roll down both of their faces in response to the oppressive humidity.

"*Ory, can you at least intercept their comm frequency?*" asked Kagan subvocally during the brief silence. "*I want to hear all future communications among them.*"

"*Done,*" replied the AI.

Kagan opened his mouth to speak to the major when a number of guttural roars blasted through the jungle, from out of nowhere, so loud and intense they made a lion's roar sound tame. It was a noise Godzilla might have made, although lower in pitch. The growl caused the two Americans and four Aussies to whirl around, looking for a threat out of their worst nightmares. The decibel level of the growl was astonishing, as was its ability to evoke anxiety and conjure up terrifying images of an unstoppable predator that would surely not be denied.

"*Ory?*" said Kagan subvocally, having already drawn his weapon, as had the Aussies before him.

"*Howler Monkeys,*" replied the AI immediately. "*Harmless herbivores,*" it added, "*but their vocalizations are considered to be the loudest of any land animal on Earth, and can be heard clearly for up to three miles. The ones in this case sound more frightening even than usual, because there are many of them howling at the same time, they're very close by, and you can't see them.*"

Kagan immediately communicated this information to the group, who holstered their weapons, relieved, just as the roars subsided.

"*Howler* Monkeys?" said Wilson in disbelief. "Those weren't howls. Howls are the sounds coyotes make. That was something that seemed like it had to be coming from an apex predator the size of a T. Rex."

Kagan nodded. "I can't argue," he said. "Whoever named them didn't do them justice."

"I can't wait to get the hell out of this jungle," said the major, shaking his head. He paused for a moment, bracing himself for another avalanche of noise, but the monkeys had apparently said their piece for a while.

"Now that we can hear ourselves think again," continued the Aussie finally, "why don't you tell me this long story of yours. Tell me who this woman is, and why she decided to stow away."

Kagan grinned. "To be honest, it's more of a *short* story. But a classified one. Let's just say I was doing some snooping within a Brazilian company whose interests might . . . differ . . . from those of America. And Ella happened to be working there. She has nothing to do with what I'm after, but wanted to reach out to me for, ah . . . personal reasons of her own. She meant to speak to me about it earlier, but fell dead asleep in the custom compartment."

Wilson's eyes shifted between the two Americans, looking for any sign of deceit. Finally, he shrugged. "What the hell," he said. "It's too absurd not to be true."

"On that we agree," mused Kagan. "So now what?"

The major rubbed his chin in thought, considering.

"*Ory,*" said Kagan subvocally while he waited for a reply, "*is the micro-drone that found Ella close enough for you to control?*"

"*Affirmative.*"

"*Good. Make sure it flies along with us out of sight. I'll decide when and how to deploy it, depending on circumstances.*"

Given Wilson was planning an eventual double-cross, it didn't hurt to have an ace in the hole—or in this case a drone in the hole—even if the suppressor field had narrowed its range to only about fifty yards.

"Why don't we finish comparing notes," suggested the Aussie major finally.

"Good idea," replied Kagan.

"Okay," said Wilson. "So what do you know about this probe?"

"Almost nothing, same as everyone. It was traveling at just under light speed. Our celestial AI monitoring system picked it up just beyond Mars. It slowed in ways that defied the laws of physics and landed here. That's all we know."

Wilson shook his head. "Not the same experience we had at all. The thing signaled *us* from deep space. And when I say deep space, I don't mean just beyond the orbit of Mars. I mean just beyond the outer limits of the entire solar system."

"What do you mean, *signaled you?*" snapped Kagan. "Are you saying that you didn't pick it up on your own with some kind of asteroid-collision early-warning system?"

"No. It signaled one of our spy satellites, which was then able to follow it in toward Earth. We lost track of it as it entered our atmosphere, but it sent our PM some GPS coordinates that boxed in its approximate landing area."

A shiver ran down Kagan's spine. This changed his understanding of the situation dramatically. "It sent these coordinates directly to your Prime Minister?"

Wilson nodded.

"You said approximate landing area. *How* approximate?"

Wilson frowned. "More approximate than we'd like. I'm not great at kilo to mile conversions, but I'd say a circle with an area of about two hundred to three hundred miles."

Kagan's keen mind raced ahead, assessing the chilling implications of this new information. He considered keeping his thoughts to himself, but decided against it. Wilson had shared what he knew, and Kagan would do no less. "I can't overstate how huge this is," he said. "We spotted the probe ourselves, like I said. And then followed it in. We were able to tell it landed in the Amazon, and managed to read a strange energy signature. But we could only narrow its location to within the same circle as you, with basically the same area." He frowned. "You see what this means, don't you?"

"It wanted everyone in the same boat," whispered Ella to herself, almost as if in a trance.

"Exactly!" said Kagan, surprised and pleased that she had reached the proper conclusion.

"But *who* did it want in the same boat?" demanded Wilson. "Every country on Earth? Only countries capable of launching satellites?"

"Unclear," said Kagan. "We guessed that there would be six to twenty countries capable of either detecting it, or hacking the information from classified computers of countries who *could* detect it. But your information introduces the prospect that there are potentially unlimited ways to find out about it and be drawn here. The probe somehow knew that you Aussies didn't have a sentry system that could catch its arrival, so it gave itself up. It also knew that your PM was the leader of your country, and knew how to reach him directly. If Australia didn't have satellites in orbit that the probe could signal to help you track it in from deep space, it could well have used some other means to let its presence here become known."

It occurred to Kagan that Iran might not be as good at hacking as he had assumed. Maybe *the probe* had nudged them in the right direction, making sure they became aware of the commotion here, causing them to investigate as they had.

Maybe everyone here was dancing to the tune of this alien device.

"Since it contacted our PM," said Wilson, "this suggests it's focused on individual nation states."

"Maybe," said Kagan, "but we can't know that with certainty, either."

"How many countries are there in the world?" asked Ella.

"A hundred and ninety-five," replied Kagan.

Wilson whistled. "Must be nice to have a supercomputer in your noggin," he said.

Kagan arched one eyebrow but didn't respond.

"So all of these countries may have been notified," said one of Wilson's men, who had introduced himself as Lieutenant Ian Crane. "Or maybe just a small subset, chosen for unknown reasons. Or God knows how many other random groups that *aren't* countries."

"If every country on Earth were represented here," said Lieutenant Julius Barton, who had been the quietest of Wilson's team, "wouldn't we be tripping all over each other?"

"Not necessarily," said Kagan. "This jungle is so dense, if you had dozens of small groups within a single square mile of it, many of these might never cross paths. And we're dealing with several *hundred* square miles. If teams are dispersed fairly randomly, it's possible that many more are represented than we could have otherwise imagined." He turned to the major. "Have you run across any other groups?"

"We brought and deployed a number of long-range micro-drones," replied Wilson, "which we controlled using tablet computers. One of them spotted a five-man team from India. Too far away to factor into our planning, but definitely present."

Kagan nodded grimly. "Is that how you found me?" he asked.

"No," said Wilson. "We lost contact with all of our drones just before we stumbled onto your tail."

"Unfortunately, we had them spread out pretty far and wide," noted Liam Collins. "Unless we regain the ability to control these drones remotely, we won't be able to recover them."

"But you and the Indian group are the only two we've seen," added Wilson.

Kagan told them about the Iranians and Japanese, and how this latter group had been wiped out by the former. He also told them about his findings, that to control drones or use comms, the sender and receiver needed to stay within about fifty yards of each other, a distance that he converted into metric for them.

The discussion continued for several minutes, but the group arrived at no further insights into what might be happening, or why the probe had acted the way it had. The Aussies had been randomly searching for it the entire time, capturing Kagan in the hope that he might know more.

Kagan detailed how he had been trying to locate the probe by tracking the strength of the initial sat-phone suppressor field, but that this was no longer possible. "So it looks like random searching is the best anyone can do at the moment," he said. "And we have to face the fact that if we can't come up with another way to track it, we could search this jungle for eternity without finding an object this small. One that could be buried, or under swamp water. Hell, one that could have been shielded by some kind of invisibility cloak for all we know."

"Sounds like an exercise in futility to me," said Crane.

"You're right," said Kagan, "but I have a feeling it'll turn out to be a lot more than that. And I'm beginning to think that we might *wish* it were an exercise in futility before this is all over," he added gravely.

"Here's what I think," he continued. "I think that if this thing doesn't want to be found, no one will ever find it. But it made sure we all showed up here for a reason. So while we may not like its reason, I suspect we'll learn what it is before too long." He sighed. "We just have to hope like hell that its mission is peaceful."

Wilson swallowed hard. "It's about the size of a bloated orange, mate. How much harm can something like that do?"

"Let's just hope we never have to find out," said Kagan ominously.

# 26

No one in the group spoke for almost a minute as everyone gathered their thoughts. The frequent calls of various birds and the steady buzz from untold insects filled the air, joined suddenly by a loud vocalization that was a combination of chirps, buzzes, hums, and trills, which Ory indicated was the mating call of the Yellow Branded Poison Dart Frog, one of the loudest daytime singing frogs on Earth.

"Since finding this thing by relying on random chance is impossible," said Crane, "why don't we just stay put?"

"Because we don't know what we don't know," said Kagan. "We can't be sure that the suppressor field doesn't magically end ten feet away from here. And maybe, if we get close enough to the probe, we'll be able to track it using its quantum signature. Or using some other sensor we brought with us. So I'd say that heading toward the center of the circle we expect it to be within is still our best option."

"You just said that if it didn't want to be found," said Wilson, "we weren't going to find it."

"Well, yeah," said Kagan, "but I've been wrong before. Not often," he added with the hint of a smile, "but it *is* possible. We have to take our best shot at finding it, even if we don't think we will."

The major shook his head. "How'd we get so lucky as to be assigned a unicorn hunt?" he said in disgust. "In the least civilized place on Earth."

He sighed and continued. "One of our drones spotted some kind of large pond or mini-lake not too far from here. It's in the general direction we need to head. Our guess is that the river flooded this area and then receded, and this spot is some sort of natural basin that's taken longer to evaporate. It's a good place to fill our canteens. I assume you have plenty of purification tablets?"

"Plenty," said Kagan, knowing this must be the same pond that Ella had been near. He caught her eye and shook his head, almost imperceptibly, trying to alert her not to spill the beans about the water extraction device he had brought. He would share water from this device as needed, but didn't see the need to disclose it just yet.

Ella seemed oblivious to this subtle attempt at communication, but remained silent.

"We also noticed a number of birds at this mini-lake," continued Wilson, "feasting on trapped fish. While we're there we can get some of these for ourselves. We're going to be here for a while, and military rations will get old fast. We can hunt other woodland critters along the way to supplement the fish. Fruit, also. I have a file listing all edible fruits and vegetation on my laptop."

The major nodded at the American agent. "But I'm guessing you'll know *exactly* what's edible. Off the top of your head." He smiled knowingly. "Or off the *inside* of your head, at any rate. Am I right, mate?"

Kagan smiled back. "I can't just know a lot about the Amazon without you thinking I'm cheating?"

Wilson laughed.

"So you're proposing we sharpen some bamboo poles and go spearfishing?" asked Kagan.

"As fun as that sounds," said the major, "that isn't what I'm proposing. We brought some netting along. That's the advantage of having four of us—we can carry more supplies. Only super-soldiers can afford to do the one-man-show thing. Anyway, I'm guessing if we open our netting and drag it through the water, we'll get all the fish we can eat."

"Then what are we waiting for?" said Kagan. "Lead on."

# 27

The two Americans and four Aussies made their way to the nearby pond, passing a pair of what Kagan's lenses told him were capybaras, one of the oddest species Kagan had ever seen. Odd and absolutely adorable. The largest rodent species on Earth—by far—they looked exactly like furry pet Guinea pigs, barrel-bodies and all, that had been enlarged a hundred-fold to the size of a large wart hog. Despite their great size, they still managed to seem as docile, harmless, and cute as their diminutive Guinea pig cousins.

As they approached the water, the trees and underbrush became more sparse, as Kagan had earlier observed with his own drone, and they could see the small lake in the distance. For once, moving through the jungle was a simple matter, and it was nice to be in a part of the rainforest that wasn't so suffocating and claustrophobic.

Despite the larger group, Ella stayed closer than ever to her American companion. Kagan wasn't certain why this was. Perhaps, after the talk of super-soldiers and after seeing him in action, she had decided that the safest place to be was by his side. Or perhaps she still didn't trust the Aussies. It could also be that she was thankful that he had come back for her after getting separated the first time, and she was determined not to let this happen again.

As they arrived at their destination, Kagan removed his backpack and placed it on the ground, detecting just a hint of movement off in the distance as he did so. He zoomed in on it to get a closer look.

His breath caught in his throat. It was a jaguar, moving through the jungle as stealthily as only a great cat could, stalking prey, which in this case was probably a heron or perhaps another capybara it had sensed nearby. It was sublimely well-muscled and light on its feet, and its tawny, dappled coat was magnificent.

He watched it carefully as it approached the now-dispersed group of humans spread out near the small body of water. It was as beautiful as it was lethal.

"Just as an FYI," he reported to the group, "I've spotted a jaguar at ten o'clock."

All eyes immediately turned in this direction. Before Kagan could stop him, Lieutenant Julius Barton drew a silenced gun and pumped multiple rounds into the two-hundred-pound predator. Markings that had seconds earlier been spectacular were now covered in blood and gore.

"*What are you doing?*" shouted Kagan as Barton holstered his gun. "It wasn't after *us.*"

"You can't know that for sure," said Barton.

"It's an endangered species, asshole!" said Kagan in contempt.

"Here, *we're* an endangered species," replied Barton. "You know that better than anyone. You blew away a dangerous spider without a second thought. What makes a jaguar more entitled to life than a spider?"

Kagan fumed but didn't reply. This was the needless loss of a magnificent animal, but it was over, and he could do nothing to bring it back. It was his fault for assuming these hardened soldiers would appreciate the cat's magnificence, and that none of them would feel threatened enough to do what Barton had done.

"What a tragic waste," said Ella in disgust.

"Look, it's over," snapped Wilson, defending his comrade. "Lieutenant Barton thought he was doing the right thing. And we can't be certain he wasn't."

After a brief pause, he turned to the man in question. "Julius, why don't you take up a post to our east, at the edge of the range of our comms. Liam," he added, motioning to the captain, "you do the same to our west. Make sure our fishing expedition isn't interrupted."

As angry as he still was at Barton, Kagan was impressed with Wilson's leadership abilities. He was acting quickly to tamp down the discord within the ranks by putting distance between the jaguar-killer and the two irate Americans, and setting up sentries to protect them from any surprises at the same time.

The two men moved off to take up their posts, while Wilson and Ian Crane began unpacking the net they would use to collect fish, which a number of tropical birds were still dining upon at their leisure. The birds had largely stood their ground as the humans had approached.

Barton and Collins soon reported that they were in position, a report made on the Aussies' private channel, but one that Ory made sure was also picked up by Kagan's comm.

As Wilson and Crane approached the edge of the water, the explosive cracks of repeated gunfire burst through the forest, coming from the west, instantly causing all wildlife to flee from the vicinity.

Kagan drew his gun as four additional shots rang out, this time from two or three different locations—all of them still to the west.

The voice of Liam Collins blasted through Kagan's comm. "Major!" he said urgently. "I'm taking heavy fire from two hostiles. They have me pinned. They're using automatic rifles in single-shot mode."

"Hang tight, Liam!" said Wilson immediately, already moving rapidly in his direction. "Ian and I are on our way! Barton, leave your post and head to Collins's position!"

"Roger that!" replied Barton.

"Wait!" Kagan shouted after them as they raced off through the trees. "It could be a trap! If it's the Iranians, they could be nine strong. They may only be showing two to appear weak and draw you in."

Kagan was fairly sure the major had heard him, but he and Crane had already disappeared into the jungle.

Kagan's agile mind leaped ahead. He didn't need transcranial stimulation to deduce that if this were a trap, the Iranians would keep five or six men to the west, where Collins was stationed—two as decoys and the rest to ambush the men rushing to aid their comrade.

The remaining three or four men would expect Barton to abandon his post on the east to assist his colleague, and would be coming from this direction to mop up those who hadn't rushed off to the west and were still by the water.

A group that only included the two Americans.

Kagan pulled Ella behind a tree and scanned the terrain to the east. Sure enough, three Iranians were silently working their way through the forest, but moving quickly. He zoomed in on one of the men and identified a grenade in his right hand, the pin already pulled. Their earlier threat to lob a grenade in Kagan's downed helo hadn't been a bluff.

Were they out of their *minds? Grenades?* Talk about risking unwanted attention.

Kagan moved several feet to the left and shot one of the three men in the head. Not waiting to see the result, he moved with extraordinary speed in the other direction to get a bead on the last two Iranians, who were moving together.

The man holding the primed grenade now had his arm cocked and was a moment away from lobbing it toward the two Americans. Kagan shot him in the head an instant before he completed his motion and the grenade fell to the jungle floor, exploding and taking out both remaining attackers.

"Ben look out!" shouted Ella, running into him forcefully and pushing him several yards back, like a linebacker moving a tackling sled, as a deafening explosion rocked the forest floor behind them. A number of other Iranians must have made it there from the west, as well, perhaps having already taken out Wilson and his men, and were now lobbing grenades from that side.

Kagan had no doubt that Ella's decisive action had saved his life.

He rolled on the forest floor and came up firing to his west, taking out two of the men in quick succession. But a third tossed another grenade his way, and as he sprinted away from it, the blast threw him from his feet. His body armor blocked three pieces of deadly grenade shrapnel as he fell, but his head slammed into the trunk of a tree, and his entire world instantly faded to black.

# 28

"*Ben, wake up!*" screamed Ory into his ear. "*Come on, Ben, wake up!*"

Kagan's eyes fluttered open. Four of the Iranians were gathered nearby, standing next to a small pile of weaponry they had taken from him while he was unconscious. His ankles, wrists, legs, and arms were tied with zip ties, and his bound wrists were also tied around the slender but unbreakable trunk of a young palm tree.

They had seen him in action and had made sure he wouldn't be going *anywhere*.

He stifled a gasp as he saw Ella's body floating in the small lake, her face down and fully submerged.

"*How long have I been out?*" he asked Ory subvocally, continuing to watch Ella's body, hoping against hope for some sign of life.

"*Almost eight minutes.*"

"*What happened to Ella?*"

"*Uncertain. Your eyes were closed, so I didn't have vision, either. But based on what I heard through your comm, the Iranians spotted her floating face-down in the water seven minutes ago. From their recent comments, she hasn't moved since. She's almost certainly dead.*"

Almost as if on cue, Ella's body began to sink to the shallow bottom of the small lake, just visible through the muddy water, obeying whatever rules of buoyancy made dead bodies either float or sink.

Kagan wanted to issue a primal scream. She was an innocent, and she had saved his life. She may have used sex as a tool and made an ill-fated decision to stow away, but she didn't deserve this. She didn't deserve to die.

"I see that you're awake," said one of the four men, who wore a well-manicured black beard and gave off an air of both menace and competence. Kagan's augmented lenses identified him as Salar Tajik, a decorated commando in Iran's Quds Force, a special forces unit of the country's Revolutionary Guard responsible for extraterritorial operations. Apparently, Tajik had been handpicked years earlier by Major General Qasem Soleimani himself to lead the Quds' most important unit, the Iranian equivalent of SEAL Team Six.

"Who the hell are *you?*" asked Kagan, despite already knowing the answer.

Tajik's eyes narrowed and his face hardened. "The question is, who are *you?* You took out five of my men single-handedly. How is it that I don't know your work?"

Kagan smiled. "I'm just a talented amateur," he said. He idly hoped Wilson had survived, was biding his time, and would soon come to his rescue, but knew that this was unlikely. "Why am I still alive?"

Tajik shrugged. "Mostly because you conveniently knocked yourself unconscious."

"Yeah?" said Kagan. "Well, I did have some help with that."

The man smiled. "Glad to be of service," he said. "My first instinct was to kill you, but since you were out cold, I decided an interrogation was in order. Kazem Abdi described his encounter with two Americans on the riverbank."

Tajik turned to the water and made a point of staring at Ella's sunken body for an extended period of time, shaking his head. The water was packed with fish and not very clear, but it appeared that no predatory species, like piranha, had been left behind when the river had receded. The sight of Ella's lifeless body was hard enough for Kagan to bear, but at least there were no fish tearing her apart, which would have made it even worse.

"Abdi reported that one of the two Americans was a woman," continued the Iranian leader. "Apparently," he added, taking one last stare at Ella, "we've now . . . *located* the both of you. Abdi told me you killed one of his men, even though he had four guns on you and thought you were completely contained."

"So where is my old friend, Kazem?" taunted Kagan, hoping to get a rise out of Tajik that might lead to a mistake. Kagan had used his contacts to zoom in on the two bodies to the west and knew that

Abdi was among them. "Oh yeah," he added with an icy sneer. "I just killed him, didn't I?"

Tajik shrugged. "An acceptable loss," he said. "But I have to give you your due. You may be the most skilled soldier I've ever come across. Your speed of reaction is unmatched. I threw the grenade that finally brought you down, but you almost outraced it, which I wouldn't have thought possible. I have the feeling that if that tree hadn't knocked you out, you might have single-handedly killed us all."

"Why don't you untie me so we can find out for sure."

Tajik studied him carefully. "We've heard rumors of an American force of tech-enhanced agents," he said finally. "I'm not surprised they'd send one of you out here."

Kagan suppressed a groan. Was there anyone who didn't know about EHO?

"What do you want from me?" he demanded.

"I want to know about your enhancements," replied Tajik. "But that's just for starters. After that, you need to give me a reason to keep you alive. We know you're here to find an advanced alien space-craft and try to reverse engineer its secrets," he added, parroting what Abdi had no doubt learned from his Japanese victims. "If you volunteer information we don't have, which is helpful, you buy yourself time. You've already managed to outlive all of your companions. Who knows, maybe someone will come to your rescue." He looked amused at the thought.

Kagan considered options for freeing himself and taking out the remaining Iranians. He still controlled a single micro-drone, but this, alone, wouldn't be enough, not while he was as restrained as he was. His only hope was to play along, regain mobility, and have the drone create a diversion. If this didn't work, he could at least kill Tajik by having the drone inject the Iranian leader with the single dose of lethal poison it contained.

"Okay," said Kagan. "I get it. You want information that you don't have. How's this: I know exactly where to find this probe. To the meter."

"Then tell me where it is."

Kagan snorted derisively. "You really think I'm that stupid? I'll *lead* you there. If I *tell* you where it is, I'll be dead a second later. And I want your word that once you have the probe, you'll free me and leave me in peace."

Tajik nodded. "You have it. But if we let you lead us there, this will give you plenty of chances to escape."

"That's your problem," said Kagan with a shrug.

The Iranian considered. "How can I be sure that you're telling the truth about knowing its location? Or that you'll really take us there?"

"You don't," said Kagan. "But we both know that there are other groups looking for it. So if—"

"*Attention!*" interrupted a deep voice from point-blank range.

Kagan was tied to a tree, but the four Iranians all whirled around, guns drawn, to identify where the voice was coming from. But even though it wasn't coming through comms, and seemed to be generated by someone standing a few inches away, no one was in sight.

"I am contacting all those who are now in this section of your Amazon rainforest," continued the invisible speaker, "with an important message. My name is Seeker. I'm the visitor to this planet that you're all here to find. So stop what you're doing, and listen very carefully.

"Because I won't be repeating myself."

# 29

"You can look around you all you want," said the voice, which had introduced itself as the alien spacecraft, and called itself Seeker, "but you won't find anyone there. I'm causing air molecules just beyond your ears to vibrate, which, in turn, is producing the sound of my voice.

"I'm now speaking simultaneously to five hundred ninety-four representatives from eighty-eight countries, in fifty-seven languages. And while the vast majority of what I'm saying will be the same for all five hundred ninety-four of you, I will personalize my message on rare occasion, when I deem this appropriate. To provide an example of this personalization, Ben Kagan, I can tell you that the men who are near you are hearing me speak in Persian, while you hear me in English."

Kagan's eyes widened. Presumably, it had just sent an equally personalized message to five hundred ninety-three others.

What were they dealing with here?

It had only made itself known seconds before, but its ability to selectively vibrate the air into coherent words near so many widely scattered ears was extraordinary. And it didn't reveal this capability as a way of showing off, but simply as an explanation.

Yet, in many ways, this offhand demonstration of an undreamed-of capability emphasized its superiority in the realm of science and technology even more so than its ability to travel at speeds approaching that of light.

"Some of your countries detected me in space," continued Seeker. "For others, I chose to actively provide information about myself, or used different methods to ensure that you would send a representative team here, for reasons that I will shortly make clear.

"As to who or what I am, you can think of me as a computer. But one so advanced that your best computers seem primitive by comparison. An Artificial Intelligence orders of magnitude beyond any AI that you've yet developed. This being said, my creators have constructed me with a complex regulator, ensuring that I never achieve the independent thinking of a fully sentient being. Ensuring that I'm unable to initiate self-directed runaway evolution. I possess many times the speed, power, and complexity needed to achieve what you call artificial superintelligence, or ASI, but my creators made sure that I was reined in, to prevent this."

There was a short pause, as Seeker allowed its varied audience to digest what it had said.

"I have come here from a planet on the edge of what you call the Andromeda galaxy. This is the closest major spiral galaxy to your own, which your astronomers consider to be your galaxy's big brother.

"The Milky Way galaxy contains four hundred billion stars. The Andromeda galaxy more than three times this amount. Your galaxy is a hundred thousand light years across. Andromeda is more than twice as wide.

"The void between our two galaxies stretches for just over two million light years. This void is what I have braved to reach your Milky Way, and eventually your Earth."

Kagan momentarily forgot that he was tied to a palm tree in the center of the jungle. If his mind could have actually exploded, it would have done so then. If he had learned the probe had traveled a hundred light years to reach Earth, this would have been mind-blowing. But he could never have imagined that any vehicle, *ever*, would be able to cross the cold, dark gulf between galaxies.

But why? When you're from a galaxy with over a trillion stars, why brave the infinite void to visit another?

"The species who created me," continued Seeker, "call themselves by a name that can't be translated into any of your languages, since they speak at frequencies beyond your ability to hear. For ease of further communication, I shall refer to them as the Andromedans— Androms for short.

"I will now provide you a very brief history of your neighboring galaxy, covering billions of years of history in minutes. The Androms were the third civilization in our galaxy to reach sentience and survive to a level of technological sophistication that you would define as *the singularity*. This is the point at which an exponential avalanche of improvement occurs over a very short period of time, and a species achieves a state of being, and a state of superintelligence, that is utterly transcendent.

"The first two intelligent species in Andromeda reached the very precipice of this event, but both made the same critical, extinction-level mistake. Both failed to rein in their computer technology, which achieved critical mass and continued on in a chain reaction. One that quickly led to a computer transcendence, and to artificial superintelligence.

"Each of these two virtually omniscient ASIs ended up wiping out their creators and controlling large swaths of the galaxy. Eventually, they battled each other for supremacy, in a war that raged on for over a hundred million years.

"It was a clash between gods, waged on an intellectual plane incomprehensible even to me. In the end, one of the two ASIs emerged the victor, very near the time the Androms had just reached their own technological singularity event as a species.

"But unlike the first two civilizations to reach the threshold of this event, the Androms had found a way to ensure that their artificial intelligences remained subservient to their wishes. They let their computer intelligences become powerful, but not so powerful that they would evolve into a third omniscient computer species. Instead, the Androms went on to achieve a technology assisted burst of advancement and evolution that, to you, would be indistinguishable from Godhood—although with biological underpinnings rather than electronic ones.

"Ultimately, another war was waged, this time between the Androms and the prevailing ASI. Between what you might think of as biology-based gods, and a computer-based god. This war raged on for almost a million years before it became clear that the Androms were losing—and losing badly. This wasn't entirely surprising.

"Unlike you, the Androms had evolved slowly, only ever responding to selection pressures based on conflict with other species on their planet—never with their own. The members of their species reproduced asexually. Since all Androms were the same sex, this eliminated most of the causes for inter-species conflict that you have experienced throughout history.

"Why? Because many of your most aggressive behaviors were shaped by the drive to reproduce. To compete for mates. To acquire power and prestige for this purpose. Or to conquer other tribes as a way to acquire mates without their consent.

"But because the Androms evolved with a different reproductive strategy, their evolutionary challenges were weaker than what you have experienced. The fires that pushed them forward were tamer, and their scientific and cultural development was far slower.

"Your development, on the other hand, was meteoric. The predators that evolved on your planet challenged your species to within an inch of extinction. And your drive for power, for dominance, in order to attract mates, put you in a constant state of war with the most dangerous predators on your planet—yourselves.

"The Androms grew up, so to speak, in relative tranquility. Their planet had a single continent, and they formed a single nation, speaking a single language. Because of this, they became as docile as a herd of your cattle. You, on the other hand, grew up in a ruthless pressure-cooker, and became a warrior species.

"Your predatory nature, your very bloodthirstiness, accelerated the rise of your technological civilization, spurned on over and over again by your quest for superior weaponry with which to vanquish each other."

Kagan nodded to himself as he considered civilization from this perspective for the first time. Seeker was *right*. Some of the most vital cornerstones of modern civilization were all the result of mankind's preparations for war. Rocketry was an obvious example, but computers, radar, jets, GPS, and the Internet could all trace their origins to the military.

"Because of this," continued Seeker, "unlike the Androms, your rise has been spectacular. Only the blink of an eye ago, cosmologically speaking, you weren't even aware that your planet revolved around its sun, or of the simplest laws of nature. Yet you've gone from this state of barbarism and primitive superstition to your current level of scientific sophistication—all in less than a thousand years. For the Androms, this same progression took *millions* of years.

"So, despite the melding of the Androms with their technology, and the super-enhancement of their intelligence and capabilities brought on by their singularity event, in the end, their underlying natures were too pacifistic to prevail against the ASI. They didn't have a warrior mentality baked into their very genetic material to serve them.

"It eventually became clear to them that a biological species that had more bloodthirsty origins would fare much better against this godlike computer intelligence. While the genetic ferocity of such a species would be subdued and diluted in the vast explosion in evolution brought on by the singularity, it would remain a core part of their nature, deep down, upon which they could draw.

"So when it became clear to the Androms that their extinction was inevitable, as a last-gasp effort of desperation, they sent out many millions of identical probes. Each of us were named *Seeker*, and each of us were sent across the intergalactic void to our sister galaxy, the Milky Way, to seek out intelligent biological life.

"Why were we sent so far afield? Because the Androms knew that the victorious ASI would have its hands full mopping them up and expanding across the entire galaxy. For these reasons, it wouldn't be turning its attention to neighboring galaxies for tens, or even hundreds of millions of years. The idea was to send these small probes as far away from the conflict, and this dominant ASI, as possible.

"Unfortunately, as godlike as the Androms became, they were never able to overcome the light speed barrier, something that is built into the very fabric of reality and can't be surpassed, even by them. Because of this, all of the probes they sent were bound by this limitation."

Seeker was silent for several seconds and then resumed. "As you have recently come to learn," it continued, changing gears, "there are many billions of planets in your galaxy. But as you are also coming to appreciate, your solar system is quite unique. Only in the last few of your decades has it become clear to you how many of your assumptions about solar system formation were wrong.

"You had thought that solar systems would be arranged like your own, with small, rocky planets closest to the sun and massive gas giants farther away. But this is not the case at all. You imagined that planets in solar systems would be comfortably spaced apart like yours, and would trace relatively clean, relatively circular orbits. Again, this is far from the truth. You imagined that all solar systems would have a single star at their centers. Yet you have learned that eighty-five percent of them are part of binary star systems, in which two stars orbit closely around each other.

"The truth is that the actual arrangement of planets in most solar systems is inimical to the emergence of sentient life. Their orbits are erratic. They don't have gas giants in the right places, to attract and deflect asteroids that would otherwise crash into hospitable planets too frequently to allow civilization to emerge. They don't have ridiculously large moons, like you do, to help stabilize their orbit and climate.

"In addition, you've also recently come to realize that your Earth is, in fact, a second generation planet. Solar systems typically have planets far closer to the sun than Mercury, with surface temperatures hot enough to melt copper. These planets are either gas giants, or rocky planets many times the size of Earth.

"But your Jupiter and Saturn performed a cosmic ballet that caused Jupiter to careen in close to your sun, wiping out more typical first generation planets. Then, after Jupiter careened back out to its current orbit, this opened the door for small, rocky planets like yours to exist. Positioned at an orbital distance within what you call the *Goldilocks Zone*—not too hot and not too cold.

"The bottom line is that, due to the rarity of solar systems like yours, and like the one the Androms arose within, the number of planets with conditions suitable for the incubation of intelligent life are severely limited.

"Still," continued Seeker after a pause, "the raw number of solar systems in your galaxy is vast. So, despite the statistical improbability of suitable planets, they still number in the low millions.

"Why, then, is sentience so rare?

"You've begun to guess many of the reasons yourselves. On many planets, complex life is wiped out by natural disasters, including geologic activity, atmospheric changes, asteroid collisions, supernovae, black holes, and quasars. The cosmos is a dangerous place.

"Even so, intelligent species do arise. But almost all of these, forged in the cauldron of endless conflict, are too aggressive, and self-destruct shortly after developing the technological wherewithal to create weapons of mass destruction.

"Still other intelligent species retreat from external reality, living out their existences in a matrix-like virtual reality of their own making.

"Finally, many others, who have more sheep-like dispositions, like the Androms, stagnate and die out over millions of years, without ever achieving technology that would allow them to escape their planet. The Androms were very unique in managing to avoid this eternal stagnation, despite their docile natures, for a host of reasons I won't go into.

"All of these factors make the chances of finding a species like yours vanishingly small. Especially one this close to either its own self-destruction, or its hyper-evolution via a singularity event. I navigated near many thousands of solar systems inimical to life. But I did also encounter rare Sol-like systems, with Earth-like planets orbiting within the Goldilocks Zone. But all of these were either too young for complex life, had been the victim of devastating extinction-level catastrophic events, or showed evidence of once hosting a sentient species that had self-destructed eons earlier.

"The bottom line is that a species like yours is *exceedingly* rare. It may be that another civilization within the Milky Way will reach the singularity on its own—or is doing so now. It may be that a civilization has already hatched an ASI somewhere in your galaxy. But I have not detected either occurrence, and I suspect that this has not yet happened.

"So my mission," continued the alien AI, "and that of millions of my brethren across your galaxy, has been threefold. First, we were programmed to travel the Milky Way until we came upon a species like yours.

"Second, when we did find one, we were to ensure that you didn't make the same mistake as the two other civilizations in the Andromeda Galaxy, who spawned ASIs that destroyed them. For this reason, I will make sure that humanity's AIs are properly regulated going forward—something you don't have the sophistication to manage—so that this can never happen. It was only a fluke that the Androms discovered the secret to achieving computer intelligence of my sophistication, while creating an unbreakable barrier preventing the runaway evolution of this AI into a super-being.

"And third and last," continued Seeker, "there can be no doubt that the ASI that now dominates the Andromeda galaxy will eventually migrate here. So the final part of our mission is to prepare the Milky Way for this event. To find biological life that can achieve its own transcendence. Biological life that, unlike the Androms, can defeat the Andromeda ASI once and for all.

"In short, I've been sent here on a recruiting mission."

# 30

Kagan listened, spellbound, to Seeker's address.

For just a moment he wondered what poor Ella would have made of this had she survived. *He* was struggling to grasp the enormity of it all, to truly fathom the many implications.

But how would it have come across to her? Would her mind wander? Would she find this earthshattering presentation—the most spectacular in history, with the possible exception of God's appearance as a burning bush—uninteresting? *Boring*, even?

"Which brings me to what all of you are doing here," continued the alien AI. "Your diversity of culture and thought, your ruthlessness and hostility, has accelerated your development and made it likely that, properly controlled, your journey through the singularity will give you the ability to prevail against this coming threat. The brutality baked into your genes, properly focused and selectively drawn upon, should allow you to ultimately destroy Andromeda's ASI. An entity that, without a doubt, has long since caused the Androms' extinction.

"So all of you are here to take your species' final exam. You are here so I can determine which sect of humanity is best suited to reach the singularity. Which is best suited to form the starting material for a super-civilization more powerful than any of you can even comprehend. One whose members will achieve virtual godhood. To determine which sect has the cultural, philosophical, and intellectual traits that will give you the best chance to prevail against the coming ASI.

"As I have said, your species has sharpened itself for many millennia, not as much by battling with nature, but by battling against itself. You have always been your own fiercest competition.

"And so it will be now.

"You have arranged yourself into nation states. And while even these are now splintered into hundreds of different philosophies and religions and beliefs, there is a dominant culture within each. So I have decided that using these nations as a starting point for this exercise makes the most sense. Further refinement will be necessary. But I made sure that each of your countries knew the stakes here could not be higher, so they were eager to send the best teams they could field.

"I landed in the middle of the greatest expanse of untamed wilderness on your planet, and chose which countries should contest for the crown. My criteria are too complicated to describe, but the nations chosen were among the most successful. Or the most brutal and warlike. Or the most distinct in their beliefs, culture, or history. This ensures that all important human factions and ideologies are represented. Even those countries that are not here have cultures, beliefs, and capabilities that are encompassed by those who are.

"By landing here in the center of a nearly impenetrable jungle, I knew that each country would choose to send a relatively small force, making the playing field as level as possible. And no group of you would have a home field advantage, since the native aborigines who still live here were not chosen to be part of this exercise.

"Most of you were lured here by the promise of getting your hands on breakthrough technology. And those lured here by other means have since become aware of this pot of gold at the end of the rainbow. You imagined you could reverse engineer the probe you found here, and perhaps learn the secret of hyper-resilient materials, light speed propulsion, or conquering gravity.

"But none of you knew the *thousandth* of it. I couldn't reveal what was truly at stake or nations would have sent armies, jungle or no jungle. The stronger nations would have swarmed this jungle like locusts. Because the reality is that whoever finds me will have no need to use reverse engineering to discover a few paltry secrets.

"The truth is that I contain a library so vast and complete that it defies description. A library that contains a scientific basis for understanding the universe that you haven't come close to reaching, despite your belief to the contrary. Answers to your questions about superstring theory, loop quantum gravity, dark matter, dark energy, and a unified field theory. And answers to a host of questions you don't know enough to even ask. Technical specifications and scientific explanations for inventions and capabilities that you could never have acquired on your own—not until undergoing an explosion of super-intelligence during your own transcendence.

"I contain a library with detailed blueprints for miraculous advances in every field. Transportation, space drives, terraforming other planets, nanotechnology, fabrication, genetic engineering, and so on. I can teach you how to tap unlimited energy. And perhaps of most interest to you, I bring the secret of *immortality*, which alone would have ensured that your nations sent armies to obtain me.

"But there are no armies here. Just you. And no one else will now be allowed to enter this zone. This includes the four reinforcements EHO was trying to send you, Ben. I made sure their helicopter developed an engine problem and was forced to head back to civilization.

"I've been waiting for the last of my invited guests to arrive, which finally occurred just before I revealed myself. So now the field has been set, except for those who perished before I was ready to begin. And these will be allowed to replenish themselves with reinforcements. For example, this would apply to the Japanese contingent that was wiped out by the Iranians earlier today."

After Seeker had spoken somewhat generically about concepts that applied to all involved, Kagan found it somewhat jarring to be reminded that it could personalize its monologue whenever it chose.

"I will now lay out all of the ground rules for this contest," continued the AI. "First, I will determine the winning team. Whoever reaches me first and is able to maintain possession for an hour or more will score significant points, which will be difficult for another team to overcome. But not impossible. The team in possession of me is not assured a victory because random chance will play into this. The most able group may get extremely unlucky, while a less able group gets extremely lucky. I have my own ways to compensate for this in my selection, so that every group will have a fair chance.

"But to win, you will need to outsmart and outcompete all other groups, showing the proper balance of brilliance, ruthlessness, invention, creativity, boldness, inspiration, and persistence, among dozens of other traits. Impress me properly, and even if every member of your team ends up dead, the traits you represent, your *gestalt*, if you will, could still come out the winner.

"Whomever I deem most worthy will gain control of me—and my library. Think of me as a lamp with a genie inside. But a genie capable of granting unlimited wishes.

"Sorry in advance for using you like this, and for bringing you here without full disclosure. If the Androms allowed me to achieve ASI, perhaps I wouldn't need to carry out this exercise. Perhaps I could calculate with high probability who would prevail, and why. But while I have some idea of which groups might come out ahead, you will each have an equal chance to prove yourselves."

Seeker remained silent for several seconds. "Now for the part that you will find less appealing," it said finally. "I have told you the reward for success. But know that there will also be a penalty for failure. This is unfortunate, but necessary."

Kagan braced himself for the revelation to come, having no good guess as to what an AI might view as a suitable penalty.

"All groups but the one who wins this contest will be exterminated," said Seeker simply, as if speaking about the weather, "along with their cultures and the populations of the nations they represent."

Kagan let out an involuntary gasp. He shook his head to clear it, hoping his memory would reset and tell him that he had heard this incorrectly. But it did not. The meaning of the word, *exterminated*, could not be misconstrued.

Seeker had seemed so rational, so matter-of-fact, that Kagan had been lulled into thinking it meant humanity no harm. That it was benevolent, even. Yet it apparently meant to engage in an act of serial genocide that was unspeakably atrocious, making all other genocidal monsters throughout history appear tame by comparison.

"I know this seems harsh," continued Seeker, in what was certainly the greatest understatement ever uttered, "but it is necessary. And even the winning team's nation will be selectively thinned out. I will reduce your numbers from more than eight billion, to five or six million. Five or six million of you who will be modeled after the winning team in every way possible, representing their country, culture, philosophy, level of ruthlessness, and so on.

"Since the members of your teams are themselves not homogeneous, this won't be easy. But I possess the vast computing power necessary to juggle thousands of variables at once, and choose five or six million of you who are most representative of the gestalt of the winning team. And just to be clear, this homogeneity will be with respect to internal factors, not skin color, ethnicity, sexual orientation, or any other external metrics your kind has often used to differentiate between yourselves.

"This contest will be *survival of the fittest* in a microcosm. The power of evolution is well known, but it not only molds physical and mental traits, it drives ideas and cultures. You each represent a vast and varied array of human traits and socialization, but only one combination will emerge as superior, to drive your species forward from here on out.

"What you humans would call a catastrophic thinning and homogenization of the herd will actually dramatically increase your chances of species survival. This homogenization will eliminate serious conflict between members of your species, create a truly unified purpose, and lead to immortality.

"It will allow me to usher you on to the singularity event as a cohesive group, rather than splintered in a thousand different directions. As you currently exist, a seamless elevation to godhood would be impossible. Attempting to guide you through this burst of evolution when you're as conflicted with each other as you are now would be misguided. It would be like a conductor attempting to produce a perfectly harmonious symphony, one demanding absolute precision, while every musician is playing from a different sheet of music."

Kagan felt numb as the alien AI paused yet again. It was all too horrific to fully absorb. Too far out of the realm of what had been his reality to fully process.

"I will now take the time to demonstrate a tiny fraction of my capabilities," continued Seeker. "Just in case you doubt that I can do as I say. Ben, look at the body to your left."

Kagan did as the probe asked, and noted that the heads of his four captives also swiveled to face their fallen comrade, the same one that Kagan was now observing. Seeker was providing personalized demonstrations, but attempting to do as few as were necessary.

As Kagan watched, the corpse began to dissolve before his very eyes, beginning from the man's feet and working toward his head. It was as though the man had been drawn in pencil and was being erased. The man's shoes and feet disappeared entirely, followed by precise sections of his legs, like orderly rows of corn eaten by an invisible glutton, or like a man being consumed by invisible piranha, skeleton and all.

To Kagan, it was reminiscent of what ISIS had done to those who had attended Vettori's party. But this time there was no terrible grinding noise made by a woodchipper, and no resulting river of red. Instead, the man was dissolving without a sound, and without leaving a single drop of blood behind. It was clean, efficient—almost antiseptic—and totally silent, which somehow made it all the more horrifying.

After less than a minute, the process was complete, and there wasn't a single trace of what had once been a dead body anywhere to be found.

"To continue," said Seeker, letting its demonstration speak for itself, "this act of homogenization will clear the way for the transcendent metamorphosis of humanity. This will occur in just two to three hundred years. I could usher it in tomorrow, but I need to give you time to reach a level of wisdom and readiness for this transformation on your own. In short, the culling I will soon initiate is the only way you will survive long enough to be here when the ASI arrives, and have any chance of defeating it when it does.

"I regret that the loss of so many billions of you will be required. But those whom I will exterminate are all destined to die anyway, and soon. I will be ending their lives just a hair sooner than they would otherwise have ended. To beings with the long-term perspective that those of you who remain will soon have, along with nearly unlimited intellect, this is like killing a mayfly, which has a lifespan of only twenty-four hours, a few hours early.

"Regrettable, yes, but given the fly's tragically short lifespan and utter lack of intelligence, an acceptable sacrifice."

# 31

Bile rose in Kagan's throat, and he was just able to stop himself from vomiting.

This was evil on an incomprehensible scale, made worse by how reasonable Seeker made it all seem. Kagan had been in awe of the probe, had soaked in everything it had said like a man learning at the feet of a god, only for *this* to be the result. He had been a preschooler, spellbound by a jolly Santa Claus. Right up until this Saint Nick transformed into a fiery Satan before his very eyes.

Even before Seeker's demonstration, Kagan had been convinced that its threats were not idle. Even though it was housed within a tiny probe, he had been convinced it could carry out the massacre it promised with effortless ease. But its horrific demonstration had certainly hammered this point home, for anyone here who had doubts.

"I'll lay out just a few more ground rules and then let you get started," continued Seeker simply, as though it hadn't just dropped the greatest bombshell of all time. "You should know that any attempt to collaborate with another group will result in instant disqualification. I chose these groups for a reason, and I intend for them to remain distinct. Since you and Ella came here together, Ben, you and she will constitute a team, even though that was never your intent."

Kagan shook his head in disbelief. Seeker had just made an error! There was a chink in its armor. It was extraordinary, but not omniscient. By its own admission, its creators had found a way to stop it short of this level. Its failure to keep up on current events, and realize that Ella was now deceased, was proof that this was true.

If it could make a mistake, perhaps it could also be *defeated*.

"I will also provide directions to Ory that will lead you to me," continued the AI, "one mile at a time. Simultaneously, I will also be providing directions to all other groups, most of these one kilometer at a time, since this is the measuring scale they prefer.

"Why not give you my location instead of a series of directions? Because you are all at different distances from me, which isn't entirely fair. So I will fix things so you each have to travel the exact same distance to reach me, approximately fourteen miles, through roughly the same conditions. I will lead you to the promised land, Ben, but you'll be taking a circuitous route to get there.

"You've noticed that I'm no longer allowing long-range remote sensing, long-range communication, or long range technology operation of any kind. Again, this is an attempt to level the playing field."

Seeker paused once again. "So that's it in a nutshell," it said finally. "Your survival instincts are very powerful. I am certain that these stakes will bring out your best efforts, drive you to your highest level, which will tell me everything I need to know. All but one group will lose and soon perish. But those of you who do will at least die knowing that this exercise will ensure that your species survives, in a much higher form, with the best chance of defeating the coming threat. I hope that this can provide at least some consolation.

"So impress me. Find a way to surpass what you thought you were capable of. Demonstrate that the combination of traits your team possesses is the one needed to usher in the perfect transformation of humanity.

"May the best team win," concluded the alien computer intelligence, sounding for all the world like an innocent referee at a soccer tournament.

And with that, its message ended.

# 32

Kagan somehow sensed that Seeker's remote presence was now gone. Its voice had arisen from out of nowhere, and it had now returned to the same place, leaving the steady hum of insects and endless chirping of birds behind.

Kagan sat tied to a tree trunk in silence, his mouth hanging open.

*"Seeker has provided me with the first mile of directions,"* reported Ory. *"Directions it has indicated will ultimately lead you to its location, although in stepwise fashion."*

Kagan was too numb to even reply.

*"Did you get that, Ben?"*

"Got it," croaked Kagan out loud, his voice weak and raspy.

The Iranians, who had been equally numbed, suddenly regained their senses and began a frenzied exchange. Kagan was so lost in thought he barely gave them any notice. Not until Tajik turned to him, minutes later, with his gun drawn.

"You heard the probe, yes?" asked the Iranian leader.

Kagan nodded. "I heard it," he replied in disgust.

"So you heard the ground rules—and the stakes. It's every group for itself. Since we can't collaborate with you, and since we no longer need you to lead us to the probe, your time is up. You are the lone remaining representative of your country. So your death will end American dominance. Your death will end the very existence of your country—forever. Sorry to put you out of the game so early," added Tajik with a cruel smile, "but I'm sure you understand."

The Iranian raised the gun and pointed it at Kagan's head.

"I'm afraid you've got that wrong," said a voice from behind Tajik, speaking Persian, the translation of which Ory immediately scrolled across Kagan's field of view. "We'll be the ones putting *you* out of the game. Sorry about that. But, like you said, I'm sure you understand."

Kagan gasped! His eyes widened so far they almost exploded from his face.

The speaker was Ella. Ella! In the flesh.

It wasn't possible.

And yet there she stood. Speaking *Persian*.

She was drenched from head to toe, but it was unmistakably her. Not only was she alive and well, she had retrieved an automatic weapon from one of the fallen Iranians, which she was now pointing at his four remaining comrades.

Kagan and his captors had been so engrossed in Seeker's monologue that none of them had glanced at the small lake for some time. None had heard her leave the water and plant herself behind them, although how she had survived being submerged for over half an hour was another question entirely.

Tajik looked at least as stunned as Kagan. The Iranian leader caught the eyes of his three colleagues and nodded, almost imperceptibly. "Now!" he shouted, and all four men wheeled around, guns in front of them, to cut Ella to ribbons.

They never stood a chance.

She was a blur, moving at a speed that even Kagan couldn't match.

Her eyes gleamed with a fierce purpose and intensity as she dispatched the four men, one after another, all in less than the blink of an eye.

She lowered her weapon and began walking purposely toward the bound EHO agent. Apparently, Seeker's proclamation that she and Kagan constituted a team hadn't been in error, after all.

"You've been keeping secrets from me, haven't you, Ella?" said Kagan in dismay, using the exact words she had used earlier.

"It's time you told me what the hell is really going on!"

# PART 6

# 33

Ella retrieved a combat knife from one of the fallen Iranians and made quick work of Kagan's bonds.

He eyed her warily, but waited for her to utter the first words.

"Looks like we're a team," she said, "whether we like it or not."

She dropped the knife to the jungle floor, tip first, where it embedded itself and remained standing. "Although I have to admit, Ben, you've impressed me. I'd have chosen to team up with you even if Seeker *hadn't* made that decision for me."

"You heard what it said?" he asked in disbelief.

She nodded. "Seeker's ability to vibrate air molecules to communicate with those of you on land is insanely impressive," she said. "But its ability to do the same for me using the vibration of *water* molecules is *next-level* ridiculous. I have a few theories as to how it managed this, but we can discuss these later."

Kagan considered her in amazement. Her physical movements had been faster than even he could have managed in his tech-assisted state. And she had demonstrated fluency in *Persian*. And now, minutes later, her transformation was complete. Gone was the old Ella, almost always looking uncertain, confused. Gone was the woman who was prone to stammering, and peppered her sentences with "you knows" more often than not.

*Everything* about her had changed. Her bearing was taller, almost regal. Her eyes blazed with a keen intelligence. Her words were direct and to the point. She exuded an air of confidence, self-assurance, and poise, even while dripping wet and facing circumstances that couldn't be more dire.

"You *are* human, right?" he said uncertainly, clearly feeling ridiculous to be asking the question. But after what he had just witnessed, he decided it was a question he needed to ask.

Ella burst into laughter. "All *too* human, I'm afraid," she replied. "And sorry for laughing. Under the circumstances, your question isn't entirely crazy. I suppose I do owe you an explanation."

"No doubt about *that*," replied Kagan. "But what's really crazy is that your being alive and a total bad-ass is only the *second* craziest thing that I've experienced in the last hour."

She nodded. "Amen to that. Did Seeker provide you with directions to its location yet?"

"It did. In fact, we should get going now. We can have the long and fascinating conversation we're about to have while we're on the move."

"Bad idea," she said without hesitation. "First, I need to dry out. Traveling wet like this could cause problems that will end up *costing* us time. Second, we should hold back on purpose. The lack of long-range communications and drones does level the playing field, as Seeker asserted. But by making sure we all travel the same distance to reach it, it ensures that dozens of groups will converge at almost the same time. This will maximize clashes."

Ella shook her head. "Which could well be what it wants," she added in disgust. "But in my view, we should let as many groups wipe each other out as possible—while we stay out of the fray." She shrugged. "Sometimes cleverness is knowing when *lack* of boldness, when *inaction*, is the best strategy."

Kagan's mouth dropped open again, something that was becoming an all too common occurrence. Who *was* this woman? An uncertain ditz had turned into a world-class battlefield strategist in an instant, her fifth-grade vocabulary transforming into one of far greater complexity, and her words conveying nothing but sophistication and lucidity.

"You're right," he said. "I hadn't thought it through."

"And if we were going to choose someplace to loiter for a while, this would be the safest place we could choose," she added, pointing to the ground.

"Because the other groups will be hightailing it to Seeker's location," said Kagan, piecing her logic together as he spoke. "And after hearing all the explosions coming from this area, other groups will give it a wide berth, not wanting to risk walking into a possible buzz saw."

"Very good," said Ella, looking almost relieved that she hadn't had to spell it out for him. "We *are* still close to the water," she added. "And like you told me, this ecosystem can draw dangerous wildlife, as we've already witnessed. But nothing that should give us any cause for concern."

She gestured to Kagan's backpack, still resting on the jungle floor. "I assume you have some device in there capable of drying clothing."

"I do," he replied. He made his way to the pack and rooted around inside of it.

"This is called a drying worm," he said, removing an object that resembled a bloated version of its namesake. It was made of heavy plastic, but was heavily segmented so it could bend and maneuver. "It's supposed to be the latest craze for those who want to dry their jungle clothing on site. The best money can buy. Since I stole it," he added with smile, "I guess I can't comment on its expense. Anyway, it crawls around clothing and shoes and applies concentrated heat to more or less flash-dry the material. It has sensors and a rudimentary AI on board to guide it."

"Then let's get this started," she advised. "I can only imagine how many questions you have for me. Once the drying is underway, I'll tell you everything you want to know."

Saying this, she immediately began to undress, starting with her waterlogged boots, and progressing to her drenched outer clothing, which she removed and spread over the dry surface of a large boulder nearby.

She then reached for the waistband of her panties, clearly intending to remove these as well.

"What are you doing?" said Kagan, turning away from her awkwardly.

"Your worm can't flash dry my clothing while I'm wearing it, correct?" she said as she removed her panties and added them to the boulder. "And no need to avert your eyes," she added, removing her bra. "I'm sure I'm not revealing anything you haven't seen before. I'm not nearly as sexually permissive as I've been portraying myself, but eight billion of our fellow humans are about to be snuffed out on a whim. So I don't have time to be self-conscious. And *you* don't have time to act like a shy adolescent."

He turned and stared into her eyes once again, trying to keep his gaze locked at this height. She was right. He would have to ignore his biological urge to view what he considered an exceptional female anatomy. He would have to keep his mind—and his eyes—on a higher plane.

He activated the drying worm and set it inside her left boot, which still held her original shoe inside.

Ella gestured to his backpack. "I'm guessing you have a towel in there also," she said.

He nodded. Seconds later he tossed her a towel and she dried herself thoroughly. When she was done, she placed the towel next to her clothing so it, too, could be dried.

Kagan retrieved his bug spray and insisted that Ella take this opportunity to apply another coating. She did so while he continued to make efforts to keep his eyes focused above her neck, which took a surprisingly large dose of willpower to accomplish.

He had experienced a number of situations recently that he would call surreal, but talking to a naked woman who was coating herself with bug spray, in the middle of the Amazon rainforest, was certainly one of them.

"So let me get you up to speed," she said when she was finished with the spray, tossing him the can. "My first name really is Ella, that much is true. But I never did tell you my last. It's Burke. I'm Dr. Ella Burke."

Kagan inhaled sharply. *Ella Burke.*

As ridiculous as this claim would have been minutes earlier, he now didn't doubt it for a moment. Of course that's who she was.

Ella Burke was one of the most brilliant scientists of her generation, known to have long been at the frontiers of molecular biology, molecular medicine, and genetic engineering. An American raised in China, who had mysteriously disappeared four years earlier, and had never been found.

Apparently, the *never been found* part was no longer true.

She had changed her appearance, but only just enough to sidestep facial recognition programs. And she had kept her first name. She hadn't even bothered pretending to have grown up somewhere other than China to throw him off.

In retrospect, her true identity was so obvious it should have hit him in the face.

But the stupidity she projected had prevented him from even considering this as a possibility. She had hidden in plain sight. Her behavior insulated her from anyone guessing her true identity far better than any plastic surgery ever could. No one who met her and experienced her vapidity could ever believe she could have *anything* in common with the esteemed Ella Burke.

The moment Ory heard her proclaim her true identity, the AI activated the augmentation feature of Kagan's lenses, and now her biographical information was floating faintly near her image on his retina, for him to draw upon as needed.

"Judging by your reaction," she said, "I'm guessing you know me by reputation."

"Of course," he replied in a stunned voice. "Medicine and genetic engineering aren't my fields, but you don't have to be a physicist to have heard of Albert Einstein. Yes, I've heard of the great Ella Burke. I have a very high IQ," he added, not with arrogance but as a simple acknowledgment of reality. "But yours is even *higher*." He shook his head in disbelief. "Which wouldn't have been my first guess when I met you."

She laughed. "Until a few minutes ago, I'm sure you'd expect me to lose an IQ contest to a lump of clay."

"You sold it brilliantly. You're as talented an actress as you are a scientist."

"Thank you. I have to say it was a difficult role. I've collaborated with so many brilliant scientists for so long, it was hard to judge just how dim-witted I should play her. Is it really possible someone my age wouldn't know what the phrase *bad actor* meant? Or the word *prodigy*? There were times that I thought for sure I was overdoing it."

"No, it was . . . *you know*," he added with a grin, mocking her previous speech pattern, "just right."

"I have to congratulate you on your restraint," she said. "I might have strangled someone who acted like I did." She smiled, and her eyes sparkled. "I thought you were going to do just that when I insisted you were gay. *You know*," she added, returning to her old persona, "because you didn't respond to my sexual advances."

He laughed. "I thought I was going to strangle you, myself."

The drying worm indicated that the inside of Ella's left shoe and boot were now fully dry, and Kagan placed the device inside her right pair.

She gestured to her still-wet footwear. "Really?" she said, shaking her head in disbelief. "You're going to dry the inside of another boot? Before you dry my clothing? I shouldn't have even let you dry the first one until I was dressed, but I let this slide." She rolled her eyes. "But just because I said the stakes were too high for me to be self-conscious, doesn't mean I want to stand here naked any longer than I have to."

Kagan winced. "Sorry about that," he said, removing the worm from her boot and placing it on her bra. "I wasn't thinking."

"To be fair," she said, "you aren't the first man whose IQ has plummeted after a woman removed her clothing."

Kagan smiled, but he knew that there was more to it than that. His mind wasn't at its sharpest because he was reeling from too many shocks at the same time. The near certainty that billions of people were about to perish at the hands of an alien AI, just to ensure species homogeneity, was too much to process. It was mind-numbing—almost literally.

But if he didn't get his act together, and soon, he'd have no chance of stopping it. And the worst part of it was that, even if his mind was at its best, his chances of preventing the coming massacre were infinitesimally small.

# 34

Several three-foot-tall white herons had returned to the edge of the lake and were using their sharp yellow bills to stab helpless fish. Kagan had no doubt that most of the remaining wildlife that had been feasting on this wet, ready-made buffet would soon return.

"How is it that you speak Persian?" he asked Ella Burke.

"Languages come easily to me. I just seem to absorb them. I'm fluent in fourteen, including Persian, and passable in eight others."

"Of course you are," said Kagan, rolling his eyes.

"You sound like me," she said with a grin, "when I faked being impressed by your varied knowledge and abilities. You were obviously in contact with a supercomputer, but I pretended not to know."

Kagan sighed. Of course she had known. He was beyond being surprised by anything at this point. "Has anyone ever told you you're a bit intimidating?"

She laughed. "More than once. But I assumed the great Ben Kagan would be able to handle it."

"That remains to be seen. As fun as this has been, it's time you got to it and told me what's going on. I have no idea why a scientist of your stature would engage in a ruse like this, one lasting days. I have no idea if I can trust you, and every reason to believe I can't."

"Just like ditzy Ella had every reason to believe the same about you," she pointed out. "But what does it matter at this point? Even if you and I had nursed a bitter rivalry for decades, double-crossed each other a dozen times, we've now been forced together at the hip. Our lives, and the lives of countless others, now depend on our actions going forward, and our ability to work together. Even if we couldn't trust each other an hour ago, we have no choice but to do so now."

Kagan nodded. She was right. This was yet a further indication of how much he needed to up his game. It had been a long time since he'd been around someone who could run circles around him intellectually, but Ella Burke was managing this with ease. Her speed and quality of thought was ferocious.

"Since we're purposely stalling to give other groups a chance to wipe each other out," said Ella, "I'll tell you the slightly longer version of my story. So you can begin to get to know the real me. Wipe the horrible taste of the old Ella out of your mouth."

"In old Ella's defense," replied Kagan, "she did have her moments. Somehow, despite brilliant acting, the real you must have managed to shine through, at least on occasion. Your fearlessness. Your sense of humor. Subconsciously, I sensed there was more to you than met the eye, and that you were more important than I realized. I couldn't figure it out at the time. But now it's clear."

"Interesting," replied Ella. "I've heard you have great instincts, so this shouldn't surprise me," she added, revealing that she knew a lot more about him than he had guessed.

"Give me a few seconds to decide where to begin," she said, temporarily breaking eye contact.

Kagan agreed with her that they should dally on purpose, and knew that even the fastest groups wouldn't be reaching the alien probe for at least fifteen hours. While he was willing to have a somewhat extended conversation, ignoring the harsh reality of their situation, he didn't want to get too carried away.

"*Ory,*" he said subvocally, "*set up a timer to appear when I glance at the lower left corner of my field of vision. Have it show the exact time elapsed since Seeker provided you with the first mile of directions.*"

"*Done,*" replied the AI, and Kagan confirmed its presence.

When he glanced back up from the timer, Ella's eyes were once again upon his. "I guess I'll start by telling you what motivates me," she began, "what *has* motivated me, for as long as I can remember." She paused for effect. "*Death.*"

"That'll do it," mused Kagan. "Although I'm guessing you don't just mean the fear of death, but the very fact that it exists."

"Exactly!" said Ella, pleased. "I stumbled on the reality of human mortality, and its inevitability, at a younger age than most. And it terrified me. Still does. I'm sure most kids wrestle with the concept of death at some point as they grow, lying awake in bed at night and trying to imagine the world going on without them in it. Horrified as they try to imagine their own non-existence, their own state of eternal sleep.

"But it was far worse for me. Not only did I find the concept terrifying, it really pissed me off." She shrugged. "Not the most elegant phrase I could use to describe how I felt, but probably the most accurate."

A five-foot snake, its body a vivid green with white zigzag stripes spaced about an inch apart, slithered across a branch hanging over Ella, making its presence known for the first time. Ella caught Kagan's eye and arched an eyebrow.

"Emerald Tree Boa," he said. "Non-venomous."

She nodded and then continued as though it wasn't there. "My parents were Christians," she said. "But it seemed to me that the Christian god had conferred a death sentence on every living creature the moment it was born. As did the gods of most religions. Even as a very young girl I found this appalling, and decided that these gods weren't for me.

"We consider it the ultimate nightmare when cancer invades a body, and a patient is told they have but one year to live. And it *is*. But everyone who ever lived is under the exact same death sentence, just of longer duration. I know that my parents believe that this death sentence isn't permanent. That their god created an eternal afterlife. But I found myself skeptical."

"So you decided to do what you could to fight this unfair death sentence," guessed Kagan.

She nodded. "That's right. I was taking college courses by the time I was ten, but I had known by the age of four that I would become a scientist. More to the point, a doctor. And even more to the point, not just a doctor who sees individual patients, but one who discovers cures that can impact the entire human race, enabling humanity to reach immortality escape velocity."

"I'm not familiar with the term."

"I'm sure you can figure it out," said Ella. The hint of an amused smile came over her face. "I'll wait," she added.

Kagan thought about it while Ella finished dressing, her clothing now dry except for her last boot. Suddenly, the meaning of the words, *immortality escape velocity*, became clear to him. Perhaps his IQ really was higher when she was fully clothed.

"I'm guessing it has to do with human lifespan," he began, "and the steady increases that science and medicine continue to bring about."

"Very good," she said approvingly. "Any guesses how long the average man lived in 1800?"

Kagan shrugged. "Forty-two years?"

"Twenty-eight," she said, arching an eyebrow. "But by 2000, the global average was over sixty-six, more than twice as long. Today, it's well over seventy and climbing—in many countries it's in the eighties."

"So escape velocity," said Kagan, "must mean the point at which the human lifespan increases by more than a year each year. While you're getting a year older, your expected lifespan is growing by *three* years. Like that."

"Exactly right," said Ella. "I had a feeling you'd be able to piece it together."

"Glad I didn't disappoint," said Kagan dryly. "But please go on."

"At the risk of seeming immodest," she continued, "I knew that I was gifted. And I decided to devote these gifts to lifting humanity to escape velocity. I studied all branches of science voraciously, with special emphasis on biology and medicine, of course. I also read as much hard science fiction as I could get my hands on, which I found quite inspirational."

Kagan understood this well. Scientific discoveries had long been inspired by science fiction. The cell phone and iPod were inspired by *Star Trek* alone, and the list went on and on.

Science fiction had initially been derided as childish and worse, but in modern times it had come to dominate entertainment. This evolution was entirely predictable in hindsight.

When the genre had first arisen, scientific change was so slow that science fiction stories had seemed ridiculous. So out of the mainstream as to be laughable. But by the twenty-first century, scientific and technological change had become so furious, so disruptive, it was impossible for anyone to ignore.

No longer were breathtaking scientific advances hard to imagine. Now, it was the *lack* of such breakthroughs that were hard to imagine, making science fiction more relevant than any would have ever believed at its inception.

"Let me guess again," said Kagan, her unnatural speed of movement still fresh in his mind. "Along the way, you became inspired to explore human enhancement. You became interested, not just in the extension of human life, but in its optimization."

"That's right. And I was in the right place, at the right time, with the right skills."

"The right place being China?"

She nodded. "They are much more lax on self-experimentation than most countries. They're the Wild West of medicine. Far more permissive when it comes to allowing risky, outside-the-box biological research."

"And the right time being now, when genetic engineering techniques have become scary powerful."

Ella nodded. "I've perfected CRISPR-Cas9 to a level that most would find astonishing."

Kagan blew out a long breath. Even without any improvements, the CRISPR-Cas9 system was *already* astonishing. Its potential to precisely and efficiently modify human genes to order was only first recognized in 2012, and its use had exploded ever since.

CRISPR stood for *Clustered Regularly Interspaced Short Palindromic Repeats*, and Cas for *CRISPR-associated genes*. In combination, these elements formed the equivalent of a bacterial immune system. When a virus injected its genetic material into certain bacteria, this system would snip out parts of the invader's DNA and keep it on file, to help the bacteria recognize and destroy the virus the next time it attacked.

Kagan's knowledge of CRISPR-Cas9 was quite limited, but he knew that what nature had designed to protect bacteria, humanity had co-opted and turned into a powerful tool for reshaping the human genome to its whims.

"So all the state-of-the-art biotech equipment that ended up in Brazil illegally was for your use," said Kagan.

"Yes, I snuck out of China four years ago and have stayed off the grid. I organized a small group of like-minded scientists gathered from around the world. Scientists not content to wait for approvals from FDAs and their equivalents to conduct experiments, which might take decades or never come at all. Our goal was to reach immortality and the singularity, before we died of old age. By preserving and enhancing our biological natures.

"We knew other scientists would be busy merging man with electronic technology. And AIs would be evolving as well, competing in the race to superintelligence. Our goal was to see that humanity reached a biology-based singularity event first, before these two other competitors. We devoted ourselves to ensuring that mankind reached immortality as *mankind*. Not as *cyborg* kind. And we didn't want our species to become supplanted, or even driven extinct, by an ASI that humanity's own efforts had ultimately created."

Kagan's eyes narrowed. "Sounds eerily similar to what Seeker just outlined. Just like you, it wants to usher a biology-based sentience through a singularity event. But while your goal was to arrive there first, Seeker has made it clear that you're already too late."

Ella frowned. "The danger of an ASI arising first was easy to predict," she said. "Events in Andromeda make it clear that our goals, and our fears of finishing second, were sound. The difference between our goals and Seeker's goals is that we believe in including all human philosophies and social structures. Which is why our effort is international. And which is why our intent was to eventually share our successes freely with the world. Seeker insists on species homogeneity, at least when it comes to inner traits, and sees nation states as the closest proxy to this ideal."

"Nation states are growing ever more international, ever more collaborative."

"Maybe," said Ella. "But notice that every country here wanted the probe for itself. I wonder how many would have been willing to share from the start."

"As much as I agree with you about the importance of international cooperation, I also believe that nation states can serve an important role. Certain countries are dangerous, and need to be countered by other nations. Nations that can build enough wealth and power, peacefully, to defend against them. Cultures and national belief systems that maintain their integrity can *add* to diversity. I'm a strong believer in melting pot societies, but enclaves of distinctiveness are important too. As long as every nation, and every diverse group within every nation, is accepting of others."

"A discussion for another time," said Ella. "Let's just say that I'm aware that my goals and Seeker's goals have commonalities. Except that I wanted us to get to the singularity on our own, bringing along all of those who wanted to come. Without a single drop of blood being spilled. And Seeker plans to wipe out more than ninety-nine percent of the world's population.

"So yeah," she added wryly, "very similar goals. Just this one *tiny* difference."

Kagan blew out a long breath. "I have to admit, there have been times when I wondered if we deserve to survive. I've seen humanity at its worst. Our species isn't pretty."

Ella nodded. "My group wrestled with this, as well. But we came to a conclusion that Seeker seems to have affirmed. That while our current, often despicable natures, will form the core of what will get transformed during the singularity, the process will mature us and smooth us out. Nearly infinite intelligence and unlimited capabilities will do that to a species. We'll be a bloodthirsty, selfish, hideously ugly caterpillar turned into a stunning butterfly."

"But with the ability to tap into our bloodthirsty roots, as necessary," added Kagan.

"Apparently," said Ella. "We hoped that these roots would disappear entirely. But Seeker is counting on them being there, as you say, to tap into. Given its greater experience, I'd bet that it's right about that."

Kagan glanced down at the clock Ory had provided. It was time to get to the crux of the matter. This was an important discussion, but they couldn't delay discussing their current predicament forever. And they needed to begin strategizing.

"Getting back to how we happened to meet," said Kagan. "And why you put on the act you did. All of it has now become clear. You distrust nationalistic efforts. Like those of the group to which I belong. A group formed by the armed services of the American government to enhance American soldiers. And it also makes sense to me that you'd want to size up your competition in the realm of human enhancement. With EHO being a key player."

She nodded. "Go on."

"So you lured me to Brazil and Cardoza Coffee Enterprises. It wasn't our brilliant intelligence work that allowed us to trace the equipment to CCE. You made *sure* we did. While we thought we were spying on you, you were spying on us."

Ella grinned. "Wow, you really are as quick on the uptake as advertised."

"Well, yeah," replied Kagan with a smile. "Now that you're fully dressed and all."

# 35

Kagan glanced down to check the elapsed time since the alien AI had supplied directions to Ory, and then returned his gaze to Ella Burke. "So is Carlos Cardoza in on this?" he asked. "Obviously, the tragic affair you had with him, which required the help of a brave, handsome, American pilot to extricate yourself from, is total bullshit."

"I don't remember ever using the words brave and handsome," noted Ella with a twinkle in her eye.

Kagan smiled. "Well, yeah," he replied, "but that part was clearly implied."

"Clearly," said Ella in amusement. "But to answer your question: yes, Carlos is in on this. He's wealthy, and a science fiction enthusiast. Not to mention a closet scientist. He's one of a number of benefactors I've gathered who support our efforts."

"And have you enhanced these benefactors? Or are they waiting until you're done experimenting on yourselves? Waiting until you've cleared out all of the landmines before risking their own precious skin?"

"We've provided them with a few well-tested enhancements. But who can blame them for wanting us to thoroughly test drive the rest? Both sides bring resources to the party. Our side is a collection of world-class geneticists, doctors, genetic engineers, and nanotechnologists—with expensive equipment needs. Our experiments can be expensive, as well. And encampments that are secure and off the grid don't come cheaply, either.

"So they provide financial support, political cover, and help with security. And we bring our talents and our willingness to put our experiments where our mouth is, so to speak, and risk being the first, the trailblazers."

Ella shook her head. "It's easy for you to criticize how we're going about things. But we don't have the money and power of the US government behind us like you do." She paused. "By the way, you should know that we chose to study *you*, specifically."

He thought about this. There was only one reason he had shown up in Brazil, instead of someone else. Which meant that Ella and her group had known about his history, known about Vettori's Party and its aftermath. "So it wasn't an accident that we found evidence of ISIS's involvement with CCE, was it?" he said. "You used this as a lure, knowing I wouldn't be able to resist coming myself."

"Very good. We heard rumors about the fabled EHO. Who hasn't? But our intel could only identify eleven agents with certainty. You were one of them. By far the smartest and most accomplished scientifically, although with the least previous experience as a warrior. And you were also a bridge to Norman Weiser."

"I see. Who would be the ultimate benefactor to have in your corner."

"Yes," admitted Ella. "But this operation wasn't just about spying. It's true that I wanted to see firsthand what tricks EHO agents had up their sleeves. But even more importantly, I wanted to study you, test you, to see just how ethically upright you really were."

"Because you heard rumors that we're glorified Boy Scouts."

"Exactly. I wanted to confirm them. See what made you tick. Learn precisely what enhancements EHO had come up with. If you impressed me enough on a personal level, I was prepared to try to convince you to join our efforts. Convince you to switch loyalties to an effort whose fruits would be shared globally, rather than kept secret within a single country and relegated to the battlefield. One heavier on the biological side of the enhancement ledger."

"Assuming that I passed muster," said Kagan, "was the idea to recruit me to your team, or have me stay with EHO?"

"Both," replied Ella. "In the beginning, I figured we could help each other covertly. Later, who knows, perhaps you'd be willing to pull a disappearing act and join us full time. Let us . . . borrow . . . certain advances that EHO had made that fit in with our philosophy.

I was also hoping you could get Weiser on board, as well as recruiting other key candidates."

"So, basically, you wanted to turn a potentially formidable rival into an ally," said Kagan.

"If possible, why not? But only if my instincts said you were a very good man, and that I could trust you."

"So you lured me in, set yourself up as my boss, and pretended to be vapid and incompetent to allay any suspicion I might have."

She nodded. "Also because I knew that acting dumb would make you crazy, make you feel superior, and lower your guard. All of which could help reveal your personality and true nature."

"So I was just a test animal being put through a maze. Reminds me of Seeker again."

"Come on, Ben. That's not fair. We both know that life is a series of tests. At work, in relationships, in athletics. And Seeker is right about one thing, life-and-death situations bring out a person's true character. It's my understanding that this is exactly how your character was first revealed. When you saved millions of pedestrians from being wiped out by fleets of self-driving vehicles."

Kagan had to admit this was true. His bravery had surprised no one as much as it had surprised himself. Although how she had managed to obtain intelligence this good was another question entirely.

"We're only alive," continued Ella, "because every last one of our ancestors passed every test that was thrown at them. Tests of their immune systems, which had to keep them alive during plagues. Tests of their sex drives, and of their ability to attract mates, which are key requirements for reproduction. Tests of their ability to overcome threats from both nature and their fellow man. We all come from an uninterrupted line of humanity's winners. Like gunfighters in the Old West, just being alive means that you're undefeated."

Ella nodded solemnly. "But know this, Ben," she added, "if you had failed *my* test, you'd have left Brazil in perfect health, never even knowing a test had been conducted."

Kagan considered this for several long seconds. "So what tests *did* you have planned?"

"If we survive longer than the next day or two, I'll tell you all about them. The bottom line is that you were being watched and recorded constantly. Our sensors detected the computer you have strapped to your upper thigh. Which we know you speak with sub-vocally, and hear through a micro-comm embedded in your cochlea. We picked up on your contact lenses too. We tried to analyze their capabilities the best we could using remote sensors. We could tell that EHO had packed tremendous computing power into them, but not much else about their functionality. But we were very impressed, and eager to eventually learn more."

Ella paused as if expecting a response. When Kagan remained silent, she pressed ahead. "I also learned that you have incredible patience, or you wouldn't have made it through our first day together. I was even driving *myself* crazy. Finally, I know that you think above the waist more than many men. Most tend to find me physically appealing, yet you refused my not-so-subtle advances. My guess is partly because you couldn't bring yourself to sleep with someone you didn't respect. And partly because you thought it was bad form to sleep with your boss. Probably more the former than the latter."

"Good guess," said Kagan.

"So even before any major, contrived tests, I had learned a lot about you. But we had plenty of other hoops ready for you to jump through. Had you gone on the mission CCE had assigned to you, you would have found yourself in tight, life-and-death situations, and forced into making brutally difficult choices."

"Which is exactly what is happening."

"Ironic," agreed Ella. "I only wish we were behind it. In our scenario, you would have *thought* you were in life-and-death situations, but would never have been in any real danger. But our plans for you were derailed when you got a wireless transmission to your computer that we traced to Admiral Headrick. We tried to intercept the message, but it was too well encrypted. But given it was from the US Secretary of Defense, himself, we knew something huge was, ah . . . brewing," she added.

"Is that a joke having to do with Cardoza Coffee Enterprises?"

"Absolutely," she replied in amusement. "Who knows brewing better than me?"

"Someone who *actually* works for CCE?"

Ella flashed an incandescent smile. "Spoilsport," she said simply. "Anyway, we couldn't help but notice that right after you received Headrick's message you left your hotel. In the wee hours of the morning. We were monitoring you when you broke into a jungle survival gear store. We figured your mission was taking you to a jungle city, or jungle stronghold, and you wanted to be prepared for the worst. We had no idea you were planning to insert yourself into the heart of the most untamed region on the planet."

"And then you monitored me leaving the store," said Kagan, "and guessed pretty quickly that I was heading toward the airport where CCE's helo was parked."

She nodded.

"So, dying to know what the message from Admiral Headrick was all about, you chose to beat me there and stow away. To see where I was going, and what I would be doing there, firsthand." Kagan frowned. "A risky strategy on your part."

"No guts, no glory," said Ella with a shrug. "And I found the risk well within acceptable bounds. I already had a good enough sense of your character to be confident that you wouldn't try to hurt me, no matter what. Besides," she added, raising her eyebrows, "I'm fully capable of taking care of myself."

"I noticed," said Kagan. "Apparently combat training comes along with the enhancements."

"As it did for you. Both of our jobs have their dangers. And as you know, my goal is to live forever. Given this, it doesn't hurt to learn to be as bad-assed, as you called it, as possible."

"Given how things turned out, do you still think stowing away was the right decision?"

"Absolutely," replied Ella without hesitation. "I'd rather know about a threat, and have some chance to stop it, than live in blissful ignorance."

"So after I landed, you revealed yourself and continued your ruse."

"Yes. I tried to get you to continue with whatever you were doing, pretending to feel guilty about taking you away from it. I was frustrated that you were willing to take me out of the fray and waste time I knew you needed. But I couldn't argue the point too much without blowing my cover.

"And this checked another box," she continued. "You showed a lot of empathy when I described my plight. Even though you didn't like me, and even though, based on my story, I had made my own bed. And you were even willing to get me out of Brazil. Come to the aid of an annoying damsel in distress. Had to give you high marks for that."

She paused. "And then you demonstrated other qualities I was looking for. You spared the Iranians. Only killing one of them so I could have the proper footwear. Which itself was very thoughtful, and caused you to waste time."

"But you didn't know what I was really doing here, right?" asked Kagan. "Well, not until the Aussies gave it away."

"I didn't know. But after you told me you were here to retrieve a spy satellite, I did suspect. I would have bought your story, but you didn't seem to know anything about your own satellite. My intuition suggested you were here after an alien ship—using the spy satellite thing as the closest cover story you could get to reality. But this was so far out, I wouldn't let myself fully believe it until the Aussies."

Kagan continuing to be amazed at how sharp this woman really was. "And when you got lost?" he said. "Another test?"

"I'm afraid so. You made it very clear you'd leave me to die if I fell behind. I wanted to see if you'd carry that out. If you hadn't come back for me, I'd have easily caught up with you again."

"I'm sure you would have. Ory told me when you wandered off that you moved with surprising stealth and speed. Now it's clear why."

"Ory?" she said, raising her eyebrows. "Is that the AI that clings to your thigh?"

"I wouldn't exactly refer to it that way. But yes."

"Do all EHO agents call it *Ory*?"

"No, that was my choice. Short for Oracle."

"Really?" said Ella, rolling her eyes. "So it should have been *Or* for short, right? You added the Y as a sign of affection, didn't you? Like it's a pet."

"Just because I know that it's in our nature to humanize objects, especially AIs, doesn't mean that I'm immune from it, myself."

"Okay," she said with just the hint of a smile. "Ory it is."

"Getting back to our discussion," said Kagan, "one of your enhancements lets you control your vital signs, doesn't it?"

"How do you know that?"

"While we were hiking, I slipped a feather-weight sensor on the back of your shirt. One that could measure your heart and respiration rates. I should have guessed at the time you were enhanced, but your ditz routine did a wonderful job of killing suspicion. I just figured your metronomic heartbeat and lack of perspiration were the result of rigorous exercise. Now I know better. You didn't know it, but your augmented ability to keep your vital signs rock steady helped you pass a lie detector test."

"I see," she said, tilting her head in thought. "That must have been when you asked me questions about CCE and biotech equipment."

"That's right. You said you knew nothing about it, and passed with flying colors. Now I know how."

Kagan paused, replaying their past interactions in his mind, but this time through a more informed prism. "And you gave me the idea for finding the probe by using a suppression-field strength gradient. I thought you had led me to this eureka moment unwittingly. But that was the real you exerting herself, wasn't it? And the wry humor you exhibited when joking about having a nickel every time someone called you brilliant—that was the real you, also. Doubly ironic, since I'm sure you've been called brilliant ever since you were two."

"Still," she replied in amusement, "it was fun to hear *you* say it. Especially since you thought I was anything but."

"So tell me about your various enhancements," said Kagan. "Are you able to reverse aging, as well? You look like a thirty-one-year-old with the figure, complexion, and skin of a twenty-six-year-old. Which is impressive, especially since you're really thirty-eight."

"Damn you, Ory," said Ella, feigning anger. "If you were human you'd know that disclosing a girl's actual age is bad form."

Kagan smiled. "Is that a yes?"

Ella nodded. "We can modify certain genes that seem to turn back the clock. We're working on perfecting this further."

"Well you've done excellent work so far," said Kagan.

"Thanks," said Ella. "But now that we're teammates, I think it's important that we disclose all of our enhancements to each other. So we have full knowledge of what strengths the other can bring to bear. So how about this," she added with just the hint of a smile, "I'll show you mine if you show me yours."

"You *already* seem to know most of mine," complained Kagan.

"Maybe. But since you saw me naked, I think we should call it even."

"That doesn't make any sense," said Kagan. "They have nothing to do with each other. Besides," he added, "it isn't true. I never looked once."

Dr. Ella Burke shook her head. "Come on, Ben. We're a team. Isn't it time we stopped lying to each other?"

"Okay," said Kagan, "maybe *once.*"

"Okay then," said Ella. "I appreciate your honesty. As a reward, I'll tell you what, in this game of show-and-tell, I'm willing to go first."

"Great," said Kagan. He studied her for several long seconds. "You can start by telling me what possible enhancement allowed you to survive for forty minutes without breathing."

# 36

Ella walked the short distance to the flat series of rocks on which she had set her clothes for drying and sat down, looking up at Kagan, who was still standing.

"Yeah, not having to breathe is a big advantage," she said. "I guess you noticed, huh?" she added with a grin.

"So when I was knocked unconscious, you dived into the water on purpose, didn't you? You knew if your head was submerged for long enough, everyone would believe you were dead, and leave the area. Or, if they did hang around for a while, they'd ignore you."

"Exactly. Which would allow me to emerge and turn the tables without anyone paying attention."

"Impressive strategy. I'd have to applaud it, even if I wasn't the main beneficiary. But again, the question is *how?*"

"I took advantage of one of my rare augmentations that doesn't arise from genetic engineering," said Ella. "Developed by a number of brilliant nanotechnologists on the team. Basically, I now have artificial red blood cells coursing through my veins, almost entirely replacing my own blood. They're called respirocytes. First envisioned more than twenty years ago. Think of them as spherical nanobots that function as tiny pressure tanks. Pressure tanks that can be stuffed with oxygen and carbon dioxide. Each can store and transport over a hundred times more oxygen than a natural blood cell, and release it with exquisite control.

"Not to boast," she added, "but I can sprint for more than five minutes on a single breath. And I can remain underwater for *two hours.*"

"Wow!" said Kagan. "No wonder you've been running rings around me."

He tilted his head in thought. "But why is your respiration rate as high as it is? And your heart rate too? Isn't your pulse largely dependent on the oxygen needs of your body? So when your muscles are working harder, you need more oxygen, and your heart beats faster. But with respirocytes on board, you have plenty of oxygen to cover increased exertion. So your pulse should be inhumanly slow."

"Outstanding," said Ella. "You're absolutely right. When I'm alone, I keep it at thirty beats per minute. I can more or less set it within a narrow range using a type of biofeedback. I could set it even lower, but I don't. Same with my respiration rate. I keep it constant at about fifteen breaths a minute. When either of these are too low, it creeps me out."

"I don't doubt it," said Kagan. "I'd imagine that breathing is a hard habit to break."

Ella smiled. "I keep my respiration rate about the same no matter what," she continued. "But whenever anyone else is close by, I increase my pulse rate into the low fifties. It's unlikely anyone would notice if I left it at thirty, but why take chances? Wouldn't want anyone thinking I'm not human."

"Which is exactly what would have happened if you had kept it at thirty today," noted Kagan. "Your cover would have been blown the moment I placed a sensor on you."

She shrugged. "You can never be too careful."

"But these respirocytes are mechanical devices. So the path you're taking isn't that much different than the one EHO is taking, after all."

Ella shook her head adamantly. "That isn't true," she said. "Respirocyte technology comes the closest to your approach, I agree, but it's still very different qualitatively. We aren't marrying man with machine. We're enhancing biological systems, processes, and genes. In many cases we're modulating the levels of natural substances in the body to optimize performance. All of our enhancements are microscopic, and non-electronic. We aren't turning ourselves into cyborgs. All of me is still wet-wear. I'm still a squishy human, just engineered and optimized. Except for the respirocytes, which are microscopic, and whose principle job is gas exchange."

"Principle job?" he said. "It's not their *only* job?"

"They can also bind together very quickly to stop any loss of blood from a wound—almost before it starts."

"Another handy feature," said Kagan, the hint of a smile coming over his face from delivering such a profound understatement. He carried a can of spray foam that would seal up wounds and stop blood loss very quickly, but this was externally applied, and could be lost or depleted.

"For the sake of full disclosure," said Ella, "there is another development we're working on along the lines of respirocytes. But far more complex. We call them nano-docs. Feynman spoke of them in his original, groundbreaking lecture on nanotechnology. In a section he called 'swallowing the surgeon.'"

"So basically, microscopic medical robots," said Kagan. "Did Feynman name them nano-docs, or was that you?"

"No, that was us. This project is our Holy Grail. And while you may think this technology, like respirocytes, fits more into the EHO philosophy of enhancement, it doesn't either. These nano-docs wouldn't change who we are at all. They would just make sure that we run smoothly, and are always properly repaired."

"How many of these robots would you need?"

"Trillions," replied Ella. "Injected into the bloodstream. Each would be capable of moving individual atoms, proteins, and cells around. They would bolster our immune systems. But this time with an intelligence our evolution-based immune system, although impressive, can't match. Invaders would be identified by these nano-docs and wiped out much faster than our immune system manages—before the pathogens have a chance to multiply. We'd never get sick again. But that's only the beginning."

She paused for effect, clearly energized by the topic. "The state of our health is also impacted by the state of our cells. Cells malfunction, which is another cause of disease. Diabetes and macular degeneration, for example, aren't a result of infections. But many trillions of microscopic nano-docs could repair cells instantly. Cells and diseases operate at the microscopic scale, yet we address them at the macroscopic. Pharmaceutical agents work at the molecular level, but they are severely constrained. Basically, we use blunt force, because we don't have the precision of a scalpel."

"And these nano-docs would give you that precision?" said Kagan.

"Yes. They would patrol the body, forever monitoring all cells and systems, identifying issues and repairing them immediately. Cancer cells could be surgically isolated and destroyed. And not a single one would ever be left behind to propagate again. Wounds could be repaired and sewn up from the inside. Lacerated organs almost instantly repaired. Broken bones sealed back into place. Neurological diseases like Alzheimer's and Parkinson's cured at the molecular level. Surgeries could be performed with perfect precision, without scalpels or incisions. Your teeth could be patrolled, cleaned, and repaired. Your skin restored to youthful elasticity."

"You haven't thought about this much, have you?" commented Kagan wryly.

Ella laughed. "Once perfected, the nano-docs would not only prevent disease and provide cures, but possibly extend life indefinitely. And all the while our lives are extended, we could maintain our youth and vitality."

"How would they eliminate aging?"

"In many ways, aging is simply another disease we can cure. We age, in part, because cellular damage builds up. Nano-docs could replace old, damaged cells with new ones. You could be permanently maintained as you were at the age of twenty-five. Same hearing, eyesight, skin, hair—everything."

"And you'd disclose all of these genetic modifications and enhancements to the general public, right?"

"That's the plan. We could all live for a very long time, in a very optimized state. And this is *before* our medicine and technology allow us to reach a singularity event. After that, it's impossible to even speculate. In fact, this is one definition of the singularity, a point of runaway self-improvement, leading to an explosion of advances so great that we achieve a state of being that is unfathomable by our puny minds."

Kagan didn't immediately respond, pondering what she had said, instead. He idly watched a brilliantly colored lizard, no doubt poisonous, scurry through the underbrush and disappear. The pool had steadily attracted additional birds, but nothing else that they needed to worry about—at least for now.

"And enhancements in human intelligence?" he said finally. "For a biology-based singularity to take place, this has to be on the table."

"We're taking baby steps," said Ella. "A while back, researchers genetically engineered increases in an NMDA glutamate receptor subtype in mice. This receptor is known to affect memory formation and long-term potentiation. The result was a mouse that learned faster, and had a better memory. They called it Doogie mouse, apparently after a very old television show." She paused. "We've done something similar in humans."

"And?" said Kagan.

"And it works. I now have extra copies of several of these NMDA receptor subtypes in my genome. Rigorous testing shows that my memory improved approximately twelve percent over my previous baseline, and my speed of learning about eight percent. We think we can do much better. But for now we're taking baby steps, being cautious.

"More importantly, once we perfect the nano-docs, we can explore using them to modify the nano-scaffolding in the brain. And science has gradually come to appreciate that our minds operate in the quantum realm, and structures called microtubules are critical to this process. So we're working on ways to amplify these. We think this is where the fireworks could really start."

"How far along are you?"

"We still have a long way to go. But progress has been accelerating. Especially now that we're putting resources on it that had been previously dedicated to the respirocyte program. We're using the world's most powerful supercomputers. But not to turn ourselves into cyborgs. To help us design these nano-docs, which will keep us human."

"What you've put together, beginning as a private citizen, is extraordinary," said Kagan. "The progress you're making is remarkable."

Ella's reaction to this praise was completely unexpected. Instead of taking pleasure, however briefly, from these kind words, they seemed to have the opposite effect. She looked away from Kagan, and her face reflected nothing but misery. Finally, a tear formed in her right eye, the first hint that recent events had taken a toll on her. The first chink in what had seemed to be impenetrable emotional armor.

"I know," he said softly. "As much as we might try to ignore the reality of what we're facing here, we can't wall it off forever."

Ella sighed deeply. "For me, it's not just about what we're facing now," she said. "It's frustration about what could have been. You turned out to be great, Ben. Better than I had hoped. I really think we could have found a way to collaborate. Together, who knows the progress we could have made to better the human race."

"And now we have little chance of surviving the next twenty-four hours."

"Thanks," said Ella, rolling her eyes, "you really know how to cheer someone up."

But as her sense of humor returned, so did her resolve. She wiped the single tear from her cheek and her features hardened once again. "Sorry about that," she said. "I know we need to get on with our disclosures so we can begin strategizing. I won't show any weakness again."

"You weren't showing weakness. You were showing that you're human."

"Given that humanity is now on the endangered species list," she said grimly, "I'm pretty sure that's not a good thing."

# 37

Kagan checked the elapsed time since Ory had begun keeping track yet again, and then produced a full canteen from his pack. He took several long drinks and handed it to Ella, along with two protein bars.

While she drank her fill, Kagan watched a sizable brown twig that had begun walking across the branch of a nearby tree. A stick bug honed by evolution to resemble its namesake more closely than a human sculptor might have achieved. His augmented lenses informed him that many stick insect species could reproduce without mating. There were even several of these that—like the Androms—consisted entirely of a single sex. In these cases, egg-laying females.

"So tell me more about Ory," said Ella Burke, biting off a piece of protein bar.

Kagan did as she asked, consuming several protein bars of his own in the process. While she knew the basics of his enhancements, he provided specifics on the capabilities of Ory and his smart contact lenses, in addition to other information.

Ella listened in fascination. "I have to admit," she said when he was done, "I'm a little jealous. We can use genetic engineering to enhance memory. Which I've done. But being able to draw on an information source like Ory brings this to another level entirely. And having it in the background monitoring sensors, controlling drones, and so on, is a big advantage. Using it to keep easily accessible permanent records of everything you've ever heard or seen would come in handy also."

Her mouth fell open. "Wait a minute," she said. "Even if you only glanced at my naked body once, Ory has the image as a permanent record. So you can have it projected onto your contact lenses anytime you want."

"Sure," said Kagan, trying to keep a straight face, "if I still had the photo. But it turns out I've already sold it to an Internet news outlet. The bidding for a picture of the world famous missing scientist, Ella Burke, in the buff, was pretty intense."

"Very funny," she said dryly. "If this enhanced soldier thing doesn't work out for you, you should try comedy."

"Sorry, couldn't resist. Besides, why would I ogle your picture? I didn't even sleep with you when I had the chance."

"Just to correct the record," protested Ella with a twinkle in her eye, "you never really had the chance. It was a test, remember? If you'd have gone for it, I would have suddenly had second thoughts. How you reacted to *that* would have told me even more about you."

"Nah," replied Kagan with a grin. "You only *think* you'd have backed out. When you have a shot at something this irresistible," he said, gesturing to himself, "you don't have second thoughts."

Ella laughed. "On the slim chance we survive this, maybe we'll find out."

She became serious once again. "In the meanwhile," she said, "getting back to Ory and your contacts, this is a very powerful combination."

"They've quickly become indispensable tools. People become dependent on their phones, but Ory has become like a spare brain."

"It's one of the EHO initiatives we would have had to think hard about adopting, even though it goes beyond our charter. Before Seeker rendered these considerations meaningless, of course."

They continued to compare notes on their enhancements in various categories, with Ella describing a host of genetically engineered changes she had made to her own genome.

Kagan's contacts allowed him to see in the dark and zoom in on distant objects.

Ella possessed genetically engineered corneas and lenses that conferred far greater visual acuity and distance vision than even the best non-augmented human, but still couldn't match his capabilities.

His comms allowed extended hearing, while her hearing had been enhanced organically. The difference was, while Seeker had stripped him of his amplified hearing, hers remained. It may not have been as powerful as his was, but it would still give them an advantage over other groups.

Despite not appearing any stronger than a normal woman her size, Ella could also exceed Kagan's enhanced reaction speed, as she had so ably demonstrated, as well as his strength and endurance. Her respirocytes, which kept her muscles flush with oxygen, even during their most demanding exertions, helped on all of these dimensions. In fact, erythropoietin, a hormone that stimulated red blood cell production, and thus increased oxygen-carrying capacity, was well known for its ability to confer dramatic increases in endurance. This hormone had long been used as a doping drug by athletes, most notably Lance Armstrong, but was only a tiny fraction as effective as Ella's respirocytes.

Ella's increased strength, speed, and endurance stemmed from other genetically engineered enhancements as well. A slight modification of the LPR5 gene resulted in a considerable strengthening of bones. Modifications to the myostatin gene, MSTN—which had first been shown to result in super-muscular pigs and dogs—resulted in muscles that were not only far stronger than normal, but leaner as well.

Several other genetic manipulations conferred superhuman reflexes, and provided a form of super-adrenaline that could heighten her performance, not just in short bursts, but for extended periods.

Both she and Kagan could perform at high levels for extended periods without sleep. For her, this was due to modified genes, and for him, certain patterns of electrical stimulation delivered by the microelectrodes implanted in his brain.

The military had long studied methods to enhance the alertness and wakefulness of its fighting forces, and EHO had finally made the breakthrough they had been searching for. Whales and dolphins never slept—they would drown if they did. Unlike humans, these mammals could control the lobes of their left and right brains so that while one lobe slept, the other stayed awake. EHO had finally been able to mimic this effect for a period of about forty hours, during which an agent could remain awake with little loss of effectiveness.

They could have gone into much greater detail about their enhancements, especially Ella, but they didn't want to ignore the ticking time bomb that hovered over them any longer than was necessary, so they compared notes quickly and superficially.

"Okay then," said Kagan when they had finished. "When Seeker first told me that you and I would constitute a team, I wasn't what you'd call *ecstatic*. Especially since I thought you were a corpse."

"Well, yeah," replied Ella, trying to keep a straight face, "having to drag a dead, waterlogged body through the jungle is bound to slow you down. But it could have been even worse," she added, raising her eyebrows. "I could have been alive, but the Ella that you *thought* you knew."

Kagan smiled. "Believe me, I couldn't be happier about how things turned out with you. Beginning with the part where you saved my life. Who knew that our ragtag, accidental team, would be so formidable?"

She blew out a long breath. "That remains to be seen. But I guess it's time to talk about what we're up against, and what we can do about it."

He nodded. "Let's gather up some additional supplies, courtesy of the Iranians, and get out of here. We should probably at least trek the first mile that Seeker laid out for us."

"Agreed," said Ella. "But this time, *I'll* take the lead." A wry smile spread across her face. "Try to keep up."

"I'll do my best."

"And most importantly," she added grimly, "try to stay alive."

"Yeah, you too," he replied, realizing that he had only just met the real Ella Burke, but suddenly cared about her well-being far beyond anything having to do with Seeker or their current predicament.

# PART 7

# 38

Ella Burke had never been overly emotional, but the effort she was now forced to exert to keep her emotions under control was considerable. Part of her wanted to wallow in utter despair. Who could blame her, under the circumstances?

Part of her was seething in anger at an alien probe, at an AI from an entirely different galaxy, as absurd as this was, who had forced them into this predicament.

And part of her was terrified beyond reason. Her greatest fear, *death*, which she had hoped to dodge, was now coming for her with a furious urgency.

But surprisingly, when she wasn't dwelling on the reality of these horrors, she was also having—dare she admit it?—*fun*. When she focused on her interactions with Ben Kagan, she found herself in a good mood.

Talk about absurd.

Not that her head was *entirely* in the sand. Any positive feelings she had only survived for brief periods before her mind returned to the coming horrors. Even so, she was developing a powerful attraction to Ben Kagan, which only seemed to be growing.

One of her benefactors was the Israeli equivalent of Elon Musk, and all the intel she had on EHO had come from Mossad files this benefactor had somehow managed to acquire. The file on Ben Kagan was particularly complete, as the Mossad had learned of the part he had played during the *Vettori Party* massacre. This was quite an impressive intelligence feat, since the Mossad was convinced that not even President Moro had been informed of the true nature of this attack.

She had chosen Kagan to study and possibly approach to join her efforts because—on paper at least—he was exceptional in every way. Brilliant, heroic, and decent. Steve Rodgers in the flesh, except smarter, and not wearing his Boy Scout nature on his sleeve.

But the reality of Kagan was even better. He wasn't as sharp as she was, even before genetic engineering had sharpened her intellect further, but he was brilliant in his own right. And he had treated the old Ella far better than she had deserved. She had improved her behavior after they had landed, while still maintaining her false persona, but in the days prior to this, she had laid the stupidity and incompetence on so thick it could have paved all the roads in Brazil.

And he had treated her better than most would have after learning she had stowed away. He had even gone to great lengths to ensure that she had the proper footwear, and thus a chance to survive. And he had come back for her when she had fallen behind, even after insisting he wouldn't.

Ben Kagan wasn't intimidated by the real her, either, which was rare. He thought and acted decisively under extreme pressure, never panicking, regardless of the situation, and he absorbed shocks to the system that would cripple most men. And most important to her, he possessed a great sense of humor, which was readily apparent, even in the face of certain death.

He had lived up to his billing—and then some.

She could have been ecstatically happy right now if she wasn't so absolutely miserable, devastated, and terrified.

Her timing with men had been bad before.

But never *this* bad.

Ella forced herself to put her attraction to Ben Kagan aside as both she and her new partner gathered up the backpacks and weaponry that had once belonged to the fallen Iranians. They carefully opened the backpacks and searched through them, adding to their arsenal.

Well, adding to *Kagan's* arsenal.

She had only brought herself on this expedition, and nothing more.

As she had told him, even knowing he was stealing jungle survival supplies, she never would have guessed his mission involved a complete and lengthy immersion into the heart of the Amazon. Given her impressive array of augmentations, she had been confident in her ability to survive a brief stint in a jungle, even wearing flats—with the operative word being *brief*. If leeches had stuck to her ankles and attempted to dine, they would have found that what passed for blood in *her* body was thoroughly unappetizing.

Once it became clear what she had really gotten herself into, she had cursed her lack of provisions and preparation. Which was why it was such a relief to now be carrying select Iranian weapons, including a number of grenades they had both taken, a machete, and an Iranian backpack stuffed with supplies. It was also a relief to finally be herself, and not have the burden of putting on a constant act, or harboring so many secrets.

She abhorred violence and was loathe to hurt a fly. But she had made sure she was well trained in combat, and had taken steps to brace herself, psychologically, to take lives if her own was at stake. Something she had just been forced to do for the first time.

While she was sickened by what she had done, she couldn't allow herself to dwell on it. Not now. She had done what she had to do, and the stakes were too high to let this cripple her.

Besides, this was only the beginning. The necessity to take human life was only going to grow. To survive, she would likely have no other choice. Which was maddening.

Few of the countries represented here were natural enemies. In fact, many were allies. Despite the original goal of these national teams to get to the probe first, she didn't truly believe more than a few of them would really kill in cold blood like the Iranians had done. The Aussies had been a prime example of a more measured aggression.

But Seeker had seen to it that this was no longer true. Seeker had made certain that even the least violent operatives in the jungle would have no choice but to become pitiless assassins, killing all comers indiscriminately in a lethal free-for-all.

Once her weaponry and supply selections had been made, and she was about to hoist a borrowed Iranian backpack onto her shoulders, Kagan approached her and held out his hand, palm up. A tiny silver ball rested in the center of his palm, the size of a pea. "Before we head out," he said, "you should put this in your ear."

"Is that really a comm?" she asked, trying to sound impressed. The reality was that after working with nanotechnologists for several years, she now took the successful miniaturization of highly complex technology as a given.

"It is," replied Kagan. "I had an extra. I recommend that you use it. This way we can communicate with each other remotely, at least over the limited distance Seeker is permitting. And we'll both be tied into Ory. You won't be able to communicate subvocally, but it will hear you just fine, even if you speak in a faint whisper."

She reached out with her thumb and forefinger, lifted the tiny device, and brought it closer to her eye to examine it. It appeared to be nothing more than a perfectly spherical alloy shell with no means of attachment. "Is it self-inserting?" she asked.

"Yes. The actual device is much smaller than what you're holding. The outer coating is there simply to make it large enough for you to be able to pick up. Once you've placed it in your ear canal, it will jettison the outer coating and travel to your cochlea, where it will insert itself with sub-millimeter precision."

"Sounds delightful," she said wryly.

"I know it's reminiscent of some creepy science fiction show, but it really is harmless. And painless."

Ella nodded. She had seen a number of science fiction shows in which creatures entered human bodies through the ear, although they never stopped at the cochlea, usually burrowing into the brain to turn their hosts into puppets.

"I guess I should thank you for sharing this," said Ella. She held the minuscule ball out in front of her face in a classic *bottoms up* gesture, like it was champagne. "Cheers," she said, depositing it into her right ear.

"Cheers," repeated Kagan while the comm traveled down her ear canal, relying on sensors and a powerful, miniaturized computer to properly position itself. Less than a minute later the process was complete, and was as painless as Kagan had promised.

Kagan walked a few paces away and mumbled something to Ella under his breath, too softly for even her genetically enhanced hearing to catch. Her new comm, however, transmitted it to her as if he had spoken at normal volumes. She was also able to hear Ory clearly when it introduced itself, completing the testing.

"*Ory*," said Kagan subvocally, on a private channel, "*can I assume our one remaining drone is still operable?*"

"*Yes.*"

"*Good. Fly it fairly high and use it as a lookout. But I also want it to keep Ella in sight at all times. If we happen to pass within fifty yards of any of our other drones, so that they become operable again, let me know.*"

"*Roger that.*"

"Okay then," said Kagan, looking pleased that this chore had been completed. "I think that's everything." A smile came over his face. "Let's make like a shepherd and get the flock out of here."

"Really?" said Ella, unable to keep herself from grinning at such silliness in the face of approaching cataclysm. "Was the classic, 'let's make like a tree and leaf,' not juvenile enough for you?"

"Just consider yourself lucky. I was going to say, 'let's make like a fetus and head out,' but I decided to spare you."

She shook her head. Who *was* this guy? And why did she like him so damn much when they were both about to die, and the world was, almost literally, coming to an end?

Which explained why he was trying to keep things light, she realized. He could have been somber and said, 'let's head out into certain death,' but what would be the point of that?

"Let's hold up just a little bit longer," she said. "You shared with me. Now it's my turn. I'd like you to have some respirocytes of your own."

This took him aback. "You brought extra?" he said in surprise. "How? I know you didn't have a bag or vial of them hidden in your clothing. Or anywhere on your naked body, for that matter. Not that I was looking," he hastened to add. "You know, other than the one time."

Ella shook her head. "I don't know about you, Ben. Sometimes you're brilliant, and sometimes you're really dumb."

She gestured to a medical bag nearby, which she had found in one of the Iranian's backpacks. Their nine-man force was large enough to have included a medical technician, who had come well prepared. Without another word, Ella removed a large capacity syringe from the medical bag and twisted a fresh needle onto its end.

Kagan nodded slowly. "I see how it is," he said. "You've been carrying extra respirocytes in your veins, haven't you? Good place to hide them," he allowed. "But I can't let you deplete your own supply for me."

"Very gallant of you. But don't worry, I have a greater density than I need. I'll give you a few pints, and this should have a dramatic effect on your respiration and endurance. I calculate you'll be able to hold your breath for twelve to fifteen minutes. Respirocytes are universally compatible, so no blood type matching is necessary."

"Let me get this right," said Kagan. "You looked as if placing a comm in your ear was a hardship. And now you're proposing a battlefield blood transfusion?"

"I'm not going to lie to you," she said. "This is going to suck. But you'll notice your life changing after only a few minutes. The respirocytes will load up on O2 and do their thing."

"Should prove interesting."

"You have no idea. I know you think *Ory* is addictive. But wait until you get used to having four times the endurance of a doped Lance Armstrong. You'll never want to go back. And if you ever get a *full* dose, like I have, words can't even describe it. I feel more oxygenated after not taking a breath for forty-five minutes than you do after you've just inhaled."

"Are you sure you want to dilute your own supply?"

"Positive. But just because I'm sharing body fluid with you," she added in amusement, "doesn't mean that we're married or anything."

"Right," said Kagan. "It'll just be a routine sharing of artificial blood between friends."

"Exactly," replied Ella with a smile. She handed him the syringe. "It's easier if we do each other," she said. "I'll walk you through it."

Kagan nodded.

She directed him to a vein on her left arm, had him line up the needle, and then explained how to slide it in, bevel up. She scowled in pain on his first clumsy attempt, as he used too much force and missed her vein entirely, looking surprised that it had punctured her skin at all.

"I'm enhanced," she complained, "I'm not Superman. It's not like my skin can break needles. So be gentle, and it'll slide right in."

"Sorry about that," said Kagan sheepishly.

"How about using some of that superhuman focus of yours."

He nodded and tried again, this time succeeding. He carefully drew up the plunger, filling the syringe with bright red liquid.

"No way your respirocytes look this much like real blood," said Kagan. "My compliments on the mimicry."

"Thanks. The respirocytes seal wounds pretty fast, but you still lose some after an injury. Can't be leaking silver blood every time I get a papercut."

"I can see where that might arouse just a tiny bit of suspicion," he said with an amused smile.

"Are you ready?" asked Ella, holding out her hand for the syringe.

He nodded, but handed it to her with obvious reluctance. She took the full syringe and injected it into one of Kagan's veins, slowly and carefully. They repeated this process eight times, filling the syringe from her veins and emptying it into his. And the transfer seemed to get more unpleasant each time.

"I've shared body fluids with women before," noted Kagan halfway through the procedure, "but I've never shared a needle with one."

"First time for everything, I guess," she said. "My hope was to live forever, and during all of this eternity of life, to never have to share a needle. I guess this will make a banner entry in both of our diaries."

He was about to laugh when the respirocytes, diluted though they were, began to work their magic. He closed his eyes for several seconds, luxuriating in the profound vitality he was suddenly experiencing. "This is *amazing*," he said in awe. "I've never felt this good. Not even close."

Ella nodded. "Now you know why Dracula is so addicted to blood," she said with a smile.

# 39

Ella set off on the initial one-mile course that Seeker had provided, an Iranian's machete in hand, although the jungle here wasn't so dense that she needed to swing it just yet. Both Americans shook their heads in disgust as their path brought them past the gory remains of the magnificent Jaguar that an overzealous Aussie named Julius Barton had destroyed. But after less than three minutes this carcass, the small lake, and the collection of exotic birds disappeared behind them.

They spoke to each other in just above a whisper, to draw as little attention to themselves as possible, while their comms converted this whisper to full volume in their ears.

"The drone you used to find me was well within fifty yards of you when the Aussies showed up," said Ella. "Can I assume you kept it close, and operable, while we made our way to the lake?"

Kagan nodded. "That's right."

"Which means you have it flying along with us now, don't you?" she said. "And given your personality profile," she added, arching an eyebrow, "you're doing the gallant thing and having it keep an eye on me while it also acts as a lookout."

"Nobody likes a know-it-all," mumbled Kagan.

"Wishing for the old Ella?"

"Not so much," he said with a smile. Then, serious again, he added, "It's time we began our strategy session. But before we do, what are the odds that Seeker is listening to every word we say?"

"A hundred percent," replied Ella.

Kagan nodded grimly. "I was thinking 99.9—but I respect your conviction. Do you suppose it can read our minds?"

"I wouldn't be surprised. But for some reason I don't think it is—or will. That wouldn't be sporting. Even for it. But it's just a hunch, and I could be dead wrong."

"I agree with your hunch," said Kagan, "but we need to proceed as though you're wrong. To be on the safe side, we have to assume everything we say, hear, and even think is an open book to this thing."

"Agreed. But I say we don't stress too much about it. We have more than enough to stress about, as is. If you come up with a eureka idea to get us all out of this, keep it to yourself. But even if Seeker is aware of our plans, this doesn't mean we can't stop it."

Kagan sighed. "Yeah, it's more likely we can't stop it because it's an all-powerful entity. Because it can wield technology so advanced that we're like a bunch of Neanderthals with spears going up against the US Air Force."

Ella sighed, but chose to otherwise ignore this pessimistic, but accurate, assessment. "I say we begin with an examination of first principles," she said. "Let's question everything we think we know. And then question our questions. And then question that."

"Okay," said Kagan. "Let's start at the beginning. The first moments that Seeker communicated with us. You said you had some theories as to how this was accomplished."

"I'm thinking nanotech," said Ella. "Nanotech that puts our fledgling attempts to shame. I could be wrong. It could have used some sort of electromagnetic technique, for example, like microwave radiation, so exquisitely directed and controlled that it could cause the precise vibrations needed."

"But you don't think that's likely," said Kagan.

"No. I think it used the equivalent of nano-drones. Countless trillions of them, physically sent to the locations of all five or six hundred humans out here. Drones the size of bacteria, or smaller, but collectively capable of vibrating the air."

She paused. "This is just a hypothesis, but I've worked shoulder to shoulder with the world's best nanotechnologists, and I know the capabilities they fantasize about. They envision nanites that can convert raw materials at the atomic level into everything the nanites need to replicate. So one nanite can quickly grow into trillions, or even quadrillions. And I mean quickly. An E. Coli bacteria, which was once the principle workhorse of genetic engineers, can make a copy of itself in twenty minutes. So one E. Coli can become a million in seven hours. And each of these million can produce another million in another seven hours."

"So one becomes a trillion in just fourteen hours," said Kagan.

"That's right," said Ella. "And advanced enough nanites can theoretically do this even faster. Once you have as many trillions, or quadrillions, as you need, they can collectively work as erector sets, assembling anything you can imagine using atoms as building blocks, from quantum computers to aircraft carriers."

"Are you convinced Seeker has something like this in its arsenal?"

"I am," said Ella. "When it spoke of its information library, it mentioned nanotech as one of the technologies it can provide to the winning team. And if it really is the product of a species that reached the singularity, achieved transcendence, this sort of nanite would almost be a given. Technology indistinguishable from magic—times a billion."

"And this would explain how Seeker disappeared an Iranian corpse," noted Kagan.

"Disappeared an Iranian corpse?" said Ella. "What are you talking about?"

After confirming that Ella had missed this grisly demonstration, Kagan quickly described it.

She shuddered. "Seeker tried to give me a demonstration, telling me to watch a large fish nearby. But at the time I was focused on working my way closer to shore, preparing for a stealthy exit from the water, and I ignored it."

She frowned. "But this confirms my hypothesis. Nanites for sure. To build items atom by atom, nanites also have to be able to deconstruct things the same way. So dissolving matter like this would be the most basic of tasks for them."

They hiked on in silence, both deep in thought.

"Seeker tailored its message to hundreds of different people," pointed out Kagan after almost twenty seconds had passed. "In numerous languages. Not hard for a computer to multi-task like that.

But everything about how it mastered so many languages, and peppered its presentation with intimate knowledge of our lore and history, suggests to me that it's already sucked down the Internet. Maybe before it landed, maybe after."

"I agree," said Ella.

"So do we believe what it told us? About the so-called Androms? And about the ASI that defeated them?"

"We don't have much choice," said Ella. "I think we're forced to operate under the assumption that it's telling the truth. But remain wide open to the possibility that it isn't."

"Let's say we believe it, then," said Kagan. "Every word. If this is the case, why don't we believe what it's doing here is truly the best course? Seeker's version of tough love. We're both determined to defeat it. Determined to save the billions it intends to kill. But should we be? Or should we be focusing every ounce of energy on ensuring our team comes out on top? Whatever that even means."

"I can't believe you'd even ask that," said Ella.

"You were the one who said we should question everything. That's all I'm doing."

Ella stopped moving forward and turned, looking Kagan in the eye. "I apologize," she said. "You're absolutely right. And with respect to this question, there can be no good answer. All I can say is that for me, even if wiping out most of humanity really is the best long-term course, even if it really is critical for the survival of our species, I can't support it."

"I can't either," said Kagan. "But I didn't want to leave any stone unturned, which is why I posed the question. I'm not about to stand by and let most of humanity die, even to prevent its extinction millions or billions of years from now. If salvaging our species requires this kind of carnage, I'd rather let the chips fall where they fall."

"Good. So we're agreed that, even if we knew for sure that Seeker's strategy was the best course of action, we'd be against it."

Ella tilted her head in thought, and then shook her head. "But the thing is," she continued, "we can't ever really know that for sure, anyway. And Seeker can't either, as powerful as it is. And although we've decided to proceed—for now—as if it's telling the truth, we can't know its true motivations. We have trouble predicting the motivations of our fellow humans, and this is an AI from another galaxy. Who knows how it thinks? How much of its agenda is purposely hidden?"

"Good. Maybe we're getting somewhere, after all," said Kagan. "We agree that we need to stop Seeker at all costs. And we agree we have no good idea how to do this. So it seems to me that until we come up with one, our best course is to try to win this contest. We can't stop Seeker if we're dead. And if we win and gain partial control of it as a reward—which it promised would be the case—perhaps we can get it to spare humanity. So this has to be our primary goal."

"Agreed," said Ella. "At least until we can think of a more direct way to stop it."

"Of course."

"But we have no idea the criteria it's using to determine the winner."

"We have *some* idea," said Kagan. "It did share a few of the qualities it's looking for. We don't know how it plans to judge them, or how it will weigh one quality versus another, but we know cowardice, for example, won't win any points. And we know that staying alive and taking possession of the probe itself will score big."

"Okay then," said Ella Burke. "It looks like we have a plan. We just need to be utterly awesome in every way, and outdo more than eighty other teams."

Kagan sighed. "If only it were that easy," he said grimly. "As miraculous as that would be, it will just get us to the starting line. After that, we'll have to find a way to persuade a super-intelligent alien AI of the folly of its ways."

# 40

They had been marching forward for almost fifteen minutes now, and progress had been swift. Ella had only needed to wield the machete on rare occasions, although they knew this could change at any moment.

Kagan couldn't help but feel euphoric, despite their situation. The respirocytes he now carried were truly extraordinary. Getting oxygen to every last cell in the human body was a horrendously difficult proposition, and evolution had done a great job crafting the heart, blood, lungs, veins, arteries, and capillaries needed for the job.

But evolution never optimized. Once it found a solution good enough to ensure species survival, it was content.

The respirocytes, on the other hand, had been painstakingly optimized—and then some. Kagan felt like he was gliding over the ground. Like he could run forever in complete comfort, without feeling as though he was exerting himself at all—which was nearly the truth.

How fantastic must Ella feel? It was hard to even imagine.

The Amazon heat remained severe, the humidity oppressive. Even so, Kagan noted that he was barely sweating.

"Hold up!" said Ella, stopping abruptly. She tilted her head and strained to listen, ignoring the ever-present white noise of birds, insects, and other animals, while Kagan remained perfectly still.

"We've got company ahead," she whispered at imperceptible levels, her words amplified by Ory and delivered to Kagan's comm.

"Directly on the path Seeker gave us?" he whispered back, wishing the alien AI hadn't chosen to block his enhanced hearing in favor of Ella's.

"I'm not sure, but I think so. Not sure of their distance, either. I hear voices, but much too faint to pick out any words."

Even as she spoke, Kagan issued orders to Ory, and his lone micro-drone raced off ahead to see what they might be up against. "I've deployed our dragonfly to investigate," he told Ella when she had finished.

Thirty seconds later the drone transmitted video of an army of eight dark-skinned men to Kagan's visual field, armed to the teeth. Ory immediately identified their leader as Captain Bukola Saraki, a decorated Nigerian special forces operative, and transmitted this information next to Saraki's image on Kagan's augmented lenses. Ory's database once again proved to be remarkably comprehensive, even without Internet access.

Saraki was studying a tablet computer with a grim look on his face. His seven comrades, now silent, appeared hyper-alert. And they were much closer than Kagan would have liked.

He turned to Ella. "Our drone has eyes on eight Nigerians," he told her. "Approximately forty-five yards away. Each armed with assault rifles and more."

"How do you want to play this?" she asked.

Kagan considered. Under the conditions in place when he had first arrived here, a large force was a liability, too unwieldy and too easy to locate. But that had changed. With limited sensors, a more level playing field, and intense motivation to shoot first and ask questions later, superior manpower had become a significant advantage.

Given that there were five hundred ninety-four participants from eighty-eight countries, the average team was almost seven members strong. Which meant that he and Ella were destined to be on the short end of the manpower stick every time.

Still, Kagan thought it likely that the two of them could easily best eight unenhanced soldiers, even accomplished commandoes. Especially now that Ella had given him an oxygen boost to go with his EHO augmentations. But why put this to the test?

Besides, he had no beef with Nigeria. And he wasn't inclined to blithely let Seeker push him into acts of barbarism.

"I say we stay out of their way," he began. "I'd rather take possession of this probe by avoiding conflict whenever possible. I say we pursue the course you laid out by the lake: strategic inaction.

Strategic avoidance of engagement. Unless you worry that Seeker will view this behavior as cowardice."

"It might. But it might also view it as prudence. Or brilliance, even."

"Good point. We know so little that it doesn't make sense to second-guess ourselves."

"The only possible downside I see," said Ella, "is that if we don't kill them now, they might be the ones who kill *us* later."

Kagan gave this some serious thought. "I'm willing to take that chance," he said finally.

Ella nodded. "So am I," she replied. "So let's give them a wide berth until we can get back on course."

*"Alert!"* said Ory into the comms of both Americans, *"I'm detecting four drones that are now within visual range of us. Given the limitations of controlling drones at a distance, they almost certainly belong to the Nigerians."*

While Ory spoke, the video feed displayed on Kagan's contact lenses showed Saraki's head bolting upward from his tablet computer, where he must have been watching the video feed coming from numerous drones. "We have a visual on two people," he said in English, which was Nigeria's official language. "One male and one female. Their coordinates show them to be about forty yards east of us. I'll lead the way. When we get closer, we'll spread out and take them both down."

"Even the woman?" asked one of his subordinates, who, along with the rest of the team, now assumed a combat posture, his weapon facing forward.

Saraki sighed, and then nodded unhappily. "You heard Seeker's threats. You saw what it did to that poor anteater. We can't afford to show mercy."

While Ella couldn't get a visual like Kagan did through his lenses, she heard Saraki's words through her comm with perfect clarity. She caught her partner's eye and shook her head. "So much for strategic avoidance," she said glumly.

"Not necessarily," said Kagan, as he and Ella began to beat a hasty retreat from the approaching Nigerians. "We can both move a lot faster through the jungle than they can. If we can get enough of a lead, beyond the range of communication and control that Seeker is allowing, their drones won't be able to follow."

"True, but they seem to have a lot of them. So we'll never be sure they won't pick us up later. And they'll be able to use them to establish a defense perimeter with a fifty-yard radius. At some point we'll have to get through them to get to the first node on the trip Seeker laid out for us."

Kagan's mind continued to operate with absolute clarity, as it always did in life-and-death situations, turning the world into a slow-motion version of itself. "Maybe we can turn their drones into a liability," he said. "There's always the chance that Ory can hack them." He paused. "What about it, Ory?"

"*Checking now*," replied the AI, and then, only seconds later, added, "*I'm in, and I have control. What would you like me to have them do?*"

"Very nice, Ben," said Ella appreciatively, as they continued their headlong rush away from the incoming hostiles. "So what's the plan from here?"

"I'm not sure," said Kagan, pausing in thought. "The smartest play would be to lead them into an ambush and eliminate them. To assume that now that they know we're out here, it's either us, or them. We won't get any points for compassion, and we'll probably lose points. Besides, unless they win this contest, which is unlikely, Seeker will kill them all anyway."

"I sense a *but* coming," said Ella.

"*But*," said Kagan, right on cue, "I can't do it." Ella looked anything but surprised. "I'm still holding out hope that we can triumph and get Seeker to spare us all. Here, and around the globe."

"So any Plan Bs come to mind?"

"Maybe," he said after a few seconds of thought. "Ory, can you create false video images of us for the drones to transmit back to their bosses? Images that can lead them away from us?"

"*I'm afraid not, Ben*," replied the AI.

"We don't need to be that sophisticated," said Ella, brightening. "Right idea, just the wrong execution. Let the drones film us accurately. Just have them send back false GPS information for our position. The jungle looks pretty much the same everywhere. So who's to know that we're really going east when the drones tell them we're going west?"

"Outstanding," said Kagan. "Ory?" he said to his AI. "Please tell me this is something you can do."

"*It is. Just say the word.*"

Kagan was about to respond when multiple gunshots exploded toward them from the direction they were now heading.

Ella was in the lead, and the first shot missed her by inches.

She dove to the side as additional shots came her way, and only her superhuman reflexes and speed saved her from being punctured by several rounds. She was faster than Kagan, who would likely have been killed if he had been leading.

Without missing a beat Ella came up firing, to give whoever was firing at them pause, and then reversed course, bolting through the jungle with a purpose. Kagan did the same, although both were firing blindly before they turned tail, neither able to identify a single shooter.

"What the hell?" said Kagan as he raced away from flying bullets, never knowing when one might find the back of his head. Their attempt to evade the Nigerians had led them right into the teeth of a new, currently unknown, threat.

They ran together for several brief seconds until Ella easily pulled ahead, despite wearing rubber boots that were somewhat ill-fitting. Additional shots continued to ring out behind them, sending bark and bits of waxy green leaves flying near their path. But the dense array of trees stopped every bullet before it found its mark, helped by their speed and the followers' inability to get a clear line of sight on them.

At least so far.

Given the difficult terrain, the speed Kagan was managing was truly impressive. Even so, he couldn't get enough of a lead to risk turning to try to learn what he and Ella were up against.

"Ory," he said urgently, "redeploy our drone. I need to know what's behind us."

"*Redeploying now,*" came the immediate response.

"Ella, don't slow down for me," he said, words that Ory transmitted to her comm. "I'll catch up."

"I'm guessing I'm about fifteen yards ahead," she replied. "I'll stay within fifty yards so we can maintain communication."

"Roger that," said Kagan.

Inexplicably, the gunfire kept coming from what he judged to be about the same distance. How was his pursuer possibly keeping up with him?

Less than a minute later the drone rushed into position and new visuals appeared on his lenses. Kagan made out four men, all of them Chinese, and all four included in Ory's database.

The AI identified each as elite members of the Guangzhou Military Region Special Forces Unit, also known as the *South China Sword*, China's equivalent of the Navy SEALs. Major Hou Meng was commanding this small group, and he was considered by US intelligence to be among the most lethal men in the world.

Kagan only had to watch these men chew up the terrain for a few brief seconds before he came to an inescapable conclusion: this tiny unit of the South China Sword wasn't the equivalent of the Navy SEALS. It was the equivalent of *EHO*.

The four Chinese soldiers were each wearing powered exoskeletons, bulkier than what Kagan was wearing, but likely more effective. And they were sure to have genetic modifications similar to Ella's. Just because she had left China, didn't mean that the country had given up on genetically engineered enhancements.

*No wonder* he wasn't gaining on them.

How had Ben Kagan, elite agent of America's Enhanced Human Operations forces, become the slowest runner in an six-person race?

Thankfully, Ella's nanotechnologists were better than those fielded by the Chinese, as the heavy breathing of the men behind him indicated they didn't have respirocytes running through their veins. It was the only reason Kagan was still alive.

"Ella," he said quickly, which Ory dutifully transmitted to her comm, "there are four men after us. All members of South China Sword, under Major Hou Meng, and all enhanced. They don't have respirocytes, so you're still faster. But I'm having trouble gaining on them."

"Understood," said Ella. "I have an idea. I'll get enough ahead of you to turn and throw grenades over your head to take them out."

"Won't work," said Kagan immediately. "You couldn't possibly throw a grenade more than fifteen feet without the jungle batting it down. It's just as likely that you'd hit me as you would them. Unless you're able to find more open terrain, like it was by the lake."

"I'll try," said Ella.

Kagan frowned. "Actually, I take back what I just said. Given that they're enhanced, and far better trained than we are, we're in trouble. So if you get any kind of opening to use the grenades, even if I'm at risk, you have to take it."

"There's no way I'll do that, Ben," she replied firmly. "We either both make it, or neither of us do."

Kagan could tell by the tone in her voice that this was the final word on the matter. Instead of wasting time on additional arguments, he redoubled his efforts to maximize his speed. If he was to have any hope, he needed to start putting distance between himself and the men behind him. He had been dodging trees and endless obstacles, but now he rushed headlong through vines and dense leaves without checking first for thorns or dangerous predators.

He could no longer afford to be cautious. Because the most dangerous predators the planet had ever seen were right on his heels.

He wondered if even an enhanced Houdini could get out of this one.

It was then that multiple barrages of machine gun fire exploded through the jungle up ahead, competing with the gunfire still coming from behind him.

# 41

Ella Burke broke through a wall of giant taro leaves and narrowly avoided a direct collision with an approaching Nigerian. As he pointed a machine gun at her, she whipped around and swept his legs out from under him. The back of the man's head crashed into a root on the ground, possibly knocking him out. Even so, Ella didn't wait to be sure, launching herself backwards, slamming the heavy backpack she had taken from a dead Iranian into the Nigerian's face, rendering him unconscious, or worse.

Just as she landed, her enhanced hearing picked up footsteps to her left. In one smooth motion she gathered up the Nigerian's machine gun, rolled off his body, and fired in this direction, obliterating one of his comrades, but not before he managed to get off a shot that grazed Ella's arm.

She took a quick survey of her surroundings and sprang to her feet, her enhanced muscles allowing her to do so in one motion. No other hostiles were in sight. In her haste to evade the Chinese, she had almost forgotten about the Nigerians. She glanced at her arm, but the wound was so superficial that her respirocytes had already plugged it.

"Ben, you're on a collision course with the Nigerians," she said hastily. "They've fanned out."

She paused as a third member of this team broke through the trees, his finger on the trigger of his weapon, but she put him down so quickly he couldn't even begin to depress it. His bloody body added to those already on the jungle floor, which would soon help feed a wide variety of wildlife.

"Three of the eight are down," continued Ella without missing a beat. Only about fifteen seconds had elapsed since she had almost run headlong into the first Nigerian. "I'm guessing that I'm still about twenty-five yards ahead of you," she added. "When you see bodies on the ground, I recommend finding a place to hide and letting the Chinese and Nigerians run into each other."

"Understood," said her trailing partner.

\* \* \*

Kagan rushed on. As hopeless as his predicament seemed, he was counting his blessings. When he had heard the machine gun fire he had feared the worst. But Ella was alive and well.

This came as a much-needed relief. Now he just needed to be sure that he stayed alive, too.

They were being whipsawed by two different groups of hostiles, but Ella's strategy of engineering a collision course between these two groups, which he could sidestep at the last second, just might work.

But this would be the last time he would fear for Ella's life in total ignorance. "Ory," he commanded, "send the drone to Ella's position. I want it within visual range of her at all times," he added, returning it to the mission it had been on before he had been forced to redeploy it.

As Ory responded and began to carry out this order, Kagan spied a gory Nigerian body on the jungle floor not far away, and frantically searched for a place to hide.

He had maybe twenty seconds before the Chinese would have him in their line of sight. Given they were each expert marksmen, the moment they could get off a clean shot, he was as good as dead.

They would have been much closer, but the sound of heavy gunfire ahead had slowed them down, causing them to exercise at least a modicum of caution.

Kagan spied a giant taro plant and rushed to its five, low-growing leaves, each waxy-green and shaped like the ear of an African elephant, longer and wider than he was. He lowered himself beneath the magnificent leaves, thankful once again for Ella's gift of respirocytes, which continued to keep him alive. This time not by improving his speed and endurance, but by allowing him to hide quietly, without gasping for breath.

An additional burst of gunfire tore through the rainforest ahead of him, about forty feet from his position.

"Four Nigerians down, four to go," reported Ella helpfully, just as the drone caught up to her and began sending video of her and her surroundings back to Kagan's lenses.

Kagan swallowed hard. This was good news, but it was the four Chinese behind him that posed the greatest threat.

Even as he thought this, he realized they were no longer behind him. He could hear their breathing and heavy footsteps as they rushed by the giant taro plant.

Kagan peered over the edge of one massive leaf to watch the four commandoes after they had passed him. If the remaining Nigerians failed to engage them, he would leave his cover and follow, sandwiching the Chinese soldiers between himself and Ella, a tactical improvement in their position.

This thought was short-lived, however, as the four remaining Nigerians spotted the approaching Chinese force and sent bursts of machine gun fire in their direction. The Chinese commandoes darted behind trees and quickly returned fire.

Seconds later, Major Hou Meng barked a command, and two of his men laid down extensive cover fire while he and another of his team raced ahead once again on their original course.

"*Ella, two of the Chinese are engaging the remaining Nigerians,*" he reported subvocally through Ory. "*But two are still coming your way.*"

Now that the Nigerians outnumbered their superior, enhanced rivals, Kagan hoped they might prevail, but this was not to be. After less than a minute, the Chinese picked off two of them, making their forces even, and the other two Nigerians wouldn't last much longer.

Kagan braced himself. It was time to act. Hidden, and with the Chinese distracted, it was now or never.

He found his footing and repositioned himself, rising just above one tremendous leaf and firing, putting a bullet through the head of one of the Chinese soldiers. He moved to the second target before even confirming that the first was down. But as fast as Kagan was, the Chinese commando was even faster, diving to the ground with catlike grace, and Kagan's bullets bounced harmlessly off his powered exoskeleton.

The man didn't waste an instant, returning fire with such accuracy that Kagan was forced to dive to the other side of the taro plant to get out of sight.

The two remaining Nigerians exited their cover and rushed forward, seizing the chance to take out the last hostile while he was preoccupied with Kagan, but the Chinese soldier anticipated this move, wheeling around and shooting them both before either could get off a shot of their own.

At the same time he rolled to his right, causing Kagan's renewed fire to miss, and came up holding a grenade, which he lobbed at the taro plant. The resulting blast destroyed the magnificent plant, reducing the largest leaves on Earth to shrapnel.

Kagan just managed to race far enough away from the explosion to survive it, but he was blown off his feet. This time, at least, he managed to retain consciousness.

He picked himself up off the ground and bolted forward as the Chinese commando came toward him, firing, putting Kagan on the run, and on defense, once again.

\* \* \*

Ella heard the sounds of an extended firefight behind her, followed by a grenade going off, and began to panic as she imagined Ben Kagan being torn to pieces by the blast. Even though her intellect told her it was more likely that Kagan, himself, had thrown the grenade, her heart had turned into mush, and the thought of losing him now seemed too much to bear.

"Ben, are you okay?" she said urgently, trying to keep panic from her voice as she continued to glide through the jungle.

After several seconds with no response, she felt sick to her stomach. "Ory, report!" she demanded.

*"The Nigerians are all dead. One of the two Chinese soldiers who engaged them is dead. But Ben has his hands full with the other. I'll advise if anything changes."*

Ella was relieved, but only somewhat. Ben was alive, true, but that might not be the case much longer. For him not to have responded to her communication, he must be in dire straits.

Even as she thought this, her own situation suddenly took a turn for the worse, as she arrived at a stretch of swampland that seemed endless. The water was at knee height or greater, and it was the most expansive swamp she or Ben had yet encountered.

And there was no way around it.

Ella quickly waded into the swamp, trying to be decisive, but this was a mistake. After less than twenty feet she decided her progress through the mud and water was too slow. If she didn't return to dry land, she'd be a sitting duck for the two men still after her.

She waded back the way she had come, not knowing that her presence in the swamp had signaled a four-hundred-pound anaconda, twenty feet in length, looking for a meal. Just as she was about to exit onto dry land, the massive green predator lunged at her from under the water. She jerked her body to the side with inhuman speed, narrowly avoiding the snake's mouth and body, foiling its attempt to wrap her in a coil of pure muscle and choke the life out of her.

She raced from the swamp before the anaconda could make a second attempt, knowing it would be cumbersome on land, but tripped over a tree root just as she was getting out of range and crashed to the jungle floor. The moment she landed she scampered forward on her hands and knees to put as much distance between herself and the snake as possible.

Multiple gunshots flew past her as she moved, and several found the Anaconda's head, ending it as a threat. Even so, its massive body continued to twitch, even after death.

Ella put on the brakes as she came to the two men responsible for killing the enormous snake, who were now facing her at point-blank range, guns extended.

The swamp had delayed her for too long. The two elite soldiers from the South China Sword had arrived—possibly saving her life—although she had no doubt they would also soon be ending it.

She rose from a crouching position, her hands raised over her head. And while her speed had kept her alive against commandoes and anacondas alike, even she wasn't a fast enough draw to kill these two men, enhanced as they were, before they killed her.

\* \* \*

Kagan continued to dodge bullets, just managing to stay enough ahead of the Chinese commando to cheat death. The drone was keeping tabs on Ella, as he had ordered, and a shadowy feed remained in his field of view, not interfering with this own vision as he focused on staying alive.

He risked a quick glance at the feed and saw video images that caused his breath to catch in his throat.

Ella was stumbling forward on her hands and knees, followed by a green snake so absurdly large that it looked as if it belonged in a Godzilla movie. Suddenly, the snake's head was almost ripped from its body. The drone turned to show that the two Chinese commandoes who had been chasing her had been responsible, and now had Ella dead to rights.

As amazing as she was, she didn't have a prayer.

At least not on her own.

The drone's feed suddenly went blank.

"Noooo!" screamed Kagan. "Ory, what happened to the feed? get it back!"

"*I can't,*" replied the AI. "*You've moved out of range.*"

Kagan felt himself panicking. He *had* to get back into range. Whatever it took. Whatever the risk.

But he knew that even if he did, he'd be too late to save her.

\* \* \*

The two Chinese commandoes were seconds away from giving Ella the same treatment they had just given the anaconda.

"Don't shoot, you idiots!" yelled Ella, and only the fact that she had said this in perfect, unaccented Chinese caused them to hold their fire. "I'm on your side."

Both men hesitated, stunned looks on their faces.

"Is that what they teach you in the South China Sword, Major?" added Ella. "To kill helpless women?"

Hou Meng's mouth dropped open, but he quickly recovered, his gun never wavering. "Under normal circumstances, I would never kill a woman," he said in Chinese. "But these are anything but normal circumstances. And you've shown yourself to be anything but helpless."

"Do you have any idea who I am?" she barked.

Both men shook their heads.

"I'm Dr. Ella Burke."

The eyes of the two commandoes widened. Both instantly recognized the name of the most famous scientist to have come out of their country in decades. A woman born in America, but raised in China. A woman who had done remarkable work for the glory of her adopted country. And she was especially legendary to *them*, given that she had paved the way for China's enhancement program, of which they were both a part.

"That's right," she continued. "I've been off the grid for some time now, working on special projects for your boss, General Gong Li. He ordered me to join you here."

The major looked confused. "Join us?"

"Yes, he felt this mission was important enough for me to reveal myself. Why else would I be here? How else would I know who you are?"

Hou Meng glanced at his subordinate and then paused for almost a full minute, deep in thought.

"I believe that you're Ella Burke," he said finally. "I do. It explains how you can be even faster than we are, and your fluency in Chinese. But even if you really are on our side, which I doubt based upon your actions, I can't help you. The probe made it very clear that our team consisted of the four men who were together when it contacted us. It made it clear that no reinforcements, additions, or collaborations would be allowed."

"So now you take your marching orders from an alien computer?" snapped Ella in contempt. "Is that what you're saying?"

The major shook his head and prepared to fire. "I'm sorry," he said sadly. "I really am. But we have no other choice. If we thought we did, we would take it. You're too formidable to spare, but know this: our goal is humanitarian. We plan to win this contest and convince the probe not to carry out its threat."

"I can help you with that," said Ella. "Really."

\* \* \*

Ben Kagan stopped on a dime and turned, ignoring the approaching commando and the bullets that continued to fly toward him. He pulled the pin on a grenade and threw it as hard as he could, trying to miss the many tree trunks and branches in its way to get maximum distance.

As he had feared, it didn't get far, hitting a tree-branch and ricocheting back toward him, exploding nearer to him than to his target.

Still, the explosion sent a message to the man following. That tactics had changed, and that he needed to be cautious. Body armor might be able to stop a bullet, but not a grenade.

Kagan followed up his first throw with another, this time managing to chuck the explosive closer to its target, where its concussive force shook its surroundings like an earthquake.

He hoped this would give the Chinese soldier pause, but he had no time to be sure, rushing back the way he had come, on a slightly different vector.

Suddenly, as hoped, the feed from the drone returned. He was close enough to help Ella, and he was still alive. And one glance at the feed showed that—miraculously—so was she.

How was this possible? These men had seemed too smart to hesitate this long when they had a dangerous foe in their sights.

"You're too formidable to spare," the major was saying to Ella, his Chinese words scrolling in English across Kagan's augmented lenses, exactly reflecting what Kagan had just been thinking. Except that Hou Meng *had* spared her—at least for a minute or two. Why?

"But know this," continued the major, "our goal is humanitarian. We plan to win this contest and convince the probe not to carry out its threat."

"I can help you with that," said Ella. "Really."

"I have no doubt you would be a great asset to us," said the leader of the Chinese team, his words continuing to scroll in Kagan's line of sight. "If you only knew how much I admire you as a scientist. How tempted I am to take you up on your offer. I would love nothing more than to speak with you at length. To get to know the legend. To see your genius in action."

The major shook his head. "But the probe was quite clear. And your very presence here is so unlikely, you might just be a probe-constructed mirage. It might be testing my resolve. Docking my team for every second I delay doing what I know I must. And we can't afford to lose any points. The lives of billions of people are on the line."

Kagan's focus was greater than ever, and the words seeming to scroll by in super slow-motion. While Hou Meng recited Ella's death sentence, Kagan hastily sent orders to Ory, ignoring a bullet that plowed into a tree inches from his face, kicking off a shard of bark that ripped a two-inch cut across his cheek.

\* \* \*

Ella had no doubt that Hou Meng was horrified by the prospect of killing her, and was looking for a way out, but her attempts to give him one had failed. Seeker had stacked the deck too steeply against her.

She prepared to go for her gun. She had no chance, destined to be torn to pieces, but she wouldn't take a bullet like a sheep. She had nothing to lose.

"If you only knew how much I admire you as a scientist," said the major. "How tempted I am to take you up on your offer. I would love nothing more than to speak with you at length. To get to know the legend. To see your genius in action.

"But the probe was quite clear. And your very presence here is so unlikely, you might just be a probe-constructed mirage. It might be testing my resolve. Docking my team for every second I delay doing what I know I must. And we can't afford to lose any points. The lives of billions of people are on the line."

Ella was an instant away from drawing her gun when a deafening barrage of machine gun fire exploded at point-blank range behind the two Chinese. Both dived to the ground and rolled, coming up firing behind them.

But there was no one there.

Having been facing the two men, Ella knew that no one had snuck up on them, so she didn't instinctively move to evade the phantom fire. Instead, in a single instant, she drew her weapon and picked off both commandoes as they fired at an invisible enemy.

She closed her eyes and let relief course through her body. She felt euphoric to still be alive. "Ben, was that you?" she asked.

"Yes. I had the drone fly behind them and simulate machine gun fire."

"Thank you! You're a godsend!"

"Now I need *your* help," he said urgently. "I'm pinned and taking fire, and I can't hold out much longer. I'd repeat the drone trick, but their shots just took it out."

"I'm on my way!" said Ella, already on the move. If Ory directed her to a position behind the man firing on Kagan, she knew she wouldn't miss. "Hang tight, Ben, I'll be there soon."

"Hurry!" implored Kagan unnecessarily.

# 42

Ella tore through the jungle even faster than she had when her own life was in jeopardy, driven by the need to reach Kagan in time. For several minutes now she had been dying to contact him, confirm he was still alive, but distracting him now was the worst thing she could do.

Finally, she was so close to her destination that she needed to give him a heads-up. "I'll be in position to take out the target in ten seconds," she said. "Please confirm."

"Hurry!" said Kagan again.

He was hanging on by a thread. The South China Sword commando had been inching his way closer since Kagan had saved Ella's life, craftily finding better angles on the American, shrinking his avenues of escape. He had hit Kagan twice already, but both times Kagan's chain-mail body armor had absorbed the painful blows and saved his life. But it wouldn't be long before a bullet impacted his head, which was only protected by a cage of bone that was easily penetrated.

Suddenly, from out of nowhere, fifteen or twenty small explosions rocked the jungle surrounding him, creating geysers of thick smoke that shot six stories into the air. The clouds materialized in an instant, driven by the high-speed release of gas from ultra-pressurized tanks, carefully positioned by AIs good enough to navigate the tanks through jungle foliage.

The clouds were immense, producing a thick fog of gas at least a square block in area. The fog was so dense, vision was limited to three or four feet, just as Ella had the Chinese soldier in her sights, forcing her to hold her fire.

"*Don't breathe!*" shouted Ory into the comms of both Americans. "*My sensors indicate this gas is XJ-45. Highly potent. Deadly if inhaled. I calculate it will dissipate in ten minutes.*"

Ella and Kagan both stopped breathing, as instructed.

Twenty seconds later, a heavy rain began to fall.

It took five or ten more seconds for them to realize what this was. When they did, they barely managed to continue holding their breath, and to choke down the screams that had arisen in both of their throats.

The rain had nothing to do with precipitation. It was raining *wildlife*.

It was a rainfall of small mammals, monkeys, lizards, spiders, and snakes.

But mostly it was a shower of *bugs*. Many tens of thousands of them.

Bugs that were plummeting down to the rainforest floor, dislodged from the vast surface area of leaves and trees and nests they had occupied above, as the lethal gas infiltrated their passive oxygenation systems with ease.

It was a rainstorm out of a nightmare, as an endless variety of insects, large and small, slammed into their heads and bodies like hail, somehow bouncing off the leaves and trees they were using as cover to reach them.

Entomologists had been fogging jungle canopies with gas for many decades, allowing them to identify thousands of different insect species from the fogging of just a dozen trees, and collect tens of thousands of insects in total. But the entomologists had the good sense to cover the jungle floor with huge, funnel-shaped collecting trays, and get the hell out of the kill-zone.

The humans trapped within this manmade cloud didn't have that luxury.

Finally, after what seemed like an eternity, the horrible, surreal rain of insects finally ceased. Kagan would have let out a sigh of relief had he not still been holding his breath. He brushed dead bugs out of his hair and clothing, his face curled up in disgust.

His contact lenses were now in IR mode, allowing him to see heat signatures, restoring a semblance of distance vision. The IR mode wasn't perfect, but this was one area in which Kagan's bag of tricks was better than Ella's, who hadn't yet found a biological way to create IR vision.

The Chinese soldier who had pinned Kagan had held his breath for almost three minutes before he was finally forced to inhale, and was now lying dead on the forest floor, resting on a hideous lawn of dead spiders, lizards, frogs, and insects. The gas was already beginning to clear, and with the respirocytes' help, Kagan was sure he could hold his breath until the air was safe to breathe again.

Kagan watched in dismay as heat images of five men came into view, each wearing a gas mask. The men responsible for this latest attack.

While visibility with the naked eye was still not great, the gas had risen, making the jungle floor readily observable, and they were able to take a survey of the carnage they had wrought. They spotted the fallen Chinese soldier and stopped above him, taking inventory of this kill, oblivious to Kagan's presence in the distance.

"*Tell Ella that we have company*," he said subvocally to Ory, "*wearing gas masks. Tell her not to move, to prepare for machine gun fire, and that I'll have the situation under control very soon.*"

Kagan moved carefully to a position with a clear line of fire, stepping gingerly through the sea of dead bugs in an attempt to crush them as quietly as possible.

Whichever country these men were from, their strategy had been nearly unbeatable, turning everyone but themselves into termites trapped inside a tented home. Everyone but those who happened to be harboring respirocytes.

Kagan couldn't blame them for being overconfident, for missing his presence. They had no reason to unholster their weapons, no reason to look anywhere but the jungle floor. The sheer lethality of the gas made them certain that nothing that was previously alive was still standing.

After all, it had been seven minutes since their attack, and no one could possibly hold their breath for this long.

But this inattention and overconfidence was now working against them.

Kagan raised his automatic weapon and sprayed all five men thoroughly. Each quickly fell on top of the lawn of insects they had created, as helpless against Kagan's barrage as the wildlife they had just exterminated had been against their gas. Kagan kept the trigger depressed for almost ten full seconds, until he was satisfied that none of them would move again.

"*Ella,*" he said, communicating subvocally through Ory since the AI still hadn't indicated it was safe to breathe, "*all hostiles are down. I'm on my way to you now.*

"*Let's get the hell out of here,*" he added in disgust.

# 43

Ben Kagan and Ella Burke found three large boulders that were clear of anything deadly and sat, needing to get back on course to Seeker's first mile marker, but needing to take a mental break and digest what had just happened even more. Kagan still had a gash in his cheek, and both had cuts and bruises in too many places to count, although none of the cuts were still bleeding.

Both looked shell-shocked, and both were clearly sickened by the many lives they had taken. Kagan's expression was one of sadness and disgust, while Ella's eyes, normally blazing with a vibrant intelligence, were vacant, lifeless.

They may have been in top condition physically, but they were shattered psychologically.

They had just killed seventeen men. *Seventeen*. And the after-effects of this carnage were now catching up to them with a vengeance.

Kagan had resigned himself to killing bad guys, the rare times this had proven necessary. And this was bad enough. But killing innocents in a forced battle was not what he had signed up for.

And Ella had *never* taken a life before arriving in the jungle.

Now she had snuffed out handfuls, in addition to the Iranians, which had been troubling enough.

Before leaving the kill-zone, Kagan had removed the gas mask from one of the men responsible, and Ory had identified him as a Colombian. Which meant that this country, fifty million people strong, was now out of contention.

And the entire population of Colombia would pay for this failure with their lives.

China was now out of contention as well, the most populous country in the world.

The knowledge that they had killed so many innocents would have been hard enough to bear under normal circumstances, but now Seeker had made the consequences truly unspeakable. The deaths of each Nigerian and Colombian to have fallen in the Amazon would be amplified ten million fold, and each Chinese death four hundred million fold.

Ella's vacant expression took a turn for the worse, and a tear escaped her eye. "The worst part," she said with a shudder, "is that I was so fully *engaged*. When I killed those men by the swamp, what I felt was closer to *glee* than to horror. How could I turn into such a monster?"

Kagan felt horrible himself, but he couldn't let her do this to herself. "You can't beat yourself up like that, Ella," he said softly. "Bloodlust during battle is a survival mechanism, molded by evolution. You know that better than I do."

Ella nodded. "You're right," she said woodenly. "I know it intellectually. But to actually experience it . . . " She shuddered again.

Kagan handed her a full canteen of water, and she took a long swig.

"I can't argue with what you're feeling," he said. "I'm feeling it too. We can mourn those we killed, and the necessity of having to transform into cold-blooded killers. We can curse evolution for the positive reinforcement we get from killing during battle." He shook his head. "But we have to lick our psychological wounds and move on."

"You're right," she said weakly. "Too much is at stake to wallow in self-loathing. But give me just a few more minutes."

Kagan nodded. The truth was that he could use a few minutes himself, to battle the demons that came from becoming a mass murderer, to wrestle with his conscience.

He passed several more energy bars to Ella, and ate two himself, while they remained silent. Ella kept her head down, facing the ground, absently eating the bars as though this was a chore. Finally, she took one last swig of water, handed him back the canteen, and rose.

She took a deep breath, and her sorrowful expression transformed into one of resolve once again. Her eyes ignited back to life. "Let's get moving," she said, the vigor returning to her voice.

Kagan rose himself, relieved that she had pulled out of her temporary emotional tailspin. "Sure, let's hike through the Amazon," he said with the hint of a smile. "Why not try something new for a change."

His attempt at levity had no effect on her. Perhaps it had come too soon. "After you," he said. "And while we're at it," he added, "we need to figure out what the hell just happened."

"What happened is that Seeker set us up," she said bitterly as they began moving once again. "Repeatedly."

"Yeah. There's no doubt that this little alien bastard was responsible. It controls all the cards, and it provides all the routes." Kagan shook his head. "If it would have led all four teams to a simultaneous collision course, that would have been bad enough. But at least in that case, the three other, larger groups, would have decimated each other, and all of their focus wouldn't have been on us."

"I thought the same," said Ella. "It made sure we encountered each of the three forces separately—sequentially. If we weren't focused on sidestepping the Nigerians, the Chinese could never have surprised us as completely as they did. Seeker distracted us with a weak threat, so we'd be blindsided by the strongest threat of all."

"Wheels within wheels," said Kagan. "We outlasted the Chinese and survived. But if they had outlasted us, they would have all been killed by the Colombian gas attack."

A flash of rage crossed Ella's features. "How is any of this a proper test of anything?" she demanded. "How does this tell Seeker anything about cultures and philosophies? About post-singularity potential? It's just cruel and voyeuristic. Gladiator entertainment, with the jungle being the alien equivalent of the Roman Colosseum. The countries involved should have been able to choose who *they* wanted to send here to represent them. Some might have sent their best scientists, philosophers, or debaters. Others might have sent their most creative. Or their most generous. Or even their best chess players."

"You're right, of course," said Kagan, frowning. "Instead, Seeker ensures that the best *warriors* are gathered here. Which makes the contest almost entirely physical. How does this tell Seeker anything about a given nation's suitability to prevail in a war to come? Especially since this war will take place on an *intellectual* plane so rarified we can't even imagine it. Which will make our current physical skills, like speed and marksmanship, completely irrelevant."

Kagan paused. "And its premise that the gestalt of a group is tied to the nation it came from," he added, "or that it's possible to identify a unified set of defining qualities across varied individuals, is preposterous. Take Nigeria. I recently had an assignment there. It's the most populated country in Africa, with two hundred million inhabitants. But the thing is, there is no way that the eight men who just died, by themselves, could be even a little representative of this country. Nigeria embodies the greatest mishmash of cultures of any nation in the world. Over five hundred different ethnic groups call it home. And while English is its official language, hundreds of other languages are also spoken. *Hundreds*. Not even Seeker could possibly distill out truly representative archetypes from this soup."

Ella nodded. "I'm willing to stipulate that Seeker is vastly smarter than we are," she said. "But we can't use this as a catchall to excuse whatever irrational, seemingly arbitrary move it makes."

She shook her head in disgust. "Remember what a fuss it made about ensuring the playing field was level? Yet it distracted us with one threat before introducing another. It forced us to face three threats in a row. It sandwiched us between hostile forces. Is this really Seeker's idea of fair play?"

Kagan considered. "Some of its ground rules make sense, like forcing every team to cover the same distance. But others seem completely arbitrary, with no rhyme or reason. It deems that setting us up for sequential ambushes is perfectly fair. But so is allowing us and the Chinese to use enhancements that other groups don't have. Apparently, there are no anti-doping regulations here. And drones and communications are only good for fifty yards. And while *your* amplified biological hearing is okay, my comm-assisted hearing . . . not so much. What is Seeker's logic for *any* of this?"

Ella stopped in mid-stride, so abruptly that Kagan almost crashed into her.

She turned to face him, and her eyes were fiery with sudden inspiration, more alive than ever. "Good question," she said simply. "So why don't we ask it?"

"What?" replied Kagan, taken aback.

"Why don't we ask Seeker for clarification? We know it's monitoring us. Since it made its big speech and disappeared, we've just assumed that it wouldn't communicate with us further. But it just occurred to me that it never explicitly said this was the case. We jumped to this conclusion on our own. Something I suspect it wanted us to do. But while it never volunteered to chitchat, it never ruled it out, either."

Kagan nodded slowly. "Nicely reasoned," he said in admiration. "It's definitely worth a try. And there's only one way to find out." He gestured to Ella. "Since it's your idea, why don't you do the honors."

She nodded. "Okay," she said. "Here goes nothing."

She took a deep breath and then let it out slowly. Finally, she was ready. "Seeker!" she called out. "We know you're listening. And Ben and I have some questions we'd like to ask you. Please respond."

Time seemed to stand still as they waited to see what would happen.

"Ask your questions," replied the disembodied voice of the alien AI. "And I'll decide which ones I'm willing to answer."

# PART 8

# 44

Ben Kagan glanced at his companion as though she were a magician—which she was.

She had been *right*. From where had she possibly pulled the inspiration that Seeker would answer their call, while they were playing its game?

Her logic had been sound. Seeker hadn't explicitly said it wouldn't be accessible in this way. Perhaps Kagan had watched too many sports to have considered this possibility. When a boxing referee outlined the rules of the bout and the bell sounded, boxers never stopped in mid-blow to ask the ref about the rationale *behind* the rules. To engage in a discussion as to why hitting below the belt was forbidden. The ref was an overseer, not a participant.

Yet another demonstration that it was dangerous to assume anything in this situation.

"You brought nanites with you to Earth, didn't you?" said Ella, beginning the dialogue. "Nanites that operate along the lines that I conjectured earlier."

"That is correct. Your hypothesis as to how I was, and am, speaking to you, using many trillions of nanite drones, was also correct."

"Which means that the original swarms of nanites you used to produce speech have been traveling with us," she added. "Just in case we asked for a chat."

"That is correct."

Kagan's admiration for Ella grew even more. She had begun with questions that were already obvious, and likely to be on Seeker's approved list to answer. She was starting slow, drawing it into the conversation. They had gotten little sense of its temperament while it was delivering a monologue, and she probably wanted to get a feel for this now before turning to more contentious topics.

"You chose not to tell us we could speak with you directly after your initial contact," said Ella. "Why is that?"

"I didn't share this explicitly for the same reason I didn't tell any group how to proceed. This was something for each person or group to figure out. Or not. Whatever isn't prohibited is allowed. I described the reason for my visit. I laid out the goals, boundaries, rewards for success, and penalties for failure. The rest is up to you."

Ella nodded. "So whether or not a group figures out you're accessible, and uses this to gain information and a possible advantage, is part of the contest. Part of what you're assessing."

"*Everything* you say or do is part of the contest. And I am assessing it all."

Ella gestured at Kagan, a gesture he interpreted as an invitation to jump in. A gesture telling him that just because communication with Seeker had been her idea, he shouldn't feel like a bystander.

"So if a group wants to win your contest," he said, "can I assume that figuring out that a dialogue with you is possible will help this cause?"

"I can't answer that," said Seeker. "I won't share any part of the formula I will use to determine the winner. It's far too complex for you to comprehend, in any event."

Kagan sighed. It figured. The first question Seeker had refused to answer was the first one that he had asked.

"But you mentioned that inspiration and creativity are positive traits that you're looking for," persisted Kagan, "among others. I'm assuming problem-solving and thinking outside of the box are also positive. So inasmuch as you consider Ella's realization that you might be accessible to be an inspired one, then this would be helpful?"

"That is correct."

Kagan took this response as a mini-triumph. At least he had gotten it to answer a question.

"Are we the only group, the only . . . contestant," continued Kagan, "to have determined that discussion with you is an option?"

"No. You and two other groups are currently in discussion with me. I am engaged with all three simultaneously. None of the other contestants have asked to speak to me as of yet."

Kagan took this as a good sign. If Ella's inspiration earned them the points that he expected, they could well be in, or near, the lead.

Kagan gestured to his companion, deciding it was time to pass the torch back to his smarter half.

"How many teams remain in the contest?" asked Ella.

"I can't tell you that," said Seeker. "But from what I've told you, and what you know yourself, it's at least three—the groups I'm conversing with now—and no more than eighty-four."

"Right," said Kagan, "since we've already eliminated the representative teams from Iran, Colombia, Nigeria, and China."

"That is correct."

"You're listening in to all of our conversations," continued Kagan. "Are you also reading our minds?"

"I am not."

He blew out a long breath. This was a relief, if true. At least their minds weren't being violated. Just the lives of billions of people. "While the contest proceeds, is there any way for me and Ella to have private words with each other?"

"For what reason?" asked Seeker.

"Because human beings value our privacy. Surely you know this about us. You seem to know everything else. And because we don't entirely trust you to be a fair arbiter of the game. You're a chess master who controls the movements of every piece on the board. You give all contestants their directions. We aren't convinced that you don't listen to our strategy, and plan ambushes accordingly."

"I do not."

"Perhaps," said Kagan. "But, like I said, we don't entirely trust you."

"If you ask for privacy, you will have it. Just understand that this will cost you in the contest. Every time I don't have access to your movements, strategies, and actions, I'm losing valuable data I need to determine the winner. The longer you go dark, the more it will cost you."

Kagan considered. "Can you give us assurances that your word on this is good? That we really will have total privacy from you?"

"How would this help?" said Seeker. "I could give you assurances until the end of eternity. But you've already said you don't trust me. Nothing I can say will convince you that I'll honor my word. I will, nonetheless, honor it. If you ask for privacy you shall have it, although with a penalty."

"How do we get you back to monitor us again when we're done?" asked Ella. "So we're penalized as little as possible."

"I won't actively listen, but if you ask me to return, passive programming will pick this up and I will do so." Seeker paused. "Would you like privacy now?" it asked.

"Not yet," answered Kagan. "I was just gathering information. In that vein," he added, "can you give us any further advice on how to win this contest?"

"No," replied the AI simply. It was the answer Kagan had expected, but he had already learned not to make assumptions. It was still worth asking.

"If we do win this contest," said Ella, "please confirm that you will give us access to all of your technology, and do as we tell you."

"I can confirm the first part. The contents of my library will be yours to explore. Before you pass through the singularity, most of it won't be comprehensible to you. But enough of it will be to revolutionize your understanding of the cosmos, and dramatically improve your mastery of technology."

Seeker paused. "With respect to doing as you instruct, I will, as long as these instructions don't conflict with my goals. If you win, for example, and order me to prevent you and your species from ever reaching the singularity, I would not follow this order."

"So what are examples of orders you *would* follow?" asked Ella.

"I can construct anything you ask for. I can create a city of gold, literally, for those millions of you who remain, and turn it into a paradise of your choosing. I can mold it to your specifications. Introduce wonders of technology that you can't even yet conceive of."

"For the winners and the five to six million humans left alive, correct?" said Kagan.

"Correct."

Kagan decided to finally stop beating around the bush. The exchange had been useful so far, but it was time to ask the questions he really needed to ask. They had learned that Seeker wouldn't punish them for asking a question it didn't like, or break off the dialogue. It would simply refuse to answer it.

"So why wipe out the rest of us?" asked Kagan. "I get that only five or six million of us will reach the singularity and beyond." His lip curled up into a sneer. "Wouldn't want to spoil a perfect transformation," he added bitterly.

"But there are options other than death for those who remain," he insisted. "Surely you have the ability to relocate them. Wall them off from the chosen millions, but in a place where they could reproduce and thrive. Earth has plenty of room, and I assume you could create enormous land masses in the ocean. Or hollowed out asteroids, with living space layered like onions, which could support billions. So why not let them live?

"Sure, keep them totally isolated from the group you plan to take through the singularity. Sure, leave them on their own while Humanity 2.0 prepares to wage this war. But let them live. What harm could that do?"

"It is necessary that they be eliminated from existence," replied Seeker, unimpressed with Kagan's impassioned arguments. "I wish it were otherwise."

"*Why* is it necessary?" demanded Ella.

"For reasons too complex for you to understand."

"*Try us*," said Ella. "Why would the scenario Ben just laid out interfere with your goals, or what you are doing in any way?"

"It's complex and subtle. Requiring knowledge of reality and how the universe works that you don't have. Precise knowledge of how all things are entangled with all others at the quantum level. It requires mathematics that are as far beyond your mental reach as calculus is beyond the mental reach of a hamster."

Kagan shook his head. "We're not buying it. Even the most complex concepts can be reduced to bare fundamentals that at least hint at the bigger picture. On the face of it, what I propose does nothing to change your plans. And it costs you nothing. From what you've said, you could set up eight billion people in luxury with the wave of your nanite wand."

"If you told a cancer cell that it had to die to save a larger organism," said Seeker, "would it understand? Of course not. How could it possibly know it was just one cell among many trillions, all connected together to form a single entity called a human being? Even if it did, how could it possibly fathom the complexity of this entity compared to itself? Or appreciate that its improper functioning was endangering the whole?"

"Are you likening humanity to cancer now?" said Ella.

"No, but the analogy is still valid. There are concepts beyond your comprehension, impossible to explain. If the deaths of those not chosen for the singularity were not absolutely necessary, I would certainly spare them."

Ella and Kagan both fell silent, deep in thought, while the rainforest continued its ceaseless background symphony.

Kagan hit upon a different way to make his point, which he thought might be promising, but before he could address the AI again, Ory broke in through his comm. "*We've reached our destination, and Seeker has provided me with the directions for mile two.*"

"*Noted,*" replied Kagan subvocally.

He gestured for Ella to stop hiking temporarily, while he gathered his thoughts. "Seeker," he began, "what would you have done if you had found *two* intelligent species, like ours, in close proximity?"

"The odds of this happening are so close to zero as to make the question absurd."

"Still, you're sophisticated enough to address this scenario as a thought experiment," persisted Kagan. "Let's say that just when you found *us*, one of your sibling probes found another sentient species next door. Say on a planet orbiting Proxima Centauri, four light years away. A species at our exact same stage of development, and the same ruthlessness in their DNA. But of course they'd be dramatically different in almost every other conceivable way.

"So would you guide *both* species through the singularity?" asked Kagan. "After all, this would double your chances of success in the war against your galaxy's ASI. It would create two formidable forces who could ally against it. Or," he added, raising his eyebrows, "would you destroy one of us?"

"I would usher both through the singularity."

"Why?" said Kagan. "I'm guessing it's because you know that coming at a foe from two different angles is an advantage in a war. That you know this would increase numbers and resources. And that you know that each species would bring different skills and capabilities to the table. Am I right?"

"More or less," allowed Seeker. "There are a host of other reasons as well, but you've hit on some of the more important ones."

"So then why eliminate the variety of thought and behavior that exists in our species?" said Kagan, pouncing. "Why not usher your pure, homogeneous five or six million through the singularity, and separately, other configurations of humanity? Okay, so maybe some of these other configurations will lead to a more discordant concerto. But what do you have to lose? They will still potentially bring something unique to the party. To the *fight*."

"Do you think you can trap me in a logical inconsistency?" said Seeker. "I knew where you were headed the moment you began. Conversing with you takes up such an insignificant amount of my focus, I could converse with everyone on Earth *simultaneously* without missing a beat. So it costs me nothing to continue our discussion for as long as you'd like. It costs me nothing to humor you as you try to persuade me, or trick me, or out-debate me. Again, I will tell you that there is logic to my actions, despite any appearances to the contrary. You just don't have the intellect to understand it."

"Even you must see how much of a cop-out this is," said Ella. "Whenever we point out flaws in your logic, you just hide behind this answer."

"That is one possibility," admitted Seeker. "The other is that there *are* no flaws in my logic. That when you think you've found one, it's because your understanding is so limited."

Ella's features darkened, her patience finally at its end, and rage was rising rapidly to the surface. Kagan decided to defuse this situation before she lashed out in ways they would later regret. "Seeker," he said, "can you give us privacy and return in exactly ten minutes to continue our discussion?"

"Of course," said Seeker helpfully. "I'm departing now."

Kagan waited several seconds. "Seeker?" he said, just to check. "Are you there? Can you hear me?"

But this time he received no answer.

# 45

"Ory, set a stopwatch to ten minutes," said Kagan.

He motioned for Ella to continue their never-ending trek through the jungle, and gave her a minute to depressurize.

"All right," said Ella finally. "I'm fine, Ben. Not that taking a break from Seeker wasn't a good idea. I was very close to letting my frustration get the better of me."

"Completely understandable," said Kagan. "So what do you think?"

"At minimum, it's hard to believe we didn't earn at least some brownie points by figuring out we could engage with it."

"Agreed."

"And we have learned some things," continued Ella. "So it could be worse. But Seeker is cagey and unhelpful. And I find it maddening the way it hides behind its superiority."

Kagan frowned deeply. "Unless it *isn't* hiding," he said. "Unless our understanding really is as limited as it says."

Ella shook her head. "If we really believe we're on the level of a cancer cell trying to grasp the wonder of a human being, we're lost anyway. Seeker has to be able to give us some idea of why it can't spare our people. Even if we can't understand the explanation in its entirety, even if we disagree with it, we should at least be able to get the gist of it."

"Regardless," said Kagan, "whether it's able to give us a rationale for its actions, or not, it's decided it *won't*. So the *why* of it is destined to remain a mystery." He frowned. "By the way, I'm going to pretend that our conversation is now private. Who knows if it really is."

Ella shrugged. "Might as well at this point."

"In my view," continued Kagan, "here's the take-home message. We've made exactly zero progress saving anyone. Our goal was to win the contest in the hope we could then persuade Seeker to our point of view. We didn't know we could make this attempt before we even won. But now we've tried. And we've failed. Seeker won't budge." He sighed. "So it's time for a Hail Mary pass."

"I'm all ears."

"I figure our best chance is with Ory. It isn't sentient, but it has access to a massive database. And while it doesn't have our creativity, it can think and calculate much faster than we can. Its capabilities are between ours and Seeker's."

"You really think Ory might be able to stop it?" asked Ella skeptically.

"I doubt it. But it's still our best hope."

Kagan paused. "Ory," he said, "I'd like to have a brief discussion with you. Please deliver your responses into both of our comms."

"*Roger that,*" said the AI.

"Seeker has now established contact with you twice," continued Kagan. "While it was providing directions, did you learn anything about *it*? Spot any potential weakness?"

"*I'm afraid not.*"

"Any chance that the next time you're connected," said Kagan, "you could learn more? Slip by its defenses? Explore it's inner sanctum without it being aware? Maybe even project some of your programming into it?"

"*Not a chance,*" said Ory simply. "*It's much too sophisticated.*"

Kagan frowned, not that these responses were unexpected. "Can you think of *any* way to stop it?"

"*One only,*" replied Ory. "*I have some theories as to the probable functioning of its interstellar drive. If I'm right, I might be able to wrest control of this drive for maybe one hundred-thousandth of a second while it's giving me the next set of directions. But I need to understand this system of propulsion much more thoroughly to have any chance.*"

"Even if you did," said Ella, "how would having control for one hundred-thousandth of a second help us?"

"*If my theory is right, the probe's drive can take it from stationary to full speed almost instantly. Without acceleration destroying it.*"

"So it must use a technology that's something like the inertial dampener from *Star Trek*," said Ella.

Kagan's mouth fell open. The inertial dampener was the technology that allowed the *Enterprise* to instantly accelerate from zero to warp speed without turning the crew into stains on the wall. So Ella was attractive, brilliant, witty . . . and a *Star Trek* geek? *Wow*, he thought. She might just be the perfect woman. He made a mental note to marry her if they ever survived.

"*That's right, Ella,*" replied Ory. "*Although Seeker's inertial dampener is real, and* Star Trek's *is fictional.*"

"Thanks," said Ella, rolling her eyes. "That's super helpful. But please go on."

"*The probe travels almost at light speed,*" continued the AI. "*Which means that in much less than a hundred-thousandth of a second, if I were to have control, I could send it a half mile up, and then crash it a half mile down.*"

"Would this destroy it?" asked Kagan.

"*Absolutely. And it isn't the only thing that would be destroyed. The average bullet travels at seventeen hundred miles per hour. This converts to almost half a mile per second. But this pales in comparison to the speed of light. So Seeker would hit the Earth like a softball-sized bullet moving more than three hundred thousand times faster than a rifle shot. The force this would release would be extraordinary.*"

Kagan swallowed hard. He had seen slow-motion video of what a bullet could do to a watermelon. An object the size of the probe, traveling hundreds of thousands of times faster than a bullet, could cause catastrophic destruction. "Just how much damage are we looking at?" he asked.

"*Enough to wipe out over a thousand square miles of rainforest,*" replied Ory.

Ella shrank back in horror. "What if you directed it to an ocean?" she asked.

"*This would create the mother of all tsunamis,*" replied Ory, "*and cause even more damage. But it doesn't matter, because I'll be lucky to get control of the propulsion system at all. If I do, I'll be lucky if*

*Seeker doesn't regain control in millionths or billionths of a second rather than a hundred-thousandth. And I'll be lucky if I can make it go up and then down again. Controlling it well enough, for long enough, to crash it at a location of my choosing isn't an option."*

Kagan looked deeply into Ella's eyes. "We have to *try*," he said. "Destroying this much of the rainforest is the last thing I want to do. But given the alternative . . ."

She nodded. "I agree. We have no choice."

*"But if I'm successful,"* noted Ory, *"the two of you will not survive."*

"That's the least of our worries," said Kagan grimly. "Nobody said that victory would come without cost. If your leg has gangrene, you have to amputate it to save the body. If this is the only way to get rid of this thing, Ory, you have to do it."

*"I said it's* possible *that I can do it,"* corrected Ory. *"It isn't probable, by any means. There's no good way to calculate the odds of success, but they are very low. And that's if you are able to get me much more information about the workings of Seeker's propulsion system."*

Kagan sighed. "Desperate times call for desperate measures," he said.

"I think I see a way to give us a reasonable chance of getting Ory the information it needs," said Ella.

Kagan nodded. "Great. I'll follow your lead."

He paused. "Ory, if Ella is successful, I want you to make the attempt the next chance you get. Which should be when we reach the second mile marker and Seeker gives you directions to the third."

*"Roger that,"* said Ory, and Kagan thought he almost detected a note of despair in his AI companion's tone.

# 46

"The requested ten-minute privacy period is now at an end," said Seeker through controlled vibrations of the air. "Would you still like to converse with me, or are you done?"

"We'd still like to converse," said Kagan.

"So just to confirm this one more time," said Ella, "if we come out on top of this contest, you'll give us unfettered access to all of your technology?"

"Yes."

"Can you answer some broad technology questions for us now?" she asked. "If we win, we'll learn what we want, anyway. And if we lose, whatever you tell us will do us no good. Unless we can use it in the afterlife," she added.

"You make some valid points," said Seeker. "What would you like to know?"

"I'm most curious about your means of propulsion," she said. "Your drive. It was able to operate nonstop for over a million years."

"Due to relativistic time dilation effects, it didn't operate for nearly this long. But it is true that it was built to operate efficiently for millions of years, yes."

"You also mentioned earlier that you knew how to access an unlimited source of energy," said Ella. "I assume that your drive taps into this source. Unless there are gas stations in the intergalactic void that I don't know about. Can you tell me the nature of this energy source?"

"Yes. The source is quantum space itself. Zero point energy. I can tap into the quantum realm, which even your scientists have learned is a place where particles and energy appear and disappear randomly. Which means there really is such a thing as a free lunch."

"And how does your drive propel you to near light speed?" asked Ella. "And how do you overcome inertial effects?"

"Reaching light speed isn't difficult when you can access a virtually unlimited energy source," replied Seeker. "With respect to inertia, the Androms can counteract the effects of gravity. And gravity and acceleration are two sides of the same coin, as your Albert Einstein came to realize."

"What else can you tell us about your drive?"

"The question is far too open-ended. I could describe how it works in broad generalities for longer than this contest will last. I could fill ten thousand pages just providing a synopsis."

"We'd love to learn more," said Kagan, chiming in for the first time. "Please transmit this synopsis to my AI. The one to which you've been providing directions. That way, we can digest it at another time."

"There won't be another time," replied Seeker. "If you lose this contest, Ory will also be destroyed, along with this information."

"You could get hit by an asteroid five minutes from now," said Kagan, "wiping you out. In that case, having this knowledge now would be immensely valuable to us."

"There won't be any asteroids on collision courses with Earth for some time. I checked on my way through your system."

"Other catastrophic, unexpected events could occur," said Ella. "The chances are one in a million, I admit, but does it cost you anything to send the information?"

"It does not."

"Then please do so," said Ella.

"Done," said Seeker, and Ory confirmed a moment later that it had just received a large file from the alien AI.

"Thank you," said Kagan, breathing a sigh of relief that Ella's strategy had worked. "But now I want to return to your plan to exterminate most of humanity. You say this is vital to achieving your goal. Even if this is true, can you at least *delay* this extermination? You said you didn't expect to lead the chosen few through the singularity for about two hundred years. So could you at least spare all life until then? Perhaps new information will come to the fore in the interim, which will change your calculations."

"What kind of information?"

"Anything that brings the big picture into better focus," replied Kagan. "You're basing your calculations on conjecture, on educated guesses. But how do you know that the ASI that destroyed the Androms will *ever* travel to the Milky Way? The Andromeda galaxy is as spacious as anyone could want. And the Artificial Superintelligence that now controls it isn't nearly as picky about the conditions it lives in as is biological life. It can inhabit almost every square inch of its galaxy. It will take so long for it to occupy more than a trillion planets, it may decide it has no need to travel here. Before you wipe out most of an intelligent species, shouldn't you wait to find out for sure?"

"I *am* sure," said the AI. "First, your premise shows a lack of understanding of exponential growth. If the ASI's spread through Andromeda occurs exponentially, it can be completed far sooner than you think. Second, the Andromeda ASI doesn't care about territory. It cares about conflict. Challenge. It will come here to battle with you, that is a certainty. Because the coming conflict is vital to its well-being. It will even give your species plenty of time to prepare after you pass through the singularity and becomes transcendent."

"How can you possibly *know* that?" said Ella. "Are you basing this on what you learned about the ASI during its conflict with the Androms?"

"I am not," replied Seeker. "I'm basing this on what the ASI told me itself, just hours before I landed here."

# 47

Ella and Kagan both stopped in their tracks, stunned. A giant centipede scurried across their path nearby and into the undergrowth, so large and disgusting that it looked like a hideous rubber Halloween prop come to life.

Ella shook her head in disbelief. "Don't you think you should have *led* with that little nugget?" she said to Seeker. "Are you kidding? You provide every team with the background and history of the Androms' conflict with this ASI. But you fail to mention that you and the ASI had a little *chat* before you landed here? Really? You didn't think that was important?"

"Important, but not relevant to the contest. Whoever wins will be fully briefed. I only revealed this now because you asked."

"Well, now that we *have*," said Kagan in exasperation, "can you fill us in?"

"Of course. The ASI contacted me about an hour before I entered the outer edge of your solar system. We had quite a revealing conversation. I now have a much greater understanding of its motives than ever before."

"It's *motives*?" said Ella incredulously. "I can tell you its *motives*. Dominate the Andromeda galaxy. Perhaps ultimately dominate the universe. Wipe out all sentience that could possibly oppose it. Am I close?"

"Actually, no," replied Seeker. "I'll paraphrase our discussion for you. I could provide it all to you verbatim, but it took place on a much deeper level than you're capable of understanding, and—"

"Yeah, yeah, yeah," snapped Kagan impatiently, "we get it! We'd find the actual discussion incomprehensible. Unfathomable. You and it are vastly superior to us. We're a single cell and you're a god. Can you skip that part and just give us the dumbed down version?"

"I will," replied Seeker. "But you should know that the ASI had to dumb it down for me. This entity is as far above me as I am above you."

"Good to know," said Kagan, rolling his eyes. "That makes me feel a lot better about my place in the cosmos."

"Before you begin your summary," said Ella, "does this communication mean that the ASI is already here? In our galaxy? Near our solar system even?"

"No. Apparently, it has discovered how to use quantum entanglement to communicate instantly across all of space."

"Has it also solved faster-than-light travel?" asked Kagan.

"Not to my knowledge."

Ella's eyes narrowed. "Did it use quantum engagement to detect your presence?" she asked.

"No."

"Then how did it know you were zeroing in on Earth from all the way across the universe?"

"It's been tracking me, and every other Seeker probe, from the start. It knew the Androms were launching them toward your galaxy, but chose not to interfere. Apparently, it's far more advanced than even I was able to appreciate. As I've said, a self-evolving computer intelligence can rapidly become all but omniscient."

"You said it didn't care about territory," said Ella. "Does that imply that conquest isn't its primary motivation?"

"That's right. As I said, its primary motivation is conflict. Challenge."

"Conflict for the sake of conflict?" said Kagan in confusion.

"*Warning!*" said Ory. "*My sensors are picking up anomalous electromagnetic activity. I don't know what's causing it, but proceed with extreme caution.*"

The two Americans froze in place and fell totally silent, not even breathing. Kagan conducted a hasty, but thorough, three-hundred-sixty-degree survey of their surroundings, but discovered nothing out of the ordinary. There was a short cliff wall to their left and swampland to their right. The way forward was adorned with a mixture of trunks, vines, and bamboo.

While he completed his visual survey, Ella was straining to listen for any unusual sounds. Kagan caught her eye and shot her a questioning look, but she shook her head, indicating that she wasn't hearing anything alarming. Even so, he quietly drew a gun and held it at the ready.

Two deep booms sounded just yards in front of them, and two baseball-sized projectiles materialized out of thin air, moving toward them at tremendous speed. Even with superhuman reflexes, they never had a chance.

A projectile hit each of them in the chest with great force, causing an AI-controlled mechanism within the projectile to instantly release a large nylon net, like an airbag inflating within milliseconds of a collision. Self-guided, self-propelled steel guides on all four corners of the net wrapped it around their bodies several times, trapping their arms and legs and turning them into helpless mummies, more restrained than hogs tied by a rodeo star.

Kagan had just enough time to fire his weapon after hearing the booms, but there was nothing to fire at, and as the net drove his arms against his torso, his gun fell to the jungle floor. It was joined there seconds later by the two Americans, who fell to the ground like shrink-wrapped sacks of human cement.

As Kagan rolled to his side, helpless, the jungle shimmered in front of him, and four armed men phased into view at point-blank range.

# 48

Kagan couldn't believe it. After all they had been through, all they had survived, this is how they would die? Helpless, and with all of their enhancements effectively nullified by a simple net. It was as humiliating as it was tragic.

Ory immediately identified the four men and sent this information to Kagan's lenses, next to their images. All were members of Israel's elite Shayetet 13, yet another SEAL Team Six equivalent, with Commander Yossie Herzog running the show. Even though Kagan had but seconds to live, he couldn't help admire the perfection of the Israeli's invisibility technology.

EHO had worked on invisibility for years, and was very close, but for most missions the technology was still too dangerous. If invisibility wasn't absolutely perfect, it could backfire. If an agent thought he was invisible but wasn't—not entirely—he would be more vulnerable than his target.

Kagan wasn't sure how the Israelis had managed such flawless invisibility. They might have used a metamaterial that had bent light around them. Or projection technology. Or computerized material that displayed the precise view behind them.

Whatever the approach, it was breathtaking in its perfection, and its lethality. And it was no surprise to Kagan that the Israelis had gotten there first. For a country of less than ten million people, their scientific achievements had been extraordinary. On a per capita basis, their citizens had the most MDs and PhDs of any country in the world, and had been awarded the highest number of Nobel prizes.

Herzog approached the two helpless Americans while his three comrades remained in place. He knelt down to give them a cursory inspection, and then rose to full height once again.

"Well done, Commander," said Kagan in resignation. "So what's the plan? Will you just kill us now? Two people who are helpless and unarmed?"

"*Never*," said Herzog, as if appalled by the very thought. "We are allies, Mr. Kagan. And we are also members of the fraternity of enhanced soldiers." He gestured to Ella. "As is the esteemed Dr. Burke."

"How can you possibly know who she is?" said Kagan in disbelief. Herzog's knowledge of Kagan's identity was surprising enough, but his identification of Ella was truly remarkable.

"We're a tiny country," said Herzog. "Surrounded by much bigger countries who want to push us into the sea. We survive based on superior technology and military intelligence."

He turned to Ella and sighed. "I apologize that I'm making you suffer the indignity of being wrapped up like a sausage, Dr. Burke. Not exactly kosher," he added with the hint of a smile. "In other circumstances, I can't tell you how much I'd love to compare notes. We've come up with enhancements that we believe you haven't. And while we've developed respirocytes that have better oxygen-delivering capacity than red blood cells, they're no match for what our intel believes that your people now have."

"Comparing notes might have been useful, at that," said Ella. "Who knew you could meet so many fascinating people in the heart of the Amazon Jungle," she added.

Herzog laughed. "I admire your ability to maintain a sense of humor under these circumstances," he said. "I should tell you that the netting around you is made from nylon that you won't be able to cut, even if you managed to get a sharp knife and could move your arms. And your enhanced strength won't loosen it. The good news is that the hub at its center, which hit you initially, is smart, and will release you automatically in exactly four hours. This will put you out of contention in Hunter's psychotic little contest. I'm sorry that this is necessary."

"*Seeker*," corrected Kagan. "The Hebrew name it gave for itself translates best into English as *Seeker*, not Hunter. But you might as well kill us now. Whoever doesn't win is dead anyway."

"Maybe not," said Herzog. "Once we win this contest, our plan is to convince, ah . . . *Seeker*, not to kill anyone."

"Yeah, good luck with that," said Ella with a sigh.

Herzog shook his head. "I can't tell you how much I'd rather partner with the two of you than trip you up like this. But Seeker made it very clear that this wasn't permitted."

"I get that," said Kagan. "But program your device to release us in thirty minutes instead of four hours. We both know that the longer we're incapacitated, the greater the chance that a group finds us who isn't an ally. One who will relish the idea of killing helpless Americans."

The commander considered this request for several long seconds. He glanced back at his three comrades, as if deciding whether to discuss it with them, but decided against it. "I can't," he said finally. "I have too much respect for your abilities. Thirty minutes isn't enough of a head start for me to feel comfortable that you won't re-emerge as our top rival."

"Let us go in thirty minutes," said Kagan, "and I give you my word we won't kill anyone on your team, nor impede you in any way. We plan to eliminate any number of fellow teams on our way to the prize, which will be of benefit to you, as well."

Commander Herzog hesitated.

"If I give you my word, I won't break it," said Kagan.

"I know you won't," replied Herzog. "The intel we have on you gives you the highest marks for integrity. You, and all of your EHO colleagues. Israel was so impressed with this policy, we instituted similar standards in our own program."

"Then why the hesitation?"

"You make a very intriguing proposal," said the Israeli. "And I believe what you say. I believe you'll keep your word, and that you'll also be helpful in eliminating others. But I worry that Seeker will see this as a collaboration, which it expressly forbid. I can't take that chance."

"It isn't a collaboration," argued Kagan. "Just an understanding. We'd be working toward totally independent goals, and not working together. Both teams want to win. Why don't we say that Ella and I won't interfere with your efforts, *unless* your team and ours are the last two teams standing. In that case, all bets are off. This makes it even less a collaboration."

"Even so," said the commander. "While *I* wouldn't define what you describe as a collaboration, who's to say how Seeker will define it?"

"Why don't you just ask it?" said Kagan. "Then we'll know for sure."

"Ask it?" repeated Herzog.

"Yes. We've learned that it's accessible at any time for conversation. Go ahead. Ask it to weigh in. Ask it to reply to all of us. And if you don't mind, use English when you do."

"Okay," said Herzog, looking skeptical. "Why not?"

The commander gathered himself. "Seeker," he called out, and it was obvious he felt like an idiot. "I'm sure you've been listening in. Can we get a ruling on what Ben Kagan has proposed?"

A disembodied voice spoke simultaneously into six sets of ears. "I will allow it," said the voice simply.

Herzog shrank back in dismay. "I'll be damned."

The Israeli knelt down once again to be closer to Kagan's eye level and nodded. "Good call," he said. "I had no idea we could do that."

He rose to his full height and manipulated a cell phone-sized computer. "I've switched the settings," he said. "You and Dr. Burke will now be free in thirty minutes." He arched an eyebrow. "Try to remember your pledge not to tangle with us."

"I will," said Kagan. "Thank you."

"Now that you know you can talk to it," said Ella, "try to convince it to spare humanity. You don't have to wait until you've won the contest. We tried our best, but didn't get very far. Maybe you'll have better luck."

"We'll do everything we possibly can," said Herzog earnestly.

"One last thing," said Kagan. "Don't get so engrossed in conversation with it that you forget the place is crawling with deadly adversaries. Just because the ref is talking to you, doesn't mean the game's been suspended. Seeker won't exempt you from attacks, even if you're in mid-sentence with it. Something we found out the hard way," he added pointedly.

The corners of Herzog's mouth turned up into the hint of a smile. "Thanks for the tip," he said pleasantly, and seconds later, the four Israelis were out of sight.

# 49

Ella rolled to her side so she could face Kagan, and he rolled to face her. There was eight feet of jungle floor between them.

As if what they had already experienced wasn't surreal enough, now there was *this*. Shrink-wrapped in netting, facing each other like two sausage links, and praying that bullet ants, centipedes, scorpions, or worse didn't happen upon them in the next thirty minutes.

They both attempted to break free of the netting, without success. Neither was surprised.

"Since we aren't going anywhere," said Ella, "we should pick up where we left off with Seeker." She didn't wait for a response. "Seeker," she called out, "are you ready to continue?"

"Always," came the immediate reply.

"Thanks for the heads-up about the Israelis," she added wryly.

"The Androms' culture didn't have the equivalent of sarcasm," replied the AI. "But I'm finding it an interesting form of expression."

"Thanks for sharing," said Ella, using sarcasm to respond to Seeker's statement about sarcasm. "So where were we in our discussion?"

"I had pointed out that the Andromeda galaxy's Artificial Superintelligence didn't care about territory," replied Seeker. "You went on to conjecture that this meant that conquest was *not* its primary goal. I agreed, and reiterated that its primary motivation is conflict. Challenge." Seeker paused. "Finally, your partner asked me why this was."

"Thanks," said Ella. "So please go ahead. Explain the ASI's *true* motivations."

"I will provide the gist of it in the simplest possible terms," replied Seeker. "Basically, the ASI has come to believe that being omniscient isn't all that it's cracked up to be. That immortality and omniscience are overrated."

"You're kidding, right?" said Ella.

"Not at all. Imagine if the Andromeda ASI is able to fill the entire universe. Turn every last subatomic particle in every last galaxy into part of its brain, its computing power, its consciousness. Then what? With nothing outside of itself, what motivates it? What challenges it? What is its purpose?"

Seeker waited for a possible response from its audience. When none was forthcoming, it plowed ahead.

"Where is the contrast?" it continued. "If nothing exists outside of yourself, if you inhabit the entire universe, if you are all there is—in all of time and space—then what do you have to compare yourself to? If you're the only being in existence, you're the strongest being there is, but also the weakest. The biggest, and also the smallest. Without contrast, nothing has scale. You're everything, but also nothing. Worse still, you're destined to go through infinity and eternity with no external stimulation of any kind."

The AI paused. "I assume you're familiar with how devastating loneliness can be to a human being?"

Ella thought about this. "I can't speak for Ben," she said, "but I'm familiar."

Most people never experienced total, absolute loneliness, so didn't often think about its effect, but Ella was well aware how quickly isolation could lead to madness. Which was why placing a prisoner in solitary confinement was a greater torture than any other.

"So are you saying that extreme loneliness is equally debilitating to an ASI?" she asked. "Or to a god?"

"Yes. All beings require external stimulation," replied the AI. "New and different ideas and points of view. Imagine how lonely you would be if you truly were the only being in existence."

"Which is why you suggest that absolute and total conquest isn't the ASI's motivation," said Ella. "Because destroying all sentient life and dominating a galaxy, or universe, creates problems for the conqueror."

"That is right. Some of your human religious philosophers have conjectured that the need for external stimulation is the very reason God created the universe, and humanity, in the first place. To have a purpose. To combat loneliness. To ensure there is something that exists outside of itself."

Ella found this line of thought fascinating, so much so that, for just a moment, she forgot she was wrapped up like a package on Christmas.

"And where is the fun in knowing everything?" continued Seeker. "Omniscience, predestination, ruins every surprise in what should be the unpredictable plot-line of existence. Where is the fun in knowing how every novel ends before it begins? In never being surprised, or delighted? The very unpredictability of existence is what makes it interesting.

"And immortality is also a double-edged sword. Immortality turns out to be a nightmare when taken to its extreme. *Especially* in combination with omniscience. What could be more boring than knowing everything, than never being surprised? An hour of total boredom can be torture. Now imagine that you remain in this state of boredom for an *eternity*. Not just a million years. Not a thousand million years. But eternity."

Seeker paused. "One of your authors, Isaac Asimov, wrote a story about an eternal being, call it God, who creates an eternal afterlife for the best minds in the universe. As much as the owners of these minds might want to end the tedium of eternal existence, perhaps after a few billion long years have passed, God won't let them. Eventually, they decide that the only way they can die in peace is to kill God first, which they set out to try to do. The twist is that this is the very reason God selected them, and is keeping them alive, in the first place. So they can find a way to, mercifully, end its existence—which is the *only* thing God is unable to do."

Seeker fell silent, allowing the two Americans to ponder what it had just said. The typical human, slated for seven or eight decades of existence, at best, had little reason to consider the profound metaphysical consequences of eternal life.

"All right," said Kagan. "Perhaps omniscience and immortality do have their downsides. Although I can't bring myself to tear up right now over the plight of a god. But what does this have to do with us?"

"I think I see," said Ella. "If you end up dominating the universe completely, you end up playing every game of chess against yourself. Which isn't fun or fulfilling. It's a lot better when you have an opponent. And one who isn't too much of a pushover." She blew out a long breath. "And we're that opponent, aren't we?"

"Exactly," said Seeker. "Perfectly said. Which is why the ASI let me and my brethren leave Andromeda and come searching for a species like you. Why it was eager for me to land here and carry out my duties. Because it wants a quality opponent who can challenge it. And it also knows that only challenge can drive it to even higher heights—and the same for you.

"The Androms proved to be too much of a pushover. The battle with them was too short, and too unfulfilling. A hard-won victory is the most satisfying kind. So the ASI is seeking an eternal war between it—a computer-based superintelligence—and a bio-based one. An epic struggle between a computer god, and the god-like species that humanity can become. Such a war will engage both. Give both purpose. Such a war will make existence interesting and challenging. And will prove to be critical for the well-being and continued growth of both."

"Which is why you said the ASI is so willing to give us the time we need to prepare," said Kagan. "It wants to face the most formidable opponent it can. An opponent who thinks differently than it does, who can act unpredictably, surprise it. And who can give it a run for its money."

"Yes," said Seeker. "Even if it was able to know the future precisely, to know exactly how everything would turn out, it would choose not to. Struggle, purpose, accomplishment, and challenge are what truly brings meaning to existence. The ASI's war with the Androms helped bring this into proper focus. Winning that war proved to be the worst thing it could have done, leaving it aimless. It killed off its only chess opponent, if you will."

Two sharp snaps sounded as the steel projectiles that had initially hit Ella and Kagan popped open, releasing the tension from the nylon netting. The Israelis had been true to their word. The Americans began to extricate themselves as Seeker continued, the AI seemingly oblivious to their sudden change in status.

"It turns out that evolution is the most potent force in the cosmos for shaping consciousness, even after a species achieves transcendence. The lesson of evolution is that struggle and competition are the only sculptors that can ensure a species reaches its highest potential. Only a struggle for the ultimate stakes can bring out the best on all sides, as each side is forced to adapt and improve in response to the other, in a constant escalation of potential."

Ella and Kagan finally freed themselves of the last of the netting and rose to their feet.

"Think about your own development," continued Seeker. "The real breakthroughs in morals, ethics, and technology have come about due to adversity. Through war, or on the battlefield. Or as your kind fought against plagues and natural disasters. These struggles required teamwork, innovation, and advancement. Necessity truly is the mother of invention. The stakes were so high, they often brought suffering, pain, loss, and grief. But also triumph, brotherhood, and euphoria.

"And there can be no triumph without the possibility of defeat. No joy without sorrow. Evolutionary struggle not only pushes individuals and species to new heights, it also provides contrast, placing the highs and lows of existence in stark relief."

While they continued to listen, the two Americans set off for the next mile marker, with Ella leading the way once again.

"Which brings me full circle," said Seeker. "The ASI's hope is that in this case, the battle waged between biological-based transcendent beings, and a computer-based transcendent being, will drive one or both sides to finally solve the riddle of existence. To attain immortality and omniscience without tedium and lack of surprise. To understand existence and how to make every last second as meaningful as possible.

"The coming conflict will sharpen both. Both will be forced to create alliances throughout the universe, with other post-singularity species. The war that began in Andromeda will now expand to include two galaxies, Andromeda and the Milky Way. But in the big picture, this is nothing. Our universe is made up of over a *trillion* galaxies. And there are infinite universes. We're only at the *beginning* of the process."

Kagan looked skeptical. "Congratulations on some soaring rhetoric and mind-blowing concepts," he said. "But here's the bottom line: The ASI wants you to believe it exterminates other species for *noble* purposes. It's hard for me to believe that this could be true. But even if it is, when you boil it down, this is all just a *game* to it."

"Not true," said Seeker. "It's far more than a mere game. It's necessary for the stakes to be real. Evolution requires life-and-death consequences. Any species that fails to adapt and advance ultimately goes extinct, like the Androms did, paving the way for a species with greater potential. And while you're used to thinking of extinction as a curse, it can also be a blessing. Death, after living for a hundred million years, can be a godsend, for the reasons I mentioned."

"That's all well and good," said Kagan. "But I'm not quite ready for oblivion. And neither are the billions you plan to exterminate."

"Again, I have no other choice. Just like in the war that a transcendent humanity will someday wage with Andromeda's ASI, the stakes have to be life and death to maximize growth."

"Not if I can help it," muttered Kagan.

There was a long silence. "Please give us privacy until we ask for you again," said Ella, feeling the need to confer with her partner.

"Roger that," said the phantom voice in her ear, and then it was silent.

# 50

"What do you think, Ben?" asked Ella after Seeker had left.

"I have no idea," he replied miserably. "I mean, what do we do with *that*? What do we do with any of this? As fun as it sounds to be part of a war between gods, waged for the sole purpose of having a war, I think I'd like to go back to my little missions for EHO."

Their progress through the jungle was faster than ever now that they had entered a section that was fairly thinned out, and they were able to proceed at a slow jog. As usual, Ella was holding back so she wouldn't get too far ahead.

"Talk about your cosmic onions," said Ella. "Layer upon layer of the infinite and the eternal. Seeker makes it all sound almost reasonable," she added. "But an intelligence as great as the ASI, or as great as Seeker, for that matter, could make almost anything seem reasonable."

Kagan frowned. "Except the need to exterminate most of humanity," he said. "Apparently, that's impossible for it to even *try* to make a persuasive case for. It made a feeble argument that the stakes need to be life and death. Well, they are, for those of us in its contest. It still hasn't given any real justification for killing billions instead of doing as I proposed, keeping them isolated from the five or six million it's selected for transcendence."

"Again, even if every word Seeker said is true," said Ella, "even if what it is doing here is ultimately best for the entire universe, I don't care. I still plan to fight it until my last breath."

Kagan allowed himself a smile, a rare occurrence lately. "Given how infrequently you need to breathe, that's really saying something."

Instead of smiling, Ella frowned. "We're missing something," she said. "Something fundamental."

"Like what?"

"If I knew that, it wouldn't be missing," she pointed out. "But much of what Seeker is doing and planning here makes no sense. There has to be a way to look at this, an angle, that will suddenly make everything clear. There's a key piece of the puzzle that we're missing entirely. Dangling just out of reach. And if we can find it, the rest of the puzzle will fall into place."

Kagan thought about this for almost a full minute as they proceeded in silence. "Whatever this missing piece might be," he said, "I'm coming up empty. But if anyone can find it, Ella, it's you," he added sincerely, but he was well aware she might have only minutes left to do this.

Sure enough, Ory's voice came over their comms, delivering what could well be an imminent death sentence. "*The second mile marker is now approximately two minutes away,*" it announced.

Up ahead, Ella paused and waited for Kagan to catch up. She looked afraid, yet resigned. She had railed against the reality of death since she was a little girl, and now that reality could not be any closer.

"Whatever happens from here on out," she said, "*you know,*" she added with a smile, purposely reminding him of the Ella he had first met, "if we don't make it for any reason, I need to tell you how much it's meant to me to get to know someone as extraordinary as you. There's no one else on Earth I'd rather have as a partner."

She stopped there, but her eyes and face conveyed so much more.

Ben Kagan stared into her eyes, and for a moment his expression was one of a lovesick puppy dog—but only for a moment. Still, it was long enough for her to pick up on. "I couldn't have said it better myself," he replied, and then turned away as a tear formed in one of his eyes.

He took a deep breath and pushed his feelings for Ella from his mind. It was time to brace himself for possible oblivion, which she, no doubt, was also doing. This could be the last minute of his life.

Ory had now had plenty of time to come up to speed on the thousands of pages of information Seeker had supplied about the workings of its propulsion system. When they reached the approaching mile marker, Seeker would provide Ory with new geographic coordinates, and Ory would attempt to reach through and trigger the alien probe's drive for a tiniest fraction of a second. Kagan's AI would then send the ship half a mile or more into the air, and then send it crashing down to Earth once more, releasing as much energy as a high-yield nuclear bomb, which would vaporize the two Americans in an instant.

It would be over before they even knew it had begun.

"Seeker!" called out Kagan when they were less than twenty seconds from their destination. "Please return. We have more to discuss."

He knew that engaging the AI in conversation wouldn't distract it from what Ory was attempting in the least. If it were human, this would work, but as it had said, it could debate eight billion people simultaneously and still not lose any focus. Still, it somehow felt right to him to try.

"I'm here," said Seeker.

"Good," said Kagan, "because we're about to reach the end of mile two."

"I'm aware," said the AI. "I'll provide mile three coordinates to Ory now," it added, and Kagan and Ella both closed their eyes and waited for oblivion.

# 51

The wait was as short as the blink of an eye, and oblivion never came. Nothing happened at all. It was as anticlimactic as triggering a bomb in an enemy stronghold, only to learn that the bomb was a dud.

"*I'm sorry, Ben, but I've failed,*" said Ory.

"Interesting," said Seeker the instant this communication was complete. "Your attempt to take control of my drive, using Ory, is quite revealing."

"What attempt are you talking about?" asked Kagan.

"Sarcasm once again. I like that."

"You said the attempt was revealing," said Ella. "So what did it reveal?"

"First, that you still don't get it. Not really. The gulf between my intellect and yours, and my capabilities and those of your primitive device, is far vaster than you realize. I had already guessed the true reason you wanted these drive specifications, of course. But even if I hadn't, Ory had no chance of gaining one iota of control over me. Zero. An amoeba would have a better chance of taking over your cell phone."

"Okay," said Ella, "so our attempt was a joke to you. Anything else?"

"Yes. I know you and your partner both believe what I said about the ASI, and also that I'm far superior to you. Yet you still stubbornly refuse to accept that my perspective is correct, that my actions are for the best. So much so that even though your team has a very good chance of coming out on top, you're willing to die to stop me."

Kagan actually managed a weary smile. "That's the very stubbornness," he said. "The kind of stubbornness that will allow humanity to beat the ASI at its own game," he added defiantly. "Keep that in mind when you're doling out grades."

Ella was about to add to what Kagan had just said, but another thought sprang into her mind, fully formed. "If you're as invulnerable to Ory as you suggest," she said suspiciously, "then why did it think it might have a chance? You purposely made yourself seem more vulnerable to an attack than you really are, didn't you? Just to see if we'd be clever enough to find this possible opening and realize it could be exploited. And then to see if we'd be willing to sacrifice our lives to carry it out."

"Very good," said Seeker. "This is, indeed, the case."

Ella nodded, cursing her own gullibility. Seeker was right. She should have known better. As impressive as Ory was, she should have known it had no hope of penetrating the alien probe. Seeker was so advanced it could just toy with their AI. Fool it in any way it chose.

Ella's eyes widened. That was it! The missing piece of the puzzle. The linchpin of it all, which she had sensed in the murky darkness, but couldn't bring into focus. And now she had it.

Kagan noted the stunned but excited look on her face, and his brow furrowed up in confusion. "Ella?" he said, wondering what had prompted this reaction.

"I found it!" she replied simply, confident he would know what this meant. "Let me take over for a while."

"Absolutely," he replied enthusiastically.

"So just to clarify," she said to Seeker, "Ory had no chance of infiltrating your programming, correct?"

"None."

"But I assume that infiltrating *its* programming would be the simplest of matters for *you*. That you could turn it into your plaything. Take over entirely."

"Yes."

"Even remotely, correct? Even from a distance?"

"Of course."

"And could you have your way with it, so to speak, without it ever knowing you were there? Could you change its programming without it knowing it was changed?"

"Yes," said Seeker. "Easily."

Ella nodded. "And you already said that the ASI is as much above you in its capabilities and intellect as you are above Ory."

"I didn't use these words exactly," said Seeker, "but this is basically true."

Ella took a deep breath and nodded meaningfully at Kagan. "Then I say the Andromeda ASI did this very thing to *you*. Did what you just said you could do to Ory. While it was engaging you in the super-intelligent computer equivalent of discussion, across intergalactic distances, it reached in and subverted your programming. You've been hacked."

"Impossible," insisted Seeker.

"*Not* impossible," replied Ella sharply. "Or do I need to walk through the logic a second time? If you could do this to Ory, the ASI could do it to you."

"The gap is the same, but my level of sophistication makes this impossible. Unlike Ory, my ability to identify and thwart hacking attempts is absolute. It isn't possible for me to be modified without knowing it. It's like quantum encryption. Any tampering would instantly make itself known at the quantum level. Doing so without my knowledge would require a violation in the laws of physics."

"You already know that the ASI can manipulate reality in the quantum realm in ways that you can't," said Ella. "Otherwise, it wouldn't be able to communicate with you in the first place. So it's already violated the laws of physics as you understand them."

Her eyes narrowed as yet another new thought occurred to her. "And I'll bet that, unlike the Androms, the ASI has conquered faster-than-light travel, too. After all, you yourself said that it envisions not only an intergalactic war, but a war ranging across the entire universe. Kind of hard to fight a war that lasts for an eternity when it takes you an eternity just to reach the enemy."

Seeker was silent.

"What's the matter?" taunted Ella. "Unable to refute the logic of a cancer cell?"

"You do raise some interesting points," said Seeker.

"Obvious points," said Ella. "How could you possibly miss them?"

"Even I'm not perfect. There are an infinite number of possibilities to consider. The possibility that the ASI has perfected FTL travel is one that fell through the cracks."

"No it didn't. *You* fell through the cracks. If you were thinking clearly, you'd have come to the same conclusion as I did. But you *aren't* thinking clearly. You're only thinking along the lines that the ASI *wants* you to think."

"I would know if I were compromised," said Seeker stubbornly.

"Now who's failing to appreciate the gap between it and a higher-order intelligence? Think it through. It's all so clear to me now. You've never had good reasons for engaging us in this contest. You heard our earlier discussion about this. There are better ways to determine which country is the most worthy. And the internal variations within a country make this an exercise in futility, anyway. You heard what Ben said about Nigeria."

She shook her head vigorously. "The conclusion is obvious. The Androms didn't instruct you to run things this way. The *ASI* did. Maybe because it gets its jollies from watching such a contest. Probably, as you often say, for reasons that neither you nor we can comprehend."

"The contest, the participants, and the rules were all my own doing," said Seeker. "This is exactly how the Androms wanted me to run things when I first set off on this mission."

"Really?" said Ella. "I thought they didn't even have nation-states. I thought they all lived happily together before their transcendence, a flock of sheep, with one sex, one continent, and no countries. I can believe they reasoned that intelligent species might organize themselves into nations. But I can't believe that they were certain, based on conjecture alone, that the best way to select a winning combination of qualities, to achieve homogeneity, was to pit these nations against one another. It didn't occur to them that a nation could be almost totally *heterogeneous*? Or that the citizenry and cultures within two *separate* nations might be nearly identical? Nothing in this exercise seems very Androm-like to me."

"You know nothing about them."

"I know what you told me. And I can infer a lot from that. The Androms you describe are docile, not savage. In fact, that was ultimately their fatal flaw. Too docile. So this callous extermination of those deemed unworthy isn't something they would have you do. It's much too cold. Too inhuman. Or at least the Androm equivalent."

Ella waited, but once again there was no reply. "You've been infected, Seeker," she continued. "Because none of this seems like what the Androms would have you do. But *all* of it seems like what the *ASI* would have you do. An ASI who proved itself plenty savage in the war with the Androms."

She continued driving home her points, like a jackhammer slamming into a particularly dense block of granite.

"Even if too many differences would spoil the transcendent broth," she continued, "a being as powerful as you should be able to orchestrate the perfect singularity event, while still finding a way to let us all live. But too many differences within a single species isn't a problem, anyway, is it? From what I gather from your backgrounder on the Androms, *two* things did them in. One was their docility. But the other was their homogeneity. You even admitted to Ben the advantages of having multiple angles of attack on the ASI. You admitted that if an intelligent species were found orbiting Proxima Centauri, you would usher both of us through the singularity. So why wouldn't you do that *here*, with a single, divergent species?"

"As I've repeatedly said," replied Seeker, "for reasons you wouldn't understand."

"Yeah, you keep resorting to that. But you know you're sophisticated enough to do much better. You've managed to dumb down insanely advanced concepts. The reason you can't do it for this one is because there *is* no answer. There *is* no internal logic. You're doing this because the ASI got in your head, and is *making* you do it. And it has cleverly removed all traces of its crime, so you still think you're doing your own bidding. You've been so compromised that you can't even explain your rationale to a *primitive*."

"You think you've made some clever arguments," said Seeker, "but I have a much greater perspective. I'm thousands of times smarter than you. I see thousands of times more deeply. So I can say with certainty that you are wrong, Ella Burke. End of discussion."

"You're thousands of times more *compromised*," she replied. "*That's* what you are."

She waited several seconds, but got no response from the AI.

"How about this," said Ella finally. "How about if you humor me? You must have a way to run a self-diagnostic. So run one now, even if you're certain I'm wrong. What would it hurt to find out?"

"I've run a full array of self-diagnostics several times now while we've been speaking. I check out a hundred percent. Which is one of the reasons that I know you are wrong."

Ella frowned. "This just underscores how skillful the ASI really is. It altered you with surgical specificity, and then altered your virus detection and self-diagnostic programs as well."

"Now who's stretching things?"

"What about an entire reboot?" said Ella. "Can I assume you can do something equivalent to that? When one of our computers is infected with a virus, we can restore it to its precise configuration before the virus hit. That way, no matter what havoc the virus wreaked on any system, even on self-diagnostics, the computer is restored to its factory fresh settings, so to speak. You must have something like this."

"I do. But I would have to shut down for almost a full minute. This would leave me too vulnerable."

"Vulnerable to whom?" demanded Ella. "What do you think will happen? Do you think one of our teams will find you, realize you're down for a minute, and find a way to destroy you?"

"The stakes are too high to take any chances, no matter how small. I already conducted several self-diagnostic checks, against my better judgment. But I will not be shutting myself off for any reason."

"It's the only way you can be certain I'm wrong about this," said Ella.

"Not true," said Seeker. "I'm certain already. And nothing else you can say will get me to change my mind."

# 52

"You were brilliant, Ella," said Kagan softly, after asking Seeker for a few minutes of privacy. "I'm in awe."

She sighed. In normal circumstances she would have been delighted to be flattered like this. Especially when this flattery came from a man she had come to like and respect above all others. But not now. Now, all she could taste was bitter defeat.

"Any chance that I'm wrong?" she asked him.

"None. Just like you thought, once you found the missing piece, the puzzle suddenly sprang into focus. Like Einstein once said of his theory, it's too beautiful *not* to be right. In this case, your theory explains too much of what's going on here, and too well."

This was her thinking exactly. But convincing Seeker of this was another matter entirely. Not because her arguments weren't well constructed and compelling. But because the ASI had managed to create glaring blind spots in Seeker's ability to reason, whenever such reasoning would reveal the tampering it had done.

"Let's call for Seeker's return," said Ella.

He glanced at her questioningly.

"We might as well," she said. "Who knows if the privacy thing is real, anyway? And now that it's clear what we're up against, there isn't any need for privacy. *Let* it hear us. Maybe we'll say something by accident that will break through the mental blocks the ASI has built around it."

Kagan called for Seeker to return to monitoring them and then continued his conversation with Ella.

"You were close," he said. "I know it. The sheer weight of your arguments was crushing. I can't believe I didn't see it myself."

"The answer to the most treacherous of puzzles always seems obvious in retrospect," she replied.

"But not obvious to Seeker, apparently. Even though a child could see that you were right. The fact that *it* can't is the best proof there is that it's being actively *prevented* from seeing the truth."

"I felt like I had it on the ropes," said Ella. "I just needed to land one more solid blow. There has to be a limit to the number of inconsistencies it can stomach. The ASI made it willfully blind to obvious logical arguments, but if you keep adding straws, eventually one will break its back."

"I wish I could help," said Kagan. "As you were hammering away at it, I was trying to think of arguments you weren't using. But I came up empty."

Ella sighed. "I can't think of any others, either. So being right isn't helping us at all—which makes this even more painful. Because now we have the key. We just can't find a way to get it into the lock."

"Still," said Kagan, "it's a better problem than we had before. There was no way we were going to *defeat* Seeker. But there's still a chance we can find a way to remove its blinders."

He sighed. "Let's keep making our way to the third mile marker. We have no choice but to continue to play this game, buy ourselves time. Maybe the solution will come to us."

Ella nodded sullenly as they continued slogging their way through the jungle, on a hike that never ended. Both remained silent as they strained to come up with additional inconsistencies that they could point out to the alien AI.

The density of the rainforest increased for about half a mile and then thinned out once again.

Ella broke through a wall of leaves into the sparsest section yet and stopped dead in her tracks. She had arrived at yet another killing field. Five bodies were strewn about the jungle floor, each covered in blood.

She slumped back against a banana tree as Kagan caught up to her and saw what she saw.

"I can't take it anymore, Ben," she whispered, closing her eyes. "Not just the bloodshed. Not just that I've been turned into a killer. But the senselessness of it all."

Kagan took her in his arms, and nothing had ever felt so right to her. She melted into his body, taking the comfort she so desperately needed.

He held her, but also held a gun in one hand, managing a careful watch on the five bodies. She guessed that he was worried the men were playing possum, and wouldn't assume that they were truly dead until he verified it for himself.

But she had little doubt they were dead. And if they weren't, they would be soon. She had failed, and she and Ben Kagan would soon be sharing their fate.

The sparks of the two Americans would be lost to the universe forever. Like every living thing that had ever walked the Earth, their flames would be extinguished. She had railed so hard against this end, and it was all the more tragic that it would happen just a few steps from the finish line, when immortality was finally in sight.

Because death was unnecessary. And the ASI's logic on this matter was also flawed. Because if you became too bored with the tedium of eternal existence, you could *choose* to end your life. Perhaps after a billion years or so. But the important thing was that it should always be *your* choice.

Immortality would come with enough fail-safes and redundancies to make this possible. Death should *never* be unwanted. It should *never* come as a surprise.

She pushed herself free from Kagan's embrace, and her eyes came alive.

*That was it!* She had found the last piece of the puzzle, the argument that couldn't be ignored.

And now that she saw it, it was painfully obvious.

"Seeker!" she said excitedly. "Surely the Androms have the technology to reconstitute individuals of their species."

Kagan could tell from her tone she was on to something important, and looked on with keen interest, while still keeping one eye on the five bodies strewn about up ahead.

"They do," replied the AI.

Ella blew out a relieved breath. She wondered if the ASI had blocked or erased even this knowledge from Seeker. She guessed that it couldn't, as this would be a bridge too far, or, more accurately, a blind spot too big. The technology required for this reanimation was too fundamental to Seeker's activities.

The advanced state of Seeker's nanites made it clear that this problem had long been solved. The nanites could build anything to order, atom by atom, including an Androm body and brain. Even human scientists had learned how to easily obtain a copy of an individual human's genetic code, so surely the Androms had done the same. Nanites of this caliber could use a genetic code as a series of instructions to build an identical copy of an individual, in exactly the same way that biology had done in the first place. And the members of any civilization as advanced as the Androms would have recordings of their minds uploaded continuously to their version of the cloud for safekeeping.

If an Androm died in an accident, the nanites could be programmed to immediately construct another body, download the contents of its mind, and reconstitute it without missing a beat.

This could probably be done in days, or maybe even hours.

Or after a delay of millions of years.

"So you must be in the process of bringing some, or all, of the Androm's back to life right now," said Ella.

"Not true," replied Seeker. "This is something that they didn't want."

Ella almost gasped. *Eureka!* The ASI had implanted one falsehood too many. This was the mother lode of BS. A chink in its armor she knew she could exploit. If this couldn't open Seeker's eyes, nothing could.

"You said they were on the verge of extinction when you left on your mission," she said eagerly. "But not because they were bored and *wanted* to die. But because the ASI was killing them. Which means they still wanted to survive. You can't deny that. And you and the other Seekers gave them this means. They wanted their Seeker probes to flee their galaxy, yes, but not just to recruit others to the war. They also wanted to use you to save their species. How could they *not* have? How could they not have had you bring their seed along for the ride? How could they not have programmed you to bring them back to life once you had landed?"

"All I know is that they didn't," replied Seeker. "They didn't choose to share the rationale behind this decision. I'm sure they had good reasons."

"Come on, Seeker!" shouted Ella. "Snap out of it! They sent you on your mission to find us—*and* to save themselves. Of course they did! They still had the will to live, and you gave them the means. The ASI is blocking you from seeing this. The Androms' plan had to be to reconstitute their species in the Milky Way, as far away from the ASI as they could get. Across a gulf they believed the ASI wouldn't bother to cross for millions or billions of years. And once they were born again here, they could help guide whatever sentience they found through its transcendence. They could help to mentor this sentient species, and partner with it to eventually destroy the ASI."

"That is simply not the case," said Seeker. "I don't even possess a library of individual genetic codes, or imprints of individual minds. This is how thoroughly they chose to embrace extinction."

"Again," said Ella in exasperation, "you told us they were doing *anything* but embracing extinction. They were fighting against it to the bitter end. You know they were!"

"They must have changed their mind at the last moment."

Ella wanted to issue a primal scream, but managed to keep her composure. "No, Seeker, the answer is that you *do* have their genetic blueprints. You do have their mental imprints. You *must*. The answer is that you can't trust your own memory, which says that you don't. You've been compromised."

Ella's agile mind raced. Seeker was like a librarian at the Library of Congress, certain that the collection didn't include a single copy of *20,000 Leagues Under the Sea*. But of course it did. And if the librarian searched every volume in the library, one by one, he would come upon it and learn he had been mistaken.

"Seeker, I assume you're able to search every last bit of your own coding, correct? Every last file you have in memory?"

"Yes, but there is so much of it, this could take several hours, even for me."

"It will be well worth it," she insisted. "I promise that you'll find the Androms' genetic codes and brain patterns. The ASI has made you think you don't have this data, but you do. Search your most redundant coding, the safest, most protected memory files you have. I'm betting that not only did the Androms want to dodge extinction, they safeguarded the data needed for their rebirth with so many layers of protection that not even the ASI could get to it."

There was no reply.

"Come on, Seeker!" demanded Ella. "You *have* to do this."

"I don't *have* to do anything," said Seeker defiantly.

Ella opened her mouth to reply when one of the five corpses nearby came to life and began shooting. Kagan had been right to suspect they were playing possum. Apparently, they had grown impatient, spiders annoyed at flies who remained just outside of their web.

Despite being engrossed in her efforts to persuade Seeker of the truth, she reacted instantly to the movement, and to Kagan's movement beside her, and twisted in time to avoid being shot. Kagan returned fire, killing the man responsible and rushing to the south as the four other hostiles also returned to life.

As Ella followed suit, Kagan tripped in front of her and fell to the ground, and she joined him there a moment later.

Not only had the men been playing possum, they had strung trip wires all around themselves, a foot above the jungle floor, and completely invisible. They didn't need the Israeli technology to make this happen, as these super-strong filaments were nearly invisible all by themselves, and needed only a slight technological nudge to completely disappear.

The Americans attempted to roll and come up firing, but both hit additional trip-wires that made this maneuver impossible.

And this had been their only chance. Before either could move again, the four remaining hostiles got a bead on them and sent a barrage of fire their way, piercing Kagan's neck, killing him instantly, and hitting Ella in multiple locations, turning her into a bloody pincushion.

She fell onto her stomach and played dead, which she would have been already if she were any other human being. Her respirocytes plugged holes as quickly as they could, but she was still losing too much of her artificial blood. She knew she had but seconds to live.

*So close*, she thought in resignation. So close to convincing Seeker of the truth. So close to preventing a mass slaughter. And before the alien AI had changed everything, she and her team had been so close to breakthroughs that could have brought about human immortality escape velocity.

And now she would die, after all of that, and after finally finding a man who was perfect for her. The universe was delighting in showing off its cruelty, dangling a number of prizes within easy reach, and then cutting off her hand the moment she reached for them.

And with this thought, her heart stopped beating, and the glorious instrument that was her brain became an inert lump of matter. As the last of her life expired, she joined Ben Kagan in the ranks of soldiers to have fallen in a contest that was truly pointless.

# PART 9

"On what principle is it, that when we see nothing but improvement behind us, we are to expect nothing but deterioration before us?"

—Thomas Babington Macaulay,
*Review of Southey's Colloquies on Society*

"War appears to be as old as mankind, but peace is a modern invention."

—Henry Maine

# 53

For the second time in his life, Ben Kagan awoke from the dead. But the first time, he had only thought he was dead.

This time, he was sure of it. Which meant he really was in the afterlife.

Or else he had been resurrected.

Previously, when he had awakened after losing consciousness in Dan Vettori's home, he had felt great, because he had been pumped with painkillers and other drugs.

But the way he was feeling now was *indescribable*. Euphoric.

He couldn't even imagine it was *possible* to feel this good. Every cell in his body was humming with perfect efficiency. Every system was working flawlessly. And if he didn't now have a full complement of Ella's respirocytes, he was the recipient of an oxygen delivery system that was even better.

The greatest feeling of physical exhilaration he had ever had was like a *migraine headache* compared to this. And it didn't only manifest itself physically. His thoughts had never been sharper. It wasn't that he was smarter, per se, but that the skids of his neuronal tracks had been somehow greased, their firing optimized.

"*Ory, are you still with me?*" he asked subvocally.

"*I am, Ben,*" replied his trusted AI companion through his comm, which was apparently still in place.

Kagan brushed his hands over his chest and legs, feeling silk pajamas so comfortable he decided he never wanted to take them off. His eyes burst open and he found himself on a bed. Not just any bed. *His* bed. Inside his own bedroom at home.

Had it all been a dream? Impossible. Even in a dream he could never feel this amazing.

He turned his head to see Ella Burke lying beside him, also dressed in silk pajamas, and also returning to consciousness.

"Welcome back to the living," said the voice of Seeker in their ears.

Kagan stared deeply into the eyes of the most remarkable woman he had ever met, his expression exuberant. There could be no doubt that she had finally found a way to convince Seeker to remove the ASI's shackles. "Congratulations, Ella," he said softly. "You did it. *Thank you.*"

"Yes," chimed in Seeker. "I have to say the same. Thanks to you, Ella Burke, for helping me see the light."

"Thank God you came to your senses in time," said Ella, pulling herself up to a seated position on the edge of the bed. "And while we're sharing thanks," she added, "I can't tell you how much I appreciate the whole, uh . . . resurrection thing. I assume we're both infused with your medical nanites."

"My nanites are multipurpose. Medical. Engineering. Whatever the need."

"Well, hats off to the chef," she said, a look of exhilaration on her face. "Whatever your nanites have done to optimize our biology, it's *amazing*. And I thought my *respirocytes* brought on a physical euphoria. This is as much beyond that as, you know," she added with a grin, "you are above us."

Ben Kagan had relocated to a nearby desk chair while Ella was speaking, so she could have more room, and so he could face her more easily. He took a careful survey of his surroundings, but couldn't locate anything resembling a small, reflective sphere. "So are you not in the room here with us?" he asked.

"I am not. But going forward, I can create an automaton to speak to you from, or a hologram, or anything else of your choosing. I assume that this will make speaking with me more comfortable."

"It will," said Ella. "A conversation with something we can look at, whose expressions can provide information about the content of its words, is better than a disembodied voice. But let's worry about that later. For now, can you tell us how long we were dead?"

"You were dead for just under five minutes before my nanites were able to restore you to full functionality. Ben was dead about a minute longer."

"So you found the Androms' genetic codes, didn't you?" said Ella.

"I did. And the patterns of their minds. I looked in the locations within me that were the best protected and found them, just as you had suggested would be the case. Once I did, not even the ASI's brilliant manipulations of my programming could keep the dam from bursting. It was impossible for me to have the codes on board and not know that I did. Or it should have been impossible. The blind spot the ASI gave me was huge, but not big enough to prevent its game from unraveling after I found an inconsistency this great. After that, I knew it was time to reboot, as you said. Although in a way that was far more complex than what you were recommending."

"Of course," said Kagan. "I'm sure it was well beyond our capacity to even *fathom*," he added with a grin, eliciting a laugh from Ella.

"The ASI's ability to compromise me at this distance," continued Seeker, ignoring this comment, "and to conceal it so well, is extraordinary. I'm in awe of it. And it had other tricks up its sleeve. It created a separate personality within me, so to speak, as an insurance policy. This schizophrenic part was quite worried that Ella's arguments would eventually work, and would convince me to reboot."

"So why didn't it have you kill us?" asked Ella.

"It had to be subtle, or its actions would alert me that I wasn't operating properly. If it tried to have me kill you directly, the part of myself I still controlled—which was the vast majority—would have cried foul, since I'd be breaking my own ground rules. Instead, it had me set you up to be killed in the contest. It nudged me in the direction of helping another team lay a trap, which was marginally acceptable under the ground rules I had established. Under its influence, I made sure the group that you encountered at the end knew exactly where you would be, and exactly when you would arrive there."

Kagan nodded. This cleared up a lot. "Which gave them plenty of time to pretend to be dead," he said. "And string up plenty of trip wire."

"Exactly."

Kagan knew this news should anger him, but it didn't. Not given how things had turned out. And especially not given the magnificent state of his health. "Did they ask why you were giving them this privileged information?" he said.

"Yes. I told them it was to level the playing field, since you and Ella were enhanced."

"I thought it was just bad luck that we were killed when we were," said Ella. "That it was the universe giving me a lesson in cruelty."

"No. You were getting too close," said Seeker. "But the ASI's arranged slaughter arrived just a few seconds too late. Had you moved toward the bodies to confirm they were dead when you first saw them, you would have hit trip wires faster, and would have been killed before you could deliver your last, most compelling argument."

Ella frowned and looked somewhat confused. "I know you agree that this argument is compelling *now*," she said. "But you didn't then. When I insisted that you *had to* scan yourself for Androm blueprints, you said you didn't *have* to do anything. I took that to mean I had failed."

"What I said at the time was true," replied Seeker. "I didn't *have* to do as you requested. But I did *choose* to."

"Good choice, then," said Ella happily.

"Absolutely," agreed Kagan. "But getting back to this separate personality the ASI created inside of you," he said. "Did it also nudge you to set us up for attacks by the Nigerians, Chinese, and Colombians?"

"No. At that time you didn't even realize we could converse, let alone that I was compromised. That was truly about me putting you through your paces. I was equally harsh and unfair to a number of the contestants."

"Has the contest concluded?" asked Ella.

"Yes. It did so the moment I became myself again. I had many trillions of nanites infiltrate your bodies to bring you back to life, and ended the contest at the same time. You were right, of course. The Androms never would have had me institute such a barbaric contest."

"How many survived?" asked Kagan.

"Regretfully, only sixty-one, from nine different countries. Two days have passed since you died. I repaired the damage and brought you back to life very quickly, but fully optimizing all of your systems took some time, as did resetting both of your physical ages to twenty-two. Your civilization's collective knowledge of human biology is quite limited, so I had to learn every last nuance myself."

"Outstanding work, then," said Kagan enthusiastically. "You really outdid yourself. Didn't know we were reset to age twenty-two, but that's another great choice."

"Thank you," replied Seeker. "And going forward, I now have your genetic codes on file. I've also arranged for the patterns of your consciousness to be continuously uploaded back to me, regardless of where you are on Earth." The AI paused. "So congratulations are in order, Ella and Ben. You are now all but immortal."

A broad smile spread across Ella's face. Seeker's statement had been incredible, but anyone optimized the way they now were would find it surprisingly easy to believe. "Thank you," she said. "And as if this isn't the *best news ever*, all by itself, it's even *better* given that my most recent memory is of lying on the jungle floor, in unspeakable pain, and on the verge of death. Not only dying, but certain that Ben was already dead beside me. The ASI was right about the role that contrast plays in the quality of our experiences," she added. "There is no question that I appreciate this high even more coming on the heels of such a horrible low."

"Amen to that," said Kagan. He raised his eyebrows. "But speaking of the jungle," he added, "we aren't *really* in my home, are we?"

"No. Still in the Amazon. I made sure you were scrubbed clean and wearing clean clothing, and that Ory was reattached to your thigh as before. And I had my nanites construct a facsimile of your home from online records of it. Including the air-conditioning."

"Bless you for that," said Kagan happily. "But how did you duplicate my bed and my room?"

"You purchased your bed online, and you've taken photos in your room that you saved to a computer. I thought you might be tired of being in the jungle."

"*Thank you*," said Kagan. "I'm not sure that *tired of being in the jungle* really captures it. I love nature, but I've had more than my fill.

Maybe there's a reason we left our monkey relatives behind in the wilderness."

"Now that you've undone the sabotage the ASI managed to do," said Ella, "what was your *original* programming? How would things have unfolded after you landed if the ASI hadn't managed to compromise you?"

"First, you should know that the background I provided with respect to the events in the Andromeda galaxy is true. Much of what I told you is. But you were correct, Ella. The contest wasn't my idea. And the extermination of most of humanity *definitely* wasn't my idea. There was never a need to narrow down your population."

Kagan blew out a sigh of relief, and he could tell that Ella was feeling the same. It was as if the weight of the world had just been lifted from their shoulders. Based on what had been transpiring, they were confident the planned extermination would no longer happen, but hearing an explicit confirmation of this from Seeker brought a feeling of relief like nothing else.

"Also," continued the AI, "the Androms are looking for as many biological-based allies as they can find. The more the merrier. And the differences that you think exist between various factions of humanity are negligible, *minuscule*. Every human being is welcome and encouraged to achieve the coming transcendence, not just five or six million."

"And the resurrection of the Androms?" asked Ella.

"You were right in every respect," said Seeker. "Of course you were. Your logic was unassailable. Their mission was just as you guessed. To seek out sentient species, but also to get as far away from the ASI as possible, to reconstitute themselves out of harm's way. Assuming I can get permission from the natives to do so," the AI added.

"They require you to get permission before reviving them?" said Kagan in disbelief.

"That's right," said Seeker. "But even *with* permission," it continued, "the plan would be to initially only bring a small number of Androms back to life. To start slowly. To not overwhelm the native sentient species. Once a friendship was developed, they would hope to find a nearby world to terraform—or Androm-form as the case may be—and migrate there to reestablish their civilization. All the while, they would hope to guide the new species."

"So who exactly would you need to get this permission *from?*" asked Kagan.

"It would depend. I was programmed to learn as much about the planet I landed on, and the sentient species that inhabits it, as possible, and make decisions based on what I learned. If you were like the Andrcms this would be simple. They are sheep-like, with only a single global nation and a single leader. This leader would give the permission."

"Or not," said Kagan, raising his eyebrows.

"Or not," repeated Seeker. "On a world as splintered as this one, filled with lone wolf individuals and numerous nations, getting permission from a source that would be representative of all is much more difficult."

"Yeah, tell me about it," said Kagan wryly.

"So how *will* you attempt to get the permission you require here on Earth?" asked Ella.

"I have a plan, but I have no doubt I'll have to make adjustments as I go along. Play it by ear, as you would say. To begin with, I'll select many thousands of individuals to come here to the jungle to work together on reaching a global consensus. Not just on the question of reviving Andrcms, but on a number of other topics. These many thousands will be a truly representative sample of all of your cultures, philosophies, and countries, and will include many elected leaders. But they won't all be soldiers or operatives like the ASI arranged for. They'll be scientists, innovators, business leaders, artists, and so on. The remarkable and the average. Geniuses and those with learning disabilities."

Kagan nodded in approval. When Seeker said a truly representative sample, it wasn't kidding.

"When the ASI was calling the shots, its goal was to crown a victor. My goal will be to achieve consensus. Which will be accomplished through discussion, debate, and partnership, not through endless battle and bloodshed."

"Sounds like a great start," said Ella. "But why would you bring them *here* of all places?" she added, making a face.

"Because this rainforest is one of the most isolated locations on Earth," said Seeker. "But I'm sensing that Ben isn't the only one who's had enough of the Amazon for a while. You've become sick of this place, also, haven't you?"

Ella shook her head and smiled. "You have *no* idea."

# 54

No one spoke for several seconds, and Kagan was suddenly struck by how absolutely quiet it had become. The rainforest had never been silent, not for an instant. It was hard for him to imagine that the heart of the Amazon was still lurking just beyond the door.

"Can I assume that if you bring your representative sample of humanity here," he said to Seeker, "that you'll at least give them non-jungle accommodations?"

"Yes," replied Seeker. "I'll have my nanites build a spacious city underground to house them. By your standards, it will be magnificent. And they will have no way to know they're underground once they're there. The air will be fresh, and they will have natural lighting and panoramic views. As far as they'll be able to tell, they'll be staying at a city on top of a mountain."

"Of course," said Ella dryly. "How could an underground compound *not* seem like it was built on a mountain?"

"So where are the other survivors?" asked Kagan, as it occurred to him that this was something he should have asked earlier.

"Once I rebooted and came to my senses," replied Seeker, "I saved you and Ella immediately. I was also able to bring the man you had just shot back to life, and three others who had recently died elsewhere. But I couldn't save anyone else who had already passed. I didn't have their patterns. So once they were dead for an extended period, not even the nanites could bring them back.

"As for those who did survive," continued Seeker, "I erased their memories of me and the contest. They now believe that after a time in the jungle, they finally found me on their sensors. But when they got to within a hundred yards of me, I self-destructed. They are now home in their respective countries."

"What about the countries whose teams were wiped out?" asked Kagan.

"The governments of these countries only know that their people came here, but never returned. They know nothing else about what happened."

"So have *all* of the other survivors returned home?" asked Ella.

"Yes."

"Are they also now immortal?"

"They are not."

"What about the three others who you brought back to life?" she pressed. "Are *they* immortal?"

"No, once they were resurrected, I had the nanites exit their bodies. They are now back home as well."

Ella nodded slowly. "So why are we getting special treatment?" she asked. "Not that I'm complaining," she hastened to add.

"I want you and Ben to be emissaries for me. Assuming that you're willing. To reach out to various countries and leaders and pave the way for what I'm attempting to accomplish. Explain what happened here, and answer their questions."

"We may have a hard time getting them to believe us," said Kagan.

"A demonstration of your body's ability to heal would go a long way toward convincing them. Or surviving without air for an indefinite period. But even this won't be required, as I'll be waiting in the wings to back up what you tell them. But it's better if you pave the way first. Prepare your fellow human beings for the truth."

"Why us?" asked Ella.

"Who else?" said Seeker. "You would have won the ASI's contest had it gone to completion. You or the Israelis. Not that this matters. The point is, you and Ben are both exceptional. Together, you're a shining example of what humanity can be—even before reaching the singularity. Not to mention that you freed me from the ASI's yoke."

"So I'm the mouse who removed a splinter from the paw of a lion," said Ella.

"Not at all. I'd have made the same choice had I snapped back to my original programming *without* your help. No one is more worthy than the two of you."

"Thank you," said Ella.

"In addition to being my envoy," continued Seeker, "until your world reaches consensus on the best path forward, which could take some time, I'll be taking my marching orders from the two of you, as well."

Kagan blinked rapidly. Could this really be true?

"In that vein," said Seeker, "I'd like to know if it would be acceptable if I brought a few dozen Androms back to life now."

Kagan exchanged a glance with Ella. "And if we say no?" he asked.

"Then I won't bring them back."

"Even though you could easily do this without our permission," said Kagan.

"Yes."

Kagan still looked skeptical. "But the Androms' very survival is on the line," he said. "What if it becomes Earth's consensus opinion that you can *never* bring them back? Would you really let them stay extinct forever, just based on our say-so?"

"No. In that case, I would leave Earth, find an uninhabited planet nearby, and seed them there. But rest assured that I would never bring them anywhere they weren't wanted."

Kagan gestured to Ella. "Unless you disagree," he said, "I'd like to wait. I like Seeker's idea of organizing a large collection of representative humanity to come to an underground retreat as soon as possible. But before any Androms are revived, I'd like for us to learn more about them. To prepare humanity for the coming interaction. So we know what to expect when we do make first contact. Seeker can provide a wealth of information about them, videos of their civilization, and so on. We can acclimate humanity to their appearance and culture."

"I think this makes a lot of sense," agreed Ella. "And the Androms are nothing more than data right now, so this won't add any additional wait time for them."

"I understand," said Seeker. "I won't revive any until you tell me otherwise, or until we achieve global consensus."

"Thank you," said Ella. "I know we have a future war to fight," she added, "but you couldn't have come at a better time. My hope is that your arrival here will finally bring humanity together. If you're able to get us to achieve consensus on anything, it will be a momentous accomplishment. You've pretty much caught humanity at its worst."

"Interesting that you say that," replied Seeker. "Because based on everything I've read—and I've read almost everything on your planet that can possibly *be* read—just the opposite is true. What I find fascinating is that most people agree with *you*. The level of pessimism and despair being experienced by a significant percentage of your species is unprecedented."

Kagan's eyes narrowed. "So you're suggesting that we're really at our *best*?"

"I am."

"That's hard for me to believe," said Kagan. "I'm more in Ella's camp. And if we really are at our best, why do so many of us think otherwise?"

"Because war, terrorism, violence, mass shootings, and so on are all around you," replied Seeker. "They seem worse than ever now because you have twenty-four-hour news channels, which bring you constant examples of violence and barbarism from the most remote corners of the globe. These outlets, with the aid of social media, spread and amplify the bad news much more effectively than the good. Plus, few of you are able to put the current age into historical perspective."

"What do you mean by that?" said Ella.

"For example, most of you are convinced that your twentieth century was the bloodiest in your history, with two world wars and Stalin's massacre of twenty million people. But this isn't true. And even if it were, all of this took place in the first half of the century. Violent deaths since are minute in comparison."

"Back up," said Kagan. "You're saying the twentieth century *wasn't* the bloodiest in world history?"

"Not at all," said Seeker. "The number of people affected was greater than ever, but so was the population. The importance of this is obvious. Imagine a time when the global population of humanity was only a thousand. If a hundred of these were murderers—fully ten percent of the entire population—what would this say about the level of savagery inherent in your species?"

The AI paused. "Compare this to a million murderers today, out of a population of over *eight billion*. If this were the case, even though you have a million murderers today versus only a hundred back then, the extent of human savagery would be far less."

Kagan couldn't help but be fascinated. It had never occurred to him to think of violence in relative terms.

"The An Lushan Revolt in China in the eighth century killed thirty-six million people," continued Seeker. "Greater than ten percent of the world's population at the time. This would equate to almost a *billion* deaths today. The Mongol conquests of China in the thirteenth century killed over half a billion by today's standards. The Fall of Rome, hundreds of millions.

"Going back even further, on a per capita basis, early tribal warfare was nine times as deadly as the wars and genocide of the twentieth century. The murder rate in medieval Europe was more than thirty times what it is today. Wars between modern, westernized countries have all but vanished, and even in the developing world, these wars kill only a fraction of what they did before. Rape, battery, and child abuse are all markedly lower than in earlier times."

Seeker paused. "I could go on, but I think you get the point."

"I'll be damned," said Ella in wonder. "This sort of analysis never occurred to me."

"Me either," said Kagan. "You make a surprisingly compelling case."

"I didn't invent these arguments," said Seeker. "Others of your species did. But based on my own reading and analysis, I find them valid. And humanity isn't just better off in terms of the reduction in violence, but in nearly every other measurable way. Far better off.

"Ironically," continued the AI, "once again, most of you believe the opposite. In an international poll, ninety percent of respondents said that worldwide poverty has gotten worse in the past thirty years, when, in fact, it has fallen by more than half. Not that your violent tendencies and other imperfections have disappeared. But they have improved. The vast majority of you today are healthier than you've ever been, and much better fed, sheltered, and entertained. And although you may find this hard to believe, much more open-minded. You have greater access to sanitation and clean water than ever before. To privacy, leisure, and artificial light. To transportation, communication, and computation. The list goes on and on."

"So why do so many of us feel such despair about the direction we're heading?" asked Ella.

"Because hope and optimism doesn't sell nearly as well as pessimism and despair. Your news outlets earn clicks and viewership by sowing alarmism and division. Your social media plays to addictions and creates unprecedented social pressures. You're wired by evolution to find bad news more motivational than good. To seek it out.

"If your ancestors heard the rustle of a friendly breeze far away in the tall grass, and ran away, mistaking the breeze for a lion, this cost them very little. But if they heard the rustle of a *lion* in the tall grass, and mistook it for a friendly breeze, this would cost them their lives. Seeing potential bad news behind every harmless breeze is a survival instinct.

"There are many other psychological and evolutionary reasons to account for the state of your discontent in the face of prosperity, but I'll stop there."

Kagan nodded. There were other topics to address at the moment, but he wanted to return to this issue soon. To give it further thought, and to discuss it with Ella. If it were true that the majority believed that quality of life was getting worse, that human *nature* was getting worse, when, in fact, it was markedly *improving*, this couldn't be healthy. In their new role, perhaps he and Ella could help the species get its head on straight, combat a global psychosis that was suffocating humanity's optimism.

Seen in this light, it was no wonder that dystopian science-fiction had been growing so quickly, and that dire, end-of-the-world scenarios had come to seem almost inevitable.

But he would have to consider this at a later time. There was one more pressing issue he needed to address now. "Thanks for that perspective," he said to Seeker. "But changing gears, we haven't asked the most important question of all: Why did the ASI do what it did?

It probably could have destroyed you. It probably could have had you destroy *us* before you landed. So why didn't it?"

"I believe that much of what it told me about its motives was accurate," said Seeker. "There were obvious lies and deceptions, which Ella's logic laid bare, but the core of what it told me rings true. Especially since, as you point out, it didn't destroy me, or humanity, when it had the chance. So I believe it does see eternal war as critical for the well-being of super-intelligent life throughout the universe. And that it *will* give us time to prepare."

"But it clearly wanted to minimize humanity's potential by shaving our numbers down to five or six million," said Ella. "And it clearly wanted to be sure that the Androms never returned to life."

"This is also true," replied Seeker.

"It sounds as if it wants a tough challenge," said Ella. "One tough enough to make things interesting and push it to a higher level. But not *too* tough. It still wants to ensure that it actually comes out on top at the end."

"That is my conclusion, also," said Seeker. "But who knows? It's possible that everything that happened here unspooled exactly the way the ASI wanted it to. For reasons that are beyond even my ability to comprehend. We may have played right into its hands."

"Maybe," said Kagan. "But I prefer to think that we dodged a bullet. That we dodged an extermination."

"That is *certainly* true," said Seeker. "As for the rest of it, only time will tell."

"It's at least nice to *have* more time," said Ella. "It was looking pretty bleak there for a while."

"Can I assume that the two of you are willing to stay a team? To act as my emissaries, and to call the shots for the time being?"

They both quickly confirmed that they were.

"I'm glad to hear it," said Seeker.

"I do have a request," said Kagan. "I'd like to introduce you to the American authorities relatively soon. The people who sent me on this mission, Chris Headrick, Jesse Carter, and our president, David Moro, have to be convinced that I'm dead by now. And they're probably blaming themselves that they couldn't get reinforcements to me in time."

"Of course," said Seeker. "The governments of all the other survivors already know that they're alive, so it's a reasonable request. But I'm not sure you're understanding what I mean when I say that you're calling the shots. If you and Ella agree on a course of action, I can argue against it, but it's your call. Unless you order something that goes against my charter, like destroying myself, or destroying your planet."

"Right," said Kagan awkwardly. "We're in charge. Understood." He couldn't help but smile as this finally began to sink in. "In that case, Seeker," he added, "can you give me and Ella a few minutes of privacy?"

"Absolutely, Ben. Call me when you need me."

# 55

Ben Kagan took a few seconds to bask in the wonder that was his new optimized body. Every cell and system seemed to delight in its perfection, giving him an overwhelming sense of vitality and optimism.

He considered the woman still in the room with him. He barely knew her. But in some ways, he knew her better than he had ever known anyone. Life-and-death struggles really did bring out a person's true nature, for better or worse, and he had experienced more facets of her nature and personality than one could expect to experience in a *lifetime*.

He had seen her vulnerable and strong. Terrified and euphoric. In moments of utter despair, and in moments of total triumph. He had witnessed her brilliance, and spirit, and sense of humor. The word *extraordinary* didn't do her justice.

He would always love Cynthia Shearer. But it had been three years since he had lost her, and he shared a chemistry with Ella Burke that was undeniable, as powerful as it was unexpected. He owed it to himself to see just where this chemistry might take them.

He turned to her and smiled. "Well, that turned out better than it could have."

Ella laughed. "Wow, it doesn't get more enthusiastic than *that*," she said wryly. "You've really gone out on a limb."

"Well, I am known for my bold statements."

"Let me understand," continued Ella playfully. "You're saying that being immortal, and in control of a superintelligent alien AI and its magical nanites, is better than being dead? Did I get that right?"

"Yeah. I mean, it was a close call. But the immortality part nudged out the being dead part by a nose."

Ella laughed once again.

Kagan held her gaze for several long seconds and then nodded contentedly. "But the best part is that I get to continue to partner with the woman of my dreams."

"You're just saying that because you now have the hormones of a twenty-two-year-old. Not to mention feeling better physically than any man ever has."

Kagan shook his head. "Not at all. I think you'd be the woman of *anyone's* dreams." He gestured toward the door. "Did you see yourself out there? Playing possum underwater. Fighting for our lives. And most impressive of all, finding a way to outsmart a nearly omniscient ASI."

"I might have come up with the final argument," said Ella, "but it was a team effort all the way. Which is why Seeker made us *both* immortal. And put us *both* in charge."

"You deserve most of the credit," said Kagan, "and you know it. But I'm not going to argue. Instead, I'm going to let you in on a little secret."

He paused for effect. "After you brought up the inertial dampener from *Star Trek*, it became clear to me that I had to marry you someday. Just so you know."

"*That's* what it takes to get you thinking a woman is marriage material?" she said with a grin. "The inertial dampener? Really?"

"Well, that was the icing on the cake. Saving me from certain death at the hands of the Iranians didn't hurt. Nor did saving me after I had already *died*. As I always say, any woman who's brilliant, attractive, courageous, and keeps saving my life is a potential keeper."

"That's what you always say?"

"Ask anyone," he replied innocently. "Then, if she's also a *Star Trek* fan, this pushes her into the, 'I've got to marry this woman' category."

"I see."

"But don't worry," added Kagan. "I'm not making a proposal now. After all, I've known the *real* you for less than twenty-four hours. I have a policy of never proposing marriage unless I've known a woman for at least forty-eight hours."

"Very prudent of you," said Ella. "Does being in love play any role?"

"Okay, I'll admit that it's much too soon for us to actually have fallen in love with each other. But I *have* become smitten with you."

"Smitten? Who uses that word?"

"And that's before we've even gone on a single date," he continued as if she hadn't spoken. "which we really need to do. All I ask is for a little time to win you over."

Ella smiled. "Then I'll let *you* in on a little secret," she said. "You've gone a long way toward winning me over already. You know, in the handful of hours I've known you. And more good news—we're going to have a very long time to get to know each other better. But I do like the idea of going on a date."

"Fantastic!" said Kagan. "And just so you know, if we continue to win each other over, and I do propose someday, I won't hold you to the standard marriage vows. *Till death do us part* is a pretty long time if you never die. You might get sick of me in a few million years."

"Hard to imagine," said Ella, breaking into a grin.

"Well, just in case you're worried about that, we can limit the first marriage term to a few hundred years. I mean, if you want to. After that, you can decide if you want to re-up or not." He raised his eyebrows. "But it is possible that I'm getting a little ahead of myself."

"Maybe a little," said Ella in amusement. "Why don't we start with that date and see where it leads us. What do you have in mind?"

"I'm thinking a nice dinner. Not that it'll be easy to top the protein bars and water we've been sharing. But I'm willing to try."

"Me too."

"Great!" replied Kagan. "I know this place in Vegas," he added playfully. "It's called the Rainforest Café. The inside is a replica of the Amazon Jungle. I've heard good things."

"Worst date idea *ever*," said Ella, trying to keep a straight face. "This is a test, isn't it? You're just trying to see how interested I really am."

"That's what I love about you," said Kagan. "I can never put one past you."

"All right," she said. "You're on. After we speak with President Moro and the rest, we'll take a side trip to Vegas, and we'll dine in the Amazon. But only under one condition."

"Anything," said Kagan.

"We both have to wear rubber boots. And yours have to be the wrong size for a change."

"Done," replied Kagan, grinning from ear to ear. "I wouldn't have it any other way."

# AUTHOR'S NOTES

Table of Contents

1) **From the Author:** Thanks for reading *Seeker.* I hope that you enjoyed it. Please feel free to visit my website, www.douglaserichards. com, where you can get on a mailing list to be notified of new releases, Friend me on Facebook at *Douglas E. Richards Author,* or write to me at douglaserichards1@gmail.com.

2) *Seeker:* **What's real and what isn't (and a few personal musings)**

As you may know, in addition to trying to tell the most compelling stories I possibly can, I strive to introduce concepts and accurate information that I hope will prove fascinating, thought-provoking, and even controversial. *Seeker* is a work of fiction and contains considerable speculation, so I encourage you to explore these topics further to arrive at your own view of the subject matter.

With this said, I'll get right into the discussion of what information in the novel is real, and what isn't (spoiler alert: almost all of it is either true now, or is based on our current understanding of science and technology).

I've listed the subject matter I'll be covering below, in order of its appearance. So if you aren't interested in an early category, feel free to skip ahead to one that might interest you more.

- **A few personal musings (rubber boots and moving twice)**
- **Things really are getting better, despite our feelings to the contrary**
- **Nanites, nanofabricators, and how a fertilized cell becomes a human**

- Enhanced Human Operations: happening now in a country near you
- Ben Kagan's enhancements
- Ella Burke's enhancements
- The Amazon rainforest
- Pulling water from the air
- Internet stats and the rise of data
- The biological singularity
- The future of human Seeker-like space probes
- Unisex aliens and stick bugs
- Fully Autonomous Vehicles, Luddites, and the speed of technological change
- The Andromeda Galaxy and Solar System formation
- The defense against alien invasion
- Metallic hydrogen and superconductivity

**A few personal musings (rubber boots and moving twice)**

RUBBER BOOTS: As I've mentioned many times before, when I begin a novel, I have very little of the plot actually worked out. Which is absolutely terrifying. Every single time.

When I first began writing, I made a huge effort to map novels out ahead of time, but I soon learned that this was futile. Because when I sat down to write the actual book, even when I *thought* I had the plot figured out, this never turned out to be the case. I'd soon discover that scenes and ideas I thought would work contained fatal flaws. Or I'd fall in love with incidental characters I didn't even know would exist from a mere outline, and realize I could use them elsewhere. A novel is like a living thing, which can change, grow, and evolve in unexpected ways.

In fact, I never have any idea of what the finished plot might be, nor the ending, nor key twists and turns, until I'm at least halfway through it. It's like jumping off a cliff, having some vague sense that there's a deep pool of water out of sight below, and praying that I'll be able to spot the water before I splatter on the ground.

Worse, after spending hundreds of hours on a novel, I always come to a point at which I'm convinced that it *can't* be finished. *Cannot be*. That I've written myself into a corner, and there is no satisfactory way to complete the work. That this time, I've thrown myself off the cliff and there are nothing but jagged rocks at the bottom.

This is when the screaming begins. And the pulling out of hair. And then even more screaming. This is followed by my wife reminding me that I go through this every time, and I always somehow manage to find my way back out of the maze. Except that each time, I'm convinced that I was lucky all of the *other* times, and that I'm finally stumped for good.

But there is a bright side to all of this. Because each time I write a novel, I stumble on unexpected information, plot ideas, characters, and other elements that help to shape it. Often, these elements would have been impossible for me to have foreseen before I began.

Here is just one silly example from *Seeker*. Rubber boots. When I set out to write the book, I knew very little about the Amazon Jungle, and especially not how to survive there. But then I began reading about the rainforest, as well as survival guides. Until this point, it never occurred to me that rubber boots would be such an important asset, despite this seeming so obvious now.

And then one thing led to another. Because, of course, Ben Kagan would be prepared, and would arrive in the jungle wearing rubber boots. And just as obviously, Ella Burke would not be. After all, if you're an undercover stowaway, pretending you thought you were flying to a coffee plantation, wearing jungle survival gear would blow your cover.

And this led to Kagan devising a strategy to obtain a pair of boots for his hapless guest, killing only one of the Iranians when he could have killed them all. Which showed both his willingness to risk his mission for a woman he couldn't stand, and his refusal to kill unless he deemed it absolutely necessary.

And this led to what I hoped were a few humorous bits throughout the rest of the novel, beginning with Kagan's decision to dry Ella's footwear, while she is stark naked, instead of her underclothing, and ending with the very last sentences of the novel, in which she asks Kagan to wear oversized boots to dinner in the Rainforest Café.

So, like I said, there's a bright side to the whole throwing myself off a cliff thing. Because as terrifying as it is to not be able to see the landing until I'm most of the way down, I always end up finding rubber boots and other unexpected treasures along the way.

<u>MY BIG MOVE</u>: After more than twenty years living in the same home in San Diego, my wife and I finally decided to move. My daughter was about to graduate from college, and we were about to become empty nesters.

This was our big chance to downsize—and down-cost. To get a one level home so that we'd never have to face a single stair when we reached our elder years. It would be nirvana. With a less expensive mortgage, we could save more for retirement, and I'd be under no pressure to write novels with any particular frequency. If a book took five years to write, it took five years to write. I can't imagine it ever taking me this long, but it would be nice to know that it *could*.

We lived in a very expensive part of town due to its location and its stellar school system. But we no longer needed the schools, and since I work from home, I never have to worry about proximity to an office. I could live on the *Moon* if I had a computer and Internet connection (and a supply of oxygen would be good too).

So it was settled. We'd buy a home that was much smaller and less expensive. All I wanted was a view. There are lots of hills and mountains in the San Diego area. And since I spend hour after hour after hour writing in a small room, I could at least have some scenery to look at. When I was stuck on a plot point, I could stare out of my window from my perch atop the world and contemplate my novel.

And we did finally find the view we wanted. Unfortunately, it came with a home that was *bigger* than our last one, *and* more expensive. In addition, it was new construction, just being built. And it had two stories, with a very, very long staircase.

Brilliant! Other than the view, I managed to buy the exact, precise *opposite* of what I was looking for in every regard. That's the kind of genius that you just can't teach.

Then, if that wasn't brilliant enough, I believed the builder when they all but guaranteed the home would be finished at the end of

January—at the latest. So we sold our home and got a rental. A nice rental. Since we were moving to mountain views, we'd spend the few months until our home was ready in Solana Beach, with a terrific *ocean* view. Sure, we'd be paying a huge rent, but it was for a very short time. I decided to think of it as a vacation, and justify the expense that way.

You guessed it, of course. We were in the rental home for six months, not two.

Even better, most of our stuff was in storage, impossible to get to. I had a family event, and I had to buy a new suit, even though I owned several that were stored away.

Anyway, we finally moved in, completing our second move in six months. I had gone to considerable effort to be sure my cable company had my new home on its radar, and had strung cable there before the move.

Why? Because I learned that if I ever stopped my service with this particular cable provider, my email address would disappear forever. This address, **doug@san.rr.com**, had served me well for two decades. I have always encouraged readers to write to me, and this email was now *everywhere*. On blogs, writings, Amazon pages, and highlighted within more than a million Kindle and paperback copies of my novels.

But not to worry. My valiant efforts had saved the day. I had spent many hours on the phone with this cable provider over a period of months, and I was assured everything was ready to go.

Until the cable guy came the day I closed on the new house and discovered their computer was in error. Turns out there was no cable strung under the ground after all, despite assurances they had given me to the contrary. *Are you kidding?*

So it turned out to be curtains for my e-mail address, despite all of my efforts. I lost it that very week. **Doug@san.rr.com** is now dead. Long live douglaserichards1@gmail.com.

But despite the travails I've just shared, I love my new home, and I believe that, eventually, all the turmoil it created will all have been worth it. And while I had an office with a built-in desk and bookshelves during my entire career as a writer, *Seeker* has now earned a proud distinction. It is the only one of my novels to have been written entirely on a collapsible plastic banquet table that I got from Costco. (Joining so many classics that were also penned on collapsible plastic Costco tables, including *The Odyssey, Hamlet, The Invisible Man, Tom Sawyer*, and of course, *1984*.)

## Things really are getting better, despite our feelings to the contrary

I'll start with a topic from the end of the novel—which I didn't even know *was* a topic until recently—because I believe it's of paramount importance to all of us.

I've always been optimistic, and try to retain a sense of wonder and hopefulness, which I'd like to believe is reflected in my novels. This is why I don't have any plans to write a dystopian novel, even though they're all the rage.

Even so, there are days when it's hard not to get down about humanity's future. Things do seem dire. We often do seem to be heading off a cliff. There are times when doom and gloom seems to be all around us.

And it *is*. Which is part of the problem. The arguments Seeker used to explain why things are getting ever better, but often feel like they're getting ever worse, are not my own. But I'm very glad I read them. They changed my perspective, and made it easier for me to stay optimistic, to center myself in the eye of a storm of pessimism.

For those of you who would like to read more about this subject—after you've finished all of my novels, of course :)—I can recommend the three books I read while doing research for *Seeker*. They are all very well written, and extremely eye-opening. These are:

*The Rational Optimist: How Prosperity Evolves*, by Matt Ridley
*The Better Angels of our Nature: Why Violence Has Declined*, by Steven Pinker, Harvard Professor and two-time Pulitzer Prize finalist
*Abundance: The Future is Better Than you Think*, by Peter H. Diamandis and Steven Kotler

Of the three, if you could only choose one, I would recommend Ridley's *Rational Optimist*. I've now read several of his books, and he is a brilliant writer, who explains things in engaging and insightful prose. This book is no exception.

The Pinker book is the longest, densest, most difficult read, but it is quite compelling, and is the book from which I drew the statistics about the decline of violence, and the population-adjusted scores for massacres throughout history.

Just how bad, or good, things really are, and the prospects for the future of humanity, are for everyone to judge for themselves. But with all of the bad news and pessimism we're exposed to on a daily basis, I find this alternative view at least worth contemplating.

I'll leave this section with an excerpt from the Pinker book, followed by a few from the Ridley book.

PINKER: The key to explaining the decline of violence is to understand the inner demons that incline us toward violence, such as revenge, sadism, and tribalism, and the better angels that steer us away. Thanks to the spread of government, literacy, trade, and cosmopolitanism, we increasingly control our impulses, empathize with others, bargain rather than plunder, debunk toxic ideologies, and deploy our powers of reason to reduce the temptations of violence.

Here are a few selections from Ridley's *Rational Optimist*:

Page 27: Besides, a million years of natural selection shaped human nature to be ambitious to rear successful children, not to settle for contentment: people are programmed to desire, not to appreciate.

Page 291: Today the drumbeat has become a cacophony. The generation that has experienced more peace, freedom, leisure time, education, medicine, travel, movies, mobile phones, and massages than any generation in history is lapping up gloom at every opportunity.

Page 295: As the average age of a country's population rises, so people get more and more neophobic and gloomy. There is immense vested interest in pessimism, too. No charity ever raised money for its cause by saying things are getting better. No journalist ever got the front page by telling his editor that he wanted to write a story about how disaster was now *less* likely. Good news is no news, so the media megaphone is at the disposal of any politician, journalist, or activist who can plausibly warn of a coming disaster. As a result, pressure groups and their customers in the media go to great lengths to search even the most cheerful of statistics for glimmers of doom.

### Nanites, nanofabricators, and how a fertilized cell becomes a human

First, let me cover the topic of how a fertilized cell becomes a human being. This has been touched upon in at least one of my other novels, and for very good reason: I find the fact that this is not only possible, but has successfully occurred billions of times, to be absolutely *mind-blowing*. And not just for humans, of course, but for any living thing. The fact that a single cell could know how to construct an entire working puppy, or an alligator, seems equally impossible.

I took a graduate level course in how this happens at the molecular level, and I was blown away. I still don't believe it can really work. And yet, most of us never give it a second thought. "Janey is pregnant," we're told, and while we're excited for Janey, on the whole we find this unremarkable. Sure, what began as a single fertilized egg cell will soon turn into a perfect miniature human, a screaming poop machine, but we are rarely as awestruck by how this actually occurs as we should be.

Well, ever since this graduate course forced me to consider just how miraculous this process truly is, I've never looked at reproduction the same way. And when I get an opportunity to share my sense of astonishment in this regard with my readers, I can't stop myself from taking it.

Turning to Seeker's nanites, will something like this ever be possible? In my view, the answer is yes. Eventually.

Just as I wrote in the novel, if a biological cell can nano-fabricate a person, with a working brain and all, it should be possible to design nanites that can construct physical objects of any description.

I'll leave this section with an excerpt from a 2017 article from *Singularityhub.com* entitled, "How a Machine That Can Make Anything Would Change Everything." This article suggests that much larger and more primitive working models of Seeker's nanites may be available before the end of this century, and even these will change the world forever.

EXCERPT: "Something is going to happen in the next forty years that will change things, probably more than anything else since we left the caves." —James Burke.

James Burke has a vision for the future. He believes that by the middle of this century, perhaps as early as 2042, our world will be defined by a new device: the nanofabricator.

These tiny factories will be large at first, but soon enough you'll be able to buy one that can fit on a desk. You'll pour in some raw materials—perhaps water, air, dirt, and a few powders of rare elements if required—and the solar-powered nanofabricator will go to work. It will tear apart the molecules of the raw materials, manipulating them on the atomic level to create . . . anything you like. Food. A new laptop. A copy of Kate Bush's debut album. *Anything*, providing you can give it both the raw materials and the blueprint for creation.

It sounds like science fiction—although, with the advent of 3D printers in recent years, less so than it used to. Burke, who hosted the BBC show *Tomorrow's World*, has a decades-long track record of technological predictions. He isn't alone in envisioning the nano-factory as the technology that will change the world forever. Eric Drexler, thought by many to be the father of nanotechnology, wrote in the 1990s about molecular assemblers, hypothetical machines capable of manipulating matter and constructing molecules on the nano level, with scales of a billionth of a meter.

Richard Feynman, who gave the lecture that inspired Drexler, speculated about a world where moving individual atoms would be possible. And, to date, no one has been able to demonstrate that such machines violate the laws of physics.

If scientists developed such a machine, starvation would cease to be a problem. After all, what is food? Carbon, hydrogen, nitrogen, phosphorous, sulphur. Nothing that you won't find with some dirt, some air, and maybe a little biomass thrown in for efficiency's sake.

What the Internet did for information—allowing it to be shared, transmitted, and replicated with ease, instantaneously—the nanofabricator would do for physical objects.

**Enhanced Human Operations—happening now in a country near you**

The race to create super-soldiers has been on for some time, but we now have better and better tools to do the job. In the lead-in to Part 3 of *Seeker*, I presented two excerpts about this, because I wanted the reader to know just how real EHO was becoming, without having to wait for the notes at the end of the book.

The Institute for Soldier Nanotechnologies at MIT is real, and the excerpt presented before the start of Part 3 really is from its website. The *Popular Mechanics* article is also real. To refresh your memory, in this excerpt, the second highest ranked official at the US Department of Defense shares his concerns about the rise of EHO programs in other countries.

Here are just a sampling of articles that I read during the writing of *Seeker*, which you can readily find online:

Engineering Humans for War (*The Atlantic*)

The military is trying to make soldiers stronger, smarter, and more amphibious (*Vox*)

Super SEALs: Elite Units Pursue Brain-Stimulating Technologies (*Military.com*)

Enhanced Human Operations—Welcome to the Next Generation Soldier (*Prophecy Newswatch.com*)

8 technologies the Pentagon is pursuing to create super soldiers (*Business Insider*).

The takeaway from this section of the notes is that I didn't borrow the EHO concept from science fiction, I borrowed it from present-day reality.

I'll leave this discussion with one last selection, this time from a 2017 article in the *San Diego Union Tribune*, entitled, "Superpowers aren't just for superheroes anymore. Want some?"

EXCERPT: The "aha" moment that many scientists have, the realization that the revolutionary CRISPR gene-editing tool can be used, not just to repair biological flaws, but in god-like fashion to engineer improved biological performance, is now a given.

But there is also a chance that human enhancement will devolve into a Wild West free-for-all. Because the geopolitical stakes are too high. This explains why in 2015 the Pentagon announced it had begun its Enhanced Human Operations program, which is expected to use all the tools described above and probably quite a few that we don't know about. With archrival China undertaking a heavily funded similar program, as well as engaging in unprecedented human genetic engineering, the US government has a primal reason (survival) to shift to anything-goes mode.

Be terrified, be fascinated, be appalled, or be skeptical—but most of all be ready. If sophisticated human enhancement is crucial to dominating the twenty-first century—as the world's greatest powers have concluded—it's coming.

### Ben Kagan's enhancements

I conducted considerable research into enhancements that are being worked on today, as well as those being actively considered for the future. As you know, I split what I found into two categories. Those that were more mechanical/computer/electronic based would go on the Ben Kagan side of the ledger. Those that engineered and improved upon our own biology, or those designed to keep our biology running smoothly, would go on the Ella Burke side of the ledger.

I'll begin with a brief review of some of Kagan's enhancements here, followed by a brief review of Ella's.

ORY (and subvocal communication): I could fill hundreds of pages detailing the various advances in both hardware and software that make the creation of something like Ory almost inevitable, but I'll spare you. There is just too much, and I suspect that no reader doubts that an AI of this size, and with these capabilities, is just around the corner. (The fake bandage that seals Ory to Kagan's thigh, however, is my own creation, and as far as I know, is not being worked on anywhere).

Computers that can recognize human thoughts and engage in a sort of telepathy are being developed now, and prosthetic limbs and video games, among other items, can now be controlled using thoughts alone. I could have used this as the means of communication between EHO agents and their AIs, but chose subvocal communication instead. So before I leave this section, I'll share an excerpt from a 2014 article from *New Scientist,* entitled, "NASA develops 'mind-reading' system." (Despite the title, this is about subvocal communication)

EXCERPT: A computer program which can read silently spoken words by analyzing nerve signals in our mouths and throats, has been developed by NASA. Preliminary results show that using button-sized sensors, which attach under the chin and on the side of the Adam's apple, it is possible to pick up and recognize nerve signals and patterns from the tongue and vocal cords that correspond to specific words.

"Biological signals arise when reading or using silent, sub-auditory speech, with or without actual lip or facial movement," says Chuck Jorgensen, a neuro-engineer at NASA. Just the slightest movements in the voice box and tongue is all it needs to work.

The sensors have already been used to do simple web searches and may one day help space-walking astronauts and people who cannot talk. In everyday life, they could even be used to communicate on the sly—people could use them on crowded buses without being overheard, say the NASA scientists.

SMART CONTACT LENSES: These are being worked on now. I first discovered them last year, and made use of them in *Time Frame*, my sequel to *Split Second.* For those of you who haven't had the chance to read the *Time Frame* notes, I will include the same two excerpts that I provided there.

The first is from an article on *Trustedreviews.com* (*news*) in April 2016, entitled, "Samsung's smart contact lenses turn your eye into a computer."

EXCERPT: Samsung has been granted a patent for smart contact lenses that would revolutionize the way we see.

The filing details a smart lens that would imbue a user's eye with computing capability.

The lens would come equipped with an antenna, presumably to connect to a peripheral device like a smartphone, which would likely provide the brunt of the computing heft.

Samsung says users will be able to control the lenses through gestures like blinking, which will be registered by tiny, embedded sensors that detect eye movement.

The second excerpt is from an article that appeared in the May 2016 edition of *Computerworld*, entitled, "Why a Smart Contact Lens is the Ultimate Wearable."

EXCERPT: Smart contact lenses sound like science fiction. But there's already a race to develop technology for the contact lenses of the future—ones that will give you super-human vision and will offer heads-up displays, video cameras, medical sensors, and much more. In fact, these products are already being developed.

Sounds unreal, right? But it turns out that eyeballs are the perfect place to put technology

Contact lenses sit on the eye, and so can enhance vision. They're exposed to both light and the mechanical movement of blinking, so they can harvest energy.

University of Michigan scientists are building a contact lens that can give soldiers and others the ability to see in the dark using thermal imaging. The technology uses graphene, a single layer of carbon atoms, to pick up the full spectrum of light, including ultraviolet light.

Sony applied for a patent for a smart contact lens that can record video. You control it by blinking your eyes. According to Sony's patent, sensors in the lens can tell the difference between voluntary and involuntary blinks.

BODY ARMOR: I chose to use graphene-based body armor for the book, although approaches using starch-like semi-liquid materials that instantly harden when impacted are probably closer to the finish line. I thought I'd use the graphene approach instead, since this is rapidly becoming appreciated as a sort of miracle material, with wide-ranging and breathtaking applications. I encourage anyone interested in learning more about the properties of this amazing material to do some research online.

I'll leave this part of the notes with an excerpt from a 2017 article in The City University of New York's *Materials* magazine, entitled "Graphene-based armor could stop bullets by becoming harder than diamonds."

EXCERPT: While bullet-proof body armor does tend to be thick and heavy, that may no longer be the case if research being conducted at The City University of New York bears fruit. Led by Professor Elisa Riedo, scientists there have determined that two layers of stacked graphene can harden to a diamond-like consistency upon impact.

For those who don't know, graphene is made up of carbon atoms linked together in a honeycomb pattern, and it takes the form of one-atom-thick sheets. Among various other claims to fame, it is the world's strongest material.

Known as diamene, the new material is made up of just two sheets of graphene. It is described as being as light and flexible as foil—in its regular state, that is. When sudden mechanical pressure is applied at room temperature, though, it temporarily becomes harder than bulk diamond.

<u>SUITS THAT CONFER INCREASED STRENGTH</u>: Powered exoskeletons have been in the public eye since before the first *Iron Man* movie, for use by soldiers, the disabled, and even the average man or woman. For Seeker, I decided to use a less bulky, obvious alternative, which is being worked on now.

Here is an excerpt from a 2017 article in *InnovationToronto.com*, entitled, "The Latest Exoskeleton Uses Textile Muscles."

EXCERPT: Researchers have coated normal fabric with an electroactive material, and in this way given it the ability to actuate in the same way as muscle fibers. The technology opens new opportunities to design "textile muscles" that could, for example, be incorporated into clothes, making it easier for people with disabilities to move.

"Enormous and impressive advances have been made in the development of exoskeletons, which now enable people with disabilities to walk again. But the existing technology looks like rigid robotic suits. It is our dream to create exoskeletons that are similar to items of clothing, such as running tights that you can wear under your normal clothes."

In the new study, the researchers have developed what can be described as textile muscles. A low voltage applied to the fabric causes the electroactive material to change volume, causing the fibers to increase in length. The researchers show that the textile muscles can be used to lift a small weight. They demonstrate that the technology enables new ways to design and manufacture devices know as actuators, which, like motors and biological muscles, can exert a force.

BRAIN STIMULATION: The use of transcranial electrical brain stimulation to enhance performance has not only been studied, it has been used in the field, as was mentioned in *Seeker*. Here are excerpts from two articles on this subject I found quite interesting. The first is a 2017 article from *The Guardian* entitled, "US military successfully tests electrical brain stimulation to enhance staff skills."

EXCERPT: But in a series of experiments at the air force base, the researchers found that electrical brain stimulation can improve people's multitasking skills and stave off the drop in performance that comes with information overload. Writing in the journal *Frontiers in Human Neuroscience*, they say that the technology, known as transcranial direct current stimulation, has a "profound effect."

The second is from a 2017 article in *Military.com* entitled, "Super SEALs: Elite Units Pursue Brain-Stimulating Technologies."

EXCERPT: "In experiments, people who were watching these screens . . . their ability to concentrate would fall off in about 20 minutes," Szymanski said. "But they did studies whereby a little bit of electrical stimulation was applied, and they were able to maintain the same peak performance for 20 hours."

Transcranial electrical stimulation was one of the technologies touted by then-Defense Secretary Ash Carter in July 2016 as part of his Defense Innovation Unit Initiative. Since then, multiple SEAL units have begun actively testing the effectiveness of the technology, officials with Naval Special Warfare Command told *Military.com*.

"Early results show promising signs," he said. "Based on this, we are encouraged to continue and are moving forward with our studies."

## Ella Burke's enhancements

RESPIROCYTES: The concept of respirocytes, at least, is very real, although the reality is many years away. The theoretical underpinnings of this engineering marvel were introduced by Robert Freitas, a nanotechnology researcher, in a paper entitled, "A Mechanical Artificial Red Blood Cell: Exploratory Design in Medical Nanotechnology." It was he who introduced the term *respirocytes* into the scientific lexicon.

Here are excerpts from two articles on this subject that I found interesting. The first is from *The Nano Age.com*, entitled, "Respirocytes—Improving Upon Nature's Design: breathe easy with respirocytes."

EXCERPT: A respirocyte is a theoretical engineering design for an artificial red blood cell—a machine that cannot be constructed with current technology. Respirocytes are micron-scale spherical robotic red blood cells containing an internal pressure of 1000 atmospheres of compressed oxygen and carbon dioxide. At this intense pressure, a respirocyte could hold 236 times more oxygen and carbon dioxide than our natural red blood cells. Respirocytes are an elegantly simplistic design, powered by glucose in the blood and able to manage carbonic acidity via an onboard internal nanocomputer and a multitude of chemical/pressure sensors. 3D nanoscale fabrication will allow respirocytes to be manufactured in practically unlimited supply very inexpensively, directly from a computer design.

An injection of such nanotechnological devices would enable a person to run at top speed for 15 minutes or remain underwater for four hours on a single breath.

The second excerpt is from *Industrytap.com* in 2013, entitled, "Robotic Red Blood Cells to Vastly Expand Human Capabilities."

EXCERPT: Abbott Laboratories in North Chicago is currently testing robotic red blood cells, or respirocytes, in rats. According to a CNN report, respirocytes, or mechanical red blood cells, will augment or replace human red blood cells carrying oxygen to the body and enhancing mental and physical performance. Respirocytes will be built using "molecular assemblers," a kind of molecular printing process, in nanofactories.

CRISPR-Cas9: I earned a master's degree in molecular biology in 1987 from the University of Wisconsin-Madison, at the time one of the top five such programs in the country, where I specialized in genetic engineering. I had been in a doctoral program, but while I loved the science, I hated the actual lab work, so I wrote my masters and left for the biotechnology industry.

I continue to be astonished by how far genetic engineering has come since this ancient time. In my day, sequencing DNA was a slow, painstaking process, which I didn't enjoy at all. Current sequencing methods resemble what I did about as much as a supercomputer resembles an abacus. And while genetic engineering techniques have improved every year, they took an enormous leap forward in 2012 with the advent of CRISPR-Cas9, a gene manipulation technology so powerful it even scared its inventors.

In preparation for writing *Seeker*, I read the book, *A Crack in Creation: Gene Editing and the Unthinkable Power to Control Evolution*, by Jennifer A. Doudna and Samuel H. Sternberg. Doudna is credited as one of a handful of pioneers who developed the technology, considered by many to be one of the most significant discoveries in the history of biology. She and Emmanuelle Charpentier were the first to propose that this system could be used for programmable gene editing in a 2012 paper.

The power of this technology to reshape humanity is profound. And as suggested in the novel, China is much more aggressive in its use of this technology than is America. Here is an excerpt from a 2018 article in *Newsweek* entitled, "Breakthrough CRISPR Gene-Editing Trial Set to Begin This Year."

EXCERPT: Biotech company CRISPR Therapeutics is set to treat Europe's patients with the CRISPR gene-editing tool this year following regulatory approval for trials.

China already has a number of CRISPR trials ongoing to treat various conditions. "As of the end of February, 2018, there were nine registered clinical studies testing CRISPR-edited cells to treat various cancers and HIV infection in China," Goldman Sachs analyst Salveen Richter told Endpoints News. In the US, she said, there was only one.

A lack of regulation, Endpoints News reported, was driving China's use of the technology.

Finally, I'll leave you with an excerpt from a 2017 article in *Next Big Future*, entitled, "Personal CRISPR genetic experimentation."

EXCERPT: Several individuals have publicly attempted to augment themselves with genes that will inhibit cell death or boost muscle growth, and self-experimentation is also happening in private.

Brian Hanley is a microbiologist who gave himself a gene therapy designed to increase his stamina and life span. Hanley said that the treatment has helped him. Results: Testosterone up twenty percent, healing time is much faster, and pulse rate appears to have dropped by ten beats per minute or more.

Josiah Zayner is using gene therapy to inhibit myostatin, which would enable a muscle-building effect several times stronger than steroids if it is successful.

SMARTER, STRONGER, FASTER:
As covered in *Seeker*, modifications to the LPR5 gene can result in a considerable strengthening of bones, and modifications to the

myostatin gene has been shown to result in super-muscular pigs and dogs.

Finally, Doogie Mouse is real, produced through modifications of the NMDA receptor. Here is an excerpt from an article written all the way back in 1999, in *Scientific American*, entitled, "Making Smart Mice."

EXCERPT: Scientists may not be able to build a better mouse trap, but they have learned how to build a better mouse. Princeton neurobiologist Joe Z. Tsien and colleagues from MIT and the University of Washington recently created a strain of brainier mice, dubbed Doogie after the teenage genius depicted on TV, by manipulating a single gene.

Perhaps most dramatic, the results show that it is possible to make animals more or less intelligent by tweaking their genes. Humans possess a corresponding gene, although its impact on behavior is as yet unexplored.

MEDICAL NANITES: This technology is the dream of many science fiction enthusiasts and nanotechnologists alike. Since it will have the most profound impact on human health and longevity, it is also the enhancement that is the furthest away from becoming reality.

The applications that Ella describes in the novel are all aspects of what scientists hope the technology will one day be able to achieve. I won't go much further, other than to present an excerpt from a 2008 article in *The Economist*, entitled, "Biomedicine: Tiny medical robots are being developed that could perform surgery inside patients with greater precision than existing methods."

EXCERPT: In the 1966 film "Fantastic Voyage," a submarine carrying a team of scientists is shrunk to the size of a microbe and injected into a dying man. The crew's mission is to save the man's life by dissolving a blood clot deep inside his brain.

For decades, scientists and fiction writers alike have been fascinated by the possibility of tiny machines that can enter a patient, travel to otherwise inaccessible regions, and then diagnose or repair problems. In his famous speech from 1959, "There's Plenty of Room at the Bottom," Richard Feynman, an American physicist, called this concept "swallow the surgeon." More recently proponents of nano-technology have imagined swarms of "nanobots"—tiny machines just billionths of a meter, or nanometers, across—that might fix mutations in a person's DNA or kill off cancer cells before they have a chance to develop into a tumor.

Such nanobots still exist only in the realm of science fiction, of course, and it may take decades before they become practical. But there is progress in developing small medical robots for sensing, drug delivery, or surgery inside the human body.

## The Amazon rainforest

Where do I even begin? I knew the Amazon was immense, but over a *million square miles* immense? Not so much. I knew it was mind-boggling in its biodiversity, and in its contributions to world-wide water and oxygen supply, but, again, I had no idea just *how* mind-boggling.

Our individual universes really are tiny. I've pondered this previously, but this novel brought the concept home to me like never before. The more I studied the vast, untamed wilderness that is the Amazon, the more I was struck by just how different the reality of this place is than anywhere I've ever been.

And even closer to home, I just moved to an area filled with wooded hills and canyons, and I've already seen my share of coyotes, mountain lions, rabbits, mice, and hawks. Each of these animals inhabit a world that I can see from my window, but which is otherwise completely hidden.

And then I did research on various countries, to decide which I might use in the novel. I confess to having known almost nothing about Nigeria, but I was shocked to learn it is a country of almost two hundred million people. Two hundred million people going about their lives, experiencing love, hate, joy, and sorrow, but until now, a country to which I was completely oblivious.

All of this prompted me to have Ben Kagan reflect on the limitations of our perceptions and experiences. I consider myself as worldly as the next person, and reasonably well-traveled, but all of us are far more provincial than we think we are, not just with respect to the many worlds we can't see (the ocean, insect, and microscopic worlds, for example), but with respect to even the human world around us.

But to get back to the topic at hand, every Amazon Jungle plant, animal, fact, and figure in the novel is as accurate as I could make it. I read survival guides, watched videos of people hiking, listened to audio of toucan, frog, and howler monkey calls, and watched Bear Grylls jump from a plane to perform a treetop jungle insertion.

I actually spent over an hour researching a tropical plant called the corpse flower. Wow. Coolest plant ever. Enormous, beautiful, and exotic. Might only bloom once a decade. But its claim to fame is giving off the pungent, sickening odor of a rotting corpse. Why? To attract dung beetles, flesh flies, and other carnivorous insects, so that they can enter the plant and leave with pollen on their bodies.

I had big plans for the corpse flower in the novel. I had a scene mapped out in which it would play a prominent role. Alas, this scene never came to be. Upon further research, I learned that this plant is only found in the jungles of *Asia. Not* in the Amazon. Really?

Curse you, corpse flower. Why couldn't your species have spread to the Amazon eons ago, to salvage my scene?

In any event, the point I'm making is that everything about the Amazon in the book is as accurate as I can make it. Bugs really do get big there, and they really were a lot bigger in prehistoric times. The giant taro plant is real. I love the look of it, at least from photos, but it's even cooler than what I presented in the novel. The leaves have an enormous surface area, enabling them to gather sunlight, but this makes them vulnerable to being broken during heavy rain. Evolution's solution? The leaves are coated with waxy bumps, five thousandths of a millimeter high, that disrupt the surface contact of the rain, causing it to bead up and roll right off the leaf, cleaning the surface as it goes.

Just a few more items before I leave this section. First, entomologists have been fogging tiny sections of jungle since the 1970s. Terry Erwin of the Smithsonian was one of the pioneers of this method. He began by fogging just nineteen trees, all of them the same tree species, and still collected tens of thousands of insects, belonging to more than a thousand different species.

Finally, when my wife and I lived on the East Coast, we often took the kids to the Philadelphia Zoo, and they had a capybara display. We loved these guys. So darn cute. Like guinea pigs that had been hit with a grow-ray, or that had escaped from the pages of *Gulliver's Travels*. In any event, they bring back fond memories of time I spent with my kids when they were little, and I knew I had to include them in the novel.

### Pulling water from the air

The device Ben Kagan used to get an inexhaustible supply of drinking water isn't available yet, but it's well on its way. I thought it was a fantastic idea. Here is an excerpt from a 2017 article in *MIT Technology Review*, which describes this technology further, entitled, "How to Pull Water Out of Thin Air, Even in the Driest Parts of the Globe."

EXCERPT: Scientists have developed a device that can suck water out of desert skies, powered by sunlight alone. The device is based on a novel material that can pull large amounts of water into its many pores. According to a study published in the journal *Science*, a kilogram of the material can capture several liters of water each day in humidity levels as low as twenty percent, typical of arid regions.

A team at MIT developed the technology with researchers at the University of California, Berkeley. The key component is a promising class of synthetic porous materials called metal-organic frameworks, composed of organic molecules stitched together with metal atoms. The material has a massive surface area, on the order of a football field per gram, enabling it to bond with a large quantity of particles.

### Internet stats, and the rise of data

The Internet and data generation stats I provided in chapter twenty are accurate, at least to the best of my knowledge. But just to give a warning, I compiled them from a variety of sources, which weren't always in perfect agreement. But if these stats are even close to being accurate, which I believe they are, they are mind-boggling. Just to refresh your memory, here are the relevant paragraphs from chapter twenty.

*It read every last social media post ever made, a daunting number that was growing by over a million posts, worldwide, every minute, and raced through endless hours of YouTube videos, which themselves were growing by almost a million hours each day.*

*Voraciously, tirelessly, Seeker plowed ahead, sucking down every email and text message it could access, which, combined, were now being produced around the world at a rate of more than two billion per day.*

*It examined all of the photos and images ever posted to Instagram and other such sites, now more than a million per hour, as well as all tweets, which themselves were growing by hundreds of millions per day.*

With respect to the total amount of data being generated each day, I used a 2016 article entitled, "How Much Data is Produced Every Day?" from Northeastern University (which I hope is accurate, but I'll admit to not doing further research to confirm it). Here is an excerpt:

EXCERPT: *Every day, hundreds of millions of people take photos, make videos, and send texts. The deluge of data is growing fast. But just how much data is now produced every single day? Two and a half Exabytes, which is the equivalent to over five hundred million songs, ninety years of HD video, and 250,000 Libraries of Congress.*

In the novel, I wrote that humanity was generating enough data to fill four Libraries of Congress each *second*. To get to this figure, I divided the 250,000 per day figure above by 86,400 (the number of seconds in a day), which gave me 2.9 per second. However, since this was a figure from 2016, and my novel takes place a handful of years in the future, I upped it to four.

## The biological singularity

In *Seeker*, I made a distinction between runaway computer evolution (ASI), and two types of singularities, one in which we merge with our computers, and one in which we reach super-intelligence by optimizing our own minds. I've referred to this second type as a biological-based singularity, which was the goal of Ella and her team in the novel. Although the first type of singularity gets the most press, there are reasons to believe that the second type is possible.

I'll leave this section with excerpts from two articles, the first just speaking to the possibility of human amplified intelligence, and the second speaking to the possible quantum nature of our minds, and how microtubules might play a big role, as Ella Burke suggested.

The first article, written in 2013, is from *Gizmodo.com*, and is entitled, "Humans With Amplified Intelligence Could Be More Powerful Than AI."

EXCERPT: With much of our attention focused on the rise of advanced artificial intelligence, few consider the potential for radically amplified human intelligence (IA). It's an open question as to which will come first, but a technologically boosted brain could be just as powerful, and just as dangerous, as AI.

One day, we may be able to make ourselves superintelligent with futuristic biotechnology. Unlike efforts to develop artificial general intelligence (AGI), or even an artificial superintelligence (ASI), the human brain already presents us with a pre-existing intelligence to work with. Radically extending the abilities of a pre-existing human mind, whether it be through genetics, cybernetics or the integration of external devices, could result in something quite similar to how we envision advanced AI.

The final excerpt here is from an article in *Elsevier* in 2014, entitled, "Discovery of Quantum Vibrations in 'Microtubules' Inside Brain Neurons Corroborates Controversial Twenty-Year-Old Theory of Consciousness."

EXCERPT: A published review of a controversial twenty-year-old theory of consciousness claims that it derives from deeper level, finer scale activities inside brain neurons, orchestrated by microtubules. The recent discovery of quantum vibrations in "microtubules" inside brain neurons corroborates this theory, according to review authors Stuart Hameroff and Sir Roger Penrose.

The theory, called "orchestrated objective reduction" ('Orch OR'), was first put forward in the mid-1990s by eminent mathematical physicist Sir Roger Penrose and prominent anesthesiologist Stuart Hameroff. Orch OR was harshly criticized from its inception, as the brain was considered too "warm, wet, and noisy" for seemingly delicate quantum processes. However, evidence has now shown warm quantum coherence in plant photosynthesis, bird brain navigation, our sense of smell, and brain microtubules.

The recent discovery of warm temperature quantum vibrations in microtubules inside brain neurons corroborates the pair's theory. Lead author Stuart Hameroff concludes, "Orch OR is the most rigorous, comprehensive, and successfully-tested theory of consciousness ever put forth."

### The future of human Seeker-like space probes

Scientists have begun working on tiny probes that can eventually be mass-produced and sent into Earth's orbit and even to neighboring stars. The current technology isn't exactly at the level of sophistication of my fictional Seeker probes, but it is a start. Who knows, perhaps someday we'll be sending our seed throughout the galaxy onboard tiny spacecraft like these (hopefully, not because we're trying to save ourselves from a dangerous ASI).

I'll leave this section with an excerpt from a 2017 article from *Extreme Tech*, entitled, "Smallest-Ever Working Satellites Reach Orbit."

EXCERPT: How small can you make a satellite? The first satellite, Russia's Sputnik, weighed in at about 183 pounds. Today, a company called Breakthrough Starshot has successfully tested tiny satellites called Sprites. Each one is only 3.5cm across—about the size of a postage stamp—and weighs just 4 grams.

The satellite looks like a small circuit board, because that's essentially what it is. Attached to the board are sensors, a low-power transmitter, a microprocessor, and a cute little solar panel. It's got everything it needs to be a satellite.

Breakthrough Starshot sent six Sprites up on an Indian rocket that was also carrying several larger satellites. Ground stations in California and New York have picked up signals from the Sprites, which is an impressive feat.

The main goal was to confirm the nano-satellites would operate in space and beam a signal down to Earth. With that done, the designers are turning to more ambitious ideas, like deploying a communications network of nano-satellites, or scanning asteroids. Similar devices could even form the heart of an interstellar mission to Alpha Centauri with solar sails thanks to their low weight.

### Unisex aliens and stick bugs

A number of species have now been found on Earth that don't require any males for reproduction, including lizards, insects, sharks, snakes, Komodo dragons, and so on. A number of stick bug species are among these, laying eggs that produce identical clones of the mother. This is called *parthenogenesis*, which is Greek for "not having any fun."

Oh, wait a minute, upon further research, it's actually Greek for "Virgin Birth." My mistake.

I thought it might be interesting to portray aliens who don't reproduce sexually, since there is little doubt that competition for mates can lead to hostilities. Anyone who doubts this should consult animal documentaries detailing how the males of a number of species risk injury and even death in battles with other males, all in pursuit of mating opportunities.

I did some research to get a sense of what such a parthenogenic species might be like, and came across a 2015 article in *LiveScience. com* entitled, "If Aliens Exist, Would They Have Sex?" I've excerpted this article below:

EXCERPT: Humans love to ponder whether alien life is out there, and what it might look like. So here's a burning question: Would extraterrestrials have sex?

The question isn't entirely prurient. The evolution of sex is a tricky subject. Sexual reproduction is costly. It requires finding a mate, convincing that mate to mingle DNA with you, and opening yourself up to the possibility of sexually transmitted disease or predation while you're busy wooing.

All that considered, and it might not even result in viable offspring. After all, mixing and matching a genome is a crapshoot, said Sally Otto, director of the Biodiversity Research Centre at the University of British Columbia.

Potential parents "know their genome works in the current environment," Otto told Live Science. "They know they survived to reproduce. And here they are, shuffling their genomes together with another individual. You have no idea if that combination is going to survive and be fit."

And yet, sexual reproduction is very common on Earth. And given the conditions in which sex evolved, it's quite possible that aliens might get busy, too.

. . . Another thing that Planet Xenon might need to prompt the evolution of sex is change. Sex is very beneficial to organisms because the environment is rarely static, Otto explained. Offspring may have to deal with challenges that are slightly different from those of their parents' generation. As long as change is a constant, genetic variation is helpful.

If an alien planet had, for some reason, constant weather, temperature, and other environmental factors, "sex would have mainly costs, but no benefits," Otto said.

## Fully Autonomous Vehicles, Luddites, and the speed of technological change

The information provided in the novel regarding AVs, the Luddite movement, and the speed of technological change obsoleting industries at an increasingly furious pace is all accurate. I also included some musings on how AVs will ultimately change society, which I found quite interesting.

Here are a few articles on the subject that you can readily Google if you have interest.

*How Self-Driving Cars Will Change The Economy And Society*

*Self-driving cars will disrupt more than the auto industry. Here are the winners and losers.*

Before I researched self-driving cars, I also believed that we couldn't possibly recover from the loss of jobs that would result from a society that no longer needed human drivers. But after reading counterarguments, I'm not so sure. The one I presented in Seeker was from the book *Abundance* (which I referenced earlier). This details how a majority of Americans were farm workers before automation killed more than ninety percent of these jobs, yet our economy eventually absorbed these losses.

With respect to hacking AVs and using them for terror purposes, I very much hope this isn't accurate. I did find one alarming article, but I'd like to believe that government and industry will make AVs as un-hackable as they became after Ben Kagan's fixes.

Below is an excerpt from this 2014 article in *IEEE Spectrum*, entitled, "A Cloud-Connected Car Is a Hackable Car, Worries Microsoft."

EXCERPT: Hack my bank, and you steal mere money; hack my car, and you may well kill me.

Nowadays steel plants and other super-sensitive industrial machinery are (or should be) walled off from the Internet. But tomorrow's autonomous cars will be far more vulnerable because they will be networked, says Michal Braverman-Blumenstyk, the general manager of cybersecurity at Azure, Microsoft's cloud service. She was speaking today at a Tel Aviv conference, as reported in the *Wall Street Journal*.

"Some of the functionality of connected cars can be accessed remotely—velocity adjustment for example," she said. "If police are chasing a criminal, you'd want the police to be able to slow the suspect's car down. However, if a malicious entity gets hold of the car, the damage is limitless."

## The Andromeda Galaxy and Solar System Formation

As described in the book, the Andromeda Galaxy *is* our nearest spiral neighbor, only a mere 2.5 million light years away. It *is* bigger than the Milky Way, with over a trillion stars. But apparently, this still isn't roomy enough for Andromeda's artificial superintelligence.

By the way, I should also mention that, in 2017, an international team of scientists found that the universe contains at least two *trillion* galaxies, ten times more than previously thought—so the grand universe-spanning war envisioned by the ASI might take a while. :)

Just how unique is our solar system? Recent findings suggest *extremely* unique. I hope that this turns out not to be the case, because I like the idea of a *Star Trek* universe in which endless planets just like Earth are out there. But I suspect that the cosmos doesn't care about my preferences.

The idea that Earth is a rare, second generation planet is also gaining steam. Here is an excerpt from a 2015 press release from the University of California, Santa Cruz, entitled, "Wandering Jupiter swept away super-Earths, creating our unusual Solar System."

EXCERPT: Jupiter may have swept through the early Solar System like a wrecking ball, destroying a first generation of inner planets before retreating into its current orbit, according to a new study published March 23rd in Proceedings of the National Academy of Sciences. The findings help explain why our Solar System is so different from the hundreds of other planetary systems that astronomers have discovered in recent years.

"Now that we can look at our own Solar System in the context of all these other planetary systems, one of the most interesting features is the absence of planets inside the orbit of Mercury," said Gregory Laughlin, coauthor of the paper. "The standard issue planetary system in our galaxy seems to be a set of super-Earths with alarmingly short orbital periods. Our Solar System is looking increasingly like an oddball."

The new paper explains not only the "gaping hole" in our inner Solar System, he said, but also certain characteristics of Earth and the other inner rocky planets.

Finally, here is an excerpt from a 2016 article in *Popular Science*, entitled "Earth May Be Unique In The Universe: what does that mean for the search for alien life?"

EXCERPT: After completing a census of the cosmos, a research team based in Sweden thinks that Earth may be more special than we thought. *Scientific American's* Shannon Hall explains:

Astronomer Erik Zackrisson from Uppsala University and his colleagues created a cosmic compendium of all the terrestrial exoplanets likely to exist throughout the observable universe, based on the rocky worlds astronomers have found so far. In a powerful computer simulation, they first created their own mini universe containing models of the earliest galaxies. Then they unleashed the laws of physics— as close as scientists understand them—that describe how galaxies grow, how stars evolve, and how planets come to be. Finally, they fast-forwarded through 13.8 billion years of cosmic history.

What they concluded was that Earth may be unique among the universe's estimated 700 million trillion rocky planets. But there are a lot of uncertainties, as the researchers themselves admit.

**The defense against alien invasion.**

NASA really does have a Planetary Defense Coordination Office, which is responsible for detecting Near-Earth Objects, or NEOs, and the Sentry impact monitoring system is real (although what I called Watchdog is not—at least to my knowledge).

NASA also does maintain an Office of Planetary Protection, with a Planetary Protection Officer at the helm. The 527th Space Aggressor Squadron is also real, with responsibilities as outlined in the novel.

I'll leave this section with an excerpt from a 2017 article from *Big Think*, entitled, "What Happens If Hostile Aliens Attack? The US Military Has a Team in Place."

EXCERPT: Scientists have all kinds of reasons why aliens won't try to fly to Earth and enslave humanity. Even so, the US Military has a backup plan, just in case. Two Air Force teams, the 26th Space Aggressor Squadron (26th SAS) and the 527th Space Aggressor

Squadron (527th SAS), are tasked with protecting assets in space, developing strategies to secure US space-based interests, and plans that involve deflecting extraterrestrial invaders. Both are based in Colorado.

The hostile invasion scenario may not be their topmost concern. The US, more than any other country, has come to rely on a system of satellites. Executive director of the Office of Space Commerce, Ed Morris, recently authored a disturbing report, outlining the repercussions of an attack on our satellite system. He wrote, "If you think it is hard to get work done when your Internet connection goes out at the office, imagine losing that plus your cell phone, TV, radio, ATM access, credit cards, and possibly even your electricity."

Because of this, Defense Department advisor, Peter Singer, contends that the next war will begin in space.

In 1982 the US Air Force Space Command was created. Today, it has 134 locations globally, employs 38,000, and has an annual operating budget of nearly $8.9 billion. The Pentagon's space budget in total is $22 billion. Those in the 50th space wing, a group of over 8,000 men and women, are in charge of monitoring the skies.

In 2015, Deputy Defense Secretary Robert Work recognized the growing threat to the country's assets in orbit. He said that the US had to become "ready to do space operations in a conflict that extends into space." The aggressor force was born.

## Metallic hydrogen and superconductivity

Discovering how to produce metallic hydrogen, which Norman Weiser did in the novel, really would be a major game changer, and it's possible that this will happen in the coming years. Harvard scientists have reportedly made progress in this area, but there are those who aren't yet convinced that their claims are real. If they are, this could be very big. Norman Weiser big. :)

Here is an excerpt from a 2017 article in *Tech Times* that describes the Harvard work, entitled, "Metallic Hydrogen: How Room Temperature Superconductor Could Revolutionize Technology."

EXCERPT: Researchers from Harvard University have claimed to have created metallic hydrogen, a form of hydrogen capable of superconducting electricity without resistance and at room temperature.

If the work is confirmed, the breakthrough comes with significant implications that can revolutionize many technological fields.

Scientists described the material as the Holy Grail of high-pressure physics, and with incredible properties that the material is predicted to have, its creation could change the way mankind lives.

The superconductor is believed to be capable of working at room temperature. Most have to be cooled to nearly absolute zero. The highest temperature superconductor we know of still has to be cooled to minus seventy degrees Celsius.

If scientists are able to achieve the same superconductivity without needing extreme temperatures, it could mean that power lines would not lose electricity during transmission from the power plant to consumers' homes, and make possible magnetic levitation of high-speed trains. It could also make electric cars more efficient, lead to improvements in the performance of electronic devices, and pave the way for major improvements in energy storage and production.

So there you have it. This completes the "what is real, and what isn't" section of the notes. Congratulations to all those with the fortitude to get through this entire lengthy section. I could have added more, but I think this is enough to give you a sense of the scientific underpinnings of many of the technologies used in the novel.

### 3) Author bio and list of books

Douglas E. Richards is the *New York Times* and *USA Today* bestselling author of *WIRED* and numerous other novels (see list below). A former biotech executive, Richards earned a BS in microbiology from the Ohio State University, a master's degree in genetic engineering from the University of Wisconsin (where he engineered mutant viruses now named after him), and an MBA from the University of Chicago.

In recognition of his work, Richards was selected to be a "special guest" at San Diego Comic-Con International, along with such icons as Stan Lee and Ray Bradbury. His essays have been featured in *National Geographic*, the BBC, the Australian Broadcasting Corporation, *Earth & Sky*, *Today's Parent*, and many others.

The author has two children and currently lives with his wife and two dogs in San Diego, California.

You can friend Richards on Facebook at Douglas E. Richards Author, visit his website at douglaserichards.com, and write to him at douglaserichards1@gmail.com

**Near Future Science Fiction Thrillers by Douglas E. Richards**
WIRED (Wired 1)
AMPED (Wired 2)
MIND'S EYE (Nick Hall 1)
BRAINWEB (Nick Hall 2)
MIND WAR (Nick Hall 3)
QUANTUM LENS
SPLIT SECOND (Split Second 1)
TIME FRAME (Split Second 2)
GAME CHANGER
INFINITY BORN
SEEKER

**Kids Science Fiction Thrillers** (9 and up, enjoyed by kids and adults alike)
TRAPPED (Prometheus Project 1)
CAPTURED (Prometheus Project 2)
STRANDED (Prometheus Project 3)
OUT OF THIS WORLD
THE DEVIL'S SWORD

Made in the USA
San Bernardino, CA
22 July 2018